**The wall of diseased flesh surged forward, spilling over cars, taking up every inch of the street.**

Starving mouths opened, their jagged teeth anxious to bite. There were too many of the monsters. There was no way five soldiers and Meg could hold them off.

"That's for Riley!" the firefighter screamed as she pulled the trigger.

Beckham scanned his team as he changed a mag. Fitz was focused, his features calm. He fired relentlessly. Garcia and Tank showed the same control. But Horn fired like a madman, a stream of lead flying from his M249.

"Grenades!" Beckham shouted. He grabbed one from his vest, plucked out the pin, and tossed it into the tidal wave of monsters. Four others sailed through the air simultaneously.

"Get down!" Beckham yelled at the civilians in the car. Every head vanished from the windows. The soldiers all crouched behind the vehicles as the deafening blasts tore through the night. The street rumbled and shook. The blast slammed into the vehicles, jerking the cars up and down.

His ears ringing and equilibrium off, Beckham stumbled to his feet and continued firing into the drifting smoke. The middle of the street was filled with chunky debris. Variants missing limbs screeched in agony and dragged their ruined bodies across the concrete. The grenades had killed over half of the monsters.

Maybe Ghost had a chance after all.

# Books by Nicholas Sansbury Smith

## THE EXTINCTION CYCLE

*Extinction Horizon*
*Extinction Edge*
*Extinction Age*
*Extinction Evolution*
*Extinction End*
*Extinction Aftermath*
"Extinction Lost" (An Extinction Cycle Short Story)
*Extinction War* (Fall 2017)

## TRACKERS: A POST-APOCALYPTIC EMP SERIES

*Trackers*
*Trackers 2: The Hunted*
*Trackers 3: The Storm* (Fall 2017)

## THE HELL DIVERS TRILOGY

*Hell Divers*
*Hell Divers 2: Ghosts*
*Hell Divers 3: Deliverance* (Summer 2018)

## THE ORBS SERIES

"Solar Storms" (An Orbs Prequel)
"White Sands" (An Orbs Prequel)
"Red Sands" (An Orbs Prequel)
*Orbs*
*Orbs 2: Stranded*
*Orbs 3: Redemption*

# EXTINCTION

# END

## The Extinction Cycle
## Book Five

# NICHOLAS SANSBURY SMITH

www.orbitbooks.net

Copyright © 2016 by Nicholas Sansbury Smith

Excerpt from *Extinction Aftermath* copyright © 2016 by Nicholas Sansbury Smith
Excerpt from *The Lazarus War: Artefact* copyright © 2015 by Jamie Sawyer

Cover design by Lisa Marie Pompilio
Cover art by Blake Morrow
Cover copyright © 2017 by Hachette Book Group, Inc.
Author photograph by Maria Diaz

Orbit
Hachette Book Group
1290 Avenue of the Americas
New York, NY 10104
orbitbooks.net

Originally self-published in 2016
Published in ebook by Orbit in February 2017
First Mass Market Edition: September 2017

Orbit is an imprint of Hachette Book Group.
The Orbit name and logo are trademarks of Little, Brown Book Group Limited.

The publisher is not responsible for websites (or their content) that are not owned by the publisher.

The Hachette Speakers Bureau provides a wide range of authors for speaking events. To find out more, go to www.hachettespeakersbureau.com or call (866) 376-6591.

ISBNs: 978-0-316-55815-0 (mass market), 978-0-316-55814-3 (ebook)

Printed in the United States of America

OPM

10 9 8 7 6 5 4 3 2 1

*To my readers—this one's for you guys.*
*Thank you for coming along on this journey with me.*
*I hope you enjoy the "end."*

"If civilization is to survive, we must cultivate the science of human relationships—the ability of all peoples, of all kinds, to live and work together, in the same world, at peace."

—*Franklin D. Roosevelt*

# 1

Sheets of rain poured down, half blinding Doctor Kate Lovato as she stared up into the swollen, dark sky. A clap of thunder echoed through the derelict city streets. In the respite from the noise came the squawks of starving Variants and the screams of their human prisoners.

It took Kate a moment to remember she was one of those prisoners.

All around her, she saw the distorted, skeletal shapes of Variants. They clambered over abandoned vehicles and skittered up the walls of nearby buildings. Snapping joints clicked and popped as the monsters lugged their prey through the dark streets.

At first Kate didn't even recognize her own wailing voice. She felt disconnected from everything, as if she wasn't even there. She couldn't feel much besides her irregular heartbeat and the cold rain pattering against her clammy skin.

As Kate struggled to focus, everything came collapsing down around her. After all she had been through, it was now, as she was being carried through the ash-covered streets of New York City on the back of a Variant, that she finally lost her sanity. Memories flooded her mind from the attack on Plum Island just hours before.

She'd lost a piece of her soul when Staff Sergeant Alex Riley had been killed by the gargantuan beast covered in bone-plated armor.

Everything seemed so surreal, and as she slipped deeper into shock, the city, the Variants, and the other prisoners around her became more and more distant.

It was the screams of Tasha and Jenny that yanked Kate back to reality.

"Daddy!" Jenny shrieked.

"Tasha! Jenny!" Kate yelled back. Staff Sergeant Parker Horn's girls were back there. Kate couldn't see them, but when she twisted around, she saw Meg Pratt. The firefighter was to Kate's right; a pair of male Variants with long limbs and hunched backs dragged her through the streets by her injured legs. Meg was still fighting—squirming and swatting at her captors, screaming, "You killed Riley! You killed Riley!"

Kate was reaching over to her when she heard Jenny wail for her sister.

"Tasha! Tasha!"

The cries broke Kate's heart. Upside down, she raised her head to scan the darkness for Horn's girls, gasping in air that smelled of sour lemons and rotting fruit. The monster carrying her bled the wretched scent. She held her breath and looked to the skyline.

*Reed, where are you?*

Even now, when all seemed lost, her thoughts gravitated to the father of her unborn child. The Delta Force operator had saved her so many times before. And while she knew he was out there fighting his way to New York, the chances of him arriving in time...

Kate's thoughts drifted to the other people Reed hadn't been able to save. Riley was gone. They'd lost Fitz and Apollo. It was just a matter of time before she and the other prisoners were killed too.

The click-clack of snapping maws and the screeches of the monsters rose as the small army worked its way deeper into Manhattan. They'd been on the move for what felt like hours, but Kate wasn't sure what time it was. It could be the middle of the night or nearing sunrise. She shifted in and out of reality, lost in memories.

*In order to kill a monster, you'll have to create one.*

Doctor Michael Allen's final words echoed in her thoughts. In her mind's eye, she watched her mentor and boss sacrificing himself by jumping out of the Black Hawk onto the lawn outside CDC as Variants closed in from all directions.

Kate's eyes snapped open to see the moon peeking through the clouds drifting over Manhattan. Its rays carpeted the streets, and Kate finally glimpsed Tasha and Jenny for a fleeting moment before the clouds swallowed the glow. The girls were both slung over the back of the same beast. It sniffed at their tiny legs with a nose frayed down the middle, flesh hanging loosely to both sides. A pointed tongue shot out of the monster's wormy lips, circled, then licked Tasha's right leg.

Kate reared back in disgust. She had to do something. She wouldn't let this abomination kill the girls.

"Let me down!" she yelled, pounding the lower back of the beast that carried her in a fit of rage. The creature howled and tightened a talon around her ankle, slicing into her flesh.

Kate bit back a scream of agony. She needed a plan—a way out of this. There had to be a way to escape. She looked back to Meg. The monsters had pulled her onto the sidewalk, but she was still fighting. At last Meg kicked one of the beasts in the face and managed to crawl away. Her fingernails dragged across the concrete as the second Variant reached out with a skeletal arm and grabbed her feet.

"No! No!" Meg screamed.

A high-pitched wail from the monster carrying Kate answered Meg's shouts. It was then Kate realized she was still pounding the beast with her fists. Meg wasn't the only one fighting.

Thunder cracked like a bomb exploding in the clouds. Kate paused her futile assault to look skyward, her gaze flitting up the sides of dark buildings. The towers extended to the heavens—and there, in the meat of the bulbous clouds, soared a winged creature.

An angel watching over them.

Kate was hallucinating. The shock was too much. She couldn't concentrate. She couldn't—

"Help me!" Tasha shouted.

"Let them go!" Meg screamed.

Kate kneed the Variant holding her in the throat. The impact caught the beast off guard. It swung her to the side, loosening its grip around her ankles. She reached out to brace herself with her right hand and covered her stomach with her left as she plummeted to the concrete.

The fall happened in slow motion, the ash and ground slowly rising toward her. She landed on her right palm and rolled to her back. She was kicking as soon as she was on the ground.

"No!" she shouted. "Leave us alone!" She knew how insane the words sounded. The Variants couldn't reason. They wouldn't show mercy to her or anyone else. They were *designed* to kill—*designed* to feed. And her bio-weapon had only made them stronger.

The beast perched in front of her. Rain pattered on its bald skull as it tilted its misshapen head from side to side. It blinked, thick eyelids closing over yellow eyes. Kate scooted backward across the concrete, prompting the creature to slash at her with one hand as it grabbed at her feet with the other. Talons scraped her shoes just as the beast carrying Tasha and Jenny lumbered by, tongue swaying from its mouth like the thumping tail of a dog.

A rattling sound pulled Kate's gaze to a third creature that strode away from the pack. The beast limped into a sliver of moonlight. Kate brushed her wet hair from her face, gasping when she saw the macabre armor plates of human bones covering the monster that had killed Riley.

The grip of talons pulled on her left boot again, but Kate was barely paying attention. A guttural roar, louder than the others, sounded through the city as the creature grasping Kate's feet dragged her across the ground.

The armored beast lumbered over on two feet, raised an arm severed at the elbow, and jammed the jagged bone into the skull of the beast holding Kate's left boot. The sharp tip tore through the monster's lips, a gurgling sound reverberating from its throat.

Kate pulled free of the dead creature's grip and fell to her back. The Alpha limped over to her and towered overhead, a thick strand of saliva dripping from his open lips.

Defeated, Kate didn't fight back. Her mind disconnected from her body. She just stared at the clouds, praying and searching for an angel she knew wasn't coming.

Drops of rain plopped on her face. She flinched as one landed in her eye, blurring her vision. Above the trumpeting roar of the Alpha and the screams of the other prisoners came a different noise—a deep rumble that was growing with every second.

The cloud cover split in two, as if a curtain had been pulled back to expose a window. In the moonlight soared the same winged creature she had seen before. Two others flew into view, gliding through the darkness.

Heart pounding, breathing labored, and body shivering, Kate was certain she was slipping back into shock. This was nothing but a hallucination.

The Alpha grabbed her with his good arm and lugged her over his shoulder. Kate's face hit the plate of human bones draped over the monster's back, forcing the air from her lungs in one burst. She put her hand on her stomach to protect the little one growing inside her, praying that it hadn't been hurt. Then she looked skyward to watch the angels that she knew couldn't be real.

A raucous roar split the air overhead as the winged apparitions soared past once again. She blinked the rain from her eyes and stilled her breathing, but her heart thumped relentlessly in her ears. Steam rose off the bloody flesh of the creature carrying her. Kate caught a drift of the rancid, sour scent radiating off the wounds that should have killed it.

The Alpha stopped midstride to look at the sky. In a moment of clarity, Kate saw the winged creatures for what they really were.

Not angels.

*Jets.*

An entire squadron of them.

Raised voices woke President Jan Ringgold. They were distant, but familiar. Exhausted and confused, she struggled to open her eyes. A shroud of overwhelming fatigue imprisoned her. She cracked an eyelid to blurry tunnel vision, as if she was looking into a portal framed on both sides by walls of blue. There was a potent smell in the air—the scent of antiseptics.

"She's sleeping, Mister Vice President, and she needs her rest."

"I need to talk to her *now*, Captain. I don't care if she's out—wake her up."

A hatch clicked shut, drowning out the voices.

The light in the room grew brighter, and the walls came into focus. They weren't bulkheads—they were curtains. Gripped by a wave of anxiety, Ringgold remembered Lieutenant Brett's haggard face in the seconds before he pulled the trigger and shot her. It was amazing what she could recall, the small details—the demented look in his eyes, the bead of sweat dripping down his forehead. Yet she couldn't remember much before that. There were fragmented memories of Doctor Carmen being stabbed to death, Kate holding her hand, soldiers rushing into the room. And blood. There had been so much blood.

Ringgold struggled to sit up in bed. Her right collarbone flared from the sudden movement, another reminder of the bullet Brett had fired into her flesh.

The hatch to the infirmary opened again, the sound of footsteps following. Grimacing, Ringgold palmed the bed and put her weight on her good hand, using it to push herself up. By the time the drape around the bed was pulled back, she was sitting up, defiant and ready for whatever news was so important that Johnson wanted to wake her up.

The vice president stood there sandwiched between Doctor Klinger and Captain Rick Humphrey. All three men were staring at her with incredulous looks.

"You're supposed to be asleep, Madam President," Klinger said.

Johnson took a step toward her bed, but before he could get out a word she said, "Don't sugarcoat it. Tell me why you look as if you just put down your dog."

There was no hint of amusement on Johnson's face, only the distraught look of a man who was losing a war. "I have some important news, Madam President."

Ringgold struggled to straighten her back. The EKG machine beeped faster as her heart rate elevated. Klinger walked to her side and checked her vitals on the monitor.

"Operation Condor was a success, thanks to Team

Ghost and the Variant Hunters. They succeeded where every other strike team failed: They captured a live juvenile specimen," Johnson continued.

Ringgold afforded all the men who had lost their lives a moment of silence. It was a tragic loss, but the mission had been successful. Yet she wasn't stupid—if they had caught a juvenile offspring, then there must be something else on Johnson's mind.

"Why are you really here?" Ringgold said, growing more irritated and anxious.

Johnson scrunched his brows together and tugged at his right cuff. "It's Plum Island, Madam President." There was a slight hesitation before his next words that Ringgold picked up on instantly. She gripped the bedsheets with her good hand to brace herself.

"There was a Variant attack on the island, facilitated by human collaborators."

A helpless squeak she couldn't hold in escaped Ringgold's mouth. She thought of the innocents there, the women and children she had thought would be protected at the facility. Johnson continued before she could ask about Kate.

"The bioreactors are safe, and we are in the process of moving them to the *George Washington*. However, the Variants overwhelmed the island, killing Major Smith and capturing Doctor Lovato and a handful of civilians. We're still searching for them, but intel indicates they've been taken back to a lair in New York City."

Ringgold's shock turned to anger. "Why are you down here wasting time telling me? Send every damn soldier you have at your disposal to get them back."

Johnson exchanged a look with Humphrey. The captain had his hat cupped under his arm. He took it out and flicked it with his finger, avoiding Ringgold's gaze.

"Well?" she asked. "What are you waiting for?"

"We are low on resources, Madam President. We lost almost all of our strike teams during Operation Condor—" Johnson began to say, but she cut him off.

"Do I look like President Mitchell to you, Johnson?"

"No, ma'am."

"Mitchell may have written a blank check to General Kennor to run the military as he saw fit, but I have not given you one. Doctor Lovato is the most important piece of Operation Extinction. We have to get her back. Now, I want you to gather every soldier you can conjure up and send them to New York City to rescue her."

Johnson nodded. "Team Ghost and the Variant Hunters are already gearing up."

"Good," Ringgold said, sighing. "Give them whatever they want. And tell Master Sergeant Beckham I have specific orders for him."

"What are they, ma'am?"

"Bring Kate back alive."

Blood. Tears. Sweat.

Heartbreak and hope.

The past six weeks had been one hell of a roller-coaster ride. With the development of Kryptonite and the capture of a juvenile Variant, Master Sergeant Reed Beckham had thought the war was close to being over, that humanity had a hope of defeating the monsters. Then, in a night of shattering terror, the grim reality of the new world had come crashing down on him.

Kate, Meg, and Horn's girls had been kidnapped. Major Smith had been murdered by human collaborators, and Riley, Team Ghost's little brother, was dead. There were a hundred things going on in Beckham's head, and none of them were good.

His dream of a better life with the woman he loved and their child had been all but destroyed. He wanted revenge for Riley, but he *had* to save Kate and Horn's girls. If he couldn't, then there wasn't anything left to fight for.

*No, you piece of shit. There's always something worth fighting for.*

Every soldier surrounding him in the troop hold had something worth fighting for: They had each other.

Sergeant Rick Thomas, Staff Sergeant Jose Garcia, and Corporal Ryan "Tank" Talon sat against the bulkhead across from him. They were down a gun with Chow back on the *GW*, in surgery, but Corporal Joe "Fitz" Fitzpatrick was here. The wounded warrior sat next to Beckham, his dented blades still covered in blood, repeating the same mantra over and over again.

"I couldn't save them. I couldn't *fucking* save them."

"It's okay, Fitz," Beckham said. "It's going to be okay." After a second glance, Beckham wasn't sure if his words were true.

Fitz had an MK11 between his legs, his head was bowed, and his fingers were laced together. Under the shadow of his helmet, his eyes were on his blades, but they were unfocused, with the haunted look of a marine who hadn't been able to save a friend.

The Variant Hunters stared at Beckham, waiting for something. Orders? A speech? Perhaps reassurance? He had nothing to offer them right now.

He avoided their gazes by reaching down and patting Apollo's head. Learning that Fitz and the German shepherd were still alive had given him a small glimmer of hope: Miracles happened. But not often.

Especially in a world overrun by monsters.

Apollo whimpered, and Beckham checked the dressing on his fur. A Variant had sliced him good, but the dog was tough as hell, and Apollo showed no sign of backing down from this fight.

Beckham shot a glance toward the open door of the Black Hawk, where Staff Sergeant Parker Horn roved the bird's M240 machine gun across the ocean. If they lost Tasha and Jenny, Beckham feared he would also lose his best friend. Horn would never stop fighting either, but a man could only stomach so much loss. With the death of his wife, Sheila, Horn was already close to the edge. Losing Tasha and Jenny at the hands of the monsters would push him into oblivion.

*That's not going to happen.*

Beckham gripped the strap of the M4 slung over his back. He rose to his feet and made his way next to Horn for a better look outside. The men were all loaded to the max with ammunition and weapons. They were going to need every round and grenade if they were to have any hope of rescuing Kate and the others.

"Be advised, Stinger squadron is reporting a group of Variants in Manhattan with civilians in tow," one of the pilots said over the comm.

Beckham's heart skipped. The F-18 Super Hornets couldn't do anything to save Kate or the others, but hearing they had been spotted out there filled Beckham with new strength.

"What's our ETA?" he asked over the comm.

"Three minutes, sir," one of the pilots replied.

"Fly this fucking can faster!" Horn shouted. He angled the gun toward the water and looked over at Beckham, his eyes smoldering with the pain of a father who was on the verge of losing everything. "We're going to get 'em back, right, Sarge?"

Beckham glanced back at Fitz and the Variant Hunters. These men needed him now, more than ever. Even Garcia looked frightened, his eyes wide in his bruised face.

*We're coming, Kate. Just hold on, baby.*

No matter what he'd lost, Beckham knew he had to pull it together—he had to bury his fear in his gut, separate his personal feelings for Kate and the other prisoners from the mission at hand, and transform back into a Delta Force operator. It was the only way he would succeed in rescuing them.

"We're going to get them back or die trying, Big Horn," Beckham said. He clapped his friend on the back and looked out over the water, ready to give every piece of himself to save those he loved.

# 2

There was no way for Meg to tell how much time had elapsed since the attack on Plum Island. In her mind, it could have been hours or days. She could only seem to focus on one thing: Riley was dead.

It wasn't fair.

The kid had died in a battle against a monstrosity that shouldn't have existed, a beast wearing armor of *human bones*. The only consolation, if she could call it that, was the way his life had ended. Despite the wheelchair and the casts covering his shattered legs, he had gone down the way he had lived—fighting to the very end.

Meg's heart was bursting at the seams. Nothing made sense, and she couldn't seem to escape her thoughts. But that's what nightmares were. That's why they were so terrifying: Nightmares didn't end. Minutes earlier she'd given up struggling against the creature lugging her through the ash-covered streets. She had to conserve her last dregs of energy to try to save Tasha and Jenny. She told herself she was going to go down fighting, like Riley, but how could she fight so many of the beasts without a weapon?

In the glow of moonlight, she counted fourteen Variants of various shapes and sizes, with two human collaborators leading the pack into Manhattan. The creatures were so filthy and deformed she couldn't identify their genders. She thought the beast carrying her might be a male, but its narrow shoulders and a few long strands of strawlike hair had her reconsidering. Whatever it was, it was strong.

All around her, the beasts hurried through the streets with their human cargo slung over shoulders and scarred backs. Even those that were injured didn't seem to slow their relentless pace. The monsters swarmed over the charred hulls of cars and scaled the toasted sides of buildings to scout for threats.

A jet roared overhead, sending whirlwinds of ash into the air. Grit peppered Meg's face and stung her eyes. The Variants darted toward the sidewalks, squawking in their evil language.

Meg dug her fingers into withered skin as the beast carrying her leaped onto a curb and plodded toward the protection of an awning. Bouncing up and down, she focused on the familiar green canopy.

Could it really be?

The creature hunched next to the cherrywood frame of a door Meg had walked through hundreds of times. This was Mickey's Irish Pub, the same bar where she had been known to slam down bottles of Jameson and Templeton Rye with her firefighter friends and her husband, Tim.

A flashback from those days caught in her throat, and she couldn't hold back the tears. It was all too much. First Riley, now these memories...

Tears fell from her eyes as the jets came in for another pass. The sight did nothing to inspire confidence in Meg. In a few hours, she and the other prisoners would be underground. Then there would be nothing Team Ghost could do, no matter how much blood they spilled.

She couldn't go back to those dark tunnels.

*I'll die first.*

The rumble of the jets faded into the night, and the sounds of human engineering once again left the city, replaced by the sounds of monsters.

Tasha's and Jenny's sobs were the only thing that kept Meg from giving up. That wasn't her. She wasn't a quitter. She was a fighter, just as Riley had been, and she wasn't going to let those little girls die. With their protector, Riley, gone, she was all they had left.

The thought of losing them sent a spike of adrenaline through her. She remembered her favorite quote:

*Firemen never die but burn forever in the hearts of the people whose lives they saved.*

Meg was going to save Tasha and Jenny, even if she died trying.

She grabbed at one of the poles holding up the awning and wrapped her fingers around it. Using all of her strength, she pulled herself up and kicked at the same time. Her injured legs burned as her shoes smacked the beast that clung to her. It reared back in anger, shrieking. She swung free, then dropped to the ground. The impact sent a second jolt of pain ripping up her legs.

The Variants in the street looked away from the sky and focused on her, apparently just as shocked as she was. Those that weren't carrying human prisoners slowly dropped to the ground and skittered around her. The beast she had kicked squatted, hunched its back, and planted its fingers like a lineman waiting to charge forward. A large diamond on its left ring finger caught Meg's eye.

A female after all.

The abomination looked at Meg with reptilian yellow eyes, the lids clicking open and shut. There was no comprehension in the creature's gaze. No memories of the person who had put the ring on its finger, no empathy for the children the other Variants were about to kill.

Only hunger.

And rage.

Meg took a step backward, her heart racing. The other beasts formed a perimeter around her. In the middle of the street, behind the monsters, stood the Alpha, with Kate still slung over his back. The doctor was docile, her body unmoving.

To the right, half a block down, the children were hanging over the shoulders of several emaciated Variants. They'd taken not only Horn's girls but the little boy, Bo, as well. Rain rushed down the creatures' naked flesh, bones protruding under pale, stretched skin. If it weren't for the Alpha, Meg was certain the starving creatures would have already devoured the kids.

The female Variant in front of her popped its lips together and let out a high-pitched squeal that sent slobber splattering onto Meg's shirt. She took another step back until she hit the shattered front door of the pub. A piece of glass crashed to the ground, breaking into jagged slivers.

A pair of Variants dropped to all fours and crawled across the sidewalk, leaving tracks in the mushy ash. They stopped ten feet away, cracking their heads from side to side.

What were they waiting for?

For a fleeting moment, Meg considered retreating into the building. She knew the layout and could possibly escape, or at least hide—but the thought vanished as quickly as it had appeared. She couldn't pull her gaze from Tasha and Jenny. The girls were still screaming for their dad, and—

"Help us, Miss Meg!" Tasha shouted. "Please!"

Meg nearly choked on a surge of adrenaline. It was the same thing she felt before running into a burning building. Fueled by the rush, Meg bent down, scooped up a shard of glass, and lunged for the female Variant. She caught the beast off guard, jamming the shard into its right eye. The glass cut into Meg's hand, but she continued driving it through the monster's soft tissue.

It unleashed a piercing howl as Meg pushed deeper. With a frantic swipe, the Variant knocked Meg's hand away and scrambled into the street, squawking in agony.

Meg limped after it into the road, gripping her injured hand in a daze, the adrenaline wearing out as the pain from the laceration and her legs took over. She shuffled toward the beasts holding the children, yelling in a voice she didn't recognize, "Let them go!"

"Please help!" Tasha yelled back.

The Alpha directed a horned finger toward Meg. Before she could react, she was tackled from the side and pinned to the ground. Her head hit the pavement with a crack, and the air burst from her lungs. Stars crawled before her blurred vision. She sucked in a breath of air that tasted like rotting fruit and squinted to see past the curtain of wet hair hanging in front of her face.

High-pitched wails amplified all around her. The sounds echoed and rose into a chorus that sounded like an army one hundred Variants strong.

Closing her eyes, she let out a breath, took in another deep gasp, and tried to focus. She opened her eyes to the stars still floating across her vision. Beyond them, the Variant she had stabbed suddenly barreled toward her, the piece of glass still jammed in its right eye. It slashed at the creatures holding her down and then climbed up and straddled Meg.

Meg had seen the look before: It was preparing to strike. She closed her eyes again, weak now in her final moments, unable to watch. The adrenaline was gone, and with it her final shreds of courage.

She wanted to fight, as Riley had, but it was all too much, and when she tried to move she couldn't budge. Her arms and legs were clamped down by the beast. The pain was agonizing. No matter how hard she pushed, she couldn't get free.

*No. Please, no.*

She squirmed again, and again.

"No!"

The screeching intensified, filling the city with the cries of the monsters that had claimed it as their home. There were faint traces of prepubescent voices as Tasha, Jenny, and Bo screamed for help that would never make it in time.

Meg took in another long, deep breath in a final attempt to find the courage she needed—the courage that would make Riley proud. She forced her eyes open and looked at the shard of glass in the beast's eye, and then to the row of gargoyles on the roof of Mickey's Irish Pub.

A drop of blood landed in Meg's eye. She blinked it away, trying to focus on the stone faces she couldn't remember ever seeing before. Squirming and kicking, Meg continued struggling under the beast's powerful grip.

The Variant snapped at her face. She met the strike with a head butt that broke its nose and drove the glass deeper into its eye. Meg used the stolen moment to gaze at the roof. There were dozens of pallid statues.

Not gargoyles.

Variants.

All at once they skidded down the sides of the building, shrieking in a war cry louder than any Meg had ever heard. The female beast rolled off her and darted toward the Alpha. All thirteen of the Variants in the pack surrounded their leader, abandoning their human prisoners in the street. The collaborators raised their rifles at the building, the muzzles roving back and forth as if they didn't know where to aim.

Meg crawled toward Tasha and Jenny. They were sitting up on the concrete, sobbing and reaching out for her. Bo's mom, Donna, scooped up her son and rushed over to the girls while the other human prisoners scattered.

A gunshot rang out, and a few seconds later, the world descended into chaos. It took a second shot for Meg to grasp what was happening. She glanced over her shoulder just as the first wave of monsters from the roof hit the sidewalk. The Alpha and its small army met the second group head on, their claws extending and needle teeth clacking.

Meg pushed herself to her feet, blood dripping from her hand. She watched the two packs of Variants crash into one another with a force that sent some of the smaller creatures tumbling across the ground. One of the human collaborators continued firing, while the other took off running.

The Alpha in his bone armor plowed through the meat of the rival group, tossing Variants aside like rag dolls with his good arm and stabbing others with his jagged stump.

A female beast suddenly leaped into the air and latched onto the Alpha's back. He bucked it off with ease and impaled it with the spear of his broken arm. The monster lifted the smaller Variant toward the sky, howling in its face through bulging lips. Using his remaining hand, the Alpha tore the creature's right arm from its socket before moving on. The female Variant crashed to the ground, blood spurting from both wounds with the force of a fire hose.

Meg could hardly move. She watched the battle in horror. At the edge of the street, the remaining collaborator emptied his magazine at a rooftop where more of the Variants were spilling over the sides. It didn't take Meg long to realize that the group that had captured her wasn't going to survive the battle. The coward struggling with a new magazine must have realized the same thing—he took off running after his friend.

"Meg!" someone shouted.

She looked over at Donna, a moment of comprehension between them. Meg had never been a mother, but she'd dedicated her life to protecting people, to saving children. She would sacrifice herself if it meant the kids had a chance of getting away, and she saw that Donna felt the same way.

"Come on!" Meg shouted. She looked for a place to hide, but all she saw was the tide of diseased flesh washing over the street. Meg found herself back at the beginning of her nightmare: trapped in the city she had called home and hunted by the monsters that had once been her friends.

"I couldn't save them," Fitz whispered.

His mind drifted from the attack on Plum Island to Iraq, back to the room where his spotter, PFC Garland, had had his face blown off. The same shithole of a building where PFC Duffy had killed two innocent children and their grandfather.

Fitz hadn't been able to help them.

He hadn't been able to save his brothers the day he lost his legs to an IED.

He hadn't been able to save Riley, Kate, Horn's girls, or—

"Coming up on target, ETA five minutes," one of the pilots said over the comm.

Fitz heard the words, but he wasn't ready to go back out there yet. What if he failed again? What if he couldn't save Kate and the other prisoners?

He sucked in a deep, raw breath that filled his lungs. Then he drew in another. After a third, he started hyperventilating. Someone was saying his name now, but he could scarcely make out any other words.

A slap to his helmet pulled him back to the troop hold. Beckham was leaning out of his seat. Fitz was only halfway conscious, but he could still see deep creases and wrinkles in his friend's face that hadn't been there before.

"You with me, Fitz?" Beckham asked. The operator nudged him in the arm with a gloved finger.

Fitz tried to nod, but inside his head the IED was exploding all over again, the blast filling his vision as if he was really back in Iraq.

*You're still alive*, he reminded himself. *You can still fight.*

Fitz looked down at his blades. They were both dented, the right one bent, but he could still run. He *could* still fight.

"Yeah." Fitz sighed. "I'm good." He pulled a magazine from his flak jacket and banged it on his helmet.

Beckham caught his gaze and offered a small, reassuring dip of his chin.

"I'm with you, brother," Fitz said.

"I know."

The Black Hawk soared over the piers and above the destroyed New York skyline. Horn rotated the M240 toward the streets, searching desperately for any sign of his family. The other marines Fitz had just met, the Variant Hunters, conducted their final gear checks. Their vests were decked out with extra magazines and M67 grenades. These men were professionals, with the lacerations and bruises to prove it.

Beckham and Horn were covered in flesh wounds too. Both men were bleeding from multiple cuts where their body armor hadn't protected them.

The floor of the troop hold was covered in crimson, and not just from Fitz's dripping blades or soiled uniform. Every man here was wounded. But there was no time for rest or medics.

One of the pilots spoke over the channel. "Stingers just reported seeing a group of Variants and possible civilians on Forty-Fourth Street."

"That's two blocks from the main library," Fitz said.

Beckham looked at him with eyes that suddenly darkened. "Fuck, that's close to the Bryant Park subway station."

Fitz nodded. "The home of the Bone Collector."

This time Beckham raised a brow, not understanding.

"The Alpha who took Kate and killed Riley," Fitz said. "Red blew off the fucker's arm, but apparently he's still alive."

Garcia rose from his seat. "That's the Alpha who led the attack on Plum Island?"

"Are you sure, Fitz?" Beckham asked.

Horn turned away from the gun to glance over his shoulder.

"Yes," Fitz said. "When we find that bastard, he's mine."

The soldiers all fell into silence. Fitz knew what they were all thinking. Same thing he was—they wanted a crack at the beast.

But this kill was his.

It wasn't the only thing they were thinking. Each man knew how insane the mission was. Insane to think they could get Kate and the others back, insane to think they could win this fucking war.

"All it takes is all you got, marines," Garcia said, his voice deep and confident.

"*Oorah*," Thomas said.

Tank nodded. "Damn straight, brother!"

Fitz almost smiled. He hadn't heard that motto for a while. Goose bumps prickled across his skin, and suddenly he felt ashamed for letting pessimistic thoughts put him off his game. He had survived hell and he would survive it again. The lingering numbness Fitz had felt since the attack vanished, replaced by his pounding heart.

He *would* save them.

Static fired in Fitz's earpiece from the pilots. "Ghost, VH, we got eyes on something below. Fifth between Forty-Third and Forty-Fourth."

Fitz joined Beckham at the open door, where he snapped the swivel-based bipod on a Knight's mount into place on his MK11. Then he brought the Leupold Vari-X Mil Dot riflescope up to search for targets.

Sheets of rain hit the inside of the chopper as it circled for a better view, and blood cascaded over the metal edge of the troop hold. Fitz moved his blades out of the flow.

"Holy fuck," one of the pilots said. "You guys seeing this?"

Beckham pointed to a mob of wet flesh in the street below. The pop of distant gunfire sounded.

"What the hell?" Fitz whispered.

He zoomed in on a small army of Variants tearing each other apart in the road, just as they had in the Bryant Park station. He tried to count them, but the creatures seemed to blend together. There had to be at least fifty, and more were joining the battle. A human collaborator ran away from the fight, twisting to fire at creatures trailing him. In the heart of the cluster, Fitz sighted the armor of the Bone Collector. He centered his sights on the monster but couldn't get a clear shot. He was very accurate up to 1,500 yards with the gun, but not from a moving bird.

The Alpha plowed through the rival group, tearing limbs away and snapping necks with its good hand. Fitz moved the cross hairs toward a pair of Variants fighting just below the helicopter. They tore into each other with their talons, opening up long lacerations visible even from the air. It was over in a few seconds, the larger beast besting the smaller creature with a slash that opened up a gash across its belly. Entrails gushed out onto the pavement.

"Do you see my girls?" Horn shouted, hysteria rising in his voice.

"Does anyone have eyes?" Beckham said with deliberate restraint. Fitz could sense he was trying to remain calm, but there was no hiding the fear in his voice.

Fitz squeezed closer to Beckham, heart racing, frantic to find the civilians. If the Bone Collector was down there, they had to be close.

Horn was screaming now. "Where are my girls?"

"Now's our chance! Kill those motherfuckers!" Garcia ordered. He raised his M4, but Horn turned and swatted his muzzle away.

"*No!*" he shouted. "Tasha and Jenny could be down there!"

Garcia crouch-walked away from the door, his gaze rueful.

There was a crackle of static over the comm, and one of the pilots said, "No sign of the survivors, Ghost and VH. I only see Variants."

"Take us down," Beckham said. He directed his gaze toward Garcia. "And hold your *goddamn* fire."

Fitz's heart skipped, landing in his throat, where it stuck. Rain pelted his forehead, and he wiped it away before putting his scope back to his eye.

The bird banked hard to the right and circled for another pass. Horn was practically hanging out the door to search the streets. His eyes were swollen and red; the water rushing down his face wasn't just rain.

On the second pass, Fitz centered his MK11 on the buildings behind the Variants. He swept the muzzle quickly over the structures, but spotted no evidence of Kate, Meg, or Horn's daughters. No bodies. No screams. Nothing.

"Come on," Fitz whispered. "Give us a sign. Just one."

White noise broke over the channel. "Eyes on possible target on Fifth Avenue and East Forty-Third Street."

Fitz roved his gun in that direction. There, on the southeast corner of the intersection, was a small group of civilians running away from the battle. Zooming in, Fitz centered his cross hairs on several small shapes that could have been Tasha, Jenny, and Bo.

He exhaled and felt the tingle of relief—only to have it suddenly ripped away, like a scab being torn off. The civilians took a left on Forty-Second, toward the library.

"Fuck! They're still heading toward the lair!" Fitz shouted.

"Get us down there!" Beckham yelled.

The chopper rolled to the left, sending Apollo sliding across the floor. Fitz grabbed the dog's collar before he tumbled out the open door. The pilots evened out the Black Hawk, and one of them shouted, "Contacts on Forty-Second!"

Blood rushing in his ears, Fitz focused his gun past the library. A herd of Variants charged straight toward the civilians. Oblivious to the new threat, Kate and the others had stopped to wave at the chopper.

Fitz alternated his gun between the Variants and the group of civilians.

"My God," he mumbled. They didn't have much time.

Beckham shouted, "Get us as close as you can!"

The pilots descended toward the street, kicking up a

cloud of ash and dust. As they lowered the bird, a crack rang out in the distance, and something suddenly pelted the side of the Black Hawk.

A flurry of gunshots followed—but not from the helicopter. It was then Fitz realized someone was shooting at them. He ducked down as the bird jerked to the left. The rotors whined in response.

"What the fuck was that?" Beckham demanded.

The pilots were yelling now too, but Fitz was too busy looking for a target to listen. They were in trouble, and they were going to be in worse shape if he didn't find whoever was firing on them.

Fitz didn't have to look far. The filthy face of a human collaborator suddenly emerged in his gun sights. The man angled an AR-15 at the bird before Fitz could squeeze off a shot. He flinched as the muzzle flashed.

Several rounds punched through the metal door. A muffled cry followed. Fitz whirled as Thomas grabbed at his chest. Blood exploded from the sergeant's mouth.

"Son of a bitch!" Fitz said. He looked back to the target, held in a breath, squeezed the trigger, and watched the collaborator's head explode. Before he had a chance to lower his rifle, the chopper whirled to the right, then to the left.

The marines and Delta operators all reached for something to hold on to as the bird spun out of control. Thomas slid across the floor, groaning and unable to stop.

"No!" Garcia yelled. He dropped to his stomach and reached for his friend, but narrowly missed the man's boot. Thomas vanished out the open door, plummeting to the street fifty feet below.

The chopper continued to spin, sending the soldiers sliding and bumping into one another.

"We're going down!" a pilot shouted.

Apollo howled, and Beckham yelled for everyone to hold on to something.

Fitz was on his back, his blades scraping across the floor. A familiar terror gripped him as the bird whirled in what seemed like slow motion. The fragmented memory of the IED that had taken his legs and the lives of his friends surfaced in his mind again. He could still feel the red-hot pain in his legs, even all these years later.

"We have to bail!" Beckham shouted. "Get ready to jump!" He grabbed Fitz by his vest and yanked him to his feet.

The street rushed toward them. Garcia and Tank jumped out of the chopper first and disappeared from view. Horn went next. Fitz waited for Beckham. The operator grabbed Apollo and yelled, "Now, Fitz!"

# 3

Doctor Pat Ellis followed a group of marines through a dark passage on the USS *Cowpens*. Everything reeked of bleach. His heart still raced with anxiety, but he'd mostly recovered from the shock after the attack on Plum Island. With his mind clear, it had finally sunk in.

Kate was gone.

She had been, in many ways, all he had left—the one person he had been able to count on besides Beckham. If she died, he would have to finish the Plum Island batch of Kryptonite with scientists he didn't even know. The thought was terrifying—and selfish. But so was the thought of letting millions of human survivors down. There were still people out there fighting for survival. He couldn't stop working now, no matter how alone he felt.

Every step down the passage was one step closer to the juvenile Variant the strike team had brought back from New York City. In his right hand, Ellis carried a small box full of syringes containing Kryptonite. He had extracted some of the finished antibodies, attached them to the chemotherapeutics, and diluted them into a solution. It was the same process they would use before loading the missiles.

In a few minutes, he would inject the juvenile with

the cocktail, and in a day or less, they would know if the weapon would kill both the adults and their offspring.

Ellis had his doubts.

The marines marched on, and Ellis hurried after them. At the end of the passage, a woman with piercing green eyes, shoulder-length red hair, and a sharp jaw waited to the left side of a doctor wearing spectacles.

"Doctor Ellis," the woman said, approaching with an extended hand. "I'm Lieutenant Rachel Davis, and this is Doctor Kevin Yokoyama."

"I'm sorry about your partner. Vice President Johnson is doing everything possible to get her back," Yokoyama said.

The comment wasn't reassuring, and Ellis simply nodded. He wasn't sure who he could trust here. After hearing about Yokoyama's inhumane experimentation on Lieutenant Brett, Ellis had built up a defensive wall that he raised whenever the doctor was even mentioned. Meeting the man in person didn't change things, and moving forward, Ellis knew he would tread lightly around him.

After they shook hands, Ellis said, "Let's get this over with. Where's the juvenile being held?"

Davis jerked her chin down another passage. "This way, Doctors."

Ellis stayed a few steps ahead of Yokoyama, but he was having a hard time keeping up with Davis. She had a long stride and walked quickly. Yokoyama tried to work his way up next to him, but Ellis wasn't in the mood to answer any questions. Pounding boots followed them through the passages, their marine escort right behind.

A few minutes later, they reached the brig. Four more soldiers were stationed here. The men were decked out in black body armor and carried shotguns with drums of ammo. Each wore a Kevlar helmet with a rectangular, mirrored visor and attached breathing apparatus. They reminded him of Imperial Stormtroopers. It gave Ellis the chills. He'd always hated those bastards ever since he first saw *Star Wars* as a kid.

Davis reached for the box of syringes. "After the incident with Lieutenant Brett, we have doubled our security and assigned a special team to administer Kryptonite to the juvenile."

The soldiers glanced in Ellis's direction, almost robotically, but said nothing. Lieutenant Davis grabbed the box from Ellis and strode over to a hatch marked CELL 6. Yokoyama joined her and pulled back the metal shutter covering the window. A guttural hissing followed, as if the doctor had just opened the door to a pit containing an anaconda.

Yokoyama shook his head in awe. "She's a remarkable creature." Then he glanced back at Ellis and grinned. "We're calling her Lucy."

Ellis almost laughed. Lucy was the name given by anthropologists to the earliest human remains ever found. "Lucy wasn't a monster."

Yokoyama took off his spectacles and tucked them into his thick hair, exposing gray roots under the overhead lights. He didn't reply; instead, he leaned closer to the glass.

"How long will this take?" Davis asked.

Ellis shrugged. "It depends. Experiments on adult Variants have ranged from a couple hours to a full day, but there are more moving targets with the juveniles. They're born with genetic mutations. That means proteins could change slightly from generation to generation. If the Superman protein is one of those that has changed in this specimen, then the antibodies in Kryptonite won't bind to it, and the drugs won't be able to get into the cells."

"Meaning what?" Davis asked.

"Meaning Lucy won't be affected," Yokoyama replied grimly. "At this rate, she'll be a full-grown adult in a few weeks."

Davis nodded as if she understood, but Ellis wasn't so sure. If the top brass knew what he knew, they would already be working on a backup plan to kill the offspring. Just hours before the attack on Plum Island, Ellis had come across worrying new information: Not only were the beasts growing at astounding rates, but their genetic makeup was evolving rapidly. If they could no longer target the unique Superman protein found in the adult Variants, then Kryptonite would be useless against the offspring.

"Sergeant Russo, are you ready?" Davis asked.

The tallest of the four men in black armor strode over. He slung the strap of his shotgun over his shoulder and tilted his face mask toward Ellis.

Davis handed the small case to the sergeant.

"You'll need to inject the cocktail into the small patch of flesh between its neck armor and—" Ellis had begun to say when Yokoyama cut him off.

"Actually, that won't work. The best place appears to be the soft tissue just below the navel. The armor never grew over that spot."

Russo regarded the men in turn, his mask shifting slightly. "You're sure? I'm only going to get one shot at this."

"Relax, Sergeant, Lucy will be sedated," Davis said.

*Relax?* Ellis thought. He wondered if the technicians and guards who'd been murdered by Lieutenant Brett were told the same thing before they entered his cell to euthanize him.

Davis pointed at the other three soldiers in riot gear. "The rest of you will secure the chains, just in case Lucy wakes up." She turned to the marine escort waiting at the end of the dark passage. "You four, keep sharp."

The marines nodded and shouldered their weapons.

Ellis felt his heart jump. There was a lot of firepower present, but the Variant offspring were different than the adults. They were stronger, faster, and more unpredictable.

Russo opened the case and pulled out two syringes before handing it back to Ellis. The soldier tucked both syringes in his left vest pocket, then unslung his shotgun.

Yokoyama backed away from the door, making room for the soldiers. All four lined up in single file to enter the room, hands on the shoulder of the man in front of them.

"Doctors, this way please," Davis said.

Yokoyama nodded and followed her down the corridor, but Ellis remained at the hatch to Cell 6.

"I haven't even seen Lucy yet," he said defiantly. "I'd really like to be present for this."

Davis hesitated. "Doctor Yokoyama, you go back to the lab. Doctor Ellis, stay close to me."

Yokoyama didn't offer any objection. He quickly walked toward the marines and vanished around the next bulkhead. So far, Ellis was not impressed with the old doctor. He was certainly no Dr. Kate Lovato.

Davis flicked her mini-mic to her lips and said, "Med One, this is Lieutenant Davis. You're authorized to proceed with sedation."

Ellis nudged his way in next to Russo at the hatch and peered through the glass. Lucy was chained to the ceiling, legs and arms stretched into an $X$. An overhead light illuminated the juvenile's grotesque body. Gray, scaly armor covered its extremities. Its cone-shaped head was angled down, chin against a plated chest where breasts would be on a normal mammal. Pointy ears tipped with fur hung loosely on the sides of its head.

"Is it sleeping?" Ellis asked.

Lucy's head slowly lifted, wide yellow eyes snapping open and ears perking toward the ceiling. A lizardlike tongue shot out of wormy lips. Hissing, the beast fought against its restraints, pulling them tight with talon-tipped fingers. The creature was four feet tall, nearly a foot taller than the juveniles he'd seen in the video from Turner Field in Atlanta.

Davis joined him at the window. "Med One, Lieutenant Davis. Do you copy? Over."

A second later, the hissing Variant was drowned out by the whisper of gas from an overhead vent. The room quickly filled with a cloud of mist, shrouding the juvenile Variant in gray.

"Get ready," Davis said, turning slightly to Russo.

She grabbed Ellis by the arm and directed him away from the hatch. The special detail of soldiers formed a perimeter around them, their rifles angled at the window. Russo pulled a key from his pocket and waited.

Beyond the window, the gas was sucked into floor vents, and the clean white walls of the room reappeared. Lucy hung limply from the chains, dry tongue hanging from its mouth like a panting dog's.

"Execute," Davis said, her voice authoritative and calm.

As the soldiers prepared to enter, Ellis felt the sting of anxiety. He wasn't sure if his heart was racing because of the monster in front of him or because of his fragmented memories of the attack on the island. In one, he was running past Riley's limp, twisted body. In another, he shot the Variant that had Fitz pinned to the ground. Ellis could almost feel the hot blood on his face. More memories came rushing over him.

The boats raced away from the island with Kate and the other hostages. A missile streaked toward the vessels still on the shoreline. The final image was the clearest, as if he was standing right there. In Ellis's mind, Fitz was on his knees in the sand, head bowed, covered in blood.

Gritting his teeth, Ellis reached for his remaining strength. Deep down, he held on to some hope that Kryptonite would work on the offspring, and deeper down, he held on to hope that Beckham, Fitz, and Horn could bring Kate and the others back.

A click snapped the thoughts away. Russo unlocked the hatch and slipped the key back in his pocket. Then he grabbed a syringe in one hand and his shotgun in the other.

"Move, move, move!" Russo ordered.

The first man swung the hatch open and burst into the room. One by one the other soldiers disappeared inside. Russo was the last to go. He slammed the metal door behind them, his visor centering on Ellis for a single second behind the glass window. There was no hint of fear in his posture, only determination.

Davis walked up to the window to watch. The men worked quickly. As instructed, three of them held the chains while Russo took a knee in front of Lucy and stabbed the syringe into her navel.

Ellis thought he saw the juvenile's eyelids flicker. He palmed the bulkhead and leaned closer for a better look. Russo quickly injected the cocktail and then backed away. The other three men retreated with him to the hatch.

"Back up," Davis said. She grabbed Ellis by the arm again and directed him toward the bulkhead across the passage. They waited there with the marine escort while Russo and his squad filed into the hall and locked the hatch behind them.

For a moment, no one said a word. Mirrored visors stared ahead. Weapons were slowly lowered toward the deck as the soldiers began to relax.

Davis put her hands on her hips and crinkled her

nose. "A lot of good men died to bring that freak back here." She glanced over at Ellis. "It better have been worth it. I hope to God your weapon works."

"I hope so too," Ellis replied. He tried to sound confident, but there was no hiding his skepticism, especially when he ducked her gaze to examine Russo's profile.

Rifles all around Ellis were suddenly raised at the glass window. Ellis turned slowly, expecting to see Lucy spitting out her guts. Instead, through the glass, a pair of reptilian eyes glared at Ellis. Lucy was awake again, tongue circling wormy lips, leaving webs of saliva behind.

"What the hell?" Davis muttered. "How is it conscious?"

Ellis shook his head. "I—I don't know, Lieutenant."

The soldiers shouldered their rifles, preparing for orders.

"It won't be conscious for long," Russo replied. "I injected the whole thing into its gut." He handed Ellis the extra syringe of Kryptonite to put back in the case.

Ellis grabbed it without taking his eyes off the little monster's pointed tongue. It shot back into Lucy's mouth, lips clamping closed over it. Davis and Russo backed away from the hatch the second they saw what Ellis did.

*No,* Ellis thought. *It can't be.*

But there was no mistaking it. Lucy's bulging sucker lips had stretched into an evil grin, touching both sides of her face. A wave of terror prickled through Ellis. The adults were, without a doubt, remarkable predators, but the offspring took it to another level. They weren't just aware, they were learning.

They had evolved into the *perfect* predator.

Beckham barely had time to look over his shoulder as the Black Hawk spun toward a four-story building. One of the pilots made a last-ditch effort to pull up, but the other opened the door and tried to bail. The chopper's nose slammed into the exterior of the brick building with the pilot halfway out the door. Flames instantly engulfed the cockpit as it smashed together and then blew apart in a massive cloud of crimson and black.

The rotors cracked in half, streaking through the air like oversized spears. A shard whizzed past Beckham's right arm. He tackled Apollo to the ground behind a car and shielded the dog's body with his own. Pieces punched into the car as the wreckage rained to the sidewalk.

Beckham said a short prayer for the pilots, but there wasn't a second to waste hiding. He waited for the final bits of shrapnel to hit the ground and then jumped to his feet to get his bearings. Horn and Fitz were tucked behind the safety of a pickup truck about twenty feet behind the twisted mess of the Black Hawk. Garcia and Tank were already firing at the herd of Variants barreling toward the civilians to the west.

"Thomas!" Garcia shouted. He unloaded a barrage of rounds and ran toward Thomas's mangled body.

Beckham took in the entire view in the amount of time it took to fire off half a magazine—from the skid marks Thomas's body had left in the ash when he had fallen from the bird to the civilians running from the Variants. In the middle of the group, Beckham glimpsed a woman who could be Kate.

"Big Horn, Fitz, on me!" he shouted. Beckham whistled at Apollo and took off in a sprint. He pulled at the strap of his M4 and raised the weapon to scope the street. The cross hairs fell on Garcia. The marine was on his knees next to Thomas's body, with his head bowed. The sheer amount of blood told Beckham that Thomas was gone. And if Garcia and Tank didn't get moving, they would be too.

"Move your asses!" Beckham shouted.

Tank threw the strap of his M249 Squad Automatic Weapon over his back and leaned down to pick up Thomas. Garcia laid down suppressing fire as they ran. They met Beckham, Fitz, and Horn in the middle of the street. An explosion rocked the building behind them. More shards of metal ricocheted off the surrounding vehicles.

"Let's move!" Beckham yelled.

Beckham strained to see over the cars blocking the road, searching desperately for Kate. The shrieking Variants drowned out the desperate screams from the civilians. Beckham ran faster. His ankles burned from the jump out of the chopper, but not even a sprain or broken bones could stop him now. He would crawl to Kate if he had to.

Bursting around a Humvee, Beckham angled his M4 down the street. He almost stopped midstride when he saw Kate's blue eyes. They saw each other at the same time, the world around them disconnecting in that moment.

Gunfire, barking, the frightened screams of children, and the screech of monsters returned them both to the nightmare. It was chaos, and Kate was right in the middle of it.

"Reed!" she shouted. Jenny bobbed up and down on her back.

The child reached out with a tiny hand when she saw Horn. "Daddy!"

"Jenny! Tasha!" Horn yelled back.

Beckham scanned the street behind Kate. Meg was carrying Tasha. Donna cradled Bo in her arms. There were two other civilians Beckham didn't recognize, but that was it.

Where the hell was everyone else?

There wasn't time for questions. An army of Variants more than a hundred strong trailed the survivors. Their talons scratched at the concrete, ash kicking up in the air. Thousands of joints snapped as the herd charged, but Beckham couldn't get a clear shot. The civilians were in his line of fire.

Garcia and Tank climbed to the top of two vehicles. Their muzzles barked to life. Beckham ran past their position, with Horn and Fitz flanking him on each side.

"Stay!" Beckham said to Apollo. "Horn, Fitz, take out the climbers!"

The chatter of gunfire broke out to Beckham's right and left, his friends training their fire on Variants scaling the walls on both sides of the street.

*Hold on, Kate. I'm almost there.*

He locked his gaze onto her face. The small group of civilians was navigating the maze of vehicles. The monsters behind them took to roofs and hoods, leaping from car to car.

Three of the beasts were catching up fast. Beckham shouldered his rifle and fired as he moved. He nailed a Variant in midair as it lunged for Meg and Tasha. The three-round burst hit it in the torso, sending it spinning away and crashing into the side of a UPS truck with a thud that reverberated over the street.

Static crackled in Beckham's earpiece. Command was trying to get a message through, but he couldn't hear shit over the gunfire. It was all just white noise and scrambled voices.

*Keep moving!*

Beckham's limbs were working independently of his brain. He fired on targets without thinking, transforming into a machine. His lungs burned as if he was at the tail end of a marathon, every breath more strenuous than the last. The fall had rattled his senses, but his aim remained true.

Shot after shot took down the beasts; brains and bits

of gore covered the abandoned cars and trucks in the street with flecks of red. The creatures were closing in, but calculated shots from Ghost and the Variant Hunters were keeping them away from the civilians.

"Kate!" Beckham yelled a second time. She ran onto the sidewalk directly underneath a scaffold. Two Variants jumped onto the metal platform. He mowed them down with a line of fire that splattered them against the wall. His magazine clicked dry as he spun to fire on another group of three beasts that emerged from the open door of a pizza joint in front of Kate.

She froze, Jenny nearly toppling from her shoulders.

Beckham slung the M4 over his shoulder, dropped to one knee, and pulled his M9 in the same motion. He squeezed off three shots that hit each of the Variants in the chest. All but one collapsed to the ground. The survivor dropped to all fours and galloped toward Kate.

"Run, Kate!" Beckham shouted. He followed the monster in the gun's sights, held in a breath, and fired at the last possible second. The rounds weren't high caliber, but they did the trick when they slammed into the beast's skull. It dropped to the ground, skidding to a stop a few feet away from Kate, who stared in shock.

"Run!" Beckham yelled again.

The suppressed crack of Fitz's MK11 sounded, and in his peripheral, Beckham saw Fitz setting up shop against the hood of a car.

Beckham chased after Horn. He caught up a few seconds later, and they ran together, side by side.

"Tasha! Jenny!" Horn shouted. "I'm coming!" He fired his M249 in arcs at the walls of the buildings on both sides of the road. Variants lost their footing and crashed to the pavement. Tank and Garcia picked off the stragglers, but still the heart of the army of beasts barreled down the center of the street, their numbers growing as more Variants squeezed out of sewer openings and came crashing out of storefronts.

"Garcia, Tank! Watch our flanks!" Beckham shouted into his headset. It only took a quick glance to see there was nowhere to escape. Even if they tried, they couldn't outrun the beasts with children in tow. He eyed a fort of wrecked cars that could offer some protection if they could set up a perimeter there.

He didn't like it, but that was their only option.

"Boss, we have to get out of here," Horn said, his chest heaving. He jammed the butt of his M249 into its nook and fired off another volley. Then he continued running.

"Garcia, set me up a perimeter at those cars!" Beckham shouted. "We'll be right there."

Horn glared at him between shots, his disapproval clear on his face.

"There's nowhere to run, Big Horn. We have to stand our ground. No telling what's in those buildings," Beckham yelled as he bolted toward Kate.

She emerged around the burned-out hull of a car, Jenny jerking up and down on her shoulders. He kept his eye on them as he changed the magazine of his M4. She was ahead of the beasts now, but not by far.

Beckham brought the rifle back up to fire on a pair of Variants skittering through the ash a few cars behind Kate. He slipped as he squeezed off a shot, regained his balance, and then jumped onto the hood of a police cruiser. Kate and the civilians were only twenty feet away now—so close it seemed he could reach out and touch her.

*Almost there, baby. Almost . . .*

She looked up and halted when she saw him standing on the car.

"Keep running!" he shouted.

Another transmission surged in his ear. "Ghost, this is Wolf Four. Do you copy? Over."

Beckham didn't have time to answer. He fired over the heads of the civilians, taking out a group of beasts that had broken away from the main mass. Then he jumped onto the concrete and continued running. He'd bought them a minute at best.

"Reed!" Kate yelled.

They locked eyes again as Beckham closed the final distance. Horn passed him on the way, running faster than Beckham had ever seen him run. He reached Kate first, taking Jenny in one arm and then lurching over to Meg to grab Tasha. Donna carried Bo with the aid of two other civilians.

"Come on!" Beckham said. He lowered his rifle and grabbed Kate's hand—something he had thought he would never do again. A flood of emotions rushed through him, but there was no time to embrace her, no matter how much he wanted to simply gather her into his arms.

"Horn, watch out!" Beckham shouted as a Variant squeezed out of a sewer opening a few feet away from Jenny.

Beckham dropped to a knee and shot the creature between the eyes. Horn slung his rifle over his back and scooped up both girls in his massive arms.

"Behind me!" Beckham yelled. Kate hugged him from behind as he continued firing. She pressed her head against the back of his neck, her warm breath sending chills through him.

"I knew you would come," she said. "I knew you wouldn't leave me out here."

"Go, Kate! Go with the others!"

She wrapped her arms tighter around him, apparently determined not to let him go.

"Now! I'll be right behind you!" Beckham squeezed Kate's hand again. He hated to push her away, but he couldn't cover their retreat and shield her at the same time. Kate was just as stubborn as he was, and he could tell she wouldn't leave.

He squeezed off two more shots at a tiny Variant that had probably been ten or eleven years old before it had transformed into a monster. It was moving faster than the others, leaping onto the backs of older creatures and clawing its way to the front of the herd. Beckham shot it in the spine and watched it somersault into the mass. The crunch of bone rang out as the larger Variants trampled the little creature.

By the time Beckham and Kate turned around, the civilians, Ghost, and the Variant Hunters were already inside the fort of cars Tank and Garcia were defending. Meg and Horn helped Tasha, Jenny, and the others inside a sedan.

A round suddenly whizzed past Beckham's left side and cracked through a target behind him. The thud of a body crashing into a car followed. He turned to see a Variant with a missing face on the ground.

Fitz had nailed a head shot on a monster that had snuck up on Beckham and Kate. He would thank the marine later.

*If we survive.*

Beckham searched the buildings for a place to escape, hope bleeding out of him. The dark structures held no refuge, only abominations. There was nowhere to run, nowhere to hide. They had to stand their ground here.

"Fitz, I want you in the bed of that pickup. Big Horn, you and Tank set up your SAWs. Garcia, you're on me. Use your grenades," Beckham ordered. He twisted to fire off a shot at the wall of Variants. Every maw seemed to open at once, a massive black oblivion releasing a discordant sound that made Kate cling harder to Beckham's arm. She halted as they came upon a barrier of cars.

"Go through the middle!" Beckham said. He turned to fire as she squeezed between two bumpers. Pulling his magazine, he reached for another, jammed it home, and then hurried after her toward the vehicles. Jenny and Tasha were already safely inside a car, their faces pressed up against the filthy back window to watch.

Garcia and Tank spread their weapons over the hood of a police cruiser. Fitz jumped into the bed of the pickup, and in seconds all three marines opened fire. The rounds slammed into the wave of monsters trailing Beckham. He jumped and slid over the hood of the pickup truck, then bolted toward Horn.

Meg helped Kate into the car. Beckham couldn't wait to watch her get safely inside. He laid his M9 on the hood of the pickup and joined his brothers as they fired into the horde.

"Give me a gun!" someone shouted.

Beckham didn't need to turn to see it was Meg, nor did he hesitate to hand her his M9. A second later she was squeezing off shots at the horde less than two hundred feet away. The creatures seemed desperate, crashing into one another as they piled over charcoaled metal. He'd seen this many times before. They were starving.

"Short bursts, head shots. Stay focused!" Beckham ordered.

He centered his M4 on a Variant perched on the roof of a minivan and squeezed the trigger. It skidded down the hood, leaving a wake of gore. Two others took its place. They were quickly cut to shreds with shots to their emaciated ribs, bones shattering and exploding away from their withered bodies.

A transmission crackled in Beckham's earpiece.

"Ghost, this is Wolf Four! Do you copy? Over!" There was urgency to the message.

Beckham flicked his headset to his lips and yelled over the gunshots, "Copy that, Wolf Four. Ghost One. We're in the middle of a goddamn firefight!"

The wall of diseased flesh surged forward, spilling

over cars, taking up every inch of the street. Starving mouths opened, their jagged teeth anxious to bite. There were too many of the monsters. There was no way five soldiers and Meg could hold them off.

"That's for Riley!" the firefighter screamed as she pulled the trigger.

Beckham scanned his team as he changed a mag. Fitz was focused, his features calm. He fired relentlessly. Garcia and Tank showed the same control. But Horn fired like a madman, a stream of lead flying from his M249.

"Grenades!" Beckham shouted. He grabbed one from his vest, plucked out the pin, and tossed it into the tidal wave of monsters. Four others sailed through the air simultaneously.

"Get down!" Beckham yelled at the civilians in the car. Every head vanished from the windows. The soldiers all crouched behind the vehicles as the deafening blasts tore through the night. The street rumbled and shook. The blast slammed into the vehicles, jerking the cars up and down.

His ears ringing and equilibrium off, Beckham stumbled to his feet and continued firing into the drifting smoke. The middle of the street was filled with chunky debris. Variants missing limbs screeched in agony and dragged their ruined bodies across the concrete. The grenades had killed over half of the monsters.

Maybe Ghost had a chance after all.

"Don't let up!" Beckham shouted. "Keep firing!" He assassinated the remaining beasts as they scattered in all directions, shooting them in their backs with no trace of emotion.

Another message flared in his ear. "Ghost One, Wolf Four. What's your location? Over."

"Forty-Second Street, near the New York Public Library," Beckham said. "Need extraction ASAP! We have civilians in tow. Where the fuck are you guys?"

The reply was lost in a hail of gunfire. Beckham grunted and focused on his firing. Once the smoke cleared, he saw there was no time for extraction. The monsters were regrouping. Dozens more emerged on the rooftops on both sides of the street. All they were doing was drawing more Variants to their location.

He met Horn's gaze, and they shared a moment that reminded Beckham of the time at Fort Bragg when they had been surrounded and down to their knives. There was dread in Horn's eyes, but there was courage there too. If they were going to die, at least they were all going to die together.

Beckham glanced over his shoulder to look for Kate as he continued firing blindly at the beasts. She had her face pressed against the cracked car window, Tasha and Jenny on either side. He was turning back to the battle when a flash of motion behind them caught his eye. To the east, a pack of Variants trailed a beast wearing plates of human bones. He didn't question how the Alpha was still alive. He simply screamed, "Our six!"

The grenades had drawn another wave of beasts.

"Fitz, Meg, on me," Beckham said. "Tank, Horn, Garcia, you keep firing to the west."

Beckham slammed his shoulder into the car behind him, angling his M4 at the Alpha. His face was covered in deep lacerations, and his yellow eyes were trained on Beckham. Opening shredded lips, he let out a roar.

The beast looked back to the Variants galloping behind his bone-armored body. He shrieked at the creatures and pounded on his chest plate with his remaining hand, as if taunting them. The monsters screeched back and continued barreling toward the Alpha. It was then Beckham realized they hadn't been drawn to the gunfire at all.

Team Ghost and the Variant Hunters weren't just trapped in the heart of New York City. They were caught in the middle of a battle between rival Variant gangs.

# 4

Lieutenant Rachel Davis had been in deep shit when Captain Rick Humphrey found out about her authorizing a Black Hawk to fly Team Ghost and the Variant Hunters to New York. She had broken protocol, deceived her superiors, and risked one of the most important remaining military assets in the world—the lives of Ghost and VH. Not to mention a Black Hawk.

"They trained the strike groups for a goddamn reason!" Humphrey had shouted when he first found out. "We can't afford to lose them!"

Vice President Johnson's response, by contrast, had caught Davis off guard. "You're a brave woman, Lieutenant, and after talking to President Ringgold, I believe you did the right thing. Same thing I should have done from the beginning. Now let's just make sure we bring our boys home."

Humphrey had glared, but Johnson had offered a grin, exposing the gap between his front teeth. She hadn't known the vice president long, but now she understood why he was so well respected. He was a risk taker, but not reckless—a leader, but not a dictator.

Davis focused her sharp green eyes on the monitor showing the juvenile Variant that Beckham and Garcia had brought back from New York. The freak was fighting against its restraints more violently than before, shaking them so rapidly it made the image look as if the live feed was being fast-forwarded. The blur of armored flesh made Davis sick to her stomach, but she had been prepared to walk the plank and jump into the Atlantic Ocean just to capture the little fucker.

When the men had returned with the beast, she had thought it would change the tide of the war. But with every step forward, the Variants had thrown a wrench into the wheel and caused more setbacks—more losses. Plum Island was destroyed, and the leader of the science team behind Operation Extinction was a hostage, or worse.

"Captain on deck," called a voice.

She whirled to see Captain Humphrey and Vice President Johnson entering through the open hatch, a squad of marine sentries right behind them.

Coming to attention, Davis stiffened and threw up a crisp salute as she scrutinized Humphrey's sunburned face. He regarded her with a cold nod that told her he was still pissed off. Not that she blamed him. She had gone against his orders.

"Follow us, Lieutenant," Humphrey said.

She hurried after them to the front of the combat information center, from where she could see out the porthole windows. A carpet of clouds drifted across the moon, bathing the aircraft carrier in darkness. The *GW* strike group was splitting through the waves toward Plum Island to recover the bioreactors and casualties. With the perimeter fences destroyed and several of the buildings ruined, there was no use wasting resources to rebuild. The bioreactors would be brought to the *Cowpens*, and the remaining scientists would finish the work Dr. Lovato had started—with or without her.

Davis waited, arms folded across her chest. Patience was something she had struggled with for the past six weeks. Watching her beloved country die and not being able to do much to stop it was devastating. But they were nearing the end. In a week or less, Kryptonite would be deployed, and they would make one final push to take back the world from the monsters.

Captain Humphrey finished talking to Vice President Johnson and turned to Davis. "What's the status of the juvenile?"

"Still alive, sir," Davis replied, dropping her arms to her sides and standing upright again. "It was injected with Kryptonite a little over an hour ago. So far the drug seems to be having no effect."

"Christ," Johnson said, massaging his forehead. After a pause, he looked out over the waves and clasped his hands behind his back. "Any word on Team Ghost and VH?"

"Air support and teams are still on their way to Manhattan, sir."

"What's their ETA?" Johnson asked.

Davis glanced at her wristwatch. "Should be there in fifteen minutes, Mister Vice President."

"Lieutenant," said a voice from near the radio equipment. Corporal Bruce Anderson was looking in her direction. Davis remembered his name because of the distinctive birthmark above his right eyebrow. Both of his brows were scrunched together now.

She knew that look. He had intel.

Davis rushed over to him, Humphrey and Johnson in close pursuit. When she got to his station, she put her hands on the back of his chair and leaned down.

Anderson cupped his hand over his earpiece and then glanced up, his youthful brown eyes hard to read.

"What is it, Corporal?" Davis asked.

"Wolf Four just reported in, Lieutenant."

"And?"

"The Black Hawk Ghost and VH took to New York has been shot down. There are survivors, but Wolf Four reports they're being pursued by Variants."

"What the hell do you mean, 'shot down'?" Humphrey asked.

Holding up a finger with one hand and cupping his earpiece a second time with his other, Anderson listened to another transmission. Davis tensed as they waited. She wanted to look out over the ocean, to search for the coastline she couldn't see.

The wait wasn't long.

Anderson glanced up again, and this time there was no mistaking the look of trepidation in his eyes.

"Wolf Four just performed another flyover. Ghost and VH are protecting a group of civilians on Forty-Second Street, but they're completely surrounded."

"How many?" Davis asked, afraid to hear the answer.

Anderson hesitated again, his gaze flitting from Davis to Humphrey and finally to Johnson.

"Hundreds. Wolf Four said the streets are full of the bastards."

Rain rinsed away the ash on the car window. Outside, every single Variant in New York seemed to descend on Team Ghost's position. The pavement trembled under thousands of pounding hands and feet.

Kate pressed her face against the inside of the muddy, cracked passenger's-side window in the back seat. Her heart was thumping, her eyes on Beckham. Her mind told her this was it: There was no way out. Escaping this army was as impossible as running through the rain and not getting hit by a single drop.

But she also knew the men protecting her would never give up. Beckham and the others fired at the approaching hordes relentlessly. Apollo, soaked and injured, barked at the monsters streaming down the sides of buildings. The pale creatures slithered into the streets from open manholes. They broke down doors and tumbled out of windows. The body of Sergeant Thomas, a marine Kate hardly knew, was sprawled out on the ground behind Garcia. All around them, the streets filled with the starving creatures, their frail bodies transformed into sacks of shriveled skin and bones.

They seemed so fragile, as if they were wasting away. But the Variants moved just as quickly as before, charging at a speed that made Apollo look slow. It was the epigenetic changes from VX-99 that kept them moving like wild animals.

From somewhere overhead came the roar of jets. The rumble was lost in the onslaught of gunfire and heavy rainfall. Kate saw Beckham and Fitz throw what looked like baseballs at the swarming Variants.

"Get down!" someone shouted.

Kate ducked and shielded Tasha and Jenny from the deafening detonations. Explosions bloomed into the air. The car shook from the blasts. Both girls buried their faces against her chest. She wrapped her arms around them, doing her best to protect the children. To Kate's right, Donna held on to Bo, but the boy struggled to look out the window.

"Where's Daddy?" he sobbed. Tugging on her arm, he continued, "Mommy, where's Daddy?" Donna stared out the window blankly, her gaze vacant. Kate recognized the signs of shock; she was pretty sure her face had looked the same way earlier. She didn't have the strength or energy to help reassure the woman. She was doing everything she could to hold it together herself.

Another grenade exploded down the street. The fiery burst sent a geyser of flesh and gore into the sky. Shrapnel broke through the car's cracked windshield, punching through the top of the front seats.

"Keep your heads down!" Horn shouted over his shoulder. Kate saw his face, strained with shock and terror.

Kate scooted lower with the girls. It took Donna a few seconds to respond, but she got down on the floor with Bo as four more small explosions rocked the concrete.

"Stay put," Kate ordered. She recognized her own voice again. It was authoritative, and it made Tasha wail even louder. Saliva stretched across the child's wide lips as she lost all control. Jenny tucked her head between her knees and rocked back and forth. The sight shattered Kate's already throbbing heart. She twisted to look out the back window. In the faint moonlight, she saw something that took away her breath.

The Alpha who had led the attack on Plum Island marched down the street, plates of human bones clanking against his muscular body. A dozen Variants sprinted across the street and raced past the enormous beast. They leaped onto burned vehicles, smashed into garbage cans, and knocked into one another. Another wave cascaded over the sides of the buildings at the other end of the street, joining a group that had emerged from an open manhole.

Beckham, Meg, and Fitz fought desperately. They killed the climbers with calculated shots and lobbed grenades that tore the creatures on the ground apart, but Kate could see there was no way they could stop them all.

Despite the overwhelming numbers of their enemy, the trio appeared calm. Beckham handed Meg another magazine and then grabbed a grenade from his vest. He tossed it at a scaffold down the street. The explosion knocked the structure loose from the building. It came crashing down, trapping four monsters.

Kate's eyes flitted to the skyline. In her mind's eye, she imagined what their position would look like from above. They were behind a blockade of four wrecked cars. Tank, Horn, and Garcia held one side, while Beckham, Meg, and Fitz fired from the other. The Variants were closing from both directions, crawling over every surface like albino ants.

Beckham was yelling now, but she couldn't make out the words. Fitz and Meg were still calm, their eyes centered through their gun sights as they fired.

Was Reed losing it? Had he gone over the edge?

The thought terrified her.

He stopped to change a magazine, still apparently talking, his head bowed. His lips were moving as he brought his weapon up and fired off three short bursts. Lowering his rifle, he suddenly backed away from the truck and rushed to the car. Opening the door, he yelled, "We have to move!"

Kate saw something in his brown eyes she hadn't seen before—something raw and deep. When he turned away, Kate finally understood. He didn't think he could save them this time.

She jumped out onto the pavement, heart assaulting her ribs. Then she turned and reached for Tasha and Jenny. The girls wouldn't budge. Both were curled up in the back seat.

"Come on!" Kate said. She grabbed their small hands and pulled them out of the car with deliberate care. Both girls stood on the street shaking and sobbing, red hair matted to their heads, pants wet with urine. They reached out for their father.

"Stay back!" Horn yelled.

Kate grabbed them by the hands and pulled them

toward Beckham. She waited behind him, eyes roving across the battlefield while he centered his rifle at the roof of the building above them. Blurred shapes of Variants raced across the edge. Two of the shadows tumbled over the side.

Muzzle flashes lit up the streets. In the glimmer, the withered, soaked flesh of the Variants spread like a shadow. Their long, skeletal limbs seemed to distort as they reached out with their talons.

The creatures were growing more desperate.

"Use the rest of your grenades!" Beckham shouted. "Tank and Horn, train your fire on the buildings. We have to get inside. Fitz, you and Garcia help me clear a path. Meg, Kate, Donna—you guard the kids."

It was almost impossible to hear Beckham over the noise. He motioned for her to get down as soon as the final grenades were lobbed into the attacking hordes.

The explosions ripped through the streets, tossing an arm that landed on the concrete in front of Kate with a meaty thud. Ears ringing, she bent down for Tasha to jump on her back. Meg grabbed Jenny's hand, and together they all ran after Beckham and Fitz. In a single-file line, they squeezed through a gap between the cars. Tank and Horn went next. The bulky marines had trouble wedging through the narrow space, their massive frames scraping against the bumpers.

Kate turned back to watch as the last of their group fled the barricade. She had to know they all made it. Garcia stopped to drag Thomas under the armpits. He got him to the gap, but couldn't pull the dead marine through the space. Garcia hesitated with one hand on Thomas's chest, and then he grabbed the man's dog tags and ripped them away. Kate choked up at the sight. She had come to understand the way these soldiers thought, to understand their fierce brotherhood and loyalty. She knew what it cost him to leave a man behind.

Tank and Horn continued fighting their way into the street, picking off the beasts darting across the buildings. Beckham, Garcia, and Fitz formed a ring to fire on the Variants closing in from the sides.

"Don't stop!" Beckham shouted, gesturing with his free hand.

Kate ran after Meg and Donna toward the shattered windows of a clothing store. Inside, charcoaled bodies reached up with burned hands. As she got closer, she saw they were just mannequins.

"Hurry! They're coming!" Beckham shouted.

Kate narrowed her eyes on him, wondering if he had finally lost it. She had never questioned him before. He was a Delta Force operator and should have been able to come up with a plan on the fly, but why hadn't he ordered them into the building in the first place? The desperation in his eyes scared her almost as much as the monsters did.

"We got thirty seconds!" Horn yelled.

The beasts rushed for their position. A cloud of smoke from the grenades shifted across the street. Several Variants lost their grip in the wet ash and were trampled by the pack. The wall of muscular limbs and open maws surged forward, rounds cutting some of the creatures down but only slowing their advance. It wouldn't even be thirty seconds before their sucker lips were clamped onto Tasha, Jenny, and Bo.

What the hell was Beckham thinking?

When they reached the sidewalk, Beckham, Garcia, and Fitz turned to fire. Horn went into the building first. He fired off a long burst and yelled, "Clear!"

Tank stayed on the curb to fire at any target that dared show its naked flesh above their position.

"Get inside!" Horn shouted.

A distant chopping sound emerged over the gunfire.

Kate lost track of the noise as she followed Meg toward the building. Tasha bounced on Kate's shoulders, her warm, wet pants soaking into Kate's drenched shirt. Donna carried Bo into the debris-ridden room.

"Move it!" Horn ordered. He gestured a massive hand toward overturned racks halfway blocking a door at the other end of the room.

"Where are we going?" Kate yelled.

"Keep moving!" Beckham shouted back.

Flashes of green suddenly ripped down the street, turning the Variants closing in on the building into chunky pulp as if they had been thrown into a meat grinder. Kate ducked under a long piece of glass hanging from the top of the store window, catching the reflection of something on the skyline.

She blinked the water from her eyes at the sight of dozens of dots on the horizon. Under the moon, in the sheets of falling rain, the sky filled with aircraft of all shapes and sizes—Black Hawks, Apaches, and smaller choppers she didn't even know the names of.

"Hurry!" Beckham shouted.

Everyone but Fitz ran for the back room. He took one knee at the doorway, his MK11's muzzle focused on the herd of beasts coming from the west.

"Move it, marine!" Beckham yelled.

Fitz roved his rifle to the right. Kate corralled the kids into a filthy stockroom that reeked of smoke, but waited at the door to watch Fitz. She followed his gun's muzzle to the center of the approaching army. At the front of the pack, surrounded by bony Variants half his size, the Alpha pushed forward.

Crack!

In the blink of an eye, the beast slumped to his knees, the front of his face caved in and the back of his skull exploding in a spray of gore.

"Run!" Beckham screamed.

Fitz lowered his smoking rifle, jumped to his blades, and bolted into the building just as the street lit up with tracer rounds. The Variants vanished in a cloud of bloody mist and body parts. The sound of gunfire and incoming aircraft hit Kate like a wave crashing into her. She cupped her hands over her ears and crouched.

Beckham waited for Fitz in the middle of the room. A grin touched the sides of the marine's lips when he reached Beckham.

"Sorry, boss. I had some unfinished business," Fitz said.

Ellis stood in front of the glass window of Cell 6. Inside, the juvenile Variant Yokoyama had named Lucy glared back at him. It was still hanging from the chains that kept it stretched in an *X*. Its thick eyelids, rimmed with scabby armor, blinked slowly. The creature tilted its head from side to side and narrowed its slitted, almond-shaped pupils at Ellis. For a second, he wasn't sure who was observing whom.

The analytical part of his mind studied Lucy with a deep fascination, but the emotional side focused on Kate. It was hard to concentrate on the beast in front of him without confirmation whether his partner was dead or alive. The only consolation was knowing Beckham was on his way to rescue her. If there was anyone left in the world who could pull that off, it was the Delta Force operator. He would use his bare hands if he had to.

"It's not working, is it?" Yokoyama asked.

Ellis shook his head. "Doesn't look like it." He let out a long sigh.

It had been several hours since Sergeant Russo had

injected Lucy with Kryptonite. So far she'd shown no reaction. If the Superman protein wasn't present in her body, then the drug particles would be moving aimlessly through her bloodstream like bullets without a target.

"Goddamnit." He ran a hand through his dark hair, pulling it back and holding it there. "The protein must have changed in the offspring."

His mind swam with questions. What came next? How could he possibly find a way to kill these monsters without Kate? And, more importantly, how could he do it in a week's time? The clock was ticking, and if they didn't defeat the Variants soon, there wouldn't be enough people left on the planet to rebuild the human race.

Yokoyama took a step closer to the glass, but they both turned at the sound of footfalls in the passage. Lieutenant Davis led a group of marines into the brig. Russo and his men greeted them halfway down. Lieutenant Davis directed her sharp green eyes at Ellis. He stared back at her, hoping she had news for him about Kate.

"So," Davis said, "do you have a sitrep or what?"

"Kryptonite doesn't appear to be working," Ellis said. When she didn't budge, he added, "Yet." He gestured toward the hatch. "Have a look for yourself."

Davis pushed her way up to the window. Lucy hissed, tongue shooting out and circling wormy lips. The juvenile's armored eyelids clicked, the sound audible from where Ellis stood.

"Yet? That thing looks pretty goddamn healthy to me," Davis said. "The president and vice president are not going to be pleased." She ran a finger across her chin. "And I'm not going to be the one to tell them. Doctor Yokoyama, you stay here and keep an eye on Lucy. Doctor Ellis, if you would follow me, I'd like this to come from you. Captain Humphrey has requested an update in the CIC. There's also something I think you should see."

"Let me know immediately if something changes," Ellis said to Yokoyama. As he turned to follow the marine escort, his heart raced. Davis didn't seem like the type of woman who would just hand over information, but he had to ask.

"Have you heard anything about Kate?"

"I'm not authorized to say, Doctor," Davis replied.

Ellis considered asking in a different way but kept his mouth sealed instead. He would find out soon enough.

It took fifteen minutes to depart the *Cowpens* and return to the *George Washington*. Davis didn't say another word until they got to the Zodiac that would ferry them to the aircraft carrier.

"You think it's possible Kryptonite hasn't had a chance to work yet?"

Ellis twisted his mouth to the side, considering his next words carefully. Perhaps he could barter for news. "I'm not authorized to say," Ellis said. Wiping salt water from his forehead, he raised a brow. "Unless you can tell me anything about Kate?"

Davis's alligator jaw remained clamped shut.

*Damn. I suck at negotiating.*

"Maybe it needs more time," Ellis said. "But I'd say it's highly unlikely. My guess is the protein the drug targets isn't present in the juveniles."

Davis nodded, and they endured the rest of the trip in silence. The moonlight sparkled over the water, and bulging clouds rolled across the horizon as a storm moved east. Jolting up and down, Ellis shielded his eyes with a hand as salty spray hit his face.

Halfway to the *GW*, Davis bowed her head and laced her fingers together as if in prayer. Ellis hadn't taken her for the sentimental type, but the show of emotion didn't last long. Davis sat up straight a few minutes later to look for the aircraft carrier.

Every wave the Zodiac crested made Ellis's heart pound harder. He couldn't wait any longer for news.

"Lieutenant, please just tell me. Have they found Kate? She's my partner. I deserve to know."

Davis grabbed a handle on the side of the boat. "I'm sorry, but I couldn't tell you even if I did know." She looked over his shoulder at the marines in the back of the craft.

Ellis didn't reply. He focused on the aircraft carrier as it ballooned in size. A chopper took off from the deck and thumped overhead. A few minutes later, Ellis was climbing a ladder to the deck. He hurried after Davis and moved into the ship, navigating the bulkheads at a brisk jog. Their pace confirmed what he already knew. Humphrey didn't just need a report on Lucy; he had news from New York.

Davis slowed when they reached the CIC. She waved Ellis through the open hatch. He was blasted by hot air as soon as he entered. In the center of the room, men and women in blue uniforms huddled around a cluster of monitors. Ellis scanned them as he approached. These were the faces of humanity's last hope: the pockmarked cheeks of a man with a receding hairline, a young officer with a birthmark over his right eyebrow, and the freckled nose of a woman around Ellis's age. There were all shapes, sizes, and colors represented in this room. The crews of the *GW* and the other vessels of the strike group were the last American forces standing between the Variants and extinction.

"Stay here, Doctor," Davis said.

Ellis stood on his tiptoes to see the monitors. They were divided into different screens, each with the green hue of night-vision cameras.

"Target coming into view in a few seconds, sir," the freckled woman said to Captain Humphrey.

Davis joined the small crowd, but Ellis remained where he was, straining to hear the conversation. "What are you hearing, Corporal Anderson?" Captain Humphrey asked.

The man with the birthmark looked up. "Lots of chatter, Captain. Still trying to get confirmation that it's Doctor Lovato and her people."

Ellis took a step forward, heart kicking at his rib cage. It felt as if he'd just downed a Red Bull and Adderall.

He pulled at his soaked collar.

On-screen, he saw four vehicles peppered with tomato-sized bullet holes outside a shattered storefront. Hundreds of smoking bodies lined the street and sidewalk. Limbs and chunks of gore speckled the concrete. Some of those bodies were still twitching. There was movement at the top of the screen where Variants were fleeing the scene. The beasts crawled into sewer openings and scaled buildings, in a frenzy to escape.

"Just got word, Captain," Anderson said. "Team Ghost and the Variant Hunters are seeking refuge in a building on Forty-Second Street, along with Doctor Lovato and several other survivors."

Ellis couldn't control his excitement. He did a fist pump as he watched the live feed, but no one seemed to notice. They were all admiring the view. The cavalry had arrived in Manhattan, just in the nick of time.

Black Hawks circled, their M240s spitting rounds at the fleeing creatures. Apaches pursued the monsters to the east and west, sending missiles streaking through the air. Little black helicopters roamed the skyline with miniguns, taking out the beasts that tried to escape to the rooftops.

The Variant army was on the run.

All around Ellis, the officers studied the feeds. He

wasn't sure if it was appropriate to smile until he saw a grin on Davis's face. She glanced over at him, her smile fading slightly, and said, "I sure hope Kryptonite starts working on Lucy. The human race could use another miracle right about now."

# 5

Fitz usually felt a rush of adrenaline after killing a monster. Man or Variant, it was almost always the same: satisfaction mixed with the slimy chill of knowing you'd taken a life.

But not this time.

This was different from what he'd felt killing Iraqi insurgents or even the Variants he'd taken down before now. The Bone Collector hadn't just been an Alpha—he had been evil. And he had killed Fitz's friend.

This rush was pure satisfaction, without any guilt.

*Rot in hell, you piece of shit.*

The anger felt good—much better than the despair he'd been living with for six weeks. It reminded him of when he'd arrived at Walter Reed to begin his long rehabilitation, when it finally sank in that his friends were dead and his legs were gone. He'd had to rebuild his life from scratch back then.

Loss wasn't new to Fitz. He'd lived with it his entire life. Friendly fire took his brother in Afghanistan. His parents had died in a car accident, and most of his brothers-in-arms had been killed in the War on Terror or by the Variants. But he still had some friends left.

He was still part of Team Ghost.

And he could still fight.

Sometimes he needed the rage and anger to remind him he was a warrior. Killing the Bone Collector had felt good, but the feeling would pass. The darkness would try to slip back over him. He had to stay ahead of it; he had to stay frosty. He had to keep fighting.

The zip of a round punching through drywall sent Fitz ducking. He stroked Apollo's bloodstained coat and tried to calm the dog.

"Everyone stay down," Beckham said. He shielded Kate with his flak jacket, hovering over her on the floor. "Central One, Ghost One, we're taking *friendly* fire. Advise your goddamn pilots again of our location."

Fitz blocked out the noise from the radio and focused on the civilians. Looking over at those inside of the storeroom, he saw the faces of men, women, and children who would have to rebuild their lives just as he had after Iraq. For some it would be harder than for others. Especially the children.

"Where's my daddy?" Bo asked.

Donna was on the floor a few feet behind Beckham, with Bo curled up in a fetal position next to her. Horn lay on his belly in middle of the room, Tasha and Jenny tucked up against him. His SAW was strapped over his back, the muzzle still smoking. Garcia and Tank were crouched next to the door, peering through the gap at the battle raging outside. Meg was the only one by herself. She was covered in ash, had her knees up to her chest, and was rocking back and forth against a wall. She held an M9 tightly in her bloody right hand. Her knuckles were white from squeezing the grip.

Two more rounds tore through the ceiling, sending panels crashing to the ground. One of the pieces landed on Beckham's back. He shook off the dust and wiped away the residue from Kate's forehead.

The air support continued circling outside, hunting down the monsters that had, minutes before, been hunting Fitz and the others. The chop of rotors, explosions from missiles, and chatter of high-caliber gunfire was music to his ringing ears. They were safe. For now. Beckham was reunited with Kate, and Horn with his daughters. There was no bringing back Riley, but maybe, Fitz thought, he could offer some comfort to Meg.

"Stay," Fitz said to Apollo. He crawled over to Meg and wrapped his arm around her. She wiped away a tear to look at him. The raw, deep pain in her eyes told Fitz how much she had cared for Riley. Hell, they'd all loved the kid. He'd been their comic relief, a ball of positive energy in Team Ghost.

"It's okay. It's all going to be okay now," Fitz whispered.

Meg heaved a skeptical sigh, but she allowed him to hold her.

They sat like that for several minutes, listening to the battle raging outside. The sounds were more distant now. Only intermittent gunshots echoed through the store.

Fitz dreaded the silence. He would rather hear the crack of gunfire than the crying of those around him. War, it seemed, had become a relief from the quiet of peacetime. That's when it was the worst for Fitz. At least, when he was fighting, he had something to keep his mind off the darkness.

A voice flared in his earpiece. "Ghost One, Central One, prepare for extraction, over."

Fitz put his hand on top of Meg's shaking hand. He tried to tighten his grip, but his own hand was shaking too.

"It's okay," Fitz said. "We're going home."

"N-no," Meg stuttered. "We're not."

Beckham looked back at them. "Plum Island is gone, Fitz. We're going back to the *GW*."

Fitz slowly pulled his hand away from Meg's. He'd forgotten: Guard Tower 4 was no longer his office. His post had been destroyed, and the island he had called home for the past month was abandoned.

"Let's move!" Garcia shouted.

Tank swung the door open and rushed through with his SAW out in front. Garcia shouldered his M4 and followed with his hand on Tank's back. They were the only two members of the Variant Hunters left. Fitz shook his head. Team Ghost was down to only two original members as well. And Chow was the only surviving member of Delta Force Team Titanium. Perhaps they would all merge under one banner soon. That thought gave Fitz the energy to scoop Meg to her feet.

Beckham whistled at Apollo, and in seconds the team was moving.

The downdraft from helicopters hit the group as soon as they were in the storefront, whipping up dust and the stench of scorched flesh. The street was covered in body parts, spread out as if some psycho killer's food truck had tipped over and spilled all of its rotten contents.

Fitz held Meg around her waist. She kept up with him, but still had the pistol gripped tight against her chest. In front of them, Beckham jogged through an inch of blood as he crossed the street. Meg gasped and stumbled. Fitz had to hold her tighter to keep them both from going down.

Overhead, four Black Hawks hovered. Apaches and MH-6 Little Bird choppers raced across the skyline, still searching for stragglers. A squadron of F-18 Super Hornets roared over the horizon, their mission complete, heading back to the *GW*.

One of the Black Hawks set down nimbly between

the wrecked bodies of two vehicles. A crew chief jumped onto the pavement, waving frantically. A marine roved the door-mounted M240 at the buildings above, searching for any monsters that had survived.

Fitz threw glances over his shoulders every few feet as he led Meg to the chopper. The sight of the civilians ducking under the shattered glass of the storefront window and running into the gory street was surreal. Horn couldn't spare his girls from the horror, and Donna shared the same lost look as Bo.

"My God, what have we done?"

At first, Fitz wasn't sure who he was talking to, or what he was talking about. He helped Meg climb into the Black Hawk and sent one last look around the ruined city street. In the near-silence under the rotor wash, Fitz realized he was talking about the human race.

Beckham slumped against the bulkhead as the Black Hawk ascended into the sky. Kate sat between his legs, turned at an angle to rest her head against his chest. Normally he would be at the door next to his men, firing on any threats, but he couldn't let go of her now. He wrapped his arms around her so tight he could smell the sweat on her neck. Bowing his helmeted head, he kissed her on the forehead. Apollo was nestled up against him, his muzzle on Kate's leg.

"It's okay, Kate. I'm never going to let go of you again. I'm never going to let anything happen to you or our child."

She glanced up at him with eyelids swollen from crying. Her blue eyes had lost their passionate spark. It wasn't the first time Beckham had seen her like this, but it was the worst. The assault on Plum Island, the kidnapping—it was enough to break anyone and drive them over the edge.

"Kate, are you with me?" Beckham asked when she didn't reply.

She managed a nod, then rested her head back on his vest. Beckham stroked her hair and took a moment to scan the troop hold. Fitz and Tank stood at the edge of the open door, their guns angled at the street. Garcia was right behind them, holding something shiny in his hands.

*Thomas's dog tags.*

Another marine lost. And this time it wasn't even to a Variant but to a human collaborator. Beckham buried the pain and focused on what seemed like a miracle: Horn still had his daughters. Donna and Bo were alive. Meg was safe. Fitz and Apollo had survived Operation Condor. And Kate was back in his arms. There was no denying things were bad, but they could have been much worse.

The pilot on the left side of the cockpit twisted and shouted, "Y'all okay?"

Beckham gave a thumbs-up.

"Name's Lewis. Hang on, everyone, I'm taking us home," the pilot said. "Harms, stay frosty on that gun. Wilson, check those kids."

"I'm on it," the crew chief said.

Apollo's amber eyes flitted upward every few seconds, pained whimpers coming from his throat.

"Hang on, boy, we're going to get you fixed up really soon," Beckham said. He looked for Wilson. The man was crouched next to Tasha.

"When you're finished, can you look at my dog?" Beckham shouted.

Wilson nodded and went back to applying a bandage on Tasha's leg. Horn was gritting his teeth, the sight of his daughter in pain overwhelming him as nothing else had. Jenny sat on his lap, her head buried against his crimson-stained flak jacket.

Outside the open door, an armada of helicopters traversed the sky. Four Apaches led the pack, with a half dozen MH-6 Little Birds racing after them like miniature beetles. Next came the eight Black Hawks.

Several of the Little Birds swooped away to chase a pack of Variants still retreating. They opened up with their M134 miniguns, 7.62-millimeter rounds plowing into concrete and slamming through the buildings the Variants were scaling.

Harms, a young marine with a neck tattoo and a scar on his right cheek, yelled, "Yeah! Kill those motherfuckers!" He roved the M240 toward the battle with one hand and pumped his other in celebration.

Tank and Garcia ignored their fellow marine, and Horn didn't bother telling him to watch his language around his girls. It was obvious everyone had other things on their minds.

Beckham hadn't known Thomas very well. The man had been quiet, but he had fought furiously and without fear. No matter how many Variants were slaughtered below, it wouldn't relieve the pain of losing Riley or Thomas.

"Holy shit, look at that!" Fitz said. He brought his MK11 up to zoom in on the view.

"My God, I've never seen so many!" Tank shouted over the rotors.

Kate suddenly pushed up off Beckham, alert. Wiping her eyes, she turned to the door, her interest piqued.

"I'll be right back, okay?" Beckham said.

Kate grabbed his hand. "I'm coming with."

Apollo and Meg followed them to the open door. Beckham narrowed his eyes on a city devoid of lights.

It was still remarkable to see New York like this. Hundreds of buildings were dark, derelict, and tattooed with scars of war. Moonlight spilled over the towers and the beasts below.

Beckham heard them before he saw them. The clatter of talons and snapping joints was audible even over the whoosh of the choppers.

Spotlights from several Black Hawks danced over the skyscrapers and angled toward the ground. The beams hit a street swelling with pallid flesh. The monsters were streaming into a massive crater.

"That's Grand Central Station," Fitz said.

General Kennor had pounded the location into the ground during Operation Liberty, after they'd learned there was a hive more than one hundred thousand strong there. Apparently those bombs hadn't gone deep enough.

There were still thousands of the monsters.

No—tens of thousands. And they were all returning to their home after being drawn out by the recent military activity. The creatures were smart. They knew they couldn't win a battle against aircraft.

The pilots of the Little Birds swooped lower, beneath the rooflines of buildings surrounding what had been the transportation hub. Those with missile launchers let their salvos fly.

"We still got any F-18s left in the area?" Beckham asked over the comm.

"They've been recalled to the *GW*," Lewis replied instantly.

As the Black Hawk shot over the street, Beckham and the other observers watched in grim silence. Beneath them was one of the largest hives the military had ever discovered. If only they had the firepower to take the creatures out while they were still in the open! Even with the 7.62-millimeter rounds and rockets, the Little Birds were only picking away at the swarm. The Apaches broke off ahead and banked to the left, Command apparently having ordered them to the fight. One by one, the Black Hawks flanking Beckham's bird peeled away.

"Ghost One, be advised, Central has requested all aircraft without refugees to pound the shit out of that hive," Lewis said. "But I could always slow down for a few minutes."

Garcia looked over his shoulder, narrowing his eyes despite the bruises beneath them. It was the marine's tell: He wanted to stay in the fight.

Beckham shook his head. He wasn't going to risk anything happening to Kate or the others now.

"Get us back to the *GW*, ASAP," Beckham ordered.

"Roger that. Command, this is Raven One, en route to home plate, over."

Their Black Hawk circled the hive one last time. The six Little Birds dropped even lower, hovering just thirty feet above the street. The beasts leaped at the choppers, talons reaching for their skids. The Variants were torn apart as they continued to jump onto cars and into the sky. Relentless and crazed, these monsters were far different from the intelligent Alphas.

Beckham went to turn away, but then he saw the rooftops were filling with the creatures. Variants jumped out of broken windows, scaled the exteriors of buildings, and climbed onto the roofs. Several of the Variants galloped to gain momentum and then propelled themselves into the air, using their back legs as springs. Most of the pilots managed to pull away from their reach, but one of the creatures landed on the skid of a Little Bird.

"Shit!" Fitz shouted.

The chopper jerked hard to the left, nearly crashing into one of the other small black aircraft. The Variant held on as the pilots tried to shake it off.

Fitz secured his grip on his rifle and took in a deep breath. He waited for the perfect moment, when the chopper seemed to be gliding in slow motion. In that moment, Beckham watched two shots that lanced away from the suppressed MK11's muzzle in his peripheral vision. The first streaked by the chopper's skids, but the second took off the Variant's head. It hung there for several seconds before falling limply to the street below.

"Holy fuck!" Harms shouted. "Nice shot, brother." He was laughing, but Fitz simply spit out the open door. Beckham rapped Fitz on the shoulder with a palm.

"You're a beast on that gun, Fitzy," he said.

The Little Birds pulled up so they were out of the reach of any more leapers before continuing their assault. Crimson tides flowed freely in the street. Rounds streaked into the mass of Variants, but it wouldn't be long before the pilots were out of ammo.

"Wolf Nine says he owes one to whoever pulled off that shot," Lewis said.

Fitz simply nodded and continued scanning the terrain with his rifle. Beckham gripped Kate's sweaty palm and laced his fingers with hers. She reached up and wrapped her arm around him to whisper something in his ear.

Beckham only heard five words over the gunfire, rotors, and shrieking monsters.

"Didn't think I'd see...again..."

He hugged her. "I'm so sorry. I should have been—"

"It's okay, Reed. This is war. We all have our missions."

Beckham heard every word this time. The strength in her voice took him off guard. This was the Kate he had fallen in love with. Her words reminded him of something Riley had told him weeks before, when he'd had to leave the wounded young Delta operator behind on Plum Island while the rest of Team Ghost went back into the field. He loosened his grip on her hand, but she quickly tightened hers on his.

That didn't relieve his pain. He had failed the kid, failed him as he had so many others. The agony was almost unbearable, and Beckham choked on the rush of pain. A tear fell from his eye. He didn't bother wiping it away. Kate did it for him.

As they left New York, Team Ghost and the civilians retreated to the center of the troop hold, taking seats or crouching on the floor. Only Fitz remained at the door, next to Harms. He raked his MK11 back and forth, scanning rooftops and windows for hostiles.

When they were almost out of the city, he pointed with his right hand. "Harms, you see that?"

"Yeah—holy shit, man!"

"Beckham, you better get over here," Fitz said.

Beckham kissed Kate on the cheek and worked his way over to the door. The husks of skyscrapers lined the horizon like metal gravestones. One building was nothing more than a skeletal frame that looked like a rib cage blown outward.

He followed Fitz's finger to one of the tallest apartment buildings in the distance. A full moon carpeted the roof with a blanket of white. But Beckham still couldn't see anything out of the ordinary.

"Here," Fitz said. He handed Beckham his MK11.

Taking the rifle, Beckham quickly zoomed in on the rooftop. His aching heart skipped a beat when he saw the plastic buckets. There were hundreds of them, all positioned carefully to spell out a message: HELP US.

Ellis left the control center of the *GW* with a spring in his step.

He didn't care that Captain Humphrey had pounded a table when he found out Kryptonite wasn't working on Lucy, or that he had yelled at Ellis for failing to have a backup plan to kill the juveniles. Nothing could mask the relief Ellis felt knowing Kate was alive.

Humanity had finally earned a win.

"Yes!" Ellis fist-pumped for a second time. A sailor working on a pipe turned to glare at him, but Ellis didn't care. His partner was coming back, and they were going to finish what they had started.

Rushing through passages and up ladders, Ellis made his way back to the flight deck, where he was escorted by a squad of six marines to a Black Hawk. He climbed inside with a smile on his face, ignoring the heavily armed men. His eyes were on the jeweled sky. The storm had finally passed, the cloud cover dispersing and the rain letting up. Ellis settled into his seat as the engine fired and the rotor's whup-whup drowned out the quieter sounds of an ocean after a storm.

"Hold on to something, Doctor," said a marine with the largest nostrils Ellis had ever seen. Ellis gripped a handhold just as the bird jolted and then ascended into the sky. In the distance, the strike group drifted across the waves. The ships surrounded him on all sides. For a fleeting moment, he felt was a sense of calm. It was a reminder of the days before the outbreak, back when he had been fighting microscopic monsters on the other side of the world. He had loved his life then: traveling, experiencing new cultures, and helping impoverished populations.

A draft of crisp, warm ocean air pulled him back to the present. The *Cowpens* grew in size as the chopper lowered itself over the vessel.

Jumping onto the flight deck, Ellis ran in a hunch after the marine with big nostrils. The man cradled his rifle across his chest when they got to a hatch. Ellis turned to scan the horizon, hoping to catch a glimpse of helicopters returning from New York. Instead, he saw nothing but a sky painted with dazzling stars.

"Doctor Ellis, if you would follow us, please. Doctor Yokoyama is waiting for you at the brig," said one of the marines.

Ellis pivoted away from the view and continued into the ship's interior. They worked their way below decks at a relaxed pace. None of them seemed anxious to get where they were going. Not that Ellis could blame them. The inside of the *Cowpens* was dark and reeked of bleach. None of the ships were inviting, exactly, but there was something about this one that gave him the creeps. The *Cowpens* had an evil history, what with the experiments that had been conducted on Lieutenant Brett, other Variants, and now, Lucy. Building 8 had given Ellis a similar chill.

Leaving Plum Island behind for this place was going to take some getting used to, but at least he was alive.

Dr. Yokoyama was waiting outside Lucy's cell when Ellis arrived. In the weak glow of the overhead lights, he saw the Japanese American doctor's face was paler than normal.

Yokoyama spun away from the cell's window, nearly jumping at the sound of footfalls. "Ah, Doctor Ellis. Thank God you're here."

Ellis stroked his goatee as he approached Cell 6. He stopped midstride and locked eyes with Yokoyama as a shriek echoed down the passage. The high-pitched noise ebbed into a low whine that was followed by a long, sharp hissing.

"Holy shit," Ellis whispered, continuing to the hatch. Those were not the sounds of a healthy Variant. These were the screeches of a creature in complete agony.

The older doctor ran his fingers through his thick hair, whispering, "It works. It really works."

Through the glass window, Ellis saw that Lucy hung from the chains. Still stretched into an $X$, the juvenile was no longer fighting its restraints. A bib of vomit rimmed its armored chest, green bile and blood frothing around its sucker lips. The flesh around its navel was bright red and splotchy. Boils prickled across the unprotected skin.

The creature struggled to lift its head; its droopy, bloodshot eyes tried to focus on Ellis. It blinked as it stared at him. Its spiked tongue shot out, then hung loosely from its lips, bloody webs of saliva dripping down its long chin.

Ellis pressed his hand against the glass, heart thumping. If Kryptonite killed Lucy, then it would likely kill all of the juveniles. Welcoming two miracles in a single day seemed like pushing his luck. Ellis wasn't used to the good fortune. His cheeks ached from the wide grin on his face; he hadn't smiled like this for months.

Lucy's lips suddenly puckered. The young Variant tilted its head back and pulled on its chains, releasing a guttural scream that sent bile exploding from its mouth. The spike of its tongue whipped around, saliva hitting the window.

Ellis leaned back. When Lucy finally looked at the door again, his smile disappeared. The juvenile's face had transformed from that of a merciless, soulless monster into something he almost recognized as human. Lines of liquid streamed from Lucy's wide, saucerlike eyes.

But it wasn't blood.

Lucy was crying.

# 6

"Get us closer!" Garcia yelled.

Beckham held up a hand to protest but fell short of it. He looked just as fascinated by the message spelled out in rain buckets as Garcia was. Everyone in the troop hold was staring. Could people have really made it this long out here?

"We can do a circle. One time," Beckham said to the pilot while he locked eyes with Garcia.

It had been two weeks since Garcia had come across any stronghold of survivors. He'd assumed they'd all fallen by now. Perhaps the survivors who had lived here were gone now too, killed by the Variants before anyone could rescue them.

Garcia closed his fingers around Thomas's dog tags. He knew his mind wasn't operating correctly. The surge of emotions ripping through him made him want to empty a magazine into the face of a Variant. But that wouldn't bring Thomas or any of his other men back.

He craned his neck to see those whom his brother had died for. The troop hold was nearly full with civilians, including three children. The man had given his life so these people could live.

Closing his eyes for a second, Garcia remembered

Thomas, his quiet brother, a man who spent his days meditating and reading dog-eared philosophy books. Thomas was a rare breed. He never bragged about his kills, like Tank or Steve-o. He never gave anyone shit. He just fought.

Garcia bowed his head, remembering all of those he had lost: Daniels, Morgan, Steve-o, Thomas. His wife, Ashley, and his daughter, Leslie. The apocalypse had stuck a knife into his gut, plunging it deeper every day, but he wasn't done fighting back.

"Get us down there!" Garcia shouted.

Beckham glared at him. "Are you fucking crazy? We don't even know if anyone is alive."

The pilots slowly circled the thirty-story tower. Garcia shouldered his M4 and zoomed his scope in on the building. The roof was surrounded by a metal wall with a makeshift barbwire fence rimming the top. From his vantage, it looked secure.

"If there's someone down there, we have to help them!" Mcg shouted.

Tank grumbled—that was Tankspeak for agreement. Garcia appreciated the hulking marine's support, but Beckham was in charge now. It was up to him, and judging by the concerned look on his face, it was going to take some convincing.

"Down there!" Fitz suddenly shouted.

In the center of the roof, the access door swung open, disgorging the silhouetted shapes of four people. They ran toward the buckets, waving.

Back at the open door, a tiny figure hid in the shadows. Others crowded behind it.

*Children.*

"Get us the fuck down there!" Garcia shouted.

Beckham stared in disbelief, then turned to the cockpit. "Can you land?"

"I would, sir, but we got a major fucking problem!" Lewis replied.

The pilots made another pass, directing the spotlight on the bottom of the bird at the exterior wall on the south side of the building. The yellow brick was covered with a horde of Variants. They looked like oversized crabs, their jointed arms and legs snapping as they climbed.

The sight chilled Garcia to the core. Harms centered his M240 on the beasts, but Garcia grabbed his arm. "Hold your fire! There could be more civilians on the upper floors."

"What the fuck do you suggest we do?" Harms asked, his eyes still on the building. "They're sitting ducks up there."

The creatures were quickly scaling the exterior, and the civilians on the roof had no idea. There was no way they could hear the snapping of joints over the rotors of the Black Hawk. They'd survived out here this long, only to have the military draw the Variants to their stronghold.

Harms let go of the M240 and cupped his hands over his mouth. "Get back inside!"

Shouting didn't help. The survivors continued waving, oblivious to the approaching threat. Five children had emerged from the open door. Garcia zoomed in on a boy no older than seven. He was gripping a ragged stuffed animal. A man in a flannel shirt rushed over to the kids. There were over twenty civilians, and more continued to emerge, far too many to extract in the Black Hawk.

"We have to do something," Garcia said. "If you won't land, get me and Tank close enough to jump!"

Beckham didn't hesitate in his response. He snapped into action. "Fitz, I want you to take out those Variants—*surgically*! Lewis, get us as close as possible. We'll take as many people as we can. Children first, then women."

"You sure about this, boss?" Horn asked.

"There are kids down there!" Meg shouted.

Apollo howled and pawed at Beckham's leg.

Horn nodded in agreement, and Fitz started squeezing off shots. One by one, Variants plummeted to the road below, shrieking for the duration of the fall before splattering on the concrete.

As the other creatures continued climbing, Garcia glimpsed flashes of motion coming from inside the building. Shit—the creatures weren't just on the outside; they were inside too. Variants scaling the building broke through windows and climbed inside to escape Fitz's precise gunshots.

"Lewis, radio in support. Tell Command we're going to need another chopper," Beckham said.

"On it."

The bird lowered toward the rooftop, wind from the rotors slamming into the rain buckets and sending them scattering. There were thirty civilians on the roof now. How that was possible was beyond Garcia. Humans were resilient, and Garcia had seen some crazy shit in the past six weeks, but this many survivors in downtown Manhattan? It gave him hope there were more in other places like this throughout the country. Hell, there might be strongholds all over the globe.

Garcia pushed the questions aside and embraced hope. Despite the fatigue and anger, he was ready to rock and roll. This was about more than revenge: Every human life was precious. He would gladly risk his own to save these people.

A little voice in his head added, *That's what happens when you have nothing to lose . . .*

Gripping his rifle tighter against his chest, Garcia prepared to jump.

The Variants continued scaling the building below.

They were just ten floors from the rooftop now. It would only be a matter of seconds before they were on the fences, and the barbwire wouldn't do much to hold them back. It took everything in him to refrain from firing on the beasts.

"Horn, get on the big gun and light those fuckers up," Beckham said. "Be careful you don't hit any civilians."

Harms protested, but Horn grabbed the marine and yanked him out of the way. The bark of the gun filled the troop hold. Kate took Horn's place at Tasha and Jenny's side. She helped them cup their hands over their ears.

Garcia worked his way to the edge of the open door, next to Tank. They exchanged a nod as the bird lowered over the rooftop. Fitz continued picking the beasts off the building's exterior, but Garcia guessed there were dozens more inside the building, blurs of flesh racing up the stairwells. There was no way of telling just how many were working their way through the guts of the tower.

The civilians backed away as the Black Hawk lowered over the rooftop, and Garcia lost sight of the monsters. He flipped the selector on his M4 to automatic, knowing goddamn well he would need to fire as fast as possible.

"Closer!" Garcia shouted.

"Nowhere to land! We have to hover," Lewis yelled back. "I'll get you as low as possible."

Garcia kept his eyes on the kids as the bird swayed back and forth six feet over the roof. The civilians backed up to the fence on the south side of the building. They reached out to the chopper, their faces ripe with terror and anxiety, eyes pleading for rescue.

Behind them, a skeletal figure leaped onto the fence, the first of the Variants. The civilians turned just as the monsters reached the rooftop.

*All it takes is all you got, Marine.*

The words fueled Garcia's next move. He jumped out of the bird and hit the ground running. Shouldering his rifle, he fired on the fence, already bending under the weight of the monsters.

President Ringgold knew she was getting ahead of herself. That was part of her nature; she didn't know how to take things slow. When she thought something was right, she put every resource into making it happen. It made her a good leader, and if she survived long enough, she hoped it would make her a good president of what was left of the United States of America.

There was a war to continue planning, and she wasn't going to let something like a bullet slow her down. A day after being shot, she'd been more than ready to get out of the infirmary and back to the action.

It had taken some convincing—and a few threats—but Ringgold was now on her way to the CIC in a wheelchair, her arm in a sling. She was aching for news of Kate and the other civilians kidnapped from Plum Island. After pressing Dr. Klinger several times, she had finally accepted that he didn't know anything.

"This is a bad idea, Madam President. I really think you should rest," he said now.

"I'm not lying in that bed another minute."

Klinger sighed and continued pushing her through the *GW*'s narrow passages. Ringgold imagined the doctor didn't much like being a chauffeur, even if it was for the president of the United States.

As they approached the hatch to the CIC, Ringgold repositioned her sling. The sudden movement earned her a jolt of pain. The painkillers were wearing off, but she had refused another dose. She needed her wits about her before returning to work.

Ahead, Johnson waited outside the CIC, surrounded by several marine bodyguards. Lieutenant Davis stepped through the open hatch.

"Welcome back, Madam President. You're already looking much better," Davis said. "How are you feeling?"

"Like I got shot."

Johnson grinned. "I'm impressed—most people would be down for days. But we both know you're not—"

"She should be resting, sir," Klinger said, frustration in his voice.

Ringgold raised her good hand. "I'll be just fine."

"Just try and take it easy," Klinger said.

"I will. Thank you again."

Lieutenant Davis took over for Klinger and pushed Ringgold into the CIC. Inside, officers had continued their routines into the early-morning hours. It certainly didn't feel like 3:00 a.m., but Ringgold had slept most of the day.

Davis maneuvered her toward a cluster of monitors at the front of the room. Captain Humphrey and his staff crowded around as Davis locked the wheels on Ringgold's chair.

"Good to see you, Madam President," Humphrey said.

Anxious for a report, Ringgold glanced up at him. "Have we heard anything about Doctor Lovato or the other civilians?"

"Yes, we have good news. Team Ghost and the Variant Hunters rescued the doctor and several civilians," Johnson said. "There were only a few casualties during the operation. They're on their way back right now."

"Actually, sir," Davis interrupted from where she

stood behind two radio operators, listening to chatter over the comm channels.

Ringgold's heart thumped.

Johnson crossed his arms. "What the hell now?"

Davis took the headset from the closest comms officer and slipped it over her ears. A few seconds later she looked up. "Raven One took a detour, sir."

"What kind of detour?" Humphrey asked. "I specifically ordered them back to the *GW*."

"Apparently they found a stronghold of survivors, sir," Davis replied. "Raven One is currently attempting an extraction."

"*Goddamnit*," Humphrey said. "Tell them to get their asses back here *now*. And recall the rest of the air support too. We need to save our ammunition, especially now that we know Kryptonite will work on the juveniles."

Ringgold couldn't believe it. First the news of Kate's rescue, and now the bioweapon was working? What the hell had she missed while she was sleeping?

"We're just going to abandon those people, sir?" Davis asked.

Humphrey regarded Davis with a meaningful look. "You already disobeyed orders by sending Team Ghost and VH into New York. Now you want to risk their lives again, and on a dubious rescue? What if they've got people infected with the original strain, like the sailors on the *Truxtun*? Or did you conveniently forget everything Beckham's team told us when we arrived? I'm waiting, Lieutenant."

Standing firm and looking the man in the eye, Davis said, "With all due respect, sir, you could send another chopper to rescue those people."

"That would put even more lives in jeopardy," Humphrey replied. "You've already risked enough on this mission—which I did not approve."

"I approved it," Johnson interjected.

"And what would you have me do, sir?" Humphrey said. His voice sounded a bit strangled.

Johnson ran a hand over his scalp and looked at Ringgold. She wanted Kate back, but at what expense? Ringgold wasn't used to making decisions over who lived and who died.

*Better get used to it*, she told herself.

Kate was one of the most important people left in the world. Humphrey was right—there was no decision.

Ringgold exhaled and said, "Get Raven One out of there."

Johnson nodded at Davis. "*Now*, Lieutenant."

She hesitated for a second, her eyes flitting to Ringgold. Then she pushed the mini-mic to her lips and said, "Raven One, you're to report back to the *GW* immediately. That's an order from the president of the United States of America."

Beckham pushed the comms link into his ear, unsure exactly of what he'd just heard. It was hard to hear with the wind blowing in his face and the rattle of gunfire echoing all around him, but there was no mistaking Davis's words, or the squadron of aircraft racing away from New York City.

The other birds had been recalled as well—apparently they weren't going to waste precious resources. They didn't see eye to eye about saving civilians. Beckham expected that from Vice President Johnson, but not President Ringgold.

When would the madness end?

With billions dead, after six weeks of intense fighting, it was clear to Beckham the nightmare wasn't going to be over anytime soon. Once again, he was dealing with leaders who did not share his priorities.

The pressure must have gotten to Ringgold—either that or she was too worried about losing Kate again to risk a rescue mission. Those were the only explanations.

While he respected the order from the president, it wasn't one Beckham could follow. He lifted his M4, picked out a target, and squeezed off a shot. The round nicked the shoulder of a beast on the fence, but it continued to climb. Tank and Garcia worked their way across the roof, shells ejecting from their weapons as they fired on the Variants scaling the fence.

Lewis suddenly pulled the bird away from the rooftop before Beckham could shout a warning to the Variant Hunters. He grabbed a handhold to steady himself.

"No!" Meg shouted as she fired the M9 Beckham had handed her back on the street. "I need more ammo," she said to Beckham. Then she glared at the pilots and screamed, "What the hell are you doing?"

"Ma'am, we have been ordered back to the *GW* immediately," Lewis replied.

"Hold on a goddamn second!" Beckham shouted back. Kate put her hand on his shoulder, and he turned slightly from the cockpit to meet her eyes. Behind her, Fitz continued firing from the open doorway, ignoring the conversation and focusing on holding back the monsters. Horn's tattooed forearms were trembling as he unloaded a barrage of 7.62-millimeter rounds from the M240.

The exterior of the building was coated with Variants like a layer of white sludge. The creatures in the interior were pulling themselves out of broken windows to join those already mounting the fence.

"Lewis, give me ten minutes," Beckham said. "That's all I need, brother. Just ten minutes."

"I'm sorry, but the order came directly from POTUS."

Beckham narrowed his eyes at the pilot. *"Ten minutes. No one has to know."*

The civilians, screaming and terrified, surged toward the chopper. Several of the men had turned to fire semi-automatic rifles and pistols at the fences.

"We can't leave these people! There are kids down there!" Kate added.

Lewis pressed his lips together, then nodded. He twisted the cyclical and lowered the bird back over the roof.

"Children first!" Beckham yelled at the top of his lungs. He got down on his belly and extended his hands. He did a quick head count of the kids. They had plenty of room for them, but they could take only a fraction of the adults.

A woman with matted hair struggled to lift her child. Beckham pulled the boy into the bird, his injured shoulder burning as if someone had stabbed the wound. Kate grabbed the child, and Beckham leaned down to pluck a girl from the arms of man. Tears streaked down her cheeks, leaving lines in the grime covering her face.

Meg dropped to her belly next to him and extended her hands toward the kids. Blood dripped freely from a gash on her palm, but it didn't stop her. She grabbed a young girl and pulled her toward the troop hold.

Harms joined them on the floor. One by one, the trio plucked the children from the roof and pulled them into the safety of the craft.

Screaming commanded Beckham's attention to the fence. Tank and Garcia were backpedaling, weapons blazing. A single Variant tore over the top of the barbwire and dropped to the ground with a scarf of flayed flesh hanging from its chest. It arched its back to strike as Tank fired a burst that blew off its legs under the knee.

Panicking, several of the civilians jumped for the troop hold. A man shoved a woman out of the way and then leaped into the air. He grabbed the metal floor and pulled himself upward.

"I said children first!" Beckham shouted. He launched a punch that hit the man in the nose. The civilian fell backward and landed on his ass. Gripping his bloody nose, he stared up at Beckham, eyes smoldering with rage. The grip of a Glock showed in his waistband.

*Maybe you should use that on the Variants, you asshole.*

Beckham leaned down to grab another child. Over the ear-splitting gunfire, he could hear the cries of the kids behind him. Tasha, Jenny, and Bo were part of the wails. This nightmare would scar the children forever. All Beckham could do was shield them as best he could from the physical threat of the Variants, but he wondered who would help them heal their mental wounds.

"Garcia!" Beckham shouted into his comms as he plucked another child from the roof. "Get your ass back here! Command has ordered us back to the *GW*!"

The marine turned slightly to look at the bird. Even from a distance, Beckham could see he wasn't going anywhere. The sergeant patted Tank on the back and shouted orders Beckham couldn't hear.

"Hurry the hell up!" Lewis yelled over the open channel.

The crowd pushed forward, and a woman was knocked to the ground. Another man pulled a long-barreled revolver from his waistband and fired it into the air, sending several of the panicked people scattering.

Time dragged to a halt as realization finally set in. Tank and Garcia were separated from the bird by a pack of desperate people—people who would do anything to get off this roof.

The Variants weren't the only threat now.

Beckham grabbed the hands of a five-year-old girl. The chopper swayed slightly, and she slid out of his sweaty grip. He caught her hand just before she fell back to the roof.

"Gotcha," Beckham said. He pulled her gently into the troop hold. Then he wrapped his hands around the wrist of a boy no older than seven. He was holding a shredded stuffed animal that was missing an eyeball. As he lifted the kid higher, the crowd suddenly surged away from the craft. Garcia and Tank were herding the civilians back toward the open rooftop door.

Beckham lifted the final child into the craft and checked the troop hold. It was almost full, but there was room for a couple more. Tank and Garcia could still make it back.

"Garcia! Move your ass!" Beckham shouted.

The marines stopped to fire on the Variants as the group ran back toward the open rooftop door. Horn and Fitz laid down suppressing fire. The fence rattled violently as the creatures on it spun into the darkness and plummeted thirty floors.

Shouting from below pulled Beckham's eyes to several men and women who had remained behind. The man with the bloody nose jumped toward the chopper again. He hadn't learned his lesson.

Behind them, the Variants were spilling over the barbwire, shredding skin and flesh. The monsters rolled onto the roof, jumped to all fours, and galloped toward the escaping mob of civilians, leaving a trail of blood. The marines pushed the crowd toward the door, shouting. "Go, go, go! Inside! Now!"

When Beckham looked back down, the man with the bloody nose was pointing his Glock at the chopper. He centered the gun on Beckham's face.

"Help me, or I'll blow your fucking head off!"

Beckham pushed himself to his knees and glared at the man. "Get that gun out of my face."

Blood gushed from his nose as the man centered the shaking gun on Beckham. "I said help me, or I'll—"

A piercing crack sounded, and an explosion of flesh, bone, and brain bloomed from the top of the man's skull. He slumped to his knees, his mouth wide open in shock. The gun fell from his hands and clattered onto the rooftop.

Gore stung Beckham's eyes. He blinked it away and pivoted to his right. Fitz nodded briefly before focusing his MK11 back on the Variants darting across the roof. He was firing again before Beckham could offer his thanks.

Beckham wiped away the blood from his face, shook off the shock, and grabbed his M4. He joined Horn at the edge of the door and looked to pick out a target. There were plenty of them on the roof. A pack of Variants darted toward the Black Hawk, and dozens more climbed the fence bordering the rooftop. It leaned further, rattled, and then crashed to the roof, kicking up a curtain of dust. The starving beasts flailed and scrambled to all fours.

With the civilians clear, Horn mowed down the wave coming from the north, but the others broke off, zigzagging around the spray. Another pack raced across the roof from the west. They were darting for the open doorway. Fitz and Harms directed their fire at the abominations.

"You got two minutes!" Lewis shouted.

Beckham fired off the rest of his magazine and looked down to the last stragglers on the rooftop.

"Help us!" shouted a teenage girl. She jumped toward the chopper, her fingers narrowly missing. Two other women reached up for Beckham. He recognized one as the mother of the first child he'd pulled into the craft.

Kate shouted something from the other end of the troop hold, and Lewis continued to yell. Apollo was howling at the Variants.

Beckham was having a hell of a time concentrating with the noise, but he knew there was no time for Garcia and Tank to get back to the chopper. Even if there was, they would never make it. The marines were ten feet from the door, laying down covering fire as the majority of the survivors ran back into the building. Variants were closing in from the west face of the building. An Alpha with a square head and bulging trapezius muscles strode into view. He halted and clamped his wide jaws together with a clicking that Beckham could hear. Yellow eyes tucked inside deep sockets flitted back and forth before homing in on Garcia and the open doorway.

*"Go!"* he roared, raising a muscular arm and directing his minions toward the marines. Hunching down, arms swinging from side to side, the beast fell into a run like that of an enraged gorilla. The other creatures spread out to flank Garcia's position.

"Harms, help the survivors. Fitz, take that Alpha down!" Beckham shouted. When he didn't hear a response, he whirled to look for Fitz—but the marine was gone.

Fitz wasn't the only one missing. Meg was gone too.

"Time's up, Beckham! We got to move!" Lewis yelled. "We got hostiles crawling all over this building."

Beckham heard the pilot, but it was just noise in his earpiece. He was staring in disbelief at the people limping toward the rooftop door. His MK11 shouldered, Fitz fired at the Alpha. One of the rounds hit him directly in the center of his throat, stopping the monster midstride. Collapsing to his knees, he reached up to stop the sheet of blood rushing from the gaping hole where his throat had been, a look of confusion on his pale, veiny face.

Across the roof, Garcia and Tank finished pushing the group into the building just as Fitz and Meg reached their position. She rushed through the doorway, but Fitz paused and raked his rifle back and forth to ensure they weren't being followed.

As the bird pulled away, Fitz locked eyes with Beckham. The torment on the marine's face told Beckham exactly why Fitz had decided to abandon the chopper. He had confided in Beckham back at Plum Island when the men had been sharing war stories. Fitz shouldered more than his fair share of guilt, and the loss of Riley had hit him hard. Beckham suspected Meg was going through something similar.

If it weren't for Kate and the children behind him, Beckham would have jumped out the open door to fight right alongside with them. He felt a hand on his shoulder and knew it was Kate. Apollo pressed up against his leg, whimpering as Fitz waved at the craft. He was gone a moment later, slamming the door and vanishing into the building.

# 7

Ellis had thought he had it figured out. He'd told Kate and President Ringgold there were three stages in the Variants' evolution: The first was physical adaptations and metamorphoses: night vision, sucker lips, talons, increased olfactory receptors, gills, fur, etc. The second was a higher level of intelligence, as displayed by the Alphas. The third was communication. But now, as he examined Lucy from behind the safety of the cell hatch's window, he wondered if there was a fourth stage.

Were Variants really capable of human emotion? Could they feel anything other than hunger and rage?

Evidence indicated they could: first Lucy's predatory smile, and now the sorrowful tears streaking down the juvenile's face. And that terrified Ellis more than the armor covering the beast. Only the most evolved mammals were capable of such emotions.

The juvenile Variants couldn't be allowed to evolve further. Every last one of them had to be killed.

Ellis continued scrutinizing Lucy. The creature hissed at him, aware it was being watched.

"Jesus Christ," he whispered.

A tap on his shoulder made him jump. Dr. Yokoyama stood in the shadows behind him.

"You scared the shit out of me," Ellis said.

Yokoyama stepped into the light. His bushy eyebrows were scrunched together, forming a network of wrinkles on his forehead. He brushed his long hair back with a trembling finger and tucked it behind his right ear, a detail that Ellis picked up on only because it was so uncharacteristic of Yokoyama's behavior.

He turned away from the door so he could look the doctor in the eyes. If something had happened to Kate . . .

"What's *wrong?*"

"There's something I think you should see," Yokoyama said. "Maybe you can explain it to me."

"Explain what?"

"We finally got the results from Lucy's blood and tissue samples."

"And?" Ellis said, to silence. He could tell his colleague wasn't going to answer him here—not in front of Sergeant Russo and his men.

"Fine, show me, then," Ellis said. He followed Yokoyama past the squad of soldiers. They hadn't moved all night, guarding Lucy as if the juvenile was Hannibal Lecter. To Ellis, Lucy was much, much worse, but these men had no way of knowing what the creature was capable of. To them, it was probably just another Variant.

It took the doctors thirty minutes to don their CBRN suits and get into the lab. By the time Ellis pressed his visor against the microscope where Yokoyama had placed the samples, he was on edge. Questions pingponged in his mind, but he couldn't seem to put a finger on what Yokoyama was keeping from him. He was used to working with a partner who shared every detail. Kate couldn't get back soon enough.

Ellis scanned the slide for several seconds. That was all it took to see what was missing. With the stain he'd used, any cells containing the Superman protein would show up a dark brown. But the cells weren't brown.

He did a second scan to be sure, then swiveled in his chair. A hot breath steamed the inside of his visor.

"So, you want to explain this to me?" Yokoyama asked. "If the Superman protein isn't showing up in the tissue samples, then how the hell is Kryptonite working?"

"I'm...I'm not sure," Ellis replied. He scratched helplessly at his helmet, the prickle of an itch on his ear. Something wasn't right. Lucy was definitely sick, but if it wasn't from Kryptonite, then what the hell was it from?

Ellis hurried to the other side of the room and sat down at his station. After keying in his credentials, he moused over to a live feed from the camera in Lucy's cell. An image of the juvenile's armored back came on screen. From the angle, it looked almost like a turtle shell, with a smooth exterior and rivet-like bumps running down the middle. It was thickest around the shoulders. Earlier, Ellis had been looking forward to dissecting Lucy, but now, he wasn't so sure. This one was different from the other Variants. It seemed too...

*Human.*

Punching in a command, Ellis manually directed the camera toward Lucy's face. The young Variant was still staring at the door, but the tears were no longer in its eyes. Bloody saliva dripped off its chin onto the floor, forming a gooey puddle between its stretched feet.

No screeches or bile came from the creature's mouth. It hung loosely from its restraints, back slouched, the weight of its arms and legs keeping the chains taut.

"Want to tell me what's going on?" Yokoyama asked. He had snuck up on Ellis again, but this time Ellis didn't flinch. He was too busy figuring out the answer to that question.

A faint cracking sound came from the speakers on the monitor. Ellis turned the volume up. It came again a few seconds later. This wasn't the sound of snapping joints.

The Variant craned its head away from the video feed and looked at its right arm. Ellis followed its gaze. What he saw shook him. The armor covering Lucy's forearm from wrist to elbow had split open, and an appendage with a thin, sharp bone on the end extended at a ninety-degree angle.

"What the hell is that?" Yokoyama asked.

Before Ellis could rotate the camera again, Lucy turned to look directly at the lens. The creature cracked its head from side to side, then launched its spiked tongue. It uncoiled and shot out, shattering the glass of the camera lens.

"Holy fuck!" Ellis shouted. He jumped out of his chair and stared at the screen incredulously. "I can't believe it." The realization was overwhelming, hitting him like a blast from a shotgun. He ran to the wall-mounted comm. Activating it, he said, "Command, this is Ellis reporting from Lab A. Does anyone copy?"

"Roger that, Ellis. This is Davis."

"Send *every* available soldier on the *Cowpens* to the brig. Right now."

There was a pause, static crackling from the speaker. "Why? What's going on down there, Ellis?"

"Kryptonite doesn't work," Ellis said. "Lucy's not really sick."

The crack of a gunshot echoed somewhere in the ship. Ellis exchanged a meaningful look with Yokoyama, but neither of them said a word. They both knew exactly what was happening.

Fitz jammed a metal bar across the makeshift lock system the survivors had rigged across the door. Panting, he put his hands on his thighs as the first creature slammed into the other side. The crack of broken bones echoed inside the stairwell, loud enough to tell Fitz that whatever had hit the metal wouldn't be getting back up right away.

He took another step away from the shuddering metal and looked for Meg. She glared back at him, a rueful but defiant look on her face. Blood oozed from her grip on the M9.

"What the hell are you doing, Meg? Why did you leave the chopper?" Fitz didn't mean to yell, but he was pissed. She should never have followed him. By the time he had realized, it had been too late to turn back.

It was difficult to hear her response over the screeching, scratching, and snapping joints outside, not to mention the fading sound of helicopter blades as their ride returned to the *GW*.

"I want to help. Just like you." Meg's fair skin flared red. She pulled a magazine from her M9, tossed it on the ground, and jammed in a fresh one. With her eyes narrowed on Fitz, she released the slide to chamber a round.

This was no time to argue with her. She was determined, and so was Fitz. They both had their own reasons, and for a second, he wondered if he'd made the wrong move. Abandoning Team Ghost to help the Variant Hunters and the survivors here was something he had done impulsively—kind of like when he had shot the civilian pointing a Glock at Beckham a few minutes prior. But he'd made both of those decisions to save his friends.

Fitz couldn't bring back Riley or all the other men and women he had failed to save. All he could do was continue trying to save those still alive, starting with these people.

*The Lord is my shepherd. He guides me in paths of righteousness.*

The prayer that popped into his head took Fitz

off guard. It was rare for him to pray, but listening to the creatures pounding at the door and standing there trapped with Meg, he suddenly felt helpless. Sometimes that was what it took to remind him of his faith.

In boot camp, he had been told that there were no atheists in a foxhole. War against the Variants had reminded him that was true.

Most of the time.

As the thuds and shrieks amplified and the sounds of the chopper grew distant, he realized he might have only delayed the inevitable for these people. He glanced down the stairs to check on the group.

Strategically placed lanterns had been set up on both sides of the narrow stairwell. In the flicker of the light, a dozen sets of exhausted and terrified eyes stared up at him, pleading.

One of the men, dressed in army fatigues and carrying an M16, pushed to the front of the group. "They're coming back for us, right?"

"They can't leave us here," said a slender woman with wild brown hair.

"My babies. They took my babies," a second woman sobbed. She pressed her head against the chest of a man who glared at Fitz as if he was the enemy.

Holding up a hand, Fitz considered offering some sort of reassurance, but the words wouldn't come. He couldn't lie to these people. He wasn't sure if Command would send anyone back for them.

The military might leave them to die. What did that say about his species? Billions were dead, but the biggest civilian stronghold they'd discovered was abandoned by the leaders who were supposed to protect them.

"Your children are safe," Fitz finally said. "And we're here to protect the rest of you."

He stood on the tips of his blades, trying to get a view

of Tank and Garcia. There was chatter coming from further down the stairwell. The marines were somewhere at the bottom, likely securing the area.

"They'll send someone back for us," Garcia said. "We just need to hold tight."

"For how long?" someone said, in a voice loud enough that Garcia turned to shush the speaker with a raised finger.

Fitz trusted that Beckham would do everything in his power to find a way to return with a new bird, even if it meant holding a gun to someone's head. But when? The Variants were already inside the building, and this door wasn't going to hold forever.

"Let's move!" shouted someone with a low, deep voice.

It was Tank, and the marine was motioning for people to follow. The group started moving down the stairs after him. The man in army fatigues took a step toward Fitz and Meg. He looked past them and examined the rusted roof-access door. Dust and pieces of concrete broke from around the trim every time a Variant slammed against the frame.

"I sure hope you know what you're doin'," the man said.

Fitz took a second to scrutinize the soldier. He was older than Fitz by about five years, with a full head of brown hair and a sharp nose. There was something about his gaze that seemed off. *But living out here for this long would break anyone*, Fitz thought.

The bar stretched across the door shook again. The locks groaned as the creatures grew more desperate.

"Come on," Fitz said. Meg checked the bolts one last time before following Fitz down the stairs. They both moved slowly behind the civilians, who had bottlenecked in the passage.

Tattered clothing that reeked of sour sweat formed a blur of different colors ahead of Fitz. Most of these people were filthy, with matted hair and grime covering their skin. He doubted any of them had seen a bathtub for weeks. As the pounding of the Variants intensified above, the group grew more desperate, pushing and shoving their way to the front of the line.

"Calm down," Tank grumbled.

The marine's voice did nothing to stop the crazed group. They continued working their way down two flights of stairs, hurrying around corners with barricaded doors. Fitz and Meg loped after them.

Fitz knew what it was like to have hope ripped away. But these people had already been through so much. To have salvation appear in front of them, only to have it torn from their grips, would leave most of them shattered.

They finally took a right into an open hallway on the twenty-eighth floor. Fitz halted on the landing to check the stairwell around the corner. The dark passage below was clogged with bookshelves, bed frames, and metal doors that had been removed from apartments. Steel planks weighed down the pile.

The light from the lanterns danced over the debris. Fitz took a step toward the pile. In the shadows, it appeared to be shifting subtly. Something was working its way up from the bottom floors.

"You seeing what I'm seeing?" Meg asked.

Fitz nodded, swallowing hard. The sounds of Variants were coming from above *and* below: scraping talons, clamping maws, and popping joints. He could almost picture the Variants squeezing through the barricades.

*Even though I walk through the valley of the shadow of death, I will fear no evil.*

Fitz patted Meg on the shoulder, glimpsing the bandages on her legs. They were weeping blood in several areas. Being dragged through Manhattan and then jumping out of the chopper had reopened the wounds. Her hand was still oozing from a deep gash too.

"You okay?" he asked.

"Yeah," Meg said with a whimper. The sweat streaming down her forehead told Fitz she was lying. Of course she wasn't okay. She was emotionally and physically at her breaking point, just like everyone else.

"Hurry up, you two," the man in fatigues said from the hallway. He jerked his chin at a door down the corridor.

Fitz patted Meg on her shoulder as they followed the soldier. Halfway down the dim passage, Tank was holding sentry duty. He angled his SAW at the stairwell.

After everyone was inside the room, Tank retreated and slowly shut the door. He helped Fitz secure it with a fifty-pound, four-foot steel bar that looked as if it was from a weight bench. Then both men clamped the bolt locks shut at the bottom, middle, and top of the steel.

When Fitz turned, he found himself inside a wide, long apartment with exposed brick walls. Mattresses lined the right wall, and an open kitchen was piled high with canned goods, jugs of water, and containers of food.

The dozen remaining civilians clustered in the center of the room, where four couches had been positioned together. Behind them, Garcia and Tank were working their way to the far end of the room to check the windows, which were covered with metal shutters and boards.

It was a bunker above ground.

Somehow, against all odds, these people had survived. It was a true testament to the strength and resilience of the human species. It also proved these people were resourceful. They'd kept the Variants out for almost seven weeks—something even most military bases hadn't been able to do. There was a glimmer of hope represented in this room—hope that maybe there were hundreds, even thousands of places just like this, strongholds that hadn't been discovered yet.

Places worth protecting.

Fitz checked his MK11 and pulled the twenty-round box magazine to check the rounds. Then he palmed it back into the gun. He still had a vest full of magazines, and with his M4 slung over his shoulder, and his M9 tucked in its holster, he had plenty of firepower. That was reassuring, but the pounding and skittering of feet on the floors above them wasn't. He ran around the group of civilians, picking up a new stench of raw sewage.

These people may have managed to survive here, but the conditions were awful, and he couldn't help but wonder if they had just gotten lucky.

"Fitz, what the hell are you and Meg doing here?" Garcia asked. He was checking the shutters and shaking them one at a time. Blood cascaded down the sergeant's bruised face. He wiped it away from a gash on his head, but it continued gushing out.

"Looked as if you guys needed some help," Fitz said.

"Beckham gave you the okay?" Tank asked.

Fitz shook his head and jerked his chin at Garcia's injury. "Looks bad."

Garcia ignored him, glancing over Fitz's shoulder to look at Meg and the civilians. "Who's in charge?" he asked in a voice loud enough for everyone to hear.

The soldier from the stairwell with the M16 walked over. "I am. Name's Trey Huff. Was a specialist with the National Guard when shit hit the fan. My unit took refuge across the street, but I was the only one who made it out. These people took me in."

Garcia wiped the blood from his face a second time. "Looks as if you guys have done okay. Pretty damn impressive, if you ask me."

"We've survived," Huff said.

"And you're going to continue to survive," Garcia replied. He checked a loose board and nodded at Tank. "Maybe," Garcia whispered, in a voice only Fitz and Tank seemed to hear.

"We'll need to reinforce everything in this room and figure out who can fight and who can't," Garcia added.

Huff scratched his long nose, turning slightly toward the civilians. "We can all fight."

Garcia nodded. "Good."

Tank pointed at an exposed pipe hanging from the ceiling. "How the hell have you kept the Variants out of those?"

Fitz examined it. Judging by the width, it was an air-circulation unit, just big enough for a baby to crawl through. But the Variants were starving and frail. It wouldn't be impossible for the beasts to tunnel through if they flattened their bodies.

"Don't worry. It's booby-trapped," Huff said. "We didn't survive out here this long by being stupid."

"Tomb," Tank grumbled, shaking his head. "God-damn tomb, I tell ya."

Garcia's eyes flitted from the shutters to the ceiling while Fitz tried to figure out what Tank was talking about.

"You led us into a tomb," Tank said. "Ain't no way we're all gettin' out of here."

"Yankee One, Ghost One. You got room for civilians? Over."

Beckham waited anxiously for the pilot's reply.

The other Black Hawks were already fifteen minutes

ahead, but he was hoping one might have the balls and the juice to turn around for Fitz, Garcia, Tank, Meg, and the others.

"Negative, Ghost One. Running low on fuel. Command has given us strict orders to return to home plate."

Beckham kicked the bulkhead, drawing the glares of several children. When he looked closer, he saw the kids weren't glaring at all. They were staring right through him—catatonic.

The troop hold had transformed into a day care for kids ranging in age between three and twelve. Wilson and Harms were checking them for injuries. Horn was back on the floor with Tasha and Jenny.

Kate put her hand on Beckham's arm. He softened at her touch. This time she didn't say a word. The warmth of her fingers was enough to relieve some of Beckham's frustration, but not enough to get him to sit. He made his way back to the cockpit.

"How far out are we?"

Lewis kept his eyes on the controls. "Thirty minutes, sir."

Beckham switched his comm channel to Central. "Lieutenant Davis, this is Ghost One, do you copy? Over."

Davis came online a moment later, her voice stern. "Copy that, Ghost One. What's your ETA?"

"Thirty minutes. You got a plan to evacuate our boys in the field, LT?" She didn't seem to respond well to requests, so he framed it as a question.

"Negative, Ghost One. Manhattan is *way* too hot right now. Can't risk the resources."

*You got to be fucking kidding me.*

Beckham clenched his jaw, doing his best not to curse at a superior officer. That wouldn't get him anywhere.

"LT, we got about a dozen civilians and four of our own in that tower. Isn't that worth the risk?"

There was a pause, static bleeding from the comm channel. "Not my call, Master Sergeant. See you when you get back."

Beckham bowed his head, containing his frustration with a discreet sigh. He had to keep it together. But he also couldn't leave them out there.

Lewis glanced back at him. "Sorry, but Lieutenant Davis is right. That building was crawling with Variants. We're lucky we got out of there in time."

Beckham narrowed his eyes at the sky. Heat lightning danced across the horizon, illuminating the ocean below. Then the blue residue faded away, and darkness swallowed the view.

*Think, Reed. There has to be a way to bring them home.*

Lewis turned back to the windshield, and Beckham retreated to the troop hold without uttering another word. He took a seat next to Kate and put a hand on her leg.

Horn wrapped his arms around his girls but didn't look over at Beckham. He leaned in and whispered something in Jenny's ear. Apollo was camped out in the middle of the kids. His presence seemed to calm them. One girl stroked his head and said, "Good doggy."

In total there were thirteen children. The farther the helicopter took them from Manhattan, the more likely it was that they'd all become orphans. It was a sacrifice his team had been willing to make.

A voice crackled in his earpiece. "Beckham, you copy?"

Beckham stiffened and cupped a hand over his ear to hear. "Copy. Beckham here. That you, Fitz?"

"Yeah. We're holed up in an apartment on the twenty-eighth floor of this building. It's me, Meg, twelve civvies, Tank, and Garcia."

"Goddamn good to hear your voice," Beckham said. "I'm working on getting you a bird."

"Not sure how much time we got."

"Just hold them off, Fitz. Hold them off as long as you can."

"Will do, boss." There was sadness in his voice. He paused and then said, "I'll give 'em hell."

"I'll see you soon, brother."

The comm channel went dead, and Beckham rested his head on Kate's shoulder. Helpless and exhausted, he felt defeated.

Horn got his attention with a snort. "How the hell are we going to get them out of that building, boss?"

Beckham shook his head. He didn't have an answer. The Variants would find a way inside, and when they did, Beckham doubted Fitz, Meg, and the two remaining Variant Hunters would be able to stop them.

Kate kissed Beckham on the cheek. He put his arm around her and pulled her close. Holding her was something he had never thought he would do again. A single sob worked its way out of his throat.

*You get to save some of them. But you can't save them all.*

But Fitz was his brother, and he cared deeply for Meg, Tank, and Garcia. Leaving them out there to die wasn't going to happen. He'd save them . . . somehow.

Sirens blared from the public-address system. A voice recalled all sailors to their stations. Ellis and Yokoyama remained in Lab A, staring at the monitor in disbelief.

"Gas her, gas her!" Yokoyama yelled. Whoever was in charge of Lucy's cell followed the order. A cloud of swirling smoke hissed into the room. The wall-mounted video camera had been splintered and knocked away by Lucy's tongue, but Ellis could still see beyond the web of cracks on-screen.

"Get Lucy back inside! Don't let it escape!"

Ellis had the channel open, and the comm picked up the

voices of Sergeant Russo and his men. Gunfire broke over the speakers a moment later. The shotgun blasts echoed through the guts of the ship. Ellis could hear each shot.

"Aim for its legs!" shouted another man.

"Sergeant Russo, you have permission to eliminate hostile," said a voice from Command. "I repeat, eliminate hostile. Do *not* let it out."

The channel filled with the crack of shotgun blasts and the screams of soldiers. The shotguns were supposed to penetrate Lucy's armor, but without a clear view, Ellis wasn't sure who was winning.

"Let us out!" someone yelled.

This time Command didn't respond.

"Open the hatch!" another soldier screamed.

Whoever was listening in the CIC didn't reply.

Ellis swallowed. They'd locked the men inside Cell 6 with Lucy. Russo and his team weren't just trapped in there with a monster, they were trapped in a room filling with deadly gas. Even if their breathing apparatus saved them, the gas would make it difficult to see.

A long, guttural howl roared over the channel. Ellis wasn't sure if it was human until a body in black armor slumped to the ground on the video feed. A rectangular visor stared up at the feed, its mirrored surface betraying nothing behind the visor. Smoke drifted across the room, blanketing the soldier.

Ellis flinched at three more blasts.

"My mask!" shrieked a soldier. He coughed into the comm, his lungs wheezing for air.

Another painful scream followed.

This one wasn't human.

Lucy had been injured.

Ellis strained for a view of the battle as a voice crackled in his helmet. "Doctor Ellis, Doctor Yokoyama, this is Lieutenant Davis. Please confirm your position."

"We're still in Lab A," Ellis replied.

"Good. Stay put. I've deployed a squad of marines to your location."

If Lucy managed to get out of that cell, the young Variant would tear through the ship. The only thing standing between it and the crew was a brave squad of men with twelve-gauge semiautomatic shotguns.

A thud echoed over the channel. Ellis bit the inside of his lip as another soldier crashed into the wall on-screen. An armored arm reached through the gas and its claws grabbed the man by the neck. Then a knife-sized bony spike popped out of the arm and stabbed the soldier through the center of his mask. Blood pooled around the entry wound and sheeted down the front of his chest. Lucy withdrew the needle and let the soldier slump to the ground, then whirled to face the others. The flash from a shotgun blast hit the creature in the side, sending it spinning out of view.

Coughing, shouting, gunfire, and the shrieks of an enraged monster overwhelmed the channel. Ellis wanted to cup his hands over his ears. Even though he knew marines were outside the lab, he felt trapped like Russo and his men.

"Shoot it in the head! Shoot it in the fucking head!" someone yelled.

There was another blast, followed by what sounded like bullets punching through tendons and bone—an awful, ripping noise that made Ellis shiver.

Yokoyama slowly sat on the stool in front of the monitor. He leaned forward and punched in several commands on the keyboard. It wasn't until the shattered lens of the camera started turning that Ellis realized what he was doing.

Ellis waited for shotgun blasts that didn't come.

On-screen, the cracked view of the room shifted

as the cloud of white gas dissipated, revealing the outlines of four bodies sprawled on the floor. One of them twitched, but the others lay still.

"Wh-where's Lucy?" Yokoyama stuttered. "I don't see Lucy."

The camera angled toward the hatch, revealing the armored back of a beast standing four feet tall. Circular cracks in Lucy's outer shell seeped blood, and one of the Variant's pointy ears was severed.

"What's Lucy doing?" Yokoyama asked.

"Oh my God," Ellis whispered. He stared in disbelief as the creature turned toward the camera. Its bulging lips widened and its pointed chin split down the middle, opening into four chattering mandibles lined with horned teeth on both sides.

Crack!

Ellis jumped at the shot. The spray from a shotgun took off a chunk of Lucy's elbow. The creature let out a screech and crouched, back hunching as it prepared to strike.

A soldier crawled into view. He aimed his gun and fired again. The second blast cracked Lucy's armor just above the navel.

The juvenile shrieked and fired its spiked tongue from between open mandibles. The tip broke through the soldier's right goggle. He convulsed on the ground, legs kicking.

Lucy ran out of view.

"What's happening?" Ellis said. "Move the camera!"

"I'm trying," Yokoyama huffed.

As he typed at the keyboard, Lucy suddenly reemerged. The creature clambered back to the hatch, stood on its legs, and reached for the lock. Its claws rotated to the right as it inserted a key it had taken from one of Russo's men.

"I don't believe it," Yokoyama said.

Ellis nearly choked on the implications. If the juvenile Variant could use a key, what else was it capable of?

Lucy's lips twisted into a grin as the hatch unlocked. Swinging it open, Lucy burst into a passage filled with marines, and straight into the gunfire of a dozen weapons.

# 8

"There's been an incident on the *Cowpens*," Beckham said. He removed his finger from his earpiece and looked at Kate. Her heart rate had finally returned to normal, but at these words, it spiked out of control again.

"The juvenile Variant broke free," Beckham continued.

"Ellis," Kate whispered.

Beckham nodded. "He's fine. Sounds as if they were able to stop it before it escaped."

Her mind was filled with questions. The first was selfish, but it was also a reminder that she still had a job to do when she got back: Had Ellis determined if Kryptonite would work before the juvenile was killed? How many men had died to extract the juvenile from New York? If Ellis hadn't performed all the necessary tests yet, then those men would have died in vain.

Her heart and mind ached from the losses. She couldn't think. Stars crept to the edges of her vision. Suddenly light-headed, she leaned back on Beckham's chest, trying to listen to his heartbeat beneath the vibration of the Black Hawk.

"ETA five minutes," the pilot said.

"It's okay," Beckham said, leaning down to whisper in her ear. "We're almost—" He stopped short of finishing, but Kate knew he had almost said *home*. Plum Island was gone, and the final hope for humanity now rested on a fleet of navy vessels drifting on the ocean. They were alone, and their resources were dwindling every day.

Kate eyed the troop hold. Horn sat in the middle of the group, hulking among them like a pro-football player turned babysitter. Most of the kids were crying or silently in shock. Some cried out for lost parents and siblings, others asked where they were going.

"Safe," Horn kept saying. "You're going somewhere safe." Jenny and Tasha were tucked up against his chest, his tattooed arms wrapped around both of them. A boy sat cross-legged in front of the girls. He stroked a tattered stuffed animal, his head bowed.

Kate carefully pushed herself off Beckham and crawled across the floor to the boy. "What's your name?" she asked, tapping him on the shoulder.

He slowly lifted his head. His eyes were blue, and his button nose was covered in freckles.

"My name is Javier," he said. "Do you know where we're going?"

Kate's heart froze in her chest. The boy didn't just share her brother's name—he was the spitting image of her little brother at that age. Everything that had happened over the past six weeks came crashing down in Kate at the sight of the child. Without thinking, she reached forward and embraced Javier in a hug.

"We're going to a new home, a safe place where there are no monsters."

As she hugged Javier, she saw the empty seat Meg had occupied an hour earlier. The three marines who had stood at the Black Hawk's open door were gone now too. It was yet another reminder that not everyone was going home.

"There she is, baby!" Harms shouted from his position by the door gun.

Long, silhouetted shapes of warships emerged on the horizon. Jets and choppers that looked like toy models were positioned neatly on the flight deck of the *GW*.

To the east, a Chinook hovered over the *Cowpens*. A bus-sized shipping container hung from a network of thick ropes attached to the bottom of the chopper and was being slowly lowered toward the helipad. As they got closer, Kate read the BIOHAZARD markings on the sides. Despite the warnings, the crate didn't bother her as it might other onlookers. The box contained a weapon that could help bring the end of the war.

Plum Island was destroyed, but the bioreactors that would help eradicate the Variants had been salvaged. She just hoped Kryptonite would work on the juveniles.

Whimpers all around her reminded her there was another key to winning the war, and it wasn't a weapon. Children were the future of the world. Innocent and full of life, they would have to rebuild when this was all over. She understood why Beckham had broken protocol to save these kids, even if it meant putting her and the others at risk.

Javier relaxed in her arms as Kate hugged him close. She remembered holding her little brother years ago and thought about the word *innocence*. These kids might have lost any chance of having it themselves, but maybe her own child would have a chance. Kate held Javier closer and hugged him harder.

In a luxury Manhattan apartment, the last thing Meg expected to smell was crap. The putrid smell of sewage was almost worse than the sour, rotting scent of the Variants. Meg wasn't sure how these people could have lived with it for so long. A flashback to the time she'd spent hiding in her old fire station with Jed and Rex emerged.

She'd been forced to make desperate decisions there.

Bringing her axe down on her best friend, Eric, was one of them. The thought made her cringe. The crack of his skull was something she would never forget.

Back then, there had been a constant smell of body odor. No matter how many wet wipes she scrubbed her skin with, she couldn't get the reek off. Antibacterial wipes could only do so much to mitigate the stench of rot and piss she had collected while hiding under the corpses in the basement of the fire station.

When her firefighter friends had joked about the apocalypse, they'd talked about what would happen, where they would go, what kind of things they would do to survive. No one talked about what happened when toilets stopped flushing and electricity shut off. They certainly didn't think about what to do if toilet paper ran out. Keeping safe and fed were the two major parts of the conversation, but keeping clean didn't seem to take priority.

Buckets, towels, and a simple curtain rigged up for privacy were how these people took care of their sanitary needs.

And it smelled awful.

At least it helped keep her mind off Riley. She still couldn't believe he was gone. She still hadn't *accepted* that he was gone. She bowed her head and closed her eyes, overwhelmed with regret and thoughts of what might have been.

"Windows are secure," Garcia said, cutting into her thoughts. She raised her head to watch him. He rested his M4 against the brick wall and pulled his M9 to check the magazine. Tank was cleaning his SAW on a chair a few feet away. Fitz stood by the windows in silence, his silhouetted frame unmoving.

Huff consoled the people in the center of the room. The group talked in hushed voices from the couches, casting skeptical looks toward the marines. Meg didn't blame them; she hadn't trusted soldiers after Jed had left her to die in the sewers. It wasn't until Beckham and Team Ghost showed up that she had started to trust the military again.

No, she didn't blame these people. She had been one of them. But at least now their children were safe. She knew they were grateful for that, even if they didn't look like it.

Huff held up a hand to silence a heavyset man who was speaking in a raised voice.

"They shot Kirk. Shot him right in his head," the man growled.

Meg remembered the man with the bloody nose from the rooftop. The bastard had pointed a gun at Beckham. He had been a threat to everyone. The coward had made his choice, and Fitz had responded to it with a 7.62-millimeter round.

Garcia slammed the magazine back into his M9, then put it back in his holster and grabbed his M4. Narrowing his eyes at Huff, he walked toward the group.

The distant screech of a Variant stopped him halfway there. From somewhere overhead came a scratching, followed by a thud, as if someone had tripped and fallen on the floor above them.

Meg was the first to raise her weapon. Garcia backpedaled with his M4 raised to follow the sound. He held up a hand when he got under the ductwork. Fitz switched out his MK11 for his M4. With deliberate care, he pulled back the slide of the carbine before pointing it at the ceiling. The echo from the thud faded until there were only the distant shrieks of monsters deep in the guts of the building.

Garcia lowered his rifle and his hand.

"Listen," he said. "It might be a while before we get

any help. So for now, we're on our own. Whatever happened on that rooftop is in the past. If any of you have a problem with us being here, then you can take it up with me. Right here, right now. Any questions?"

The heavyset man sitting on the edge of a leather couch looked at the tile floor, his cheeseburger cheeks flaming red.

"I'm glad you're here," Huff said. He stopped to correct himself. "*We're* glad you're here."

"Good," Tank mumbled. He stood and held up his clean SAW. "'Cause now we need a plan to get out of here."

"I thought you just said they'd come back for us," Huff replied.

Garcia and Tank exchanged a glance, then looked at Fitz.

With all eyes on him, Fitz sucked in a breath. "Beckham said he would come back for us when he can."

"What the hell does that mean?" Huff asked.

"It means what it sounds like," Garcia added. "I told you, we're on our own right now."

"Fucking military," the fat man scowled. He scratched at his neck. "They never helped us from the beginning."

"They left us here, again," said a young woman standing behind the couches. "This isn't the first time. They've seen our buckets on the roof. They knew we were here." Both her arms were dressed with bandages that were stained red. Sweat dripped off her forehead. Meg recognized the signs of infection immediately. She needed antibiotics.

"Don't be stupid," another man said. He had a metal pipe in his hand and wore a tank top that read I'M NOT A PLAYER, I JUST BLOG A LOT. "No one is coming back for us."

A young woman with braided red hair nodded. "Our

kids are safe, but we're not. We're never going to see them again."

Meg finally broke her silence, blurting, "Will you shut up? All of you!"

"Keep it down," Fitz whispered.

Meg massaged the handle of her M9. "Look, I used to think the same thing you're all thinking: that the military, sworn to protect us, had actually abandoned us. But there are *good* soldiers left out there—*good* marines. Men like the ones I decided to follow into this building to help you. Many more have already died to save people like you and me."

Huff cracked his head to the side and licked his dry lips. "She's right. She risked her life for us, and so did these marines. If they say help is coming, then we should trust them."

"Help will come, but the Variants could get in here before it arrives," Tank said. "That's why we need a plan to get out of here on our own if we have to."

The other civilians were fidgeting, nervous, and frustrated. Some held rifles, but most simply carried knives. The man with the tank top changed hands with his pipe. How he had survived this long was a mystery. Meg almost said something about his ridiculous shirt, but she turned to Fitz instead. The marine was messing with his headset.

"Beckham, Fitz. Do you copy? Over."

Meg leaned her head toward his helmet so she could listen. Static filled the marine's earpiece. It lasted for several agonizing seconds, and when a voice finally emerged, it sounded distant.

"Copy, Fitz…Beckham…What's…status? Over."

"Safe for now. But we're still holed up in this apartment. How's that bird coming along?"

"Working on it, Fitz. You hang in there."

"*Oorah*," Fitz replied. He gave a thumbs-up to Garcia.

It was hard for Meg to gauge the sergeant's expression with all the bruising around his broken nose. The bleeding from his forehead had mostly stopped, but there was enough crusted on his face to make him look like a bloody raccoon. A pissed-off, bloody raccoon.

"A'ight, you heard Beckham. He's working on getting us help," Fitz said.

Tank draped his SAW across his chest, his arm muscles flexing. His large nostrils opened as he snorted his response.

Garcia shot him a glare, but Tank wasn't deterred.

"We need a plan to get out of this tomb. Not later. Now," Tank said.

Taking off his helmet, Fitz ran a hand through his auburn hair. "What do you suggest? Fight our way back to the roof?"

"We're going to have to eventually," Tank said. "For now, we should get the layout of the building, see what's passable and what's not. Then we form a plan. If and when the choppers come back, we'll probably need to get topside on our own."

Garcia gestured for Huff to join them at a long table covered in trash. "You got a map of this place?"

"Maybe I can help," Meg said. "I was a firefighter. Figuring out escape routes was part of the gig."

Huff used an arm to clear off the table. Then he motioned to a man wearing a pair of blue coveralls and black-rimmed glasses. "This is Pedro. He's the building's engineer."

Pedro scratched his full beard. He was a bit nerdy looking, but his muscular frame told Meg this man could hold his own. Anyone who had survived this long could—even the guy in the blogging shirt.

"I was working on the boilers when the outbreak

happened. Hid in the basement for a week. Almost died down there," Pedro said. "After we sealed off the bottom stairwells with furniture, I flooded the ductwork with gas."

Meg raised a brow. "You flooded the ductwork with *gas*? Do you realize how dangerous that is?"

"Calm down, miss," Pedro replied, holding up a filthy palm. "It's only the bottom fifteen floors."

Meg didn't like his tone or his attitude. "So you turned the bottom half of the building into a ticking time bomb. Do you know what will happen if a single bullet penetrates those floors?"

Pedro formed a wide arc with his hands. "Boom."

"Jesus," Meg replied.

"Yeah, I get it," Pedro said. "But it's saved us this far, and it was worth the risk. Any Variant that's tried to crawl through the ductwork has died from the fumes."

"I saw some of them on the upper floors when we were hovering in the Black Hawk," Fitz said.

"That's your fault," Pedro said in a nonchalant voice. "They climbed the exterior and broke through windows above us when they heard your choppers. You drew the bastards right to us."

Meg thought about apologizing for a split second, but that wouldn't do any good. She couldn't change their situation; she could only help fix it.

Huff pointed at a blueprint of the building he had spread out. "We've booby-trapped these floors and the ductwork with a variety of homemade contraptions. But it's only a matter of time before they get through the stairwell. That's our Achilles' heel. The roof-access door won't hold forever either."

"We have a few hours, by my estimate," Pedro said. "Maybe less than that before they get to us."

As if in response, a boom sounded on one of the floors above. A strangled shriek followed.

Pedro jerked his chin toward the ceiling and grinned. "Got one of 'em."

Meg studied the engineer with grim fascination. She had worked with crazy firefighters before. Hell, anyone who ran into burning buildings for a living had to be a little crazy. Pedro had that same cocky, adrenaline-fueled look.

Another thud rang out above, and Pedro's grin widened. Meg could only imagine what kind of traps he had set for the beasts. The noise continued to echo. She pictured a human-sized mousetrap with a frail Variant twitching in it.

Pedro's right eye twitched. He scratched at it and said, "They'll eventually find a way inside this apartment. I agree with the big guy over there. We should come up with a Plan B."

"All right," Garcia said. "Meg, see if you can find us a way out of here."

Pedro unfolded a second set of blueprints and then marked a stairwell with a yellow highlighter. "This is the only route back to the roof that we can use."

Meg scrutinized the map, checking each stairwell and floor. Those marked in red were the levels Pedro had sabotaged. There were several other ways to the roof, including an elevator shaft, but those were filled with gas.

She continued going over the blueprint slowly, remembering what her fire chief used to say: *When shit hits the fan, you must be aware of your surroundings as you are of your own body. The building is a living, breathing thing. Every floor, every stairwell, every room can become your salvation or a death trap.*

Meg put her finger on a vertical vein from the first floor to the top that hadn't been marked.

"Anyone been inside of this?" she asked.

Pedro and Huff leaned in. Both men shook their heads.

"Not even sure what that is," Pedro said. He ran a finger over his mustache.

"Some of these older buildings have skeletal ladders built inside old coal chutes that were abandoned when they were renovated," Meg said. She looked in the bottom right corner of the blueprint. "Built in 1915. I bet this building has one."

"We still have to take the main stairwell to access it," Huff said.

Meg nodded. "But that's our out. If things go south, we fight our way to this room and take the ladder to the roof."

Garcia tipped his helmet and nodded. "Works for me. I think we can manage the creatures above us, but what about below? No way in hell we can stop two assaults."

Pedro smiled a wide grin that exposed coffee-stained teeth. "I have an idea about that."

Tank shook his head as if he knew what the engineer was going to say next.

"We blow up those floors and every Variant on them," Pedro said. He reached into his pocket and pulled out a homemade timer with a switch on it.

"That will likely take down the entire building," Meg said. "It will blow us *all* up."

"I know. It's a last resort."

"It's not going to come down to that," Garcia said. "Now, if you're all done chatting, we have work to do." He patted the table and pulled Tank aside. Fitz took a seat on a chair near a boarded-up window and reached down to check his blades.

Meg strolled over to him. When she looked down, Fitz met her gaze with cold, sad eyes. It was then she saw his dented, blood-covered blades. She hadn't noticed that the right one was bent at the bottom. She took a seat next to him and looked at her own bloody legs. Not long ago, they had carried her one hundred and forty miles to complete an Ironman triathlon. Now she wasn't sure she would even be able to limp out of this building. To make things worse, she was having difficulty holding Beckham's gun in her injured hand. The wound pulsated with her heartbeat. The gash was deep, and Meg knew she would need stitches. She just hoped she would be able to fire the pistol when the time came.

All of a sudden, their plan didn't sound all that great. She didn't know how many more miles her legs or Fitz's blades would take them. Running up stairs certainly wasn't going to help.

"We're still in this fight, Meg," Fitz said when he saw her looking. He put his helmet on and rested his back against the wall. Meg could see the same darkness creeping over him that she'd seen on Plum Island. And deep down, she felt it crawling through herself too. She didn't dare close her eyes, knowing that if she did, she would see Riley in his final moments.

# 9

*Don't leave, Rachel.*

The words appeared in Lieutenant Davis's mind, emerging from the vault where she had stored them since the outbreak. The world had ended while she was on leave in Boston with her husband, Blake, and her nephew, Ollie.

There were other words too—words that reminded her of the worst day of her life.

*Lieutenant, you have been ordered back to the GW. Report to Hanscom Air Force Base by 1430 for airlift to your duty station.*

Duty to country came before family. That's what her superiors had drilled into her head. When shit hit the fan, there would be only soldiers to stand between those families and whatever evil threatened them. There would come a time when America's fate rested in the hands of the few.

That time had come. Davis had answered the call, leaving Blake and Ollie behind.

She'd left them behind to die.

Now, nearly two months later, she was sitting in a room with men and women who had made the same sacrifice. All were here because they'd abandoned their loved ones for their posts. But what if they could go back? What if *she* could go back? Would she have done her duty? Or would she have spent the last few days of her life with Blake and Ollie?

*And died along with them? Ripped apart by monsters?*

Or made into a monster by VX-99, just like Lieutenant Brett.

Ever since she was a kid, Davis had believed there would come a day where she would be faced with a life-changing decision. Never had she imagined it would be between saving the world or holding on to her loved ones. The question of whether she'd made the right choice wasn't the only thing pecking away at her guts. The intel she'd reviewed minutes before consumed her thoughts. Hearing how fucked things were worldwide made her ask another question: Was it too late to save the human race?

The door to the conference room swung open, and her superiors filed in. Now was not the time to be questioning her decisions or worrying about the future. Davis settled her nerves. She'd made her choice. It was done. Her job was to fight, even if fighting seemed all but hopeless.

An image of Ollie's curly locks and bright blue eyes vanished from her mind, replaced by the freshly shaved faces of the men tasked with leading the war. The scent of aftershave drifted into the room.

"Good morning," Captain Humphrey said.

Everyone in the room stood as Vice President Johnson wheeled President Ringgold to the head of the table. Officers flanked them on both sides. Lieutenant Colonel Marsha Kramer was there, her hair in a severe bun. Davis had never liked Kramer much; she was a hard, cold woman who inspired loyalty among her own men but treated everyone else like shit. General Tom Davis, who had helped plan Operation Liberty, stood to Kramer's left, the lines on his forehead as deep as battlefield trenches.

Ringgold cradled her injured arm, which hung in a white sling. Despite her injuries, she looked presidential in a white button-down shirt, black slacks, and an American-flag pin on her collar, right above the area where Lieutenant Brett had shot her. She smiled when she saw Dr. Lovato and gestured to the doctor with her free hand. Lovato hurried over and leaned down. They exchanged a few words that Davis couldn't hear before the doctor returned to her seat between Dr. Ellis and Dr. Yokoyama.

"Good morning, all," Captain Humphrey said. "And welcome home, Doctor Lovato and Team Ghost."

Ringgold raised her hand again and winked at Master Sergeant Beckham and Staff Sergeant Horn. They were in clean uniforms but clearly hadn't had the chance to shower. Davis could smell them from where she sat.

Beckham simply nodded back at the president. The two men were all that was left of the original Team Ghost. And from Davis had recently learned, the Variant Hunters were down to two original members also.

*Two damn men.*

The magnitude of loss was hard to fathom. Between the sight of the battle-bruised Delta Force soldiers and the numbers she'd just seen in a confidential report, Davis felt overwhelmed, and demoralized. An enthusiastic voice pulled her back to the room. At first she couldn't believe it belonged to the vice president.

"We have entered a new stage of this war—a stage that will determine, frankly, whether our species survives or perishes."

Johnson laced his hands together and waited for the news to sink in. Davis went over the numbers in her mind, anxious for her turn to speak but unsure how her news would be received.

"I'm breaking this meeting up into three parts. The first will address the current situation worldwide: projected numbers of survivors, adult Variants, and offspring. The second will focus on Kryptonite. The third will be our plan moving forward." Johnson jerked his chin toward Davis. "Lieutenant, you're up."

Standing, Davis acknowledged the president and vice president in turn with formal nods. She resisted the urge to pull at her cuffs and instead focused on making her back as rigid as possible.

"Madam President, Mister Vice President, this morning we received updated numbers from our sources around the world. The Variant population is projected to be around half a billion. Human survivors have been reduced to approximately one million, a drastic drop from our previous estimates. In a month, that number will plummet to hundreds of thousands of humans, and soon there will not be enough survivors in any one place to ensure the survival of our species."

Davis spoke over the hushed exclamations that followed her announcement. "There is a bit of good news: The Variants aren't breeding at the rate we thought they were. Only about one percent of their population is healthy enough to produce offspring, and while the gestation period is only weeks, we put the juvenile numbers at about five hundred thousand."

Several conversations, less hushed now, broke out around the table.

"Five hundred thousand juveniles is not good news," said Lieutenant Colonel Kramer, scowling. "Will Kryptonite kill them all?"

Davis kept her jaw locked. Kramer was baiting her for info, and she wasn't going to fall for it. Looking at

Dr. Ellis, Davis said, "I'll defer to our science staff to discuss Kryptonite."

Before Ellis spoke, he carefully ran a hand through his hair to fix his side part, then took off his glasses and stuck them in his shirt pocket.

"In short, Kryptonite doesn't work on the offspring," he said.

All around Davis, the room erupted into chaos. Officers spoke out of turn, the drastic development and lack of sleep transforming these stoic soldiers into panicked men and women.

Kramer stared at Ellis with wide eyes. "Kryptonite *doesn't* work? Then I hope to God your team has a Plan B to kill five hundred *thousand* armored Variants, because we don't."

Johnson put an end to the discussion with a fist to the table. The impact resonated through the room. "Give the doctor a chance to speak."

Ellis fidgeted nervously and pulled his glasses from his pocket. He put them back on and continued. "I wish I could tell you that we had another option, but we don't. We've been forced to work with guns to our heads. Now we're simply out of time." He paused, fidgeting again with his glasses. "There's more bad news, and everyone in this room needs to hear it. You need to understand what we're dealing with. The observations Doctor Yokoyama and I made over the past twenty-four hours change everything I thought I knew about these creatures."

Davis clasped her hands behind her back. She had never liked science growing up, and now she liked it even less.

"Previously, my theory was that the Alphas possessed a level of intelligence based on the severity of their Ebola infections before VariantX9H9 was released over the United States, that those that hadn't suffered brain damage from the virus retained some intelligence after VX9H9 that allowed them to speak and perform basic tasks. The offspring, however, are born without any of the health problems their parents may suffer from. On top of that, they've evolved at remarkable rates. The protein that the drugs in Kryptonite target is not present in these second-generation creatures."

Ellis paused to let the information soak in. He glanced over at Dr. Lovato for a split second. She raised both brows at him. Davis hadn't been sure if they'd even had a chance to speak yet—that they hadn't was evident now.

"Go on, Doctor," Johnson said.

Nodding, Ellis continued. "The juveniles aren't human, but Lucy, the juvenile that was brought back from New York, is—or was—capable of human emotion. Before Lucy was killed, we learned quite a bit. First and foremost, Lucy was growing at an astonishing pace. In Variants, development from conception to birth to what we would consider adulthood takes approximately two months— which means most of the juveniles will be full grown by the time we deploy Kryptonite. The adults will die, but the remaining offspring will be much more dangerous than their parents."

"Jesus Christ," Johnson muttered.

Davis watched Dr. Lovato's facial reactions, but it was hard to get a read on her. With her head slightly bowed, eyes swollen, and hands on her lap, the doctor looked worse than Davis had ever seen her.

"That's not all," Ellis added. "Lucy was intelligent enough to pick a key off a dead soldier and unlock a hatch. What's even more frightening is the fact that this specimen was able to *deceive* us into thinking it was sick—that Kryptonite was actually working. These are cunning creatures, far more intelligent than the average human killer. Think of the most deranged sociopaths through-out history—serial killers like Ted Bundy, Charles Man-son, or Richard Speck. Lucy makes these men look like amateurs."

"So how do we kill them?" Johnson asked.

Dr. Lovato rose from her seat and looked toward Beckham, then to Ringgold. "Doctor Ellis and I haven't had a chance to discuss the development of another weapon. But frankly, there isn't time, and I'm not even sure that we could design something if there was."

"What are you saying, Doctor?" Johnson asked. "That we have no way to fight them?"

Dr. Lovato folded her arms across her chest, reveal-ing a long gash on her right arm that was only partially wrapped. "Kryptonite will be ready in two days," she said. "As Ellis stated, it will kill the majority of the adults but it will leave behind the offspring. In the past, we have relied on science to win this war. Now, I'm afraid, we must rely on the military."

Ellis and Yokoyama both nodded their agreement.

"I see," Johnson said. He leaned slightly back, then forward. After a moment of silence, he pivoted in his chair toward his command staff. Among the six uni-forms, there were at least fifty medals for victories in for-eign lands, wars that had been fought when Davis was still in diapers. Even with all that experience, it was hard to believe they could craft a plan to kill five hundred thousand individual combatants, each with the cruel intelligence of a serial killer.

"All right, people. You heard the doctor. I want a plan drafted as soon as possible. In it, I want every available resource we have left," Johnson ordered. "Secondly, I want to know which cities are salvageable. Some were hit hard during Operation Liberty."

"I know this won't be a popular question, but have you

considered nukes, sir?" Kramer asked. "General Kennor was looking into the option. Perhaps we should—"

"You fail to remember, Marsha, I am *not* General Kennor," Johnson quickly replied. "I'm not going to nuke our own soil unless it's a last resort."

Kramer wasn't satisfied. "What do you consider a last resort, sir? Because according to what I just heard, we've already reached that point."

Johnson shook his head, apparently ignoring Kramer's insubordinate tone. "Last resort means we have no men or women left to fight."

Davis wasn't used to seeing the vice president frustrated, but the situation was more fragile than a house of cards in a cornfield with a tornado barreling toward it. Every decision from here on out would determine the fate of humanity.

A voice from the back of the room broke the brief silence. "With all due respect, we're wasting time. There are still survivors out there." The voice, which Davis now recognized as Beckham's was low at first, but the master sergeant's next words were powerful. "We have a duty to save *everyone* we can."

Davis nodded at Beckham approvingly, but Kramer and the other officers glared at the Delta operator as if he didn't have a right to be here. In Davis's mind, Beckham had more of a right than anyone else in the room.

"Go on and speak, Master Sergeant. We're listening," Johnson said.

Beckham and Horn stepped closer to the end of the table to face the president and vice president.

"As you know, on our way out of New York, we came across a stronghold with more than thirty survivors. We rescued a dozen children but were forced to leave the adults and four of our own behind. Meg Pratt, Corporal Fitzpatrick, Sergeant Garcia, and Corporal Talon have risked their lives to protect those people."

"Master Sergeant, you know I and everyone here appreciate your efforts. We understand your losses, and we sympathize with you. But we have much bigger problems on our hands," Johnson said, ruefully.

"Sir, if I—"

"Look," Vice President Johnson said. "I'm grateful for the valor you and your men showed out there, and I'm thrilled you were able to bring back Doctor Lovato. But our focus now is on killing the juvenile Variants. We can't risk resources to save every survivor in the field. Kryptonite did not kill Lucy. We will need every drop of gas, every round, and every rocket to defeat the monsters."

"That's what you don't understand, Mr. Vice President," Dr. Lovato interjected. "What matters now is saving lives. The future of our species depends on it."

Before Johnson could reply, President Ringgold scooted her wheelchair away from the table. She used her good hand to push herself out of her chair. Johnson stood to help her, whispering, "Madam President, you should stay seated."

"*No*," she said sternly.

When she was standing straight, Ringgold looked at Beckham and Dr. Lovato in turn. What she said next gave Davis the chills.

"Everyone, I want you to see what I see." Ringgold paused until all eyes were on the Delta Force operator and the doctor. "This man and this woman have done everything in their power to save our species, since the beginning. Master Sergeant Beckham was there on day one. He rescued Dr. Lovato from Atlanta, and they have worked through blood, sweat, fatigue, and extreme loss to ensure we still have a future. We're sitting in this room, ladies and gentleman, because of them."

Beckham grabbed Dr. Lovato's hand, squeezing it so everyone could see.

"They have taught me that every life is precious, and I want to take a second to thank them." Ringgold smacked the palm of her injured hand with her good hand, slowly, then faster, until the claps echoed in the room. Everyone else joined in, and one by one, the highest-ranking members of the United States military stood and applauded as well.

With her eyes still on Beckham and Dr. Lovato, Ringgold said, "In two days, we will deploy Kryptonite in a wide sweep to kill the adults. Vice President Johnson, I want you to work with your team to build a strategy to kill the offspring. In the meantime, we *will* focus on saving *every* life that we can—starting with our compatriots and the survivors stranded in New York City."

Beckham picked up his radio the moment he left the conference room and kissed Kate goodbye. She hustled to the *Cowpens* with the other doctors, parting from Beckham as they both were recalled to their duties.

Opening a channel to Fitz, Beckham said, "Fitz, you copy? Over."

"'Sup, boss?" came the reply.

Beckham almost smiled. Instead, he gritted his teeth, remembering how long Davis had said it would take to get a bird and strike team to Manhattan.

"Good news and bad news, brother. We got a team gearing up to come bring you back. Lieutenant Davis has authorized two birds for extraction. But we won't be there for another three hours. Think you can hold off the Variants for that long?"

There was only a short crackle of static. "Not a problem, boss." The silence that followed told Beckham there was something else on Fitz's mind.

"You good, Fitz?"

"For now."

Static. Horn glanced over at Beckham, worry on his freckled face.

"You said *we*," Fitz finally said. There was something odd about his voice, almost as if he felt guilty.

Beckham bit the inside of his lip and checked with Horn. The big man nodded stoically.

"I'll be on one of the birds," Beckham said. "Might have Big Horn with me too."

"No," Fitz said abruptly. "Staying behind was my decision. You have families to protect. Don't risk that."

"Fitz, I'm not leaving—"

The radio crackled, and Fitz cut him off before he could finish. "No, Beckham. *Please.* Promise me you'll stay on the *GW.* I can't live with any more guilt, man. If something happened to you, I would never forgive myself."

Beckham looked at the floor. Kate had told him it was okay to go. That sparked his own guilt: He had all the faith in the world in Fitz, but he was trapped inside a building crawling with monsters, and Beckham didn't trust another team to do what Team Ghost did best.

"Promise me, Beckham," Fitz said.

This time Beckham was the one to grumble. "You better fucking come back in one piece, man."

Fitz chuckled. "I'll be fine, brother. See you soon."

The grip of a strong hand pulled Beckham to the passage. Horn had that uncertain look on his face—the one that told Beckham he had something to say.

"I just got my girls back, and they're in shock. I felt guilty about leaving them with a babysitter to go to the goddamn briefing. And I know you want to go back out there, even though Fitz told you not to go."

"Big Horn—"

"They're just kids," Horn growled. "*My* kids. I can't let nothin' happen to them again. I can't lose them like I lost Sheila."

Beckham scratched at the stubble on his face that was dangerously close to becoming a beard. He'd only seen Horn like this a few times, but they were Delta Force operators. Their job was to save people, to fight. The members of Team Ghost who suffered the most were the ones with families. It had always been that way.

"We both know we can't sit on this ship and wait for the war to end," Beckham finally said. He grabbed the back of Horn's neck and brought their heads together until their foreheads touched. "Even if we don't go out there to get Fitz, we will go back into battle soon."

Horn pulled away, nodding. There was still fight in his eyes, despite everything he'd lost. They would always have each other's backs. That was what friends did. That was what *brothers* did. They took care of one another. They were family. Fitz was part of that family too. Trusting others to bring him back wasn't going to be easy.

But Beckham had another family to think about now.

"Wanna go see Chow?" Horn asked.

Beckham nodded. He hurried through the passages of the ship with Horn. Traffic was dense, and Beckham flattened his body to squeeze past sailors and soldiers working in the narrow, dimly lit space.

When they got to the makeshift infirmary, it was overflowing. This was not the same place President Ringgold had been taken to when she was shot. The main infirmary was already completely full. Captain Humphrey had ordered a second one set up below decks. The long room had served as an exercise facility before. Weight machines had been replaced with cots and medical supplies.

Beckham had seen some shitty field hospitals in his day. In Afghanistan, Team Ghost had fought on a joint mission alongside the locals in a battle to take a small but strategically important village. Five Americans had lost their lives in the Taliban ambush there. Twenty Afghani fighters had been killed. Overall, counting civilians, the death toll had reached almost a hundred. The temporary field hospital Ghost had helped establish had looked like something from a Civil War photo: pans filled to the brim with blood, buckets overflowing with amputated limbs, and bugs. The flies had been everywhere.

As soon as Beckham stepped inside the infirmary, he thought he'd gone back to the Korengal Valley. He and Horn passed beds filled with soldiers missing legs. During Operation Liberty, Beckham had witnessed a Variant rip a marine's arm clean out of its socket, but the chaos of battle had kept Beckham moving then. When he had a chance to see the results of war in a quiet moment, it was hard to stomach.

Somewhere above decks, another wounded warrior was recovering: Apollo was receiving his own medical care. It hurt knowing he couldn't be down here with the others, but at least the dog was safe. Beckham would visit him as soon as he could.

He stopped at the bed of a sleeping marine just old enough to be considered a man. His smooth, wrinkle-free face reminded Beckham of what he had looked like as a teenager, back when he would spend his free time in the mountains. Long before the War on Terror or the Variants.

Shaking his head, Beckham looked down. Beneath the white sheet covering the marine were two stumps wrapped with bloodstained dressings.

"Are you looking for someone?" a nurse asked. She stopped behind Horn. The red cross on her shirt was barely visible beneath the bloodstains.

"Staff Sergeant Jay Chow," Horn said.

"He's right over there," the woman said, pointing.

Beckham followed her gesture across the room, but centered his focus on a cluster of beds where two of the people he'd saved from New York were recovering.

Bo was there, sleeping peacefully, his mother by his side. Donna sat in a chair alongside Bo's bed with her hand on his arm. Beckham shook his head. Bo was another child who had lost a parent, and before this was all over, there would be more orphans.

The marine in the bed in front of Beckham struggled to open his eyes. His face turned red and his eyes brimmed, as if he was ashamed to be seen in his injured state.

A flashback to the tunnels beneath Fort Bragg rose in Beckham's mind. He saw a red-haired kid with his back to the wall and a blanket covering prosthetic legs. Hours later, Beckham had handed that man a rifle and asked him if he wanted to fight. In the weeks that followed, Fitz had saved countless lives.

"What's your name, marine?" Beckham asked.

"PFC Tunnis." His eyes brightened when he saw the Delta Force Team Ghost patch featuring a skull wreathed in smoke on Beckham's arm. "Holy shit, you're with Team Ghost?"

Beckham nodded. "I'm Master Sergeant Beckham."

"Why are you here?" The marine said, his face showing signs of worry. He struggled to sit up, pushing at his bed and grimacing further as he moved what was left of his legs.

"To say thank you," Beckham replied. "And to remind you that a marine can still fight without his legs. One of my best friends has killed more Variants than I have, and he's done it with prosthetics."

A weak grin touched the sides of Tunnis's lips. "Thank you. I hope someday I can fight alongside you."

"Me too, son," Beckham said. He patted Tunnis on the shoulder and turned to follow Horn and the nurse to Chow's bed. In a sea of injured soldiers, it wasn't easy to spot him. Most of the wounded were unrecognizable in the bandages that covered their bodies. Those lucky enough to survive combat with a Variant typically had long, deep gashes to show for it. Talons and needle-sharp teeth could do a number on human flesh.

Many of the soldiers who did survive later died of infection. Those talons weren't just razor sharp, they were coated with bacteria, and antibiotics were in short supply.

"Over there," the nurse said. She pointed at a bed in the northeast corner of the room. "He's the second one on the right."

As Beckham approached, his heart thumped. There was a reason the woman had been obliged to point out the bed. Chow looked like a mummy, wrapped in bandages from head to toe.

"Fuck," Horn mumbled.

Chow was sleeping when they arrived. His chest moved up and down, slowly enough to make Beckham's heart kick even harder. He turned to Horn, and they exchanged a worried look.

"Did you bring them back?" asked a faint voice.

Beckham looked down to see Chow squinting up at him. A long bandage seeping pus covered Chow's right cheek. Another stretched across his forehead. His chin was hidden behind another wrap.

"Yeah," Beckham said. "We brought Kate and Horn's girls back. But Meg, Fitz, Garcia, and Tank are trapped out there. Thomas was killed, and we also lost…" The last name was too painful to say.

"I know," Chow said, coughing. "The kid's gone."

There was a moment of silence that hurt worse than any physical injury a Variant could inflict.

*Why couldn't I have been there? I should have fucking been there!*

"Riley was a good man," Chow said, shaking his head.

Horn put a hand on Beckham's shoulder, and the three shared a moment of silence to remember the kid. At least they had something to bury this time. They would lay Riley to rest as soon as his body was brought back from Plum Island. After a few moments, Chow looked to Horn and then to Beckham.

"There's something else too," Beckham said. "Kryptonite doesn't work on the offspring. Vice President Johnson is cooking up a plan, but it sounds as if whatever soldiers the military has left will be sent back into the meat grinder. We *will* play a role in the final battle."

Chow tried to reach up to touch his face but then slowly lowered his arm. He cringed from the pain of the short movement.

"When can I get out of here?" he asked.

"Not for a while," Beckham said. "You earned yourself a break." He considered cracking a joke to lighten the mood or reassure Chow, but honesty always seemed to be the best way of dealing with injured brothers.

Horn used a different approach. "You look like a carved-up turkey on Thanksgiving, man. Good thing girls like scars," he said. Reaching up, Horn wiped sweat from his brow, nervously, back and forth.

Chow chuckled and then coughed again. "I'll be back in the game in no time."

Instead of lying, Beckham kept his mouth shut. Chow picked up on his silence.

"These aren't that bad," Chow said. He lifted up his arms. "I'll be back on my feet soon."

They were the same words Riley had used. Beckham crouched next to Chow's bedside and grabbed his hand. "I'm sorry, brother. You wouldn't be lying here if I hadn't gone AWOL."

Another laugh came from Chow's chapped lips. "You're right about that, man."

"I'm so—"

Chow gripped Beckham's hand back even harder. "Don't you do that, Beckham. I wouldn't be here at all if it weren't for you. You made a mistake, but you've saved my life countless times. Don't blame yourself, man. I'm going to have some scars, but I'll live." Chow managed a grin without even grimacing. "I'll be back out there with Team Ghost for the final battle. You'll see."

Beckham nodded. Part of him actually believed Chow. The end was coming, and when it did, what was left of Team Ghost would face it together.

# 10

Garcia didn't want to go back to the *GW*. What the fuck was there to go back to? His wife and daughter were dead, and now almost his entire team had been killed. Tank was all he had—a single brother out of a group of six men Garcia had spent the past decade fighting with.

That was a different kind of pain than being shot to pieces.

"Sarge," Tank grumbled, "you better take a look at this." He stood next to one of the boarded-up windows on the west side of the apartment. The first rays of sunlight were sneaking in around the boards. But that wasn't what Tank was looking at.

A flurry of movement ten stories down commanded Garcia's attention. Placing his eye against the split between the boards, he watched pallid bodies climbing into a hole and entering the building. The beasts were still scaling the tower.

"How can they not smell us in here?" Garcia asked in a whisper. It made no sense the Variants wouldn't know exactly where they were.

Huff and Pedro walked over to the windows.

"I tricked them," Pedro said. "I dragged some corpses into the ductwork when I started setting traps. The scent of rot confuses the beasts. They like fresh meat. We're, like, protected by a rot shield."

*Lord help this man.*

Garcia was seriously impressed, but also a bit disturbed. He didn't trust the look in Pedro's eyes. Everyone out here had screws loose; spending six weeks in hell would do that to the strongest of men. But Pedro was different from the others. The forty-year-old engineer was seriously off. He didn't seem scared—he seemed excited.

Garcia turned back to the window. From his vantage, the Variants looked like ants as they entered the building. They had to number in the hundreds now.

"So the gas will kill them?" Garcia asked.

"Might take a while, but it should."

"How do you keep the flow going?" Tank asked. "And how does it not escape?"

Pedro looked at Tank as if he was stupid. He shifted his black-rimmed glasses up onto his nose and shrugged. "Some of it does escape, but the natural-gas line to this building never shut off when other services did. We have a constant flow."

"We're sitting on dynamite with a short fuse," Meg griped. "It wouldn't take much at all."

Pedro shrugged again. "Better than getting discovered and torn apart, right?"

Tank mumbled something that Garcia hoped no one else could interpret. He looked away from the boards and glared at Tank, then jerked his chin back toward their rucksacks. It was time to get packed up. Two hours had passed. The sun would be coming up soon, and the birds from the *GW* were getting closer. And if Pedro's estimates were correct, the Variants would be too. It wouldn't be long before the monsters found their hiding spot.

They were down to the wire.

Garcia grabbed his bag and set it on the table with the blueprints.

"Fitz, Huff, Tank, gather 'round," he said.

Meg grabbed a hatchet with a long handle that she had accepted earlier from one of the survivors. She lugged the handle up on her right shoulder and shot him a steely gaze that would have given him the chills in any other situation. He had almost forgotten she was a fire-fighter in her past life.

"Fine, you too, Meg," Garcia said.

She joined the men at the table while Pedro retreated back to the group of civilians. Most were sleeping on the couches, but a few were pacing back and forth nervously. Garcia didn't like that. Everyone needed to keep as quiet as possible. He pointed at the man carrying a pipe and then put a finger to his lips as if to say, *Keep it the fuck down*.

"You said everyone here can fight," Garcia said to Huff, his gaze still on the man.

Huff nodded.

"Has anyone here actually had any formal gun training?"

Hesitating, Huff turned back to the group. "No. Just me."

"That's what I figured," Garcia said. "I'm worried these people pose more of a threat to each other in close quarters than the Variants."

Huff tilted his head slightly. "Probably right about that."

"Then this is the plan," Garcia said. "When air support arrives, we will wait for them to clear the rooftop. At that point, Fitz, Tank, and I will clear the stairwell and the upper floors—"

"I'm coming too," Meg said.

"Figured you'd say that." Garcia didn't dare look at her. Her gaze would break him. "Huff, you lock that door behind us. Once we clear the upper floors, we will link up with the strike team and return for the civilians."

Tank snorted and cradled his SAW across his chest. "I don't like it, Sarge. We don't know how many Variants are out there."

"You got any other ideas?"

A wild screech somewhere overhead cut Tank off before he could reply. They all glanced up at the ceiling.

"Got another one," Pedro said from a few feet away. He'd walked over when Garcia wasn't looking. Shit, he hated it when people snuck up on him.

"One of a hundred," Tank groused.

Meg studied the blade on her hatchet. Her M9 was tucked into her pants. If it weren't for her injured legs, Garcia would have been the one asking for her to join them. She looked like Xena fucking Warrior Princess.

"This shit is crazy," Tank said. "They're already above us, and it's just a matter of time before they break through that roof-access door."

Garcia brought a finger back to his lips and furrowed his eyebrows so hard his eyes bulged. Tank was right. It was remarkable the Variants hadn't found them yet, even if they were camouflaged by rotting corpses.

Pulling his finger away from his mouth, he pointed to his eyes, then to Tank and Fitz. They all pulled fresh magazines and jammed them into their primary weapons and handguns.

The civilians watched in silence, and Garcia glanced up every few seconds to scan their faces. He could pick out those who were parents: Knowing their kids were safe had relieved some of their anxiety. The guy still wearing slacks and shivering was obviously a lawyer or businessman of some sort. Only a Wall Street banker would still have on dress pants six weeks into the apocalypse.

After holstering his M9, Garcia glanced at his wrist-watch. Forty-five minutes until extraction.

Another thump and screech sounded above them. Outside the room, in the stairwell, a boom rang out almost simultaneously. Garcia's eyes darted from the ceiling to the secured door. A crack of metal sounded; the echo bounced off the walls as if a gong had been pounded inside the bunker.

The Variants were getting closer.

"Get ready," Garcia said. "Tank, you got point. Meg, you take rear guard. Stay *behind* us."

She raised her M9 in her trigger hand and the hatchet in her other. With her sleeves rolled up, Garcia could see her biceps flexing. She wasn't one of his fallen Variant Hunter brothers, but he was glad to have her at his back.

Garcia waited for Fitz and Tank to flank him. Standing side by side, the three marines walked through the center of the apartment with Meg right behind them. The civilians watched them with frightened, skeptical eyes as they moved.

As soon as they were at the door, Garcia checked Tank and Fitz. Both marines offered reassuring nods. They were good to go. Meg mimicked their actions, but Garcia saw the pain in her eyes. He remembered that she'd lost someone important to her too. If they could all channel their pain into anger, then they might just have a chance of making it out of here in one piece after all.

"Meg, you use that hatchet on anything we fail to kill," Garcia said.

She twirled the weapon in her left hand. The blade whooshed through the air. "Try to kill most of 'em," Meg replied.

Garcia grinned, but Tank shook his head. Fitz didn't

say a word. His face was a mask of calm even as the noises of hunting Variants intensified inside the building.

Garcia checked his watch every few moments.

Thirty minutes to extraction.

It was 0500 hours, and Garcia hadn't slept for over twenty. Half of those he'd spent fighting or hiding. There were days in Iraq and Afghanistan where he only saw a few minutes of sleep, but killing evil men was easier than killing monsters. Facing a building full of starving beasts in dark passages, especially after losing Thomas, was going to be like fighting while coming off a drug high. He felt off—Simultaneously enraged and lethargic.

Over the next fifteen minutes, the building came alive with the noise of prowling Variants. Glass shattered, wood creaked, and the snapping of joints filled the tower. They were getting closer, but Garcia still didn't hear anything in the hallway outside.

Earlier, he hadn't trusted the barricade Huff and the others had used to block the stairwell to the lower levels. Now, he was impressed. With the gas, the deceiving stench of rot, and the debris pile clogging the stairs, the Variants still hadn't reached them from below. What surprised him the most, however, was the rooftop-access door. It was only four floors above, and he still hadn't heard it break open.

The marines and Meg stood in complete silence for another five minutes, stilling their breathing and waiting. Garcia noticed Fitz was struggling to keep his balance. His bent blade made standing difficult, and his thighs were trembling. Sweat poured down his face. Tank was putting most of his weight on his left foot. He had hurt his right during the helicopter crash. Looking at it now, Garcia could see it was injured worse than he originally thought.

Garcia closed his eyes and said a prayer for their fallen brother who hadn't survived, knowing in his heart that Thomas was truly in a better place.

*Be strong and courageous. Do not fear or be in dread of them, for it is the Lord your God who goes with you. He will not leave you or forsake you.*

The distant bark of gunfire forced Garcia's eyes open. A bang followed, and the shriek of metal on metal echoed from the stairwell outside. All at once, the high-pitched whines of Variants flowed into the building as the monsters from the roof finally made their way inside. These were not the cries of monsters charging into battle; they were the crazed screeches of beasts retreating from it.

The cavalry had arrived.

Garcia flashed a nod at Tank. The marine lifted the steel bar off the door and handed it to Huff.

"Good luck," Huff said, his voice shaky. He backed away, standing to the side so he could lock the door as soon as the marines and Meg were clear.

Fitz pulled back the slide on his weapon at the same moment Garcia did. The echoes of an intense firefight coming from the rooftop filled the stairwell. He grabbed the handle of the door and nodded at Tank, Fitz, and then Meg.

Raising his M4 in one hand, Garcia greedily accepted the adrenaline rushing through his veins. He twisted the door handle and charged into the stairwell.

*All it takes is all you got, Marine.*

Kate couldn't remember a time when Ellis had hugged her. Not this hard, at least. He'd wrapped his arms around her the moment they reached their lab on the *Cowpens* and still hadn't let up.

"I thought the worst. I thought you weren't coming back," Ellis whimpered.

Kate patted his back softly, as she would Tasha's or Jenny's. Ellis could be a sensitive man, and she had a lot of respect for him, but they didn't have time to sit around and cry.

They had a juvenile Variant to dissect.

She didn't want to seem coldhearted, but earlier that day she'd faced certain death. She'd been given a second chance. A lot of men and women had given their lives to protect Plum Island and the bioreactors, and now it was time to do her job.

"I'm fine, Pat," Kate finally said. "Really, I am."

He pulled away, knowing she only used his first name when she meant business.

"You've missed a lot in the past twenty-four hours." He put his glasses back on. "Where do I even start?"

"The bioreactors. You told me before the briefing that we're on track with other labs in the United States to produce enough Kryptonite to launch in two days."

"That's right," Ellis said.

"What about other countries?"

"Still working on it."

"Goddamnit, *who's* working on it?"

"She was shot," Ellis replied coldly.

Kate remembered the words President Ringgold whispered to her before the briefing: *I told you there's always hope. Together, we will persevere. The war will be over soon.*

Those words filled Kate with strength—resolve she so desperately needed now. Kate had fought to get Kryptonite deployed worldwide, but it wasn't going to happen simultaneously with the weapons deployment over the United States. VX9H9 had been launched over other countries much later, and the surviving governments and militaries had fallen like dominoes as a result.

Europe, Asia, South America: They all needed

America's help, but right now the United States had to focus on saving its own citizens before they could lend resources overseas. It was hard to stomach, but it was reality. Politically, things weren't much different now than when Kate had worked in third-world countries— resources would always go wherever the United States felt there was a priority.

After all that she had been holding in, Kate simply said, "Bring me up to speed."

"Doctor Yokoyama and his staff have already started working on Lucy's body. They just finished using a perfusion pump to shoot contrast into her blood vessels. We also used optical coherence tomography over areas of exposed flesh. That's where things get interesting." Ellis crinkled his nose inside his helmet. "Kate, the juveniles have an extensive network of what look like glands. I haven't seen anything like it—not even the adults have so many. Yokoyama's technicians ran a contrast through those too. We can look at the results after the autopsy."

"What's interesting about that?" Kate asked. "Isn't it just part of their lymphatic system, to help with hormone delivery and the increased immune-system activity?"

"You'll just have to see for yourself."

Kate nodded. "Okay, what else you got?"

"That's about it for now."

Kate could see the excitement in Ellis's eyes. He was ready to see what was under Lucy's armor, and so was Kate.

She turned toward the observation glass that looked over Lab A. Days before, Kate had been in the same spot, next to President Ringgold, watching as Lieutenant Brett brutally murdered Dr. Carmen and attacked Dr. Yokoyama. The flashback faded, and in its place she focused on a cadaver-dissection table in the center of the room. Two technicians were prepping Lucy for the autopsy. They turned the body on its back and tucked the armored arms against its sides.

"Doctors, please get suited up. We're ready," said a voice through the wall speaker. Yokoyama entered at the far end of the lab, through the same doors Brett had used.

Fifteen minutes later, Kate and Ellis joined everyone in Lab A. The technicians prepared tables full of a wide variety of autopsy tools. Some were more advanced, like the Stryker saw that was used to cut through skull in a way that protected soft tissue. Others were traditional: bone saws, rib cutters, skull chisels, toothed forceps, and scissors.

But this was no ordinary autopsy. The cadaver on the table wasn't human. It hardly even looked like a Variant. Kate would need the barbaric-looking tools to cut through the armored plates covering Lucy's body.

The doctors walked to the table together, Kate's breathing rapidly increasing as she focused on the four-foot-long beast.

"Remarkable creature," Ellis said.

Kate stepped up to the table. She reached out, but hesitated.

"It's okay," Ellis said, as if he could read her thoughts. "She's deader than a doornail."

There was no doubt about that. The creature's armor was riddled with cracks and holes where the marines had emptied their magazines into it. But what scared Kate even more was what they would discover when they pried off its outer shell.

Evolution had proven to be a very dangerous thing.

Kate put a gloved hand on Lucy's right leg. Even through the gloves, she could feel the rigid exterior. She ran a finger over it, tracing it back and forth. The texture was smooth in some places, like a turtle shell, and rough like bark in others.

Yokoyama leaned over the corpse and said, "Let's start by removing the armor on the left femur. Ronnie, get me a bone saw."

The technician retrieved the tool and gave it to Yokoyama. With the utmost precision, Yokoyama made a long stroke over the center of the plate covering Lucy's femur. The saw made a piercing screech as the blade cut through the rough shell.

Starting slowly at first, Yokoyama worked the tool back and forth, cutting a narrow trench. Ellis exchanged a flicker of a glance with Kate, his brows raised, before turning back to Yokoyama. They watched their colleague struggle for several minutes.

Grunting, Yokoyama finally took a break.

"Good God, the plating is stronger than bone," he said. "It's got to be an inch thick."

Kate examined the shotgun blasts that had cracked Lucy's armor. The spray had broken the shell, cracks spreading around the impact area. Frayed flesh hung from the more severe wounds, but in most places, the armor had deflected the shots. It was a 5.56-millimeter round that had finally taken the Variant down, and that was only because it had hit the creature in the right eye.

Stepping closer, Kate examined its face. The bony plating crested its skull and ran down the nose. It looked oddly like a Spartan warrior's helmet. Lucy's wormy lips were sealed, and Kate could only see a faint trace of where the juvenile's armored chin had cracked open to reveal mandibles.

Ellis leaned closer with a long pair of tweezers. "Stay back," he said, without looking at Kate.

Every muscle in Kate's body tightened, time halting around her as Ellis seemed to reach forward in slow motion. He inserted the tip of the tweezers into a nearly invisible crack in the middle of Lucy's chin. All at once, four mandibles popped open around the creature's bulging lips and twisted tongue. Kate jumped at the snapping sound.

Lucy's deflated right eye seeped out of its socket like an egg yolk as the mandibles deployed. The left eye still stared up at the ceiling. Almond-shaped, with a yellow iris, it was much wider than that of an adult Variant. If Lucy's parents could see in the dark, Lucy might have developed even better vision. Perhaps the creature could see heat signatures or spot prey from a mile away. The possibilities were endless.

But it was the mandibles that Kate couldn't look away from. The horned teeth rimming both sides were coated in plaque and bloodstains. Morbid thoughts filled Kate's mind. She wondered how much human flesh the beast had consumed.

Yokoyama glared but then went back to sawing away. "Almost...got...it."

Kate put her hand on her stomach and stepped away from Lucy. When her heart stopped pounding, she joined the other doctors again.

In her most powerful voice, she said, "Once we get through this armor, I want to perform every test we can think of. We're going to run panels of chemical analyses and expose its flesh to all ranges of radiation. If this juvenile has a weakness, we're going to find it."

A sharp crack echoed through the room. Yokoyama peered at the long ravine he'd sawed in the armor covering Lucy's femur.

"I'm through," he said, his voice awed. "Ellis, you use a hammer to finish breaking through this piece. I'll get started on the arms."

Kate supervised the autopsy from a distance, breathing steadily. Crunching noises filled the lab as the men slowly broke away Lucy's armor. There was a lot on

Kate's mind, but those words from the past once again found their way through the mess:

*In order to kill a monster, you'll have to create one.*

"Ghost Two, this is Whiskey Four, approaching target. Please state position, over."

The transmission was hard to hear over the roar of the Variants, which had sharpened into a whine louder than an air-raid siren. Fitz acknowledged the transmission by screaming into his headset. "On our way to the roof. Stand by!"

In the flicker of light from the lanterns, two twisted Variants emerged from the shadows. The beasts jumped onto the landing, crouching and tilting their heads at the approaching marines.

Their skulls were suddenly flung back, one after the other, Garcia taking out both creatures with head shots. Brain matter splattered the wall behind them, and the corpses slumped to the ground. Scratching talons followed as more Variants from the roof poured into the stairwell. Fitz couldn't see them yet, but he guessed there were at least two dozen, judging by the macabre cacophony of shrieks and snapping joints.

Fitz checked the pile of debris clogging the stairs that led to the floors below. It wasn't moving, as far as he could tell, but there was a sound reverberating from the pile, like the fins of a massive fish hitting the bottom of a dock.

Meg caught his gaze, her eyes widening. They didn't have much time. He limped after Tank and Garcia, his right blade creaking with every step. Shit, he didn't want to look down at it.

*Don't look down.*

Fitz snuck a glance.

The carbon-fiber blade had a crack near the dent. He

wasn't sure how much longer it would hold—especially if he had to run for his life.

"Goddamnit," Fitz whispered. He brought his scope up and centered the red dot on the landing just as a Variant skittered across the ceiling. Garcia and Fitz fired at the same time, pumping the creature full of rounds that jerked its body as if it was being hit by electricity. It collapsed onto the two downed beasts, blood gushing from a dozen holes.

Meg stuffed her pistol into her waistband as she crept past Fitz. Then she brought her hatchet down with both hands on the twitching monster's skull as if she was chopping wood. The blade split open the top of the Variant's head like a ripe melon. The crack of bones made Fitz wince.

Ahead, Garcia flashed an advance signal to Tank. The massive marine nimbly leaped over the corpses, bounded around the corner in a defensive position, and then opened fire.

A Variant missing an arm bounced off the wall next to Tank and crashed to the landing. Meg brought her hatchet down on the beast's spine. It screeched in pain, pale legs kicking and arms flailing like an albino cricket. She withdrew the blade, flipped it over, and swung an uppercut that hit the monster's chin, silencing it with the graceful blow.

"Multiple contacts!" Tank bellowed.

Fitz and Garcia hurried around the corner, rifles shouldered. The narrow passage was swarming with creatures. Every inch of the walls, ceiling, and stairs crawled with them. Blood dripped from wounds the monsters had accumulated on the rooftop.

Two dozen lips seemed to open all at once, revealing broken, jagged teeth and maws dripping with saliva. The marines fired into the mass. A river of blood gushed down the stairs as the creatures were torn apart. Meg pulled her pistol and nailed two consecutive head shots.

"Short bursts!" Garcia yelled. "Conserve your ammo! Meg, watch our six!"

The wounded, starving Variants didn't stand a chance against the well-trained marines. Fitz, Tank, and Garcia had fought enough of them by now to know exactly how to handle the beasts in close quarters. They went from the defensive to the offensive, advancing up the stairs and pushing the Variants back toward the rooftop. Meg swung her hatchet in smooth arcs, decapitating or fatally maiming monsters that still had air in their lungs.

Fitz wondered if the beasts felt any sense of fear, or if their retreat was fueled only by basic survival instincts. A female squatting on the landing above stared at him right as he squeezed the trigger. It didn't even flinch when the bullet hit it in the forehead. It was almost as if the creature had accepted its fate.

Tank moved past the dead female and pivoted toward the open door to Floor 29 with his SAW. "Clear!"

He stomped on the face of another downed beast before he continued around the corner to the next flight of stairs. One less for Meg to take care of.

Fitz continued up the next stairs carefully, eyeing his cracked blade. Four Variants were waiting above, their webbed hands plastered to the ceiling, microscopic hairs allowing them to cling to the concrete. Another half dozen loped down the stairs on the tips of their talons.

The passage filled with echoes of what sounded like hundreds of pitchforks being dragged over rocks, overshadowed only by the agonizing howls of dying monsters. Fitz's nostrils were still burning from the scent of raw sewage back in the apartment, but a draft of rotting fruit quickly took over. Even their blood reeked.

"Changing!" Garcia yelled.

Fitz's M4 went dry at the same moment. He slung it over his shoulder with one hand and grabbed the strap of his MK11 with the other. He raised the sniper rifle and was firing three seconds later.

The suppressed cracks echoed in Fitz's ears as he fired. He counted each shot and watched the same number of heads explode with satisfaction. They only had two floors to go before they hit the rooftop, and so far they hadn't run into any snags.

He thought of his blade again, but this time resisted the urge to look down. He squeezed off a round that lanced into the chest of a creature that had tried to get past Tank by scurrying above him. Whatever was inside its rib cage caked the ceiling with muddy sludge. It fell limply to the stairs behind the larger marine.

"Thanks, little man!" Tank slaughtered five more beasts as they came bounding around the next corner.

Garcia was firing again, M4 in one hand and M9 in the other. Fitz used the stolen moment to change the box magazine in his MK11. Then he swung the rifle over his back, grabbed his M4, and changed that magazine.

By the time he'd finished, seven more Variants were bleeding out from mortal wounds. Some of them swiped at Tank as he ran past them. Each time Meg brought her hatchet down on their puckering lips, leaving no question that the Variants left behind wouldn't be flanking them.

Tank stopped on the final landing and fired into the hallway. Sunlight streamed from the open door above, something Fitz hadn't been sure he would ever see again.

Fitz felt a grin coming on. He was almost to the top.

Before he had a chance to fire another shot, something grabbed his right blade and yanked so hard it broke the carbon fiber in half. He fell face first to the ground, his helmet smashing into the concrete. His heart slammed against his rib cage.

He'd been so focused on getting topside that he hadn't noticed one of the beasts behind them was still alive.

*Stupid! So fucking stupid!*

Fitz reached for his side arm, pulled it, and twisted as something pulled on his other blade. He almost squeezed the trigger, but then he saw Meg's frightened eyes. She was on her back, looking at him, her neck craned at an awful angle.

"Help!" she choked.

A Variant had her pinned to the ground, maw descending toward her neck. To its right was a second beast missing its left arm and a chunk from the top of its skull. A flap of thick skin hung loosely over its right eye. The left eye homed in on the piece of Fitz's blade it held in its good hand. Croaking, the creature tossed the piece down the stairs.

"Son of a bitch!" Fitz shouted. He shot the creature in its good eye and watched a piece of himself clank down the steps in what seemed like slow motion. His heart hammered, but not because he'd just lost his mobility. When he roved the barrel to shoot the monster on Meg, it was already pulling her down.

"Meg!" he shouted.

She reached up, screaming in horror as the creature dragged her down the stairs. It was there, at the bottom of the flight where his blade had come to a rest, that Fitz spotted a pack of Variants charging up the passage, their bodies distorted in the light, twisting and bending, shadows growing in size as they raced toward Meg.

"No!" Fitz shouted. "Garcia, Tank! Help!" He squeezed off calculated shots, dropping monsters to her left and right. Light from the lanterns danced over a small armored lump that made Fitz nearly shit himself.

It was then that he understood. This pack wasn't just adult Variants; it was full of juveniles. They had bulldozed through the debris pile and opened a gateway for the others to follow.

Fitz aimed his M4 and M9 at the beast as it galloped up the stairs toward Meg. Dozens of adults and offspring followed, talons screeching over concrete.

"Help me!" Meg shouted.

Spent shells ejected from Fitz's weapons and rounds streaked down the passage, ricocheting off the juvenile's armored body. It grabbed the adult that was dragging Meg, tossed it against the wall, then grabbed her legs and pulled her backward.

Fitz dropped his pistol and gripped his M4 with both hands, trying to line up a shot, but Meg's head was in the way.

"Please move, Meg. Please."

For the first time in Fitz's career, he couldn't line up a shot. The wave of pallid flesh obscured Meg a second later, rushing over her and slithering up the stairs toward Fitz in a solid lump of ropy muscle and bulging lips.

He fired his weapon on full automatic, rounds lancing into flesh and coating the walls with sticky crimson. By the time he finished off the magazine, she was gone. Tossing away his rifle, he swung his MK11 from his back, screaming, "Meg! I'm coming! Hold on!"

*You can still fight. You can still save her.*

Fitz pushed himself up using the muzzle of his MK11 like a crutch. He grabbed the wall and then raised the gun. The first shot threw him off balance and he crashed to the stairs, sliding on his butt. Shouldering the weapon, he fired from his back into the mass charging toward him, frantically searching for any sign of her between shots.

"Tank, Garcia! They got Meg, they fucking got Meg!"

The only reply came in the shrieks of the monsters. There might have been a human scream of agony, but it was too hard to tell. He squeezed off another shot and then felt a pair of massive hands that could have only been Tank's underneath his armpits. The marine yanked him up a step as Fitz kicked with his broken blade.

"We have to move!" Garcia shouted.

"Meg's down there!" Fitz yelled back. "We can't leave her!"

Fitz fought in Tank's iron grip, squirming and firing his MK11 at the same time. The pack of monsters that hadn't stopped to feed advanced, led by three more armadillo-like offspring.

"No!" Fitz sobbed as Tank pulled him up the stairs. "God, please, no."

Fitz had failed his friends again, and this time he couldn't even run back in to help.

# 11

For the first time in six weeks, Beckham had nothing to do but worry. He paced on the flight deck of the *GW* as the sun came up. The amber glow crested the waves on the horizon, spreading warm light over the ocean. On any other day, Beckham would have marveled at the glorious sight.

The sail of the USS *Florida* cut through the waves to the north. It submerged a few moments later, vanishing under the sparkling teal water. An Apache helicopter shot over the *Cowpens*. From this distance it sounded like a dragonfly. Two more gunships raced after it.

Beckham took a knee next to Apollo and rubbed the dog's head as the birds sped away from the strike group to deal with an unknown threat. The dog was lucky. The tactical vest he wore had mitigated some of the damage from the wound he'd suffered on Plum Island, but he still had a nasty gash that had required a dozen stitches. Knowing Apollo, Beckham was certain the injury wasn't going to slow him down.

"You did good back there, boy," Beckham said. "You helped save Fitz. If it weren't for you, our friends would be dead."

Apollo craned his head to the side, his dark eyes with flecks of amber locking with Beckham's. His tail whipped back and forth. Beckham envied the dog. Apollo had no idea how bad things were: Riley was gone. Chow was in bad shape, Fitz was still out there with Meg and the Variant Hunters, and Kryptonite didn't work on the juveniles.

Hope was always the last thing to go, but Beckham was starting to wonder how much more he could take before he lost it for good. Delta Force training had taught him to lock the emotions away, to keep fighting despite the losses, but that was before the apocalypse—before his friends and his world were torn apart by monsters.

Beckham ran a hand over the back of his short-cropped hair, working his fingers to the top of his skull where the hair was longer. When he pulled them away, his hands were shaking. His eyes flitted to his trigger finger, and for the first time in months, he wondered how many men and beasts he'd killed.

*I can't remember.*

Before the outbreak of the hemorrhage virus, Beckham could recall every Taliban member, Al-Qaeda operative, Iraqi insurgent, and terrorist he'd killed. Since then, he'd gunned down human collaborators and Colonel Wood's guards. In total, he'd killed around five hundred men. Some were more evil than others, but all deserved their demise. Still, taking a life could change a man. Taking five hundred could ruin one.

Apollo whimpered as if he could sense his handler's thoughts.

"It's okay, boy," Beckham said. He stroked the side of the dog's coat where he was unharmed. The soft fur felt good against his battered fingers.

Pounding sounded over the wind. These weren't the clacks of officers' boots. They were the sounds of flight crews performing their morning checks.

Apollo sniffed the air and studied the small army of

orange jumpsuits as they strolled toward the F-18 Super Hornets three hundred feet away. The dog watched them work for a few moments, then turned back to bask in the glow of the rising sun with Beckham.

Horn was inside with his girls, comforting them and probably attempting to catch some shuteye. Chow was healing below decks, and Kate was in the lab with Ellis. Beckham, however, couldn't have slept even if he wanted to. He'd been out here since the Black Hawks had left to get Fitz, Meg, Garcia, and Tank, and he would stay until the birds brought them home.

Ringgold stared out of the portholes of the CIC, sipping a cup of steaming coffee. The brilliant sunrise was one of the most beautiful things she'd seen in a long time, but now she couldn't look away from the flight deck.

"A man and his dog. If that's not a symbol of everything we are fighting for, then I don't know what is," she whispered to herself.

"Madam President," said a stern voice.

"Yes, what is it?"

Vice President Johnson stood behind her, holding his own cup of coffee. "May I join you?"

"Please," Ringgold said with a smile.

"Is that Beckham?"

Ringgold nodded. "He's been down there for a while."

"That man deserves some damn rest," Johnson said, bringing the coffee to his lips. He took a gulp and then wiped his mouth with the back of his hand.

"Doctor Lovato hasn't slept since she got back either. She's in the lab performing an autopsy on Lucy. Now you know why I said what I did back in the briefing."

"Absolutely, and I—"

A sharp female voice cut Johnson off. "Mister Vice President, may I have a word, please?"

The reflection of Lieutenant Colonel Marsha Kramer appeared in the window. Ringgold kept her gaze on Beckham. The old soldier reached up to his face and dragged his arm across an eye. Then he stood and looked skyward.

"What is it, Kramer?" Johnson asked.

"A *private* word, sir?"

Ringgold resisted the urge to turn around and give Kramer a piece of her mind. She wanted to see how Johnson handled his subordinate without her intervention. Their situation was still so new that she hadn't had a chance to see Johnson in action with his officers—especially one he seemed to disagree with.

"Whatever you have to say to me can be said in front of President Ringgold."

In the reflection, Kramer twisted her lips to the side. After a brief pause she said, "Very well, sir."

Ringgold turned and regarded Kramer with a frosty nod. The lieutenant colonel replied with the tightest grin Ringgold had ever seen. She pivoted ever so slightly away from Ringgold, a small, intentional gesture that showed a much larger lack of respect.

"Mister Vice President, I would highly advise that you reconsider using our nuclear arsenal on the juveniles," Kramer said. "Assuming Kryptonite kills the majority of the adult population in two days, the offspring are the biggest threat to our species now. We don't have the ground troops or resources to kill them all."

Johnson gulped his coffee, then crushed the cup in his hand. "You better have a damn good reason for bringing this up again."

"Sir, I've been going over the reports Lieutenant Davis compiled. There are several cities that we have no hope of recovering, cities where the juveniles dwell in higher numbers. Places like Chicago, where the outbreak started. Atlanta is another. New York also has a high concentration. There is simply no way we can take those cities back. If we don't destroy them, we risk the juveniles migrating to areas we *can* salvage."

Ringgold drew in a discreet breath through her nostrils, managing her frustration with Kramer the same way she'd always dealt with rogue politicians. The woman certainly had nerve, especially after what Ringgold had said during their briefing just hours before.

"What about stranded civilians?" Johnson asked. "Have you put together a plan to rescue them before you would rain nuclear fire on our cities?"

"Collateral damage," Kramer said, a bit too quickly. "Casualties of war in an end game to save our species, sir. I think we need to look at the big picture: A lot more innocent people are going to die before this is all over."

"Sacrifice the few for the greater good," Ringgold said, her voice cutting. She cradled her sling with her good arm. "I'm not a big advocate of that philosophy. It's what got us where we are today. Lieutenant Brett's platoon in Vietnam was a perfect example of how that philosophy works."

Kramer shook her head. "With all due respect, Madam President, you have no military experience. We're fighting a war against an unprecedented enemy."

"And you're talking about nuking American cities. Have you thought about the fallout?" Ringgold clenched her jaw and glared at Kramer. They stared at one another defiantly, neither of them flinching or backing down.

Ringgold and Kramer weren't that different on the surface. They were both crisply dressed and well groomed, even in this chaos, and were about the same age. They'd both spent their careers in public service. But they couldn't be farther apart when it came to fighting this war or protecting American lives.

"We would set the nukes off underground to mini-mize fallout," Kramer replied. She remained calm, her back stiff and features stoic.

That made Ringgold even more furious. They weren't talking about the potential for civilian casualties in some drone attack—they were talking about killing thousands, if not more, of their own citizens.

"Your comments have been noted," Johnson said, shutting down the conversation.

Kramer's jaw moved, but she said nothing. Offering a nod, she turned and strode across the CIC with her heav-ily armed guards following her.

"What's with her entourage?" Ringgold asked when Kramer was out of sight.

Johnson shrugged. "She's been paranoid ever since the Variants took down Central Command. So paranoid she was ready to evacuate. It saved the lives of most of her staff when Offutt AFB was overrun. Now she's given most of them guns. They follow her everywhere, as if she's the Pied goddamn Piper."

Ringgold narrowed her eyes.

"Best to take her with a grain of salt," Johnson said. "It's probably hard to believe, but she does have the best interests of our country in mind."

"General Kennor, Colonel Gibson, and Colonel Wood supposedly did as well," Ringgold replied. "Forgive me if I don't extend her the benefit of the doubt." She took a deep breath and turned back to the window. Beckham was still in the same spot, his hand on Apollo's head as they waited for their friends to return from a city Kramer wanted to destroy.

"No! Let me fucking go!" Fitz shouted. He continued squirming, but there was no escaping Tank's mitts. He had an iron grip, so Fitz did the only thing he could think of. He shouldered his MK11 and fired at the Variants as Tank dragged him down a hallway. It took every ounce of Fitz's willpower not to give up, but seeing his broken blade and thinking of Meg being torn to shreds threatened to throw him over the edge.

*You can still fight. You can still…*

But he couldn't still fight like he could before, and he couldn't save her. If it weren't for Tank, Fitz would be dead too.

*I* should *be dead.*

"In here! In here!" Garcia shouted.

Tank yanked Fitz around a corner, throwing off his next shot. The round hit an overhead bank of lights, shattering them into a hundred pieces.

*Goddamnit!*

Out of Fitz's three shots, only one had killed a juvenile. The 7.62-millimeter rounds penetrated their armor, but only head shots took them down for good. Lining up kill shots while being lugged down a hallway was almost impossible.

A stream of rounds fired over Fitz's head, punching into the ceiling and wall as two juveniles barreled into the dark passage. In the light of the muzzle flashes, he watched them drop and curl into balls and somersault forward. Garcia hit the beast to the left with a volley of shots, sending it spinning into a wall.

Sweat from Tank's face dropped onto Fitz's nose as the marine continued pulling him down the hallway.

"Shoot the other one!" Tank shouted.

Holding in a breath, Fitz waited for the second juvenile to stop rolling, but the beast kept coming. It was moving so fast it was just a blur in the flashes from Garcia's rifle. Fitz was down to only five rounds in his magazine.

"Take it down!" Tank yelled.

Fitz fired a shot that hit the creature somewhere in the back. The impact sent it skidding into the beast that was recovering behind it. They both crashed into a door with a thud.

A third juvenile leaped over the two creatures, arms spread like a bat. It clung to the ceiling, tucked its head to its chest, and skittered forward at an astonishing speed.

Fitz aimed his rifle and fired a shot that lanced into the ceiling tiles. He squeezed off another just as the other monsters leaped back to their feet and charged.

Behind the three creatures, a white wall of veiny flesh exploded into the hallway. Dozens of adult Variants chased the offspring. Fitz's eyes roved back and forth, taking in the sight, terror striking at his gut.

This was it. There was no escaping.

The juvenile on the ceiling dropped to the floor and crouched. Fitz centered the muzzle on the creature's face just as its sucker lips popped. Its chin suddenly split down the middle and opened into mandibles with horned teeth on both sides. Another set of needle sharp teeth clattered behind those.

"*Shoot it!*" Tank bellowed.

Squeezing the trigger had never been so simple. A round zipped into the beast's open mouth. There was an awful cracking sound as it broke teeth and shot out the back of the creature's skull.

Somewhere behind Fitz, a door opened, and then he was being pulled into a dark room. He let out his breath as the juvenile skidded to a stop a few feet from his broken blade, just outside the entrance to the room. Tank dropped Fitz on the floor and shouldered his SAW while Garcia kicked the door shut.

Tank grabbed Fitz under an arm with his other hand and pulled him deeper into an apartment that smelled like a slaughterhouse in summer. Somewhere behind them, light bled through a gap in closed curtains. The rays were just enough to illuminate a family room covered in trash and a filthy rug. It reminded him of the hotel room in Iraq where PFC Duffy had killed two Iraqi children and their grandfather.

All three marines angled their weapons at the door, breathing heavily, sweat pouring down their foreheads.

"Get ready," Garcia said between gasps. "This isn't going to hold long."

Automatic gunfire rang out in the distance. The snaps and pops seemed to grow louder with every beat of Fitz's pounding heart. He changed the magazine in his MK11 as a thud rattled the gray metal. The first of the Variants pounded on the door, relentless.

Dust rained from around the trim, and a dent in the shape of a skull popped out of the center. A juvenile speared the door with its armored skull again, breaking one of the locks. Fitz readied his rifle in shaking hands.

His earpiece flared to life. "Ghost Two, this is Whiskey Four. Strike team is in the building. Where the fuck are you guys?"

"Trapped in Apartment 909!" Garcia replied.

"Hold tight, we got—"

The transmission ended in a surge of white noise. A second message quickly replaced it over the open channel.

"Fitz, do you copy? Over."

Beckham's voice was drowned out by an explosion. The door flew off the hinges and crashed to the ground next to Fitz's broken blade.

Heart stuck in his throat, Fitz jerked his rifle up and fired a shot into the ceiling. Light streamed into the dark room and a slender figure ducked into the open door.

"Hold your fucking fire!" someone yelled.

For a moment, Fitz expected to see an Alpha, but it

wasn't a Variant. This was a soldier. The figure, covered with Kevlar plates, strode into the room with a hand out. The soldier lifted up a face guard with the other hand and screamed, "What the hell are you waiting for? Let's move, motherfuckers!"

Fitz lowered his weapon, staring in shock at the chiseled face and sparkling green eyes of Lieutenant Rachel Davis. Behind her, two other soldiers helped hold up a woman covered in so much blood Fitz didn't recognize her at first. If it weren't for the hatchet hanging loosely in her right hand, Fitz wouldn't have known who it was.

"M-meg?" Fitz stuttered.

Davis snapped Fitz from his shock. She held out a hand toward him, and Fitz took it.

The whine of a drill sharpened inside the lab as Ellis pressed the Stryker saw down on Lucy's skull. After an hour of working on the juvenile, Kate was starting to get used to the noises, but it still made her shudder every time the bone saw got stuck.

In her gloved hands, she held a section of Lucy's breastplate the size of a small laptop. According to the calipers she was using to measure it, the armor was a little more than an inch thick, but it was surprisingly light and flexible. She flipped it and put it on a table to study the underside. Thick veins covered a rosy block of flesh like the back of a scab that hadn't had time to heal.

Using the tip of a stainless-steel knife, Kate cut into the flesh, peeled it back, and scraped the blade against a cartilaginous substance. There was something below that too, a second layer between it and the thickest part of the armor.

Across from Kate, the technicians waited patiently. Ronnie, a forty-year-old man with a handlebar mustache, followed her graceful movements with eager brown eyes. She carefully handed the plate to him after she finished examining it.

"Separate each of the layers. Then prepare them for testing. You know the drill," Kate said.

Ronnie whisked the piece to a lab station. She watched him prepare the sample with a critical eye, still unsure if she could trust Yokoyama's staff.

When Kate turned back to the cadaver table, Ellis had exchanged the Stryker saw for the bone saw. He was halfway through the crest of Lucy's skull when Yokoyama waved them over.

"Take a look at this," he said.

Ellis left the saw in Lucy's forehead. It wobbled for a few seconds, the metal groaning before finally coming to rest.

"What is it?" Ellis asked. He looked over Yokoyama's shoulder for a better view. The older doctor slowly lifted Lucy's right arm. He'd inserted a clamp in the opening he'd made in the armor covering the radius and ulna. Fishing inside with a gloved finger, Yokoyama pulled out a cluster of what looked like small brown eggs the size of peas.

"What do you make of these, Kate?" he asked, holding them to the light in the palm of his hand. "Extraordinary. I've never seen anything like them."

Yokoyama carefully set them in a tray on the table next to him. Before Kate could respond or protest, he stuck his fingers back into the gap in Lucy's arm and dug inside. There was a mushing sound, and he withdrew a glove covered in slimy brown sludge.

"What the hell?" he said, wiping it on his suit. The front of his chest was already covered in black, grainy blood.

Kate considered lecturing the doctor about proper lab protocol, but she was too tired to think, let alone issue basic instructions to a scientist who should have known better. It didn't help that she needed a fresh bandage on her arm.

"Get a few more of those for sampling," Kate said, pointing at the balls he'd left on the table. "I want to start testing immediately."

Yokoyama held up his hands, stretching his fingers apart. The brown goo turned into a tangle of spider webbing. The material snapped as he spread his fingers. Reaching down, Yokoyama put his right hand back into the split in Lucy's arm.

"Careful you don't puncture your glove," Kate said, unable to stop herself from correcting him. She walked across the lab to check on the technicians. Ronnie was slowly removing a layer of pink flesh from the back of the plate Kate had handed him. He hesitated when he saw her watching, but then continued working, slowly and precisely. That was good; he had been paying attention earlier. At least someone in the lab was competent.

He used the sharpened edge of a thin blade to cut away the tissue. He put it in a dish and handed it to another technician, who took it to a separate station.

"Doctor Lovato, there's more of those things," Ronnie said. He had peeled back another layer of flesh speckled with brown, egg-shaped balls. "Any idea what these are?"

Kate shook her head. "We're going to find out."

Using a pair of tweezers, Ronnie reached for one of the balls.

"Careful."

Ronnie nodded and slowly plucked one of the balls from the flesh. He held it under the bank of overhead lights to scrutinize the small object. Kate tilted her helmet. It was translucent and filled with . . .

"Looks like some sort of an egg," Ronnie said. He

slowly set it in another dish and handed it to one of the other technicians.

Kate squinted to focus on the brown blobs dotting the layer of pink flesh. She was leaning closer for a better look when a rough, wet pop sounded from the autopsy table.

An excruciating scream suddenly filled the lab, followed by a crackling that sounded like burning fire logs. She whirled around to see that the clamp that kept Lucy's right arm open had popped off, locking Yokoyama's hand inside the arm. The armor seemed to be melting around the doctor's trapped hand, tendrils of smoke rising from the opening.

"Help me!" Yokoyama shrieked.

Ellis grabbed his wrist and pulled, but that just made Yokoyama scream even louder. The three technicians hurried away from their stations, boots pounding the floor.

Petrified, Kate stared for several seconds before she burst into action. In the time it took to grab a knife from the nearest table, Lucy's arm had started sizzling. The snap of tendons echoed in Kate's helmet. Above the hellish sounds, Yokoyama screamed in agony.

"Kate, I need help!" Ellis yelled, without taking his eyes off Yokoyama. He yanked on the doctor's wrist to no avail. It was stuck, and whatever was happening to Lucy's arm was spreading throughout her body. Spider webs broke across her outer shell like fault lines rupturing a street. Her mandibles jiggled, and the bone saw still jammed in her forehead rattled back and forth, squeaking.

Yokoyama dropped to his knees, holding his trapped arm with his good hand and crying out in Japanese.

"Do something!" Ronnie shouted.

Kate gripped the handle of the knife tightly and

focused on the slot in Lucy's arm. More smoke fizzled out from the small crack.

*Shit. Shit. Shit.*

She couldn't see an opening that wasn't too close to Yokoyama's wrist. Every second she hesitated, Lucy's armor melted further, drawing screams from her colleague. Kate jammed the tip of the knife into a tiny gap and twisted it to the side to try and force the shell open.

There was a thud as Yokoyama's skull banged against the side of the table. His screaming rose to a high, piercing wail.

Kate worked the knife back and forth, desperate to free her colleague. Sweat dripped off her forehead as she worked. She was steaming hot now, a dramatic change from the chills she'd had just minutes before.

A section of armor covering Lucy's clavicle cracked off and slid to the floor, exposing a patch of bubbling flesh. The same brown eggs Kate had seen earlier were exploding like miniature grenades. Sludge splattered Yokoyama's helmet. His eyes suddenly bulged and his face twisted into a mask of pain as the goo ate through his visor.

"Hurry!" Ellis shouted.

Kate grunted, pushing with all of her strength. The knife felt lighter, as if the tip had melted, and before she could react, the blade broke off. She stumbled away, still holding the handle, heart beating so hard she thought it would burst.

Time seemed to slow around Kate as she stared incredulously at the scene unfolding in front of her. Smoke radiated off Yokoyama's helmet. He began pawing at his visor with his good hand, and in the same moment his trapped hand at last popped free. Covered in brown sludge, Yokoyama's limb was almost unrecognizable. He pulled it away from Lucy, screaming in horror, and Kate finally saw why: His hand was gone. All that was left was a stump of frayed flesh and a white nub of melting bone.

Kate dropped the handle of the knife and backed away. Overhead, the sprinklers suddenly fired, sheets of rain and disinfectant cascading over the lab.

Ellis retreated from the table as Lucy melted like a block of cheese in an oven. A siren screamed from the wall-mounted speakers. Yokoyama collapsed to his back, his boots twitching and an awful gurgling sound coming from his throat. His lips puckered as he struggled for air.

"Stay back!" Kate shouted as Ronnie moved toward Yokoyama. The right side of Yokoyama's helmet suddenly caved in, and one of his eyeballs plopped out onto the floor.

Ellis, covered in blood, backed up against Kate. Looking down, she saw her suit was covered in a sticky layer of red too. Her heart continued to fire out of control, but her mind quickly reassured her that whatever was happening to Lucy and Yokoyama hadn't spilled over to them.

At least not yet.

Her stomach churned as she stood there, terrified. Ellis and the technicians weren't the only ones inside the lab exposed to the toxin that had killed Yokoyama— Kate, and the child she carried, had been exposed too.

# 12

Fitz tried to get a look at Meg before two soldiers whisked her away. She was in bad shape, but she was alive. Lieutenant Davis had managed to do what Fitz couldn't—she'd saved Meg from the monsters.

*For now.*

"Go with them!" Davis shouted.

Fitz shook his head. "I'm still in this fight."

Instead of arguing, Davis turned to her squad. "Let's move!" She jammed several shells in her shotgun and pushed her face guard back over her mouth.

"You're heavier than you look, little man," Tank griped.

Fitz used the larger marine as a crutch as they worked their way back down the staircase. Dead Variants riddled with bullet holes clogged the narrow passage. The bloody staircase stank of rotting fruit and sewage. Fitz grabbed onto Tank as his remaining blade slipped on the blood. Somewhere, a floor below, the crack of a shotgun rang out. The intermittent pop of small-arms fire had echoed through the building ever since Davis showed up with the reinforcements.

"Where are the others?" she shouted.

"Twenty-eighth floor," Garcia said. He ran in front

of her at a dangerous pace. All around Fitz, soldiers wearing the same black armor as Davis hurried down the stairs, boots pounding the sticky floor. They carried Benelli M1014 twelve-gauge semiautomatic shotguns and had M4s with modified magazines slung over their backs.

These were the new weapons in the war against the evolving Variants. With a broken blade and both of his weapons low on ammo, Fitz felt grossly unprepared to face the monsters again. He went back to searching for the broken piece of his blade as Tank helped him down the stairs.

A human scream cut through the gunfire. The soldiers ahead of Fitz increased their pace, loping down the stairs, weapons clanking on the backs of their armor.

"You gonna be okay," Tank grumbled.

Fitz wasn't sure if Tank was telling him or asking him, so he simply nodded. He stopped searching the carnage-filled stairwell for his blade after they passed the first landing. It was gone, lost in the debris of flesh and bone.

*You are still whole. You can still fight—with a little help*, Fitz thought.

He tightened his grip around Tank's back and aimed his MK11 toward the stairs with his other hand. The weapon was heavy, almost impossible to hold steady, and even more difficult to aim with his tired arms.

He barely had time to move the gun as a claw punched out from under a pile of bodies to swipe at Tank's boot. In a swift motion, Fitz pulled away from Tank, planted his back against the wall, centered his gun on the corpses, and fired into the mass. The monster screeched and withdrew its talons before it could tear through Tank's flesh. Fitz squeezed off two more shots into the stack, just to be sure.

Several of Davis's soldiers turned with their shotguns. "Clear," Fitz said.

"Keep an eye on these bodies," one of the soldiers shouted.

Tank reached out to help Fitz, and offered his thanks with a dip of his helmet. They hurried down the next flight of stairs. Normally the strike team would have taken a stealth position—hunched and quiet, careful not to draw attention—but the Variants knew they were here. Fitz hoped it wasn't too late to save the civilians they'd left locked in the apartment below.

At least Meg was alive. But he couldn't get the image of her covered in blood out of his mind. Humans were capable of surviving massive amounts of blood loss if they got help quickly, but they were far from help here.

Another gunshot reverberated through the guts of the building. A flurry of pops followed in rapid succession. That was good: It meant Huff and the others were still fighting.

Garcia reached the door to the secured room first. He grabbed the handle and pushed, but it was locked. More gunshots rang out on the other side.

"Out of the way," Davis said.

She strode forward, reaching into a cargo pocket, and pulled out a small square of C4 and a short coil of detonating cord with a blasting cap on the end. She pushed the cap into the white block of explosive and stuck it on the door. Everyone retreated to the landing and the stairwell above.

Davis winked at Fitz as she pulled the detonator. There was a muffled explosion. The team was moving before the door crashed to the ground. Smoke swirled outside the entrance, masking the stink of raw sewage, but not the sour scent of the Variants.

Ears pounding, Fitz's world slowed to battle time. He

wanted to close his eyes and protect himself from the bloodbath he feared they were walking into. He knew damn well that if the Variants had gotten inside the room, Huff and the others wouldn't have been able to hold them off for long.

Tank pulled him through a swirling curtain of smoke. A wall of sunlight hit Fitz. The boards over the windows were gone, allowing blinding rays inside. He squinted into the glow, scanning the space for hostiles. Bodies were sprawled across the far end of the room under the windows—piles of them.

Fitz shielded his eyes from the sunlight. At one of the windows, a figure splattered in crimson pointed a shotgun toward the street. A blast sounded, and the gun discharged a shell.

The screech of a Variant plummeting to its death followed in the ringing echo.

As his eyes adjusted, Fitz saw most of the bodies on the floor were monsters. There were only three humans. One of them was still moving, hand clutched over gut.

"Over here!" someone shouted.

Davis led a team of three soldiers toward a group of survivors hiding behind the couches. "Get them out of here!" she shouted.

Tank and Garcia hurried over to the windows. Huff turned to glare at them, his eyes wide from the adrenaline rush and the sight of reinforcements.

"Thanks for coming back!" he shouted. "I didn't think we were going to make it." A grin touched the side of his lips. Fitz could see something change in the hardened soldier's eyes. It was the rekindled flicker of hope that he was finally leaving this place.

Huff had just lowered his shotgun and taken a step away from the window when a pair of claws grabbed the frame behind him.

"Behind you!" Tank shouted. He let go of Fitz as the bulbous lips and yellow eyes of a Variant's face emerged over the boards still strung across the bottom of the window. Strands of thin hair clung to the bald, veiny skin on the beast's forehead. It sniffed with a pointy nose that made its ropy lips jiggle.

It was one of the ugliest Variants Fitz had ever seen.

The attack happened so fast he didn't have time to react. But he missed the hope vanishing from Huff's face. His eyes widened, realization gripping him. He tried to move as the beast peeled back the boards, tossed them aside, and latched onto his shoulder. The wood sailed into the sunlight and the creature dug its claws into flesh.

Tank grabbed Huff's left hand, but Fitz crashed to the floor as he reached for his right. He quickly pushed himself up and clutched Huff's leg.

Garcia rushed over to get a shot just as the beast pulled Huff back to the window, turning him into a human shield. Blood spurted from the soldier's back. He wailed in pain and fell backward, pulling Fitz and Tank with him. He hit the window frame with a thud and grabbed onto the side with his right hand while Tank pulled on his left. Garcia roved from side to side, still trying to find an angle to shoot the creature.

Hanging outside the window, the monster lost its grip on Huff's shoulder. Talons ripped through flesh as it fought desperately for something to hold on to.

The scream that followed echoed through the apartment.

"Shoot it!" Tank shouted. "Shoot it, goddamnit!"

"I can't get a shot," Garcia yelled back.

From the floor, Fitz saw the monster pulling itself up using Huff's back as a ladder. Garcia moved again, but still couldn't find a shot. He finally gave up and grabbed the front of Huff's shirt.

Together, all three marines tugged on him, but the beast was stronger than it looked. A second set of claws wrapped around the right side of the window frame. Fitz's face was inches away, and he could see the yellowed, jagged nails digging into flesh.

"There's another one!" he shouted.

In the blink of an eye, the left side of Huff's uniform tore clean off. Tank and Garcia lost their grips, and Huff was yanked backward. Fitz held on to his boot, the force dragging him to the wall under the window. The second beast peeked over the side, staring Fitz right in the face. Hot, rancid breath that smelled like scorched flesh and dead fish hit his face.

A gunshot rang out right next to his ear. He clenched his jaw in pain, the echo ringing deep inside his skull. He jerked his head away just as an explosion of warm liquid hit the right side of his face.

Blinking, he caught a glimpse of the Variant as it fell, a bullet hole in the center of its head spewing blood mixed with brain matter.

Tank grabbed Huff's right boot and pulled.

"Hold on!" Fitz shouted.

With his face pressed against the wall, Fitz slowly inched his head up and looked over the side. The Variant Garcia had shot in the head smashed against the road below, bursting like a tomato thrown against a tree. The other beast was still clinging to Huff's back.

Movement below revealed half a dozen creatures climbing the building. Upside down, with his back and head hanging outside the window, Huff saw them too. He screamed while Garcia fired at them. The shots knocked several of them away. They spun backward, flailing for something to hold on to before crashing to the pavement.

Working with Fitz, Tank pulled Huff halfway back

into the room, but the Variant was pulling too. It let go with one hand, swung back, and then used its upward momentum to clamp the free claw around Huff's neck.

"Pull me up!" Huff yelled, his voice cracking. "Pull me—" Blood exploded from his mouth, and his eyes bulged as the beast tightened its talons around his neck, cutting through his jugular vein.

Garcia angled his rifle to shoot the beast just as Huff's boot slipped from Fitz's hands. Fitz fell, his eyes flitting toward the sun. Tank let out a grunt and pulled harder.

As Fitz pushed himself back up, the monster climbed up Huff's chest and then his waist. It swiped with a free claw at Tank. The talon ripped across the marine's face.

A shot sounded as Tank let go of Huff's boot and stumbled away, clutching his right eye with both hands. The huge man crashed to the floor, screaming in pain.

"Huff!" Garcia shouted. He rushed forward, but it was too late. The soldier was gone. His body hit the sidewalk a moment later. He didn't make a single noise as he fell, but Fitz wasn't sure if that was because the beast had slit his throat or because Huff was too proud to cry out.

Fitz closed his eyes for a second. When they snapped open, he saw a new face staring at him a few feet away. It was Pedro, the engineer, and he was gripping his stomach with a glistening hand. In his other, he held his homemade detonator. His face twitched, and he sucked in labored breaths that crackled in his chest.

"Better get moving," he said, squinting in pain. "Not sure how long I can hang on."

"You're coming with," Fitz said. He reached out, but Pedro shook his head.

"No." He pulled his hand up to reveal his exposed guts. Fitz could smell the fatal wound.

"My eye! I can't fucking see," Tank shouted.

Garcia was still at the window, firing on the remaining

Variants below. He backpedaled and turned to check Tank.

"Hold on, brother," Garcia said. He turned to hand a pistol down to Pedro. "Just in case they get to you before you can detonate that thing."

Pedro took the gun with his sticky hand. "I got you. Now get out of here."

In Fitz's mind, there were two types of people at the end of the world: Those like Red, who bravely stood and protected their families and fought to the end, and those like the human collaborators who did anything to save their own skin. Pedro was somewhere in the middle, but he was one of the good ones. Fitz threw up a quick salute to a man who wasn't even a soldier.

Pedro cracked a smile and returned the gesture. He looked away, straightened his back against the wall and tightened his grip on the detonator.

Fitz knew he had no choice but to leave him there. He pushed himself up and did a quick scan of the room. Davis's team was already leading the other civilians into the stairwell. She stood in the open doorway, shouting, "Move it, marines!"

Reaching down, Fitz grabbed Tank under an armpit with one hand and used his rifle as a crutch with the other.

"Hang in there, big guy. You're not as heavy as you look," Fitz said.

Tank grunted.

"You're going to be okay," Fitz reassured him. This time it was definitely a statement, not a question. He made sure of that as he strengthened his grip around Tank's shoulder. They were both getting the fuck out of here, together, even if they weren't leaving in one piece.

Davis remained behind her team, sticking close to Fitz, Garcia, and Tank. She checked on them every few steps as they worked their way up the flights. The moment the first rays of sunlight hit Fitz, he felt a wave of guilt. Once again, he was going home—once again, he had survived when brave men like Huff had died.

The whoosh of chopper blades should have been music to his ears, but instead it only amplified the guilt tearing through him. He searched for Meg, and started hopping quickly to the bird where he found her.

"Slow down," Tank said.

By the time they got to the Black Hawk, she had vanished behind a sea of civilians. Two soldiers in the open door turned and waved the marines to the second Black Hawk.

"No room, get to the other bird!"

Fitz tried to glimpse Meg through the fort of bodies, but he only saw a sliver of her bloody shirt and the hatchet she still gripped in her right hand. Behind the bird, another wave of Variants climbed onto the roof over a brick ledge. The door gunners unleashed a barrage of 7.62-millimeter rounds that lanced through diseased flesh and punched holes in the red block of the wall.

Garcia screamed over the chop of the blades. "Keep moving!"

Fitz helped Tank over to the other chopper. As soon as they had piled inside, he loosened his grip under Tank's armpit, and they both crashed to the floor.

Tank growled, hand still covering his eye, blood weeping through the fingers. He was hurt, and hurt bad. Fitz couldn't see the wound, but the amount of blood told him Tank was going to lose the eye.

Garcia knelt next to them and put his hand on Tank's shoulder. "Let me see it, man."

Fitz couldn't understand Tank's response, but Garcia nodded and sat cross-legged on the floor, shoulders sagging, his M4 draped across his chest.

Fitz didn't need to be a mind-reader to guess what Garcia was thinking. *Three marines left.*

As the choppers ascended into the sky, Fitz looked down. The rooftop was dotted with corpses. There were a few human bodies speckled across the graveyard, but most were those of the oddly jointed, pallid Variants, strewn about like crabs washed up on a beach.

The building dwindled until it was just another tinsel tower on the skyline. They were two minutes out when a blast wrapped out around the third floor. Fire burst out the windows. The fourth floor went up a beat later, and then, in one massive detonation, the entire first third of the building imploded.

Fitz flinched, thinking of Pedro and wondering what had happened in the man's final moments. An image of Huff falling to his death replaced the thought. He tried to shake away the memory, but it was glued there, tattooed forever on Fitz's mind, along with memories of all the other people he had watched die.

In the distance, the top floors of the building plummeted earthward, tendrils of fire and smoke reaching into the sky. Somewhere inside the ruins, Fitz had lost a part of himself. But it wasn't the carbon fiber of his blade; it was another piece of his soul. He hadn't been able to save Huff or Pedro, just as he hadn't saved Riley. And if it weren't for Lieutenant Davis, Meg would be dead too.

Sunlight washed over Manhattan, and as their bird raced away from the city, Fitz forced himself to remember the final look in Huff's eyes when the man realized he wasn't going to escape. It was awful way to die—to have hope ripped away.

Fitz bowed his helmet and closed his eyes. Once again, he was returning to safety, a place he felt he didn't deserve to be.

\*    \*    \*

Beckham strode down the passage toward a Medical Corps soldier standing guard outside the laboratory wing of the *Cowpens*.

The man threw up a hand. "Master Sergeant, please stop where you are. This is a quarantine zone!"

Beckham continued without slowing, determined to get to Kate. When he'd heard the SOS over the comms, he'd commandeered a Zodiac and raced over to the *Cowpens* on his own. No one was going to stop him.

"I've been ordered to prevent anyone from entering this passage! Please turn—"

"Out of my way," Beckham said.

The soldier moved to the left, blocking Beckham from entering the next passage with his bulky CBRN suit.

"I'm warning you," Beckham said. He tried to step around the man, but the soldier grabbed him by his right arm, gloved fingers clamping around the fresh bandage on Beckham's wrist.

"Get your fucking hands off me!"

The man loosened his grip and held up both of his hands in a nonthreatening manner. "Sir, you need to step back from the quarantine zone. We're at Level One lockdown right now."

"Let me pass," Beckham growled, in a voice he didn't even recognize.

"I can't do that." There was restrained anger in the man's voice, obscured partially by his breathing apparatus. Beckham eyed the M4 swung over the man's back, but his next action wasn't marred by a single second of hesitation.

Using his palms, he shoved the Medical Corps soldier's shoulder against the wall and then drew his revolver. The soldier grunted and reached for the strap of his rifle, but by the time he went to unsling it, Beckham had the barrel of his Colt .45 pointed at the man's visor.

"Don't even fucking think about it," Beckham snarled, putting his thumb on the tip of the hammer.

"Whoa, take it easy." The man immediately pulled his fingers from under the strap of his weapon. Very slowly, he raised his hands and held them above his head. "I'm not a soldier. I'm just a microbiologist who was ordered to stand guard. I don't want any trouble."

Beckham let out an exasperated breath when he saw the man's eyes. They were very young—and also terrified.

Gritting his teeth, Beckham moved his thumb away from the hammer.

The scientist's lips were trembling, his eyes centered on the barrel. "Could you please point that somewhere else? I'm not a big fan of guns."

Beckham slowly lowered the weapon toward the floor, tucking it against his right side without holstering it.

"Is there a problem down there, Anthony?" shouted a voice from the opposite end of the hallway. In Beckham's peripheral, two more Medical Corps soldiers wearing CBRN suits emerged. Both had their rifles cradled across their chests. They couldn't see Beckham's Colt .45 from that angle—at least he didn't think they could. He tucked it against his side, trying not to be obvious.

"No problem, Jake," Anthony replied in a confident voice. "I was just about to escort Master Sergeant Beckham here inside the quarantine zone for him to suit up."

"You know who I am?" Beckham whispered.

The other two soldiers lingered for a moment at the far end of the passage but at last disappeared around the bulkhead. Their footfalls faded to weak echoes.

Anthony shrugged. "Didn't at first, until you shoved me into the wall and pointed that monster pistol in my face. That gun has almost as much of as reputation as its owner."

"I'm sorry," Beckham said. "Kate—Doctor—Lovato is in that lab. I need to get to her."

Anthony nodded his understanding. With the weapon out of his face, he jerked his helmet toward the quarantine zone. "I'll take you to her. Follow me."

Beckham holstered his weapon. He was embarrassed, but it was water under the bridge. If Anthony wanted to help, he wasn't going to turn him down.

"Do you know what's happening?" Beckham asked.

Anthony hesitated, turning his helmet slightly before replying. "It's the juvenile Variant. Apparently it had some sort of self-destruct mechanism. Doctor Yokoyama was killed during the autopsy, and everyone in the lab has been quarantined until we figure out exactly what happened."

Beckham passed Anthony when he saw the entrance to Lab A around the next bulkhead. His gut tightened, as if his intestines were twisting and churning. There were a dozen suited individuals outside the first hatch. Overhead, a sign read, AUTHORIZED PERSONNEL ONLY. Hazmat and radiation symbols marked the bulkhead.

"Let me handle this," Anthony said as they approached.

Beckham hung back, heart pounding, trying to imagine what was going on inside the lab. The thought of losing Kate now, after just having gotten her back, made him want to open the hatch and run into the lab.

Anthony spoke to one of the other scientists-turned-soldiers. They both glanced back at Beckham several times before Anthony finally waved him over.

"It's all good. We just need to get you into a suit." He hurried to a hatch and pulled his key card.

Inside, Beckham grabbed a suit hanging on the wall. He fucking hated these things. Anthony helped zip up the back and secure his helmet.

"Thanks," Beckham said. "Seriously, man, I appreciate it."

"Don't mention it."

They moved back into the passage and followed a Medical Corps soldier to another hatch. The man grabbed the wheel handle, twisted it, and opened it to reveal a small office with observation glass.

Two other suited soldiers were already inside, talking on an intercom system. Beckham's heart flipped when he saw Kate and Ellis through the glass. They were at the west end of the lab, sitting on stools next to three technicians in blue suits.

"Sergeant Garrett," Anthony said, "this is Master Sergeant Beckham. He's Doctor Lovato's..."

"Boyfriend," Beckham said when Anthony paused. There was no time to worry about the heat rising in Beckham's cheeks. It wasn't from embarrassment, anyway—it was from fear.

In the center of the lab, the smoldering remains of Lucy lay cooking on a gurney. There wasn't much left, only a pile of charcoaled bones. Part of the metal table had melted. Silver drops fell to the floor next to Dr. Yokoyama's body. The right side of his helmet had dissolved over the remains of his skull.

Garrett turned from the intercom and gestured Beckham forward.

"This is the only way we have to communicate with them right now," Garrett said.

Heart in his throat, Beckham punched the button. "Kate, it's me. Can you hear me?"

Across the room, Kate slowly rose to her feet. Beckham couldn't see her face, and that hurt more than anything. He placed his hand against the window, the desire to hold and protect her overwhelming him. The helplessness was crushing. He had to get in there.

"Stay where you are, please, Doctor," Garrett said.

Kate took another step forward, then hesitated, her visor angled toward the observation window.

Beckham whirled to the sergeant. "You have to let me in there."

"That's not possible right now, sir. We're still running tests. The lab hasn't been cleared."

Anthony cleared his throat. "Sarge, at this point, what does it matter? If he's willing to risk it, then I think we should let him. If that was your wife in there, wouldn't you want to be with her?"

Garrett turned to look at Kate, then at Beckham. "Goddamnit." He sighed and shook his helmet as he walked over to another hatch leading to a compartment that opened into the lab.

"Good luck, Master Sergeant," Anthony said.

Beckham took a deep breath of filtered air and looked through the narrow window. His suit seemed to tighten around his chest. Inside that lab was an enemy he couldn't fight. The lab was Kate's battlefield, and most of the time he was glad to leave her to it. Biological and chemical warfare had always made him uneasy, and since the Variants, that unease had blossomed into full-fledged fear. But the unconditional love he felt for Kate helped him push past the fear. No monster, big or small, would stop him from being by her side.

Opening the hatch, he stepped into the tunnel and hurried toward Lab A.

# 13

A pool of steaming blood surrounded Dr. Yokoyama's corpse. Kate darted around it and ran for the plastic door leading to the tunnel that connected to the offices and observation room. Beckham was preparing to enter through a secure hatch.

Despite the filtered air she breathed, Kate could smell the reek of burning flesh as she crossed the lab. There was another smell too, reminiscent of something she'd encountered in 2007 when her medical team had come across an open mass grave of malaria victims. Diseased, rotting flesh under the heat of the sun had a distinct odor.

The memory made her shiver, and she hurried past Lucy's smoldering remains. By the time she reached the door connecting to the tunnel, Beckham was already inside.

"Stop!" Kate held up her hands and waved. The soldiers sealed the hatch behind him, and a chirp sounded on the other side of the door. A light overhead switched from red to green inside the tunnel. He continued to the door that opened into Lab A.

Kate put her gloved hands against the window of the entrance. "Reed! Don't come in here! It's not safe!"

He said something Kate couldn't make out. They locked eyes, and for a moment she was lost. On the other side of the door was the man she loved more than she had any other in her life, the man who was willing to risk his life, again, just to be with her and their unborn child, even if it meant suffering an excruciating death like Yokoyama's.

Beckham held her gaze while he unlocked the door. He stepped inside the lab, eyes flitting to Lucy's and Yokoyama's remains for a split second. Undeterred, he continued forward and hugged her.

The feeling of Beckham's arms around her filled her with strength. She needed that more than anything right now.

"Are you okay? What the hell happened?" Beckham asked. He pulled away so their visors touched and they were face-to-face.

"We still don't know," Kate said. She craned her helmet toward what was left of Lucy. "The juveniles have some sort of self-destruct mechanism."

"Were you exposed?" Beckham leaned back to look at her suit, up and down. She glanced down at the blood on her chest and arms. Then she saw the smear she had left on Beckham's shoulder.

*How could you be so stupid?!*

Stumbling backward, Kate held up her hands again. "Stay back."

"Kate, no. It's okay."

"No, it isn't. I told you not to come in here. We've all been exposed to whatever killed Yokoyama!"

Beckham's gaze lowered to her stomach as she continued to retreat toward Ellis, Ronnie, and the other two technicians.

"We're in this together now, Kate," Beckham said. He reached out for her and took a step closer.

The nightmare on the *Truxtun* flashed in her memory. Beckham had been covered in infected blood when they had extracted his team from the ship. But that hadn't stopped her from holding him then, and she knew nothing would stop him from holding her now.

She reached out for Beckham as static surged from the intercom.

"This is Captain Humphrey speaking. Air scans have revealed an unknown toxin inside Lab A. To those inside: Please remain calm, and keep away from Doctor Yokoyama's and the juvenile's remains. We're going to use an experimental chemical spray to try to destroy the toxin."

*Experimental?*

Kate took a step toward Beckham and slipped in a pool of blood. She flailed for his hand but came up empty and landed on the floor.

"Kate!" he cried out.

She looked up, dazed but unharmed. The angle provided her a view of what had once been Yokoyama's brain. Now it was nothing more than steaming mush spilling from his helmet.

Beckham's hands gripped Kate under her armpits and pulled her to her knees. She didn't resist, but she couldn't look away from Yokoyama. His left eye was centered on her. For a fleeting moment, she thought he had blinked.

"Kate, it's okay. Everything is going to be okay," Beckham said. "We're together, and that's all that matters."

The words were reassuring, but it was all too much. As the jets overhead began to hiss, spraying them with the experimental wash, Beckham sat behind her and pulled her to him so she was sitting with her back against his chest. He hugged her from behind, their helmets side by side as sheets of liquid rained from the sprinklers.

White foam streaked down her visor. In seconds, she couldn't see past it, as if she was sitting in a car wash, watching through the windshield as she was slowly sealed off from the outside world.

*Never leave a man behind.*

The motto was sacred to Garcia. It had meant something six weeks ago.

Before the monsters.

Since those things had emerged from the pits of hell, Garcia had betrayed his oath to bring the fallen home. Four of his men were rotting out there, and Tank was in bad shape.

Garcia looked down at Thomas's dog tags in his gloved hand. It was all he was bringing home of the marine, but it was something. He had nothing of Steve-o but the memory of his broken body slung up on the sewer wall.

The voice of one of the pilots broke Garcia's concentration.

"Home plate in fifteen minutes."

Closing his fingers around the dog tags, Garcia carefully put them back into his vest pocket. He leaned down to check on Tank. The man was on his back, hand still cupped over his eye. In the few seconds he had pulled it away, Garcia had seen the slash. The Variant had cut right through his iris. Garcia didn't need an optometrist to tell him that Tank wouldn't see out of that eye again.

"How you doing, brother?" Garcia asked.

"Fuckin' hurts like hell."

"Hang in there, man, we're almost back." Garcia patted Tank on the shoulder and crouch-walked across the floor to check on Fitz. The marine sat cross-legged, with his helmet tucked between his hands. He slowly rocked back and forth, whispering something that sounded like a prayer. It was the first time Garcia had heard Fitz pray.

"Yo, Fitz, buddy—you okay?"

Fitz stopped rocking, pulled his hands away from his helmet, and nodded. "Yeah. I'll be fine."

Garcia saw right through the lie. "Meg's going to be okay. That wasn't your fault, Fitz. What happened to her could have happened to any of us."

"She's not a marine, *Sergeant*," Fitz said, replying through clenched teeth. "She's just a civilian. An injured one. We shouldn't have let her come with us."

Fitz's eyes blazed with anger. Garcia knew the man well enough to recognize it as uncharacteristic for the Southern gentleman. He also knew nothing he would say could relieve that burning rage. He patted Fitz a second time, then turned toward the open troop door to study the bulbous clouds drifting across the skyline. They were almost home. What they all needed right now was some chow, a little rest, and a bathtub full of bleach. Before that, though, Garcia would get Tank to the infirmary on the *GW*, and then he'd find Beckham and Horn. They needed to know about the juveniles and their continued evolution. It was only a matter of time before everyone would be going back out there to make their final stand.

The final battle would be upon them before they knew it.

"There she is!" Davis shouted. "Prepare for landing!" She stood and walked over to Fitz. Squatting, she put a hand on his back and said, "Don't worry, we're going to get you a new prosthetic."

Fitz didn't bother to look down at his broken blade. He simply watched the toy-sized shapes of the *GW* strike group that dotted the horizon. The vessels coasted through the sparkling teal water. As they got closer, the flight deck of the *GW* filled with medical personnel. Teams of medics and soldiers swarmed below with gear.

Garcia bent down to help Tank up. The moment the bird touched down, a team rushed to the troop hold.

"Who's hurt?" one of the men yelled over the whoosh of the blades.

"Are you blind?" Tank asked.

Garcia almost laughed. He handed Tank off reluctantly to two medics, hoping neither would walk away with a black eye. As Garcia suspected, Tank put up a fight the moment they tried to get him to sit in a wheelchair. He swatted at them with his free hand and growled, "I can walk, goddamnit."

It took a few moments for the men to convince him to sit. By the time they did, the younger medic was rubbing his bicep where Tank had elbowed him.

"Staff Sergeant Garcia," said a sharp voice. "As soon as you got a minute, I want a debriefing."

The words came from Davis. She was helping Fitz a few feet away. He leaned on her for support.

"Where's Meg?" Fitz muttered in a strangled voice.

"Just behind us," Davis replied. She turned to look at the sky. Over the wind came the sound of a second helicopter. A second Black Hawk burst through the clouds and descended to the deck.

The warm ocean air rustled through Garcia's filthy fatigues as he stood and watched.

"Do you see her? Does anyone see her?" Fitz asked.

Davis brought a hand to her eyes to shield them from the sun. The chopper disgorged a dozen soldiers and civilians, but Garcia didn't see Meg's bloodstained form in the mix. He pivoted to the left for a better view.

Behind the departing group, three soldiers were bent down in the troop hold of the Black Hawk, working on two people lying on the floor. Several more medics piled into the craft to help.

Blood dripped onto the flight deck. Meg wasn't the

only one hurt badly. Someone else had been injured on the way out. The crew chief moved to reveal an injured marine on his back inside the chopper next to Meg. The medics were already cutting away his fatigues.

It was hard to see much past the mob of civilians. Sailors herded them away from the choppers. Most of them looked like frightened, lost livestock, eyes roving and wide.

At least some of them had made it. It helped lessen the pain of the loss of his men. They had died for something.

Fitz pulled away from Davis's grip, limping on his single blade back toward the chopper. "I have to see Meg." He crashed to the ground and pushed himself back up as if he was doing an up-down. "Meg!"

"Fitz, get back here!" Davis shouted.

Garcia reached toward Davis. "You should let him go, LT."

Davis pulled off her helmet and let her shoulder-length red hair down. It caught in the breeze, blowing behind her head in a halo. Together, Garcia and the lieutenant watched Fitz struggle, jumping on one blade and using his MK11 as a crutch. He moved like a man possessed.

Tank groaned from the wheelchair.

"I'm going to get him inside," Garcia said as he went to join Tank. "Make sure Fitz is okay."

Davis slipped her helmet back on. "Hang in there, Corporal."

The marine grumbled as the medics pushed him through the open hatch. Five minutes later, they arrived at the makeshift infirmary. The room was bustling with activity. A nurse and a soldier Garcia had never seen before wheeled a gurney toward a hatch at the other end. A white cloth stained with blood was draped over a sailor who would never see the ocean again. They pushed the body past an area that had been cordoned off by large plastic walls marked with biohazard signs.

"What are those for?" Garcia asked one of the nurses.

"Preparation. You didn't hear what happened?"

"Hear what?"

"There was an incident on the *Cowpens*. Several doctors were exposed to a toxin during an autopsy. One of the Delta Force operators is quarantined in the lab with them right now."

*Beckham, you son of a bitch.*

Garcia shook his head. Just when he thought things couldn't get any worse. He looked away from the clean room and back to a row of empty beds along the starboard wall. The sheets were white, but he could still see the bloodstains that bleach couldn't get out.

The medics pushing Tank's chair helped him onto the bed next to Chow. The operator reached over with a hand dressed in bandages as a nurse hurried toward them.

All around him, Garcia heard the moans of injured soldiers, shouts from doctors trying to save patients, and the frightened voices of civilians who hadn't seen military personnel for six weeks.

Garcia took it all in, wondering exactly how much more humanity could take. He prayed that Dr. Lovato and Beckham were still in the fight. He was terrified of being the last soldier standing.

Beckham hated not being in control. Fighting Variants was one thing—at least he could direct his aim. But sitting on the floor in a BSL4 laboratory, covered in chemicals and holding the mother of his unborn child in his arms, made him feel helpless. To add to the pressure, he still hadn't heard anything about the mission to retrieve Fitz, Meg, and the Variant Hunters from New York.

The wait was torture.

The last message they'd had was from Captain Humphrey, announcing the use of the experimental wash, and that was fifteen minutes ago. Whatever his people were doing to get them out of this lab wasn't working. Foam was still raining from the overhead jets, which told Beckham that whatever toxic shit was floating around hadn't been destroyed.

Ellis took a seat next to Kate and Beckham. He didn't say anything. He just sat there, staring at Lucy's remains. The bones were covered in a white residue that reminded Beckham of drywall. The liquid streaming out of those jets was hardening on everything it touched. A thick layer covered the lab floor. He wiped away the streaks on his visor.

"How much longer?" Ellis finally asked.

Beckham wasn't sure if he was talking to himself or to Kate. There was no way anyone in the other room would have heard him.

Every second that passed made Beckham feel more helpless. He needed a plan. Training had taught him to always leave himself an out. On every mission, from Operation Liberty to raiding Raven Rock, he had had an out. But the only plan he'd had when he walked into the lab was to be with Kate. What came after that was out of his hands.

Beckham watched Ellis stand and walk to a lab station.

"Where are you going?" Kate asked.

"To work. If we're going to sit in here, I might as well get something done."

The three technicians had stayed seated on their stools around the lab stations. Foam crept down their blue suits.

"Ronnie, where's the sample Kate gave you?" Ellis asked.

"Over here, Doctor." The technician stood and led him to another station.

Kate scooted away from Beckham and pushed herself to her feet. Beckham rose with her, considering telling her to stay put, but he saw the defiant look that had returned in her eyes. Instead of protesting, he followed her toward the lab stations. Maybe there was something he could do after all.

"Look," Ellis said in a voice just above a whisper. "I don't know what the hell is going on outside, but with Yokoyama dead, I'm not going to just sit here and hope Captain Humphrey's people know what they're doing."

Kate nodded. "I agree. We need to find out what these eggs are."

The jets suddenly shut off overhead. Everyone looked at the ceiling, waiting for the message they all knew would follow.

As if in answer, the wall intercom barked. "This is Captain Humphrey. Despite our attempts to destroy the toxin, air scans reveal it's still present. We're working on something else, but for now, we'd ask that you remain as far away from the juvenile and Doctor Yokoyama as possible."

Ellis and Kate exchanged a glance. Beckham could tell they weren't going to listen. That was fine by him. He wanted to get the hell out of here.

"Let's get to work," Kate said. "But be extremely careful."

Ellis issued orders to the three technicians. They wiped down their workstations and keyed their credentials in to their computers. Undeterred, they began testing samples.

Beckham took a seat on a stool and watched the team. This world was as foreign to him as the Afghani mountains and Iraqi deserts were to Kate. They came from completely different backgrounds, but they both shared the same goal—to protect America from enemies domestic and foreign.

The only difference was the type of enemies they fought.

Fifteen minutes passed. Then half an hour. Beckham watched diligently, trying not to focus on his labored breathing. His suit seemed to be shrinking around his muscular chest. He could feel it pressing in on his ribs.

Beckham stood. Kate and Ellis were crowded around a station together. He looked over Ellis's shoulder.

The doctor stuck his hands into the gloves of a bio-safety cabinet. Inside was a small petri dish containing several small brown balls. Using the internal gloves, Ellis picked up a pen with a razor edge in his right hand and a small tube in his left.

"Careful," Kate said.

Ellis paused for a moment. In a deliberately slow movement, he split open a tiny brown egg and pushed the open end of the tube toward it. Sludge oozed into the container. The egg deflated like a punctured balloon as the liquid emptied out.

"Got it," he said. He set the pen down next to the remains of the egg and put the cap on the tube.

"Let's get this under a scope ASAP," Kate said.

Ellis carefully removed the tube from the box. He cupped it in his hand gently, as if it contained the deadliest chemical known to man. Beckham wasn't sure what was inside, but he had a feeling that wasn't too far from the truth.

Beckham followed Kate and Ellis to a third station. They walked slowly, Ellis taking one step at a time. The technicians were waiting. They watched Ellis carry the tube, wide eyes following his every movement. Ronnie reached out, but Ellis shook his head.

"I'm doing this," he said.

"Not going to argue with you there, Doctor," Ronnie replied.

Using thoughtful care, Ellis deposited part of the sample on a slide and sealed it within the biosafety cabinet. Then he sat down in front of the connected microscope. A few minutes later, he looked up at Kate and nodded.

"What now?" Beckham asked.

"We wait," she replied.

# 14

President Ringgold cradled her injured arm and stepped closer to the CIC observation window. The *Cowpens* was surrounded by Zodiacs and smaller boats. A helicopter circled overhead.

"Captain, I want a sitrep right now," she said.

"Working on it, Madam President."

Humphrey looked up from a combat station across the room and waved Lieutenant Davis over, then went back to studying a report. He was multitasking, with ten different fires to put out. An hour earlier, he'd dispatched three Apaches to a derelict vessel full of shipping containers and a crew infected with the hemorrhage virus. He'd ordered the strike group to change course and the Apaches to hold their fire. There was no use wasting rockets on a ship that wasn't a threat.

Ringgold had questioned that assessment but kept her mouth sealed. Humphrey was a busy man and now had thirty new civilians from New York to look after. He was understaffed, running low on sleep, and visibly anxious. Ringgold could see it in his eyes and actions. She had decided to pick her battles carefully—especially with Lieutenant Colonel Kramer hovering in the CIC like a hawk. She was still flanked by two hard-looking men carrying massive shotguns.

Lieutenant Davis strode over to Humphrey wearing a fresh uniform. Her hair was still wet from the showers. She clasped her hands behind her back and whispered something to the captain that Ringgold couldn't hear.

There was no hint of emotion in Davis's features, nothing to tell Ringgold what intel she had. What Ringgold did see was a woman who wasn't afraid to speak her opinion—a woman who backed those opinions with actions. She hadn't been ordered to New York to extract survivors; she had volunteered. And she had returned to the bridge as soon as she was finished washing the blood off her uniform. Davis had helped secure a win, but Ringgold needed more wins. A lot more. And she needed Kate and Beckham back from the *Cowpens* safely.

"Sorry, Madam President," the captain said. Humphrey and Davis walked over to the observation windows side by side. "I apologize, but right now I don't have a new sitrep for the *Cowpens*. We're still—"

"That's unacceptable, Captain," Ringgold interrupted. "We have some of the best remaining American scientists on that ship. I want—"

This time Humphrey interrupted Ringgold. "With all due respect, we *had* the best. Doctor Carmen and Doctor Yokoyama are dead. Doctor Ellis and Doctor Lovato are quarantined, and our three best technicians too. I have a team of scientists from the Medical Corps working diligently on getting them out of there, but we're in uncharted waters. Half of those men only have undergrad degrees in biology."

Ringgold held in a sigh. "Our main priority—*your* main priority is to get Doctor Lovato and her staff out of that lab safely, ASAP. Do I make myself clear, Captain?"

"Yes, ma'am." Humphrey brushed a strand of silver hair away from his tanned forehead as Davis leaned over to whisper something in his ear.

"Goddamnit," he muttered. She handed him a pair of binoculars, and he quickly centered them on the horizon. "I thought I ordered all ships away from that vessel."

"You did, sir," Davis replied. "We changed course thirty minutes ago."

"Then why does it look like…?" Humphrey's words trailed off as he slowly lowered the scope and looked at Davis.

Ringgold gestured for the binoculars while Humphrey and Davis spoke. Using her good hand, she pushed them to her eyes. A vessel loaded with multicolored shipping containers filled the oval scopes. From a distance, it hardly looked as if it was moving at all. Then she saw the wake.

By the time she understood what was happening, a trio of Apaches shot over the CIC. The sleek black choppers raced across the skyline, their mounted miniguns rotating toward the vessel.

"Get it done, Lieutenant," Humphrey said.

Davis snapped to attention and hurried away. Ringgold watched her leave in the reflection of the window.

"What did I miss?" called the voice of Vice President Johnson. He stood in the center of the room, rubbing tired eyes.

"A lot, sir," Humphrey replied.

"I was only asleep for an hour."

Ringgold followed the Apaches with her binoculars. "We have a problem, Johnson. Have a look."

Humphrey pointed to the colorful ship in the distance. "We located a vessel that has infected all over the decks. Not Variants—people infected with the hemorrhage virus. Apparently there's also someone who's *not* infected on board. And they're headed right for us."

"Jesus. I was just briefed on the situation on the *Cowpens*, and now this?" Johnson said. "Someone bring me a cup of coffee. Black coffee. None of that decaf horseshit."

Ringgold zoned out from the conversation to focus on the Apaches. When they arrived at the vessel, they circled like turkey vultures over a dead carcass. The ship continued to cut through the water, undeterred by the birds.

"Captain, is there a reason that—" The Apaches suddenly pulled away, and before Ringgold could finish her thought, the ship exploded in a brilliant fireball. Shipping containers shot into the air like firecrackers, then plummeted back to the ocean, lost to the currents that would take them to a new home.

At first Ringgold thought the ship might have been carrying a bomb, but then she saw the finned sail of the USS *Florida* cutting through the water.

"One shot, one kill. Nice hit," Humphrey said.

He turned to Davis, who was leaning over two officers at a battle station. "Recall the Apaches."

"Sir," Davis said, "I just got an update on Lab A. The toxin is dissipating. We should be able to get the scientists out shortly."

Ringgold almost exhaled. It didn't mean Kate and the others were out of the water yet, but as the crimson fireball vanished on the horizon, Ringgold decided she would chalk it up as another win.

Kate heard Captain Humphrey's voice over the intercom, but she wasn't really listening. She should have been happy. They were cleared to leave the lab, and Fitz was apparently back from New York City with Meg. But she couldn't seem to move. It was no wonder scans couldn't determine the identity of the unknown toxin. Technically, it didn't exist.

"What exactly are we looking at?" Kate asked. She bent down to look at the computer screen Ellis was facing. Beckham paced behind them anxiously. Kate could tell he was ready to get out of the lab and be washed down in the detox facility, but she couldn't leave just yet.

"I've seen something similar before, but this has a much higher concentration of enzymes," Ellis replied. He swiveled his chair around to face Kate and the technicians. "These eggs contain a type of venom that's much stronger than what's found in spiders."

"I don't get it," Ronnie said. "Why?"

Ellis offered a meaningful look. "What's the one thing Variants can't do?"

Ronnie thought for a moment. "Seems to me they can do a whole hell of a lot."

"They can't speak," Kate said. "At least not yet. Or not like the Alphas."

Ellis shook his head and spun back to the computer screen.

"They can't shoot," Beckham said. He had stopped pacing.

"*Exactly*," Ellis said. "I believe the venom is yet another example of metamorphosis. Their armor protects them from bullets, but as of right now they can't shoot back."

"I don't follow," Kate said. She glanced back at Lucy's corpse. Her mind was working in slow motion, like a lagging computer.

"The enzymes in this venom will digest proteins like a hungry stomach," Ellis said. "Think of proteins as scaffolding for your tissues and organs. They're crucial to holding everything together. When you tear that scaffolding apart..." He jerked his chin toward Yokoyama's corpse.

Kate nearly choked on an epiphany. "You think the juveniles will evolve to fire the venom like a weapon?"

Ellis shrugged. "Doesn't do a lot of good inside of them, right?"

The technicians behind her broke into a hushed conversation, but Kate didn't reply. There was no evidence that the juveniles could shoot the venom. If Lucy had been able to do so, the creature would have used it on Sergeant Russo's men. At least, that's what Kate kept telling herself.

"Kate, can we get out of here?" Beckham said.

"Yes, I'm sorry. Just a few more minutes," Kate replied. "We're almost done."

Ellis punched at the keyboard. "I'm downloading all of the data. But before we continue our research, we'll need to fractionate the different components to separate the molecules by size. To further identify the compounds present, we need to perform mass spectrometry."

"Why? What's the point?" Ronnic said. "We already know what we need to know. Those things aren't just armored killing machines; they're poisonous. There's no designing an antidote to stop a venom stronger than anything found in nature."

"He's right," Kate said. "We need to focus on Kryptonite and warn Command about this new development. Anyone going into the field should be aware of what we've discovered. We're not going to waste time trying to create an antidote. Our focus should be finding a weakness—some way to kill these monsters."

Ellis looked unsure, but Kate wasn't going to spend any time trying to convince him. They all needed a break, and Kate wanted to see Fitz, Meg, and the others.

"Let's get out of here." She grabbed Beckham's hand and pulled him away from the station. Her heart was pounding, but his simple touch calmed her. They were finally leaving.

Together.

But not everyone was as lucky.

Yokoyama had joined the ranks of the dead. His grisly end was a reminder of the threat they faced when they left the lab. The juveniles weren't just deadly when they were alive—they were equally as deadly when they were corpses. And if Ellis's theory was correct, the juveniles were about to add another weapon to their already terrifying arsenal.

Ronnie opened the hatch to the clean room, and all six of them entered the shower facility. On the other side of the next hatch, a team of Medical Corps soldiers and scientists waited.

One of them stepped up to the wall intercom. "Doctors, once you finish rinsing off your suits, please discard them in the infirmary chute."

Kate gave the thumbs-up sign.

Thirty minutes later, she was shivering in her underwear. She stripped and tossed them into a bag a Medical Corps soldier held. He looked away.

"I'm going to need this back," Beckham said. He was holding his uniform out toward the Medical Corps soldier with the bag.

"Your clothes have to be destroyed, sir."

Beckham put his clothes on a bench and began digging through them. Kate didn't need to see him pull the picture of his mom from a pocket to know exactly what he was looking for.

"Everything needs to be—"

"It's my last one," Beckham said. "No way in hell you're taking this from me."

The soldier looked over his shoulder and sighed. Holding out the bag, he said, "Fine. Just put your clothes in."

Shaking from the cold, Kate reached into the locker

and pulled out a white jumpsuit. The warmth of a towel suddenly spread over her back. She grabbed the sides and pulled it around her. When she turned, she was face-to-face with Beckham. He had a towel wrapped around his waist, but wore nothing else. His barrel chest was covered in bruises, and scabs had formed around the stitches on his shoulder. Both of his forearms and calves were covered in scrapes and gashes, some so deep they should have had stitches by now. He was going to have a lot of scars.

"Ready to get out of here?" he asked.

Kate smiled as warmly as she could. She slipped into the provided jumpsuit and waited for Beckham to change. When they were finished, they joined Ellis, Ronnie, and the two technicians. The squad of Medical Corps soldiers and scientists waited for them in the passage outside.

"Good to see you, Master Sergeant," one of them said. Beckham reached out to shake his hand. "Thanks for what you did earlier, Anthony. I appreciate it."

"Happy to help." The man looked at Kate and grinned. "You know who your boyfriend is, right?"

Kate felt another smile coming on, but she didn't let it. She was too tired, and now didn't seem like an appropriate time for small talk. Instead, she nodded and grabbed Beckham's hand.

Anthony led them above decks, where they were met by a marine escort in CBRN suits.

"This way!" one of the men shouted, pointing toward a Black Hawk.

They took the bird back to the *GW* and quickly made their way to the makeshift infirmary. The room was packed to the brim with new faces. Many of them were children. The massive space quieted as they entered. Every nurse, doctor, and patient seemed to stop what they were doing to stare in Kate's direction.

In the center of the room she saw Donna and her son, Bo. Tank was set up in a bed next to Chow. Garcia stood at its foot. Horn was there too, holding Tasha's and Jenny's hands. The girls looked over and waved at Kate. She couldn't believe it, but they were both smiling.

Even President Ringgold was there. She finished shaking the hand of an injured soldier, then wheeled toward Kate. An escort of three marines trailed Ringgold through the maze of beds, moving fast to keep up.

Beckham waved to his men, a gesture that said he was okay. He scanned the room with Kate, both of them realizing at the same time that there were two missing faces.

"Where are Fitz and Meg?" Kate asked.

Beckham shook his head. "I—I don't know."

Horn left his girls with a nurse and walked over with Garcia.

"Goddamn, it's good to see you guys," Beckham said.

Horn snorted and raised a brow. "That was pretty bold of you, telling me you had to take a dump and then rushing to the *Cowpens*."

Beckham blushed when Kate looked at him. "I knew you would try and stop me, Big Horn."

"You're okay?" Garcia asked. His black hair was matted to his skull, and bandages covered his forehead. His broken nose was swollen worse than before.

"I should be asking you the same question," Beckham replied. "You look like hell, Marine." He searched the room a second time. "Where are Fitz and Meg?"

Garcia shook his head. "Things got bad out there."

Kate's heart flipped. She squeezed Beckham's coarse hand.

"Meg was hurt. Hurt bad. She's in surgery. Fitz is waiting for her to get out," Garcia said. "That's all I know. She's been under the knife for a while."

Kate let go of Beckham's hand as President Ringgold approached in her wheelchair. He walked over to his men and patted Garcia on the back. She heard him asking about Tank, Chow, and the other soldiers just as Ringgold arrived.

"Doctor Lovato," said the president, "you never cease to amaze me. I'm only going to say this once. I want you and Master Sergeant Beckham to rest. Take a nap. A *long* one. Then report to the CIC."

Kate considered protesting, but Ringgold held up her uninjured hand. "That's an order, Kate."

"We just need to run a few tests on them before they're cleared to leave," Anthony said.

Ringgold reached up and put a hand on Kate's left arm. "I'm glad you're okay."

The marines behind Ringgold drew back, startled.

"Madam President, please refrain from touching Doctor Lovato right now," Anthony said. "She's been cleared, but..."

Ringgold kept her hand on Kate's arm and smiled. "I'll see you soon, Kate."

"Thank you for your concern, Madam President." Kate smiled back and patted Ringgold's hand.

"This way, please," Anthony said.

Beckham finished his conversation and joined Kate in the single-file line. Ellis and the technicians were already heading toward the plastic tent marked with biohazard signs across the room.

"You think Meg's going to pull through?" Kate asked Beckham as they walked. Meg had never stopped fighting the monsters. It didn't seem fair for her to survive the Bone Collector and everything else, only to perish now.

He clenched his jaw and rubbed at his forehead. "She's tough."

Kate focused her thoughts and continued after Ellis toward the makeshift biohazard facility. The temporary infirmary smelled like sweat and blood, but it represented everything they were fighting for. The new faces were civilians, people who Fitz, Meg, and the Variant Hunters had risked their lives to save. As Anthony opened the plastic door to the room, Kate nearly gasped. Kryptonite was almost ready, and there were still people alive out there to save.

People who were still fighting.

Stepping through the door, she allowed a dangerous thought to enter her mind: Maybe the human race could be saved after all.

# 15

Numb and drowsy, Meg shifted in and out of consciousness. If it weren't for the shouts and the beep of an EKG machine, she would have thought she was dead.

"We're losing her!" someone yelled. The voice was distant and muffled, as if whoever was shouting was in the middle of a windstorm.

She felt the world spinning around her, fading away and then rushing back, full of pain. Meg couldn't remember where she was or how she had gotten there. Her eyelids were weights. She didn't have the energy to open them.

Fragmented dreams surfaced in her mind as she struggled against the warm darkness that tried to welcome her, like sleep after hours and hours of being awake.

*Meg opened the back door to her in-laws' vacation home in Martha's Vineyard. It was mid-July, and a warm breeze rustled the white blouse she wore over her swimsuit. She stepped out onto the lawn that separated the property from rolling beaches of creamy sand. The ocean sparkled in the distance, beckoning her.*

*"Meg, the water's great!" shouted her husband. Tim hopped through the surf and dove into the water.*

*A smile crested her face. She loved watching him swim: his graceful strokes, the way his body glided through the water. He was a natural. It had taken an Ironman triathlon for Meg to enjoy the sport. And even after completing one, she still didn't love the water like Tim did. But today, she wasn't swimming 2.4 miles with a thousand other triathletes. It was just her and her husband on a beach devoid of everything but seagulls.*

*She stripped off her blouse as she ran to the water, toes slipping into the warm sand. Nothing beat running barefoot on the beach. Pounding concrete in her running shoes or pedaling her triathlon bike down a straightaway was heaven. But this—this was what she loved more than anything else. It gave her a natural high.*

*Meg spent the afternoon and evening on the beach with Tim. They ate dinner at dusk, then ran back into the surf with a full moon overhead. She stood knee-deep in water with her back to his chest, his arms wrapped around her stomach. The waves slapped against their legs in the sparkling twilight, and she turned for a kiss that seemed to last forever.*

*That night they made love for hours. It had been months since they had come together so intensely. With demanding careers, they were almost always exhausted at night, and the weekends they spent catching up on everything else. Feeling Tim lust after her reminded her why she had fallen in love with him years ago. She lost herself under his muscular body, his every kiss caressing her skin.*

"Give me the paddles!"

A powerful shock jolted Meg awake. Fire raced across her skin, burning her. She forced her eyelids open to a brilliant white glow. Two faces wearing surgical masks hovered over her. Blinding pain ripped through her extremities, tingling and sharpening until she couldn't stand it anymore. The agony slowly forced her eyelids shut, the faces overhead blurring until they vanished.

*Meg reached out for Fitz's hand. His eyes flitted from the Variant that had her legs to the bottom of the stairwell. She could hear the beasts climbing, their talons striking the concrete, joints snapping with every movement.*

*This was no different than being chased by the flames inside a burning building. Her only option was to keep moving forward.*

*Fitz fired a shot into the face of a Variant that had broken his right blade. Then he reached out to grab her, but she was sliding. Pain lanced up her raw legs, and her chin hit a stair as the monster holding her pulled her away from Fitz.*

*Shouts echoed through the stairwell. Garcia. Tank. Someone else. She could see figures rushing to help her, but there was no time. The marines faded into the shadowy stairwell as she was dragged toward dozens of chomping maws.*

*The Variant Hunters and Fitz couldn't help her now. She had to protect herself.*

*Still holding her hatchet, Meg rolled to her back and used the blade to strike at the wrinkled face of a female Variant. Crunching bone echoed, and warm blood sprayed her face. A horrifying, deep shriek followed, and a pair of talons yanked at her hands.*

*Her hatchet was her strength. Without it, there was no holding back the terror. As the claws cut through her flesh, she screamed out for help.*

*Gunshots rattled above. More blood peppered Meg's exposed skin. She wasn't sure if it was hers or the beast's.*

*"Meg, hold on!" Fitz screamed.*

*The swarm consumed her before she could respond. Desperate, she squirmed, punched, bit, and scratched. She tore a chunk of flesh from the monster holding her down, then dug her fingernails into the creature's neck, pulling away diseased skin.*

*Blood dripped into her eyes, forcing them shut. The*

*weight of the beast suddenly lifted, only to be replaced by what felt like a dozen Variants all at once. She blinked away the sticky gore to the sight of a single face with almond eyes and barklike skin.*

*If it weren't for the pressure on her chest, she would have screamed. What came out was a strangled whisper. In her peripheral, the rest of the pack raced by her and up the stairs toward the marines, leaving behind a wake of rotting, sour flesh. Meg writhed under the armored monster, but there was no budging under its weight.*

*She watched, with one eye open, as the beast's jaw split. Four mandibles extended to reveal barbed teeth. A blast of rancid breath hit her in the face. Meg searched the ground for something to fight back with. Her fingers brushed the cold steel of her hatchet.*

"Ma'am, can you hear me?"

Meg gasped for air, her eyelids snapping open to the same bright infirmary. A partially obscured face leaned down. The man waved a thin object in front of her eyes. The pain came back, and stars drifted across the darkness.

"We're losing her again!"

*Meg fired her M9 at the empty bottles. She could see Riley staring at her from his wheelchair. Blushing, she fired off another three shots.*

"Damn, you're a natural."

"I thought I told you to stop looking at me," Meg said.

*Riley turned slightly, but she could still feel his gaze.* "I'm sorry," *he said.* "It's just . . ."

*Meg pulled the magazine and handed it to Riley, her eyes locking with his.* "Just what?"

"You're the most beautiful woman in the world to me."

*A moment of silence passed between the two of them. Meg wasn't sure how to reply. It had been a long time since any man told her she was beautiful. After they'd been married*

*for a few years, she and Tim had let their romance all but
fizzle out, both of them wrapped up in their careers and their
busy lives. They'd talked about taking a trip, just the two of
them, to rekindle the spark. They'd never gotten the chance,
and Meg had resigned herself to never seeing a man look at
her with desire again.*

*Then she'd met Riley.*

*"Sorry," he said, blushing.*

*Shaking her head, Meg said, "Don't be." She gestured for
another magazine, and Riley fumbled with one sticking out
of his vest pocket. He handed it to her with shaky fingers. It
was odd, seeing the elite soldier show such vulnerability, and
it was then that Meg knew how deeply he cared for her. She
realized she felt the same.*

"Goddamnit, get him out of here!" screamed a voice.

The sharp eyes of a doctor Meg didn't recognize
replaced Riley's carefree gaze. She was back in the infirmary and felt herself slipping away, but it was the intense
sadness of her memories that hurt the worst. She was
afraid to close her eyes again—terrified that she would
see Tim, transformed into a monster, being gunned
down, or the life leaving Riley's blue eyes on Plum Island.

"Meg, it's going to be okay," said a second, softer
voice. There was urgency and fear in the words, enough
to confirm what she suspected—she was dying. Using
every ounce of strength, she tried to twist her head in
the direction of the voice. A nurse restrained her with a
palm Meg couldn't feel.

"Please stay still, ma'am," the nurse said sternly.

The slight movement provided Meg a view of her
body on the operating table.

She scarcely recognized her muscular legs, the Ironman tattoo on her upper right thigh, or the abs she had
worked so hard for. Her body was covered in long, bright
lacerations. Two doctors and a team of nurses were

working on her. One of the doctors was bent next to her right side. She could feel something inside her.

"I can't get this artery . . ." the doctor began to say. His words trailed off as the pressure increased on her guts.

*Are those his fingers?*

Meg fought for a better look. The EKG machine chirped louder, her heart rate elevating at the sight of an open gash along the right side of her stomach.

"Don't move, ma'am!" the nurse entreated.

Meg opened her mouth to yell at the woman, but all that came out was a croak. Shades of red encroached on the sides of her vision.

"Jesus Christ, will someone put her back under?!" a doctor yelled.

The same soft voice from earlier called her name. This time she saw the face it belonged to. Fitz was standing to her right. A nurse turned toward him, her hands outstretched. He crutched past her and limped toward the table.

"It's okay, Meg, I'm here," Fitz said. "And I'm not going anywhere." His eyes flitted to her injuries for a split second, just as they had in her memory right before she had been pulled from his reach by the Variant that had maimed her.

This time he grabbed her hand and held on. There were no more monsters to drag her away. Only terrifying memories and the sobering reality of her injuries.

She wasn't going to get up from this table, and they both knew it.

The chirp of the EKG machine sharpened. Meg knew the sound. She'd heard it dozens of times when she lost patients before they made it to the hospital. Oddly, she had felt more fear for those people than she did for herself.

"You're right," Meg whispered to Fitz. Despite the

numbness, her words came out remarkably clear. "It's all going to be okay. Don't blame yourself. It's not your fault. You haven't ever failed *anyone*."

Fitz gripped her hand tightly, his sweat mixing with her blood. "Hang in there. You're going to pull through. You *have* to pull through." He looked over at the doctor, but Meg squeezed his hand, forcing him to hold her gaze.

The doctor leaning over her yelled, "Get this man out of here!"

A second nurse approached Fitz, grabbing him by the arm.

"You have to leave, now, sir!"

"No, I'm staying with her!" Fitz shouted back. He yanked his arm away.

Meg had always been told your life flashed before your eyes when you died. But besides a few memories of Tim, her thoughts were all about the past six weeks. She thought of Tasha and Jenny, how they had been a light in the darkness. She had cherished her time with the girls, even though it was short. Their resilience had given her hope that the human race would survive.

"Tell Tasha and Jenny I love them," Meg said, her voice dwindling into a whisper again.

"You can tell them that yourself," Fitz said. "You're going to be *fine*."

Fitz looked sweet when he lied. It was the same way Riley had looked when he told her it was going to be okay.

Meg's heart rate amplified, the noise from the EKG machine filling the room. Her body was shutting down, but she felt no fear. She wasn't scared anymore.

Fitz massaged her hand with his thumb. His features hardened from the guilt he had lived with since she met him.

"Don't let it win, Fitz. You're a good man. The *best*,

just like Riley. You didn't fail us. You saved us with your friendship and kindness."

A nurse reached down with a needle toward Meg's left arm. The pain was slowly washing back over her, the drugs wearing off. But Meg still had a little fight left in her. She grabbed the nurse's hand.

"No more drugs," Meg mumbled.

The doctor and nurse exchanged a conflicted look. He nodded, and the woman slowly withdrew the needle. Meg turned back to Fitz. His eyes had softened again, and a tear streaked down his filthy cheeks.

"Please, Meg," he said. "Don't give up. Please don't leave us."

"I'm tired, Fitz. And I miss Tim. I miss my friends. I miss Riley." Meg felt her own tears falling down her face.

Fitz blinked long and hard. His dry lips opened, and he leaned down next to her face with her hand still in his. Trembling, he struggled to stay up on his crutch as he kissed her on the forehead.

Meg could feel his lips on her skin. The warmth reassured her that everything really would be okay. She could rest now.

A smile touched the side of her mouth. "Tell Beckham and Kate—"

A sharp jolt ripped through her chest. She gasped for breath, the room slipping away as whiteness filled her vision.

"Meg!" Fitz shouted.

"We're losing her again!" yelled another voice.

Meg blinked rapidly and squeezed Fitz's hand.

*Meg sat on the steps of Building 1 on Plum Island, watching Fitz and Riley train the troops heading to New York. Tasha and Jenny were curled up against her sides, both of them sleeping peacefully. She held them tight against her body. The warm ocean breeze rustled through her hair.*

*After they had finished the training, Riley and Fitz both turned and waved. She smiled, not daring raise a hand from Tasha and Jenny's still bodies. Riley smiled back, clearly excited about his new mission. He wheeled over to the stairs with that shit-eating grin of his. It was the happiest she had seen him in a while. Butterflies sent both warmth and chills through her. The sensation reminded her how much she had learned at the end of the world, from things she never thought she would experience.*

*She had learned what it felt like to take care of children. She had met some of the strongest and most brilliant men and women on the planet—from Beckham and Horn to Kate and Ellis. Even more important, she had learned to love again. She'd never expected to find love at the end of the world, but she guessed it was as likely a place as any.*

The memory of Plum Island slipped away as her heart finally gave out. But her final thoughts were not plagued with fear or regret. They were happy, hopeful. Beckham, Kate, and Fitz could save the world without her. She knew they would.

The last thing she heard was Fitz's voice asking her to save a seat for him up there, and to tell Riley and his family hello.

"Tell them I'll never stop fighting," he said.

Meg smiled weakly, and then she was gone.

Fitz limped to the CIC with a broken blade and a broken heart. Meg had died right in front of him, but before she passed, she had given him the most precious gift of all—she had lifted the heavy burden he'd been carrying on his shoulders ever since Iraq.

He had killed countless times, and before this war was over, he would kill many more times to protect his friends. At least now, he would do so without the raw guilt that had been eating him alive.

For an hour, Fitz strolled through passages of the *GW* aimlessly, lost in his thoughts and hardly aware of the stares he was drawing. It wasn't surprising, considering he was covered in blood and hopping on one blade. The clanking echoed through the interior of the ship. He didn't bother looking for the rest of Team Ghost or the Variant Hunters. Everyone would be dealing with the fallout of New York in their own way. Most of them would probably be trying to rest in their quarters.

But he hadn't even been assigned a bunk yet. He had nowhere to go, so he continued to wander through the passages until a voice called his name.

"Fitz, where the *hell* have you been? I've been looking everywhere for you."

Lieutenant Davis came rushing toward him.

"I was in…" Fitz grimaced at the thought of seeing Meg take her final breaths. "I was with my friend."

"How is she?"

Fitz bowed his head.

"I'm sorry, Fitz," Davis said. She put a hand on his shoulder. "But we can't mourn for her or anyone else right now. We have a mission to plan. And I need you. Follow me."

The thought of another mission distracted him momentarily. Davis was right. There was no time to slow down now. They had to push on despite the losses. Those who had died would have wanted that.

Meg had wanted that.

Davis stopped around the next bulkhead and knocked on a hatch. "Master Sergeant, Doctor Lovato, are you awake?"

Fitz stepped out of view as they waited. The hatch creaked open a few seconds later and a groggy Beckham looked out, his hair mussed and face pale. Kate stood behind him, rubbing at her eyes. In the back of the room Fitz thought he saw Apollo's tail thumping.

"You going to let us out of here so we can see Meg now?" Beckham asked. "We're fine. Anthony's team cleared us."

Davis locked her jaw.

"LT?" Beckham said. He stepped into the passage barefoot and noticed Fitz.

"Holy shit," Beckham said. He wrapped his arms around the marine, embracing him in a strong hug. "Goddamn, it's good to see you, brother."

"You too," Fitz replied softly.

Beckham pulled away. "What's wrong?"

Fitz shook his head, choking on his words. "She didn't make it."

Kate gasped and cupped her hands over her mouth.

"Fuck," Beckham muttered. Guilt filled his eyes, the same guilt Fitz felt.

"It was peaceful," Fitz said. "I was there for the end."

Beckham glared at Davis. Fitz didn't blame him. She hadn't let Beckham or Kate close to the infirmary after their exposure to the juvenile Variant. They hadn't even had a chance to say goodbye.

Beckham pulled Kate close. "I'm sorry, brother."

"Me too," Fitz said. He felt the urge to apologize further, but doing so would have disrespected Meg's final wishes.

Kate put her head on Beckham's shoulder, whimpering.

"I'm sorry for your loss, truly I am," Davis said. "But President Ringgold and Vice President Johnson have requested your presence in the CIC."

"Right *now*?" Kate asked.

"Yes, Doctor."

Kate slowly slipped back into the dark room, and

Beckham shut the hatch behind them. When he opened it again, they were both fully dressed. Kate was pulling her hair into a ponytail, but she looked dazed.

Apollo poked his head out from between Beckham's legs and wagged his tail when he saw Fitz.

"Hey, buddy," Fitz said. He balanced on his crutch to bend down and pet the dog.

"You have to stay here, Apollo," Beckham said.

The shepherd whined, but retreated into the room and sat. Fitz smiled at the dog, remembering everything they had been through.

"Let's go," Davis said. She led them through the passage at a hurried pace, stopping only to collect Ellis and Horn. By the time the six of them arrived at the CIC, over eight hours had passed since Fitz had left New York. It was midafternoon, and rays of sunlight gleamed outside the portholes.

They were directed into a conference room already packed with bodies. Chatter about death tolls and Kryptonite filled the space. President Ringgold stood at the front of the table and held up her good hand. Hushed voices dwindled into whispers, then silence. Everyone stared at Fitz, their eyes taking in his bloodstained clothes and broken blade.

Davis gestured toward the back of the room. Fitz squeezed in behind several officers in neatly pressed uniforms. He followed Beckham and Horn into the back corner where Garcia was already camped out. Ellis and Kate joined Davis at the other end of the table.

"Thank you all for coming," Ringgold said. "I'm happy to report that I have good news: The other three facilities working on Kryptonite have finished their batches, and ours should be complete within a few hours. When it's done, we will immediately prepare them so they can be loaded into missiles. The diluted Kryptonite inside those missiles will mix with Earthfall, the modified weather agent designed to cause massive rainfall.

"As you may remember, there are sixteen strategically placed facilities designed to manipulate weather on a global scale. Tomorrow evening, at dusk, a team from the *GW* will meet three other teams at an Earthfall facility in Colorado. The strike teams will enter and secure the building. They will then load the missiles and launch them over the United States."

Fitz attempted to stiffen his back, hoping he was here because he was going on that mission. Being part of something so big was beyond anything he could have ever imagined.

"Once the missiles are airborne, recon teams in the field will monitor the effects of Kryptonite on the adult Variants," Johnson added. "We expect the weapon to kill most of the adults within a period of twenty-four to forty-eight hours. During that time, I'll be working with remaining military assets across the United States to launch a coordinated offensive in several strategic cities that will target the offspring. Now that we know they possess venom, it's been decided we must destroy them before it's too late. Assuming everything goes according to plan and we eradicate the majority of the adult population, in five days we will launch the final stage of Operation Extinction. The Marine Corps Recruit Depot at Parris Island will be the staging ground for this offensive. It's one of our final remaining bases and has been fortified by engineers familiar with the Variants."

Several voices rose over Johnson's, but his glare cut them off. Fitz grimaced as he continued working on straightening his sore back. His entire body hurt, and a gash on his forearm was bleeding freely. He wiped it on his pants, smearing his blood over Meg's.

Johnson continued, "Lieutenant Davis will be leading

the strike team to Colorado. Sergeant Garcia and Corporal Fitzpatrick will join her. Team Ghost will remain behind to help plan the final mission."

Out of the corner of his eye, Fitz scrutinized the Delta Force operators. Horn rubbed at one of his biceps, but Beckham didn't so much as flinch. A few feet over, Garcia had his arms folded across his chest. Rolled up sleeves exposed a newly tattooed cross on his left arm, still glistening with fresh ink that read *Rick Thomas*.

Davis stepped up to the table, and Fitz returned his attention to the officers. She opened a folder and glanced down.

"Good afternoon, everyone. As the vice president already noted, we will be staging most of our operations out of the Marine Corps Recruit Depot at Parris Island. I've been in contact with General Willis there, and he's guaranteed the safety of our troops."

Fitz saw several skeptical brows raised across the room. He didn't blame them. The Variants had managed to infiltrate and destroy nearly every military stronghold throughout the country.

Davis didn't seem to be fazed by her skeptics. "We have approximately ten thousand remaining soldiers in fighting condition. We're dividing them up to invade five cities strategically selected by our best intel officers. Reports indicate there are smaller populations of juvenile Variants in San Diego, Des Moines, and Portland. Atlanta and Washington, DC, have higher numbers, but both are high-level targets due to their importance in rebuilding society and reestablishing our federal government in the—"

"How much higher?" Lieutenant Colonel Kramer interrupted. "I want to hear numbers."

Davis glanced down at her folder. "Our troops in San Diego, Des Moines, and Portland will face even odds against the juveniles, and with mechanized units, air support, and Special Forces, I'm confident we will prevail without—"

Kramer interrupted Davis a second time. "Lieutenant, you're not answering my question. What about DC and Atlanta?"

Johnson glared at Kramer. He wasn't the only one. Ringgold was staring her down with a ruthless gaze.

"Soldiers on the ground in DC and Atlanta will face three times their numbers," Johnson said calmly.

Kramer shook her head. "Three times? You expect our men to take back Atlanta and DC facing those kinds of numbers? I'm sorry, Mister Vice President, but that is suicide. We would be better off using our nuclear—"

Johnson pounded the table. The rattle echoed through the room. Kramer's mouth opened, but she didn't speak.

"Enough," Johnson said. "I will not tolerate any more talk of using nuclear weapons. And if that's not clear enough, the next time I hear that kind of insubordination, I'll be replying with a charge of treason during wartime. That's Articles Eighty-Eight, Eighty-Nine, and Ninety in the Uniform Code of Military Justice, Lieutenant Colonel. If you need to review them, you can use the copy in my quarters."

Kramer's face betrayed her shock, but her eyes flashed with anger. Ringgold put a hand on Johnson's arm. He leaned back, her touch seeming to calm him instantly. After a few seconds of silence, Ringgold took Johnson's place at the head of the table.

"Some of you may doubt the plan moving forward, but we can all agree that the time to take back our country is now. It won't be easy. But as Lieutenant Davis tried to say, we *will* prevail. We have a chance of finally stopping the monsters that have taken over our country and our world. Vice President Johnson and I will not destroy our cities and poison our farmlands with radiation from the fires of a nuclear holocaust. We will take them back the old-fashioned way and fight for every inch with flesh and blood."

Kramer raised her hand as if she was about to lecture a private. "With all due respect, Madam President, we have already poisoned our cities by playing God with VX-99. By sending in troops, you will only poison our streets with something else—the blood of our remaining soldiers."

There was venom in Kramer's words that seemed to make Ringgold even more furious. Johnson's eyes lit up as if he was ready to order Kramer's arrest—or have her shot on sight. But Ringgold spoke first. "I guess I have more faith in our armed forces than you do."

The president pointed to the back of the room with her good arm. Fitz's heart raced at the gesture, warmth washing over his body.

"If you haven't noticed, Lieutenant Colonel, we have some very good men left to take back our cities, and I have the utmost confidence they will be successful." Ringgold finished with a smile aimed at Team Ghost.

# 16

A low growl woke Beckham. His eyes flipped open to the pitch-black interior of a cold room. Instinct told him to reach for his gun, but instead of his holster, his fingers scraped against his boxer briefs. He flipped from his back to his side. The warmth of another body touched his bare chest.

"What's wrong?" whispered a voice.

His mind slowly reassembled at the sound of Kate's voice. He was in the quarters he shared with her aboard the *GW*. The growl wasn't from some grotesque Variant—it was Apollo. The dog probably needed to take a leak. Beckham did too. He slid his legs over the side of the bunk and searched the darkness for the shepherd.

"Come here, boy," Beckham said.

A wet muzzle brushed against Beckham's fingertips. He stroked the dog's head, careful not to touch the fresh stitches in Apollo's back.

"What time is it?" Kate whispered.

Beckham stepped onto the cold floor. "No idea. Close your eyes, I'm flipping on the lights."

He waited a few seconds before switching on the overhead. A bank of lights lit up the cramped quarters.

Apollo looked up, squinting, his tail whipping back and forth.

"Jesus," Beckham said. "It's 0700 hours." They had actually slept through the night. It felt like an insult to everyone they had just lost, but their bodies had no longer been able to fend off the exhaustion. The moment Beckham's head hit the pillow the night before, he'd passed out.

"Shit," Kate blurted out. She sat up and rubbed at her eyes. "Kryptonite will be finished by now."

Beckham suddenly remembered the painful truths from the night before as reality came crashing back over him. He'd wanted them to be nightmares, but the evil dreams *were* real.

He climbed back into the bunk and curled up next to Kate. Then he patted the bed and motioned for Apollo to join them. With the dog at his back, Beckham wrapped his arms around Kate and put his palms on her stomach.

"We need to get up," Kate groaned. She turned to kiss Beckham on the cheek.

"Kryptonite can wait, right? You finished your work. I just want to lay here with you a few more minutes."

Kate didn't object as he caressed her. He still couldn't quite believe there was a part of him growing inside of her. The warmth of her body brought with it a sense of relief, like the safety and comfort he'd known as a kid. But there was no stopping the mental agony today. The pain worked its way to the front of his mind. He couldn't stop thinking about Meg and Riley. Losing the kid hurt so badly he couldn't stand it. To lose Meg too seemed surreal. What hurt even worse was picturing the future they could have had together. He'd noticed the way Riley looked at her, and their constant teasing and bickering had been tinged with growing attraction. Even Beckham had seen that they were falling for each other.

"She's really gone, isn't she?" Kate asked, echoing his thoughts. She turned on her side to face Beckham.

He knew they needed to get above decks, but moments like these were rare, and Beckham wasn't sure how many they had left.

"Yes," Beckham finally replied. "She's gone."

The firefighter he'd plucked from the sewers of New York had been through so much, in the end, it had pushed her over the edge. He'd seen it happen when soldiers lost their brothers in battle. He'd recognized the change in Meg's eyes after they'd rescued her in New York, and Beckham wished he had said something, done something, to help her then.

He sighed. "Watching Riley die broke her. I've seen it before. She'd lost her will to live. That's why she jumped out of the chopper and followed Fitz."

He caught his reflection in Kate's blue eyes. Meg wasn't the only one who had changed. If he lost Kate, he wasn't sure he would want to go on either.

*No. I wouldn't. But I would have to.*

"I saw it too," Kate said. "Meg was ready to give her life for Tasha and Jenny, almost eager to go down fighting. When she jumped, I had this gut-wrenching feeling I wouldn't see her ever again."

"She risked her life to save others. She died the same way Riley did."

In the silence, the anguish tightened its grip on him. He shook it away and prepared to tell Kate something they had both wanted to deny.

"The time will come where I will have to risk my life again for you and our child. For Horn's girls. For everyone."

Kate avoided his gaze. "I know."

Using a finger, Beckham lifted Kate's chin.

"I love you, Kate Lovato."

"I love you too, Reed Beckham."

That precious word still didn't seem like enough. *Love* couldn't describe how he felt about Kate. It was much more than that—a deep, raw feeling that he'd never experienced this intensely before. Thoughts of the future raced through his mind as they kissed.

Could he have it all with Kate? Kids, marriage, a home? Thinking of such things at the end of the world seemed naïve.

A rap on the hatch interrupted them, and Beckham slowly pulled away. After changing into his uniform, Beckham cracked open the hatch to see a sailor he didn't recognize.

"Master Sergeant Beckham, we're starting to assemble the strike team for Colorado on the flight deck. Lieutenant Davis has requested your presence."

Beckham nodded. "I'll be up there in a few minutes."

When he closed the hatch, Kate was already changing into a pair of white scrubs.

"I need to get to the lab. Ellis is probably already there working."

"On what?" Beckham asked. He grabbed his M4 and slung it over his back. Then he holstered the Colt .45 he'd left on the side table.

"We're trying to find out if the juveniles have a weakness. Something that the military will be able to use when they send troops to take back the cities." Kate wrapped her hair into a bun. "There has to be something—something you can..."

She paused and bowed her head slightly.

Beckham went to her and tilted her chin up again. "When I do go back out there, I'll be prepared. I promise. We're going to have a shit-ton of firepower and mechanized units. Way more than we had during Operation Liberty. And even more important, not some green-ass lieutenant who's never seen combat. I'll lead the damn platoon if I have to."

He sealed the promise with a kiss. Then Beckham whistled at Apollo. The dog followed them as they worked their way up the ladders until they reached the hatch leading to the flight deck. As soon as Beckham swung it open, the sound of pre-combat drills filled the open passage. A draft of warm air rushed inside with the familiar noise.

Kate paused in the entryway to watch from a distance. The crimson morning sun illuminated a Chinook racing away from the *Cowpens*. Flight officers jogged across the deck of the *GW* to get into position. They waved their orange sticks to direct the pilots as they lowered a crate marked BIOHAZARD.

Kate grabbed Beckham's hand.

"Is that the Kryptonite?" he asked.

"Yes."

Apollo squeezed between Beckham and Kate. He sat on his hind legs, looked up at the box, and let out a low growl, as if he knew what the shipping container held.

"I'll be back before Davis and her team take off for Colorado," Kate said. She kissed Beckham on the cheek, glanced at the shipping container one more time, and then hurried off to catch her ride to the *Cowpens*.

Beckham kept an eye on her as she left. Sometimes he still couldn't believe he was lucky enough to find her. As her chopper ascended into the sky, he waved, then continued with Apollo toward a trio of Black Hawks where several strike teams were assembling. Fitz was already there, sitting on a box with his back to Beckham.

"Mornin', Fitz."

The marine's broken blade clanked against the box as he swiveled. Beckham hardly recognized the man who turned to face him. Patches around Fitz's light eyes were swollen and bruised. He blinked eyelids red with irritation and centered his gaze on Beckham as if he was trying to see him from a distance.

"What are you doing out here?" Fitz asked. He used a crutch to push himself up on his left blade. He reached down with a shaky hand to pet Apollo's head.

It was subtle, but Beckham was used to reading the signs of battle shock. Fitz wasn't ready to go back out there. He needed sleep and probably a couple of sessions with a counselor.

"Lieutenant Davis asked me to join her up here," Beckham said. "Do you know where she's at?"

Fitz shook his head. "Haven't seen her yet."

Beckham almost cringed at the silence that followed. He had thought of all the things he would say to Fitz when he saw him again, but standing here now, none of them seemed right.

"How ya holding up?" Beckham finally asked.

"Primed and ready."

That was the response Beckham had anticipated. The downtime between combat missions was always the worst, especially in the aftermath of losing brothers and sisters. After weeks of intense fighting, neither Beckham nor anyone else knew what to do in the stillness and silence. Going back into the fray was a relief from being stuck in the mental prison of depression and survivor's guilt.

Fitz strained his eyes again. He was no longer looking at Beckham, and a tiny grin touched the sides of his mouth. Beckham wondered if it was an optical illusion. The last thing he expected to see was a smile on his friend's face.

The chatter of pounding boots commanded Beckham's attention. Davis led a small group of marines across the deck, carrying metal cases. She cradled two gleaming weapons across her chest.

Fitz crutched forward, mouth partially open. "Are those...?"

Garcia, a bandage on his forehead, ran after the group. "LT, hold up!" the man shouted.

Davis halted and waited for Garcia to catch up. She turned away from the sun, and Beckham saw that the things she carried weren't weapons at all—they were brand-new prosthetic legs for Fitz.

"LT, I can do that," Garcia said. He grabbed a crate from one of the other marines. The gunmetal blades in Davis's hands sparkled in the sunlight.

Beckham crossed his arms and took a step back as Davis and her entourage approached. They exchanged a nod before she handed the blades to Fitz.

"Told you I'd get you a new pair," she said. "Hope they fit."

Fitz took a seat on a crate and, with deliberate care, reached up to grab the blades. His lips trembled as if he couldn't find the right words.

For a moment he just sat there, staring at the prosthetics. Unlike his old blades, these had a curled foot with a diamond-shaped spur on the tip.

"They're made of carbon fiber and steel. You'll be fast and strong, and that spike will break through a skull," Davis said.

"Beautiful," Fitz said, glancing up. "They're absolutely beautiful. Thank you, LT."

Davis twisted her lips to the side, uncharacteristically shy, as if she wasn't sure how to reply. Then she winked and said, "Try them on."

Fitz pulled off his old blades and tossed them onto the deck. Apollo sniffed at the broken metal and pushed it to the side like a bone he didn't want.

A few minutes later, Fitz had the shiny blades secured to his legs. He stepped onto the deck, the diamond tips pointing toward Beckham. The other marines had stopped to watch. These men weren't staring because of Fitz's disability—they were admiring the warrior in front of them.

Garcia stepped away from the group and pulled a hatchet from his rucksack. "Thought you might like this too. Meg held on to it all the way from New York to the *GW*. One of the pilots found it in his chopper."

Fitz grabbed the handle in one hand and studied the blade. "Thanks, Sarge," he said with a smile. He wiped a tear from his eye with the other hand, and looked back to Davis. "Y'all are too kind."

The sight made Beckham tear up too. The prosthetics—not to mention Meg's hatchet—seemed to have given Fitz the confidence he needed, and it showed in his face. The color had risen in his cheeks, overshadowing the bags under his eyes.

Beckham couldn't hold back a grin. He was no longer looking at a marine damaged by war. Fitz was whole again, and he looked like a man who was ready to save the fucking world.

Kate stood outside the hatch to Lab A in a snug CBRN suit. The extra layers were designed to prevent direct contact with a range of contaminants, but she doubted it would protect her from the juvenile venom.

The lab was spotless. Every inch of floor, wall, and ceiling had been scrubbed. At first glance, the average onlooker would have had no idea what had occurred hours earlier.

In her mind's eye, she pictured Yokoyama's final moments. His screams in Japanese and the reek of his smoldering flesh would stick with her forever. State-of-the-art air filtration systems and buckets of bleach couldn't remove that stench from her mind. She knew the phantom smell wasn't real, but it was just as powerful as if it were.

Kate continued across the room to a station where Ellis and Ronnie were already working. They were huddled around a computer monitor, their bulky suits blocking the screen from view.

"Hey, Kate," Ellis said without turning. "Did you get some sleep?"

"Too much."

"Good, because I'm about to drop a bomb on you." He looked up from the monitor. "We already found a weakness. Ronnie, you want to explain?"

The technician stepped away from the computer to make room for Kate. "It's pretty simple. We ran panels of chemical analyses and exposed tissue samples to a broad range of radiation. Remember how the adults are sensitive to ultraviolet light?"

"Yes, of course," Kate replied.

"Well the juveniles seem to be extremely sensitive to gamma radiation. The ionized radiation tests revealed something remarkable. Watch this."

On-screen, a dime-sized sample of Lucy's flesh rattled and shook inside the radiation delivery machine. Within minutes, the sample began to hiss.

"I'm only using a few rads," Ronnie said.

Kate couldn't believe her eyes. That much radiation would have little short-term effect on a normal human, but it was cooking the sample right in front of them.

"Do we know if their armor will shield them?"

Ellis nodded. "It does to an extent, but not much."

Kate continued to study the screen. "Tests on the adult Variants have shown the exact opposite—a strong resilience against a wide range of radiation. So why are the offspring more sensitive?"

"You're right," Ellis said. "It doesn't make much sense."

"Well that's just the beginning. We found something else too." Ronnie looked at Ellis.

"I think I can now prove that the eggs aren't a self-destruct system," Ellis said.

Both men gave Kate meaningful looks—the type that told her they were about to give her some very bad news.

"Take a look," Ellis said. He punched at his keyboard and pulled up the results from a CT scan. An overlay of Lucy's vascular and glandular systems filled the computer screen. "We got the results back from the CT scan that we ran before the autopsy. Remember those glands that we pumped the contrast into? They weren't all glands, Kate."

She processed the development quickly. "It's connected to the venom, isn't it?"

Using a gloved finger, Ellis pointed to shadows. "I think what we thought were glands were, in some cases, the eggs holding the venom."

"They're all over Lucy's body," Ronnie added. "Her arms, legs, chest..."

"And what are those?" Kate asked. She ran her finger over a network of small tubes that connected to the shadows.

"I'm not sure," Ellis said.

"There's no way to know now that her corpse is so damaged," Ronnie said.

Kate's mind went into overdrive as she studied the images. For the first time in days, she felt like her old self. Her brain was functioning at the level it had before the outbreak. Her own theory quickly emerged. She wasn't an expert in reading CT scans, but she did recognize the darker tubes connecting to the pouches of venom.

"They were still growing," she said. "Do you see those?"

Ellis and Ronnie leaned in and followed her finger.

"I knew it," Ellis whispered. He turned to Kate, eyes wide with awe. "The venom is a weapon, but Lucy's delivery system wasn't fully functional. She was still growing…"

Kate was crossing the room before Ellis finished his thought. "Where are you going?" he shouted after her.

"To the CIC. We have to warn the strike teams heading to Colorado," Kate yelled back. "I have a feeling President Ringgold is going to want to hear this from me in person."

# 17

"Take care of my dog, Fitz!" Beckham hollered from the deck of the *GW*. He shielded his eyes from the sun with one hand and waved with the other. A crowd had gathered around him to watch the three Black Hawks and Chinook take off to Colorado.

"He takes care of me!" Fitz replied from inside one of the Black Hawks.

Apollo scuttled to the open door, nails dragging across the metal, eyes on Beckham as the Black Hawk ascended into the sky. Fitz grabbed the German shepherd's collar and pulled him back just as the dog leaped toward the door.

"It's okay, boy, we won't be gone long," Fitz said. Apollo sat on his hind legs, but his eyes didn't leave Beckham.

"Damn, loyal dog," Garcia muttered. He tilted his black helmet to get a final look at the *GW* strike group. The USS *Florida* surfaced below, its sail rising through the waves. Several figures climbed out of the hatch and looked up at the birds. Every sailor, civilian, and soldier on the vessels watched.

The human race was counting on a handful of soldiers to complete the next stage of Operation Extinction.

Fitz was right there in the thick of it with Apollo and a troop hold full of marines. It sure as hell didn't seem like enough, but this mission didn't require an army, only a small squad of well-trained, experienced men and women.

And that's exactly who Fitz had around him right now.

As the pilots changed course, Fitz got his first good look at the members of Strike Team Spartan, the name picked out by Lieutenant Davis.

Sunlight filled the troop hold, casting a warm glow across the men and women decked out with armor and weapons. Like the other soldiers, Fitz wore plates of dark impact armor that covered him from his thighs to his chin. It was lightweight and durable, yet strong enough to stop the claws of a Variant. Each plate locked or fastened together across all vital areas. Beneath the armor, he wore matte black fatigues that were already wet from his sweat. He cradled his helmet against his chest, avoiding the reflection in the mirrored visor. He'd rather look at Davis.

She slid her helmet over her shoulder-length red hair, pushing it down to obscure her green eyes and her sharp jawline. Reaching down, she flipped up the face guard so Fitz could see her lips.

But Davis still hadn't said a word. She was staring in the direction of the *GW*, the place she had made home for the past six weeks. Fitz didn't know much about her, but what he did know, he liked. She had pulled Meg out of that building and helped save innocent civilians.

To her right sat another impressive woman. Marine Staff Sergeant Jeni Rico had proven herself during Operation Liberty and was now called up again to fight on the front lines. No one complained about her non-regulation hair or the blue highlights frosting the tips. She'd *gone rogue*, to hear her tell it, right after the Variant threat emerged. And besides, Fitz thought, shit like regulation hairstyles didn't matter anymore. Even better, Rico's contagious smile and sense of humor were a welcome addition to the team.

The two marines sitting next to Garcia were Staff Sergeant Dan Murphy and Corporal Marcus Hoffman. They were both in their mid-thirties, although Fitz wouldn't have known it. Hoffman had more wrinkles and gray hair than most men his age. Murphy, on the other hand, looked as if he was in his twenties, with a clean-shaven face and big eyes. Both were well built, with defined muscles under their armor.

Unlike their team's ancient namesake, these Spartans wore all black. But like the warriors of ancient history, every man and woman aboard this chopper knew the brutality of war. Their helmets hid their haunted eyes and the high-tech armor covered their scars, but they were all, in their own ways, walking wounded.

Even after it's over, war has a way of changing people. Physical wounds heal with time and treatment, but the mental anguish is too often left to fester. It surfaces when you least expect it.

Everyone dealt with it differently, and some, Fitz knew, took the only way out they could see and ended the pain themselves. Fitz had even thought that might be how he'd go out. That was before Team Ghost had pulled him from Bragg and gotten him back in the game. He didn't think like that anymore. The ache was there still and probably always would be. But Fitz wasn't going to walk away from his life and his duty, and neither were the men and women with him now.

They all hurt, and they all licked their wounds in their own ways. Rico twisted her blue-frosted hair and chewed bubblegum. Davis stared stoically out the door at the water below. Garcia kept his head bowed in prayer. Fitz simply patted Apollo's head.

Three minutes out from the *GW* strike group, the pilots banked to the left and followed the other two Black Hawks. All three gracefully swooped into position to surround the Chinook and its precious cargo. Inside the bird were the finished cases of Kryptonite, resting in six-foot long containers that reminded Fitz of coffins. All Team Spartan had to do was load the weapon into missiles and hit the launch button.

When the *GW* strike group was a blot on the horizon, Davis patted her helmet to get everyone's attention. Then she crouch-walked to the center of the troop hold. Cracking her neck from side to side, she said, "Listen up. We have a little over six hours before we get to the target. I'm Spartan One on the comms; Fitz, you're Two; Garcia, Three; Rico, Four; Murphy, Five; and Hoffman, Six. We're meeting three other teams: Lightning, from Texas; Saber, from Oregon; and Wolverine, from Florida. Rendezvous time is 2000 hours, but it sounds as if we're going to be the last team there. The other three will have already secured the facility by the time we touch down."

"So what's our job?" Garcia asked.

Davis pointed at the Chinook that was now flying adjacent to their Black Hawk. Fitz followed her gaze.

"We guard what's in that bird," Davis said.

Fitz looked past the Chinook to one of the other Black Hawks in their group. He didn't know most of the marines onboard, but he recognized Sergeant Jack Lynch and Sergeant Bobby Adair. He'd heard they'd saved a lot of lives during Operation Liberty.

Garcia scooted forward in his seat, apparently unsatisfied with Davis's response. "LT, I'm assuming someone knows how to operate the Earthfall facility, right?"

Davis tipped her helmet to look him in the eye. "I've seen the specs; I know how the system works."

"Guess we better watch your ass then. I'm not good at reading instruction manuals, and we all know that's probably horseshit 'bout the area bein' Variant free. Last I checked, those freaks could camouflage their skin," Garcia said with a grin. The smile faded when he saw her reaction. "No disrespect meant by that, LT."

"The facility is dark. Nobody's on the comms, and recon runs show no signs of Variants or their offspring," Davis replied. "With that said, I'll be watching *your* ass once we land, Sergeant. No telling what's inside that building."

Rico chuckled and shifted the gum in her mouth to the other side.

That was good. It meant tensions weren't reaching a boiling point, as they had on so many other missions. Even Apollo was calm. He rested at the edge of Fitz's blades, muzzle on his front paws. The dog was in some obvious discomfort, shifting every few seconds, but he hid his pain well. Animals always did. Showing weakness made them targets to other predators.

"Hang in there, buddy," Fitz murmured.

Silence filled the troop hold for the next few hours. They stopped at a small military outpost fifteen minutes west of Chicago, one of the last safe zones the military had managed to cling to in the Midwest. Fitz quickly saw why: The post was protected on all sides by an electric fence. From the sky it looked like a massive Faraday cage. Guard towers surrounded the perimeter with mounted M134 Gatling guns and M260 rocket launchers.

"Hard to believe anyone's still alive all the way out here," Garcia said.

A skeleton crew of exhausted-looking soldiers fanned out onto the tarmac to refuel the convoy as the birds put down within the safety of the fences. A second group of men in battle armor jogged out after them. They surrounded an officer wearing a Chicago Cubs hat and tennis shoes.

Fitz had heard stories about this man over the past few weeks. Lieutenant Jim Flathman had made a name for himself by keeping the Variants at bay since the outbreak. He was a crazy son of a bitch who was known to break rules—probably one of the reasons he was still alive.

"Fitz, you're with me. Everyone else stay put and keep frosty," Davis ordered. She jumped onto the concrete and waited for Fitz to join her.

Rico, Murphy, and Hoffman remained at the door, weapons cradled across their chests. Everyone kept an eye on the woods outside the barrier of the fences. Garcia stayed in his seat, his scope pressed to his eye as he scanned the forest. Fitz wasn't the only one who had seen what the monsters could do to electrical fences. Every member of Team Spartan knew the feeling of safety at this place was nothing but an illusion.

"Welcome to Deadwood, Lieutenant," Flathman said, with a slight dip of his chin.

Davis returned the gesture. "Thanks for the juice." She looked over his shoulder at the cluster of three buildings in the distance. "Pretty remarkable that this place is still standing."

Fitz hung back, alternating his gaze from Flathman's guards to the fence and woods behind them.

Flathman pulled off his baseball cap to run a hand through cropped gray hair. "No shit. It's the Wild West out here, hence the name. When we aren't holding back Variants, we're fighting outlaws."

"I'm hoping to change that," Davis said. She jerked her chin toward the Chinook. "Kryptonite's going to kill the adult Variants."

Flathman eyed the convoy skeptically. "I just hope Command can figure out a way to kill the juveniles. They've been prowling the forest out there. It's just a matter of time before they attempt an attack."

Fitz kept his eye on the woods, occasionally glancing back at Garcia and Rico in the chopper. They hadn't let their guard down, and wouldn't the entire time as the birds were refueled.

Finally, the crew chief shouted that they were good to go.

Fitz checked the Black Hawks. Garcia and Rico were still on point, watching for any signs of Variant activity.

Flathman slipped his baseball cap back on. "I'd tell you to give 'em hell out there, but I already know you will. You got a reputation, Lieutenant."

Davis grinned. "Not as big as yours, sir." She jerked her chin at Fitz, and together they ran back to the chopper.

When the birds were airborne Fitz stood in the open door with the other members of Spartan, watching as Lieutenant Flathman and his tiny fort disappeared on the horizon. The forests and cities seemed to blend together as the convoy continued west.

Murphy and Hoffman remained at the door, glaring at the derelict cities below. Fitz had seen it all before, but mostly at night. Seeing it in the daylight was a new experience.

"Which city is that?" Hoffman shouted.

"Des Moines," one of the pilots replied.

"Iowa, right?" Murphy asked.

Hoffman nodded. "I had a cousin who lived there. Great place to raise a family."

"Not anymore," Fitz whispered to himself.

A brown skyscraper with gold windows sparkled in the sunlight. In the windows' reflection was a city dotted with decayed corpses. Tattered clothing flapped from bones that had been picked dry. Dark maroon streaks tattooed the streets where blood had been spilled weeks before. The rain still hadn't washed it all away.

Garcia made the sign of the cross over his armor. "Our father, who art in heaven, hallowed be thy name... Lead us not into temptation, but deliver us from evil."

Fitz said a mental prayer of his own.

"We did this, you know," Garcia said. "We're responsible for the end of the world."

"Duh," Rico said. She continued chomping her gum.

"We're also going to put things right," Davis said sternly from across the troop hold. She gave Fitz a meaningful look before turning back to the view. The convoy of choppers flew through the heart of the city.

"Think we'll ever build anything like that again?" Rico asked. She pointed toward a building cresting a hill in the distance. Its golden dome dazzled in the sun. The side of the building had a gaping hole from a rocket. The Iowa State Capitol was a reminder of the beautiful architecture humans were capable of creating—and also of tearing down.

"I saw Rome a couple years ago," Rico said. "It was crazy how some of their buildings have lasted thousands of years. The Colosseum and the Pantheon. And this harbor city, Ostia Antica." She cracked a mischievous grin. "Sometimes I wonder if Variants will be touring our cities like that."

"You're crazy, Rico," said Hoffman.

Her faced hardened, and she twisted a blue strand of hair with her gloved fingers. "That's why I'm here. That's why I'm fighting. To protect what we built."

Garcia rolled his eyes and turned away, but Fitz continued listening. He appreciated history, and she was right; it was worth fighting for. But first, they had to save the human race. Then they could think about rebuilding.

Maneuvering to the right, the pilots flew on the south side of the capitol. The building was surrounded by mounds of sandbags and concrete barriers. Tanks, Humvees, and armored trucks sat abandoned, bullet casings surrounding the vehicles on all sides. A battle had raged at the top of the hill, right below the golden dome. Bodies piled four and five high surrounded the barriers. Fitz wondered how long the soldiers had held back the Variants before they were overrun.

"Couple more hours," one of the pilots said. "Team Wolverine and Team Saber just stopped to refuel. Team Lightning is en route. We'll be there about thirty minutes after the other teams land."

Fitz rested his helmet on the bulkhead. Hopefully he could catch a few minutes of rest. The second he closed his eyes, thoughts of Meg invaded his mind. He tried to push them away, but an image of the Bone Collector picking Riley up by his neck replaced Meg's bloodstained face. Fitz couldn't shake the nightmarish scenes no matter what he did. The only way to keep his mind frosty was to stay active.

Moving over to the door, he crouched next to Murphy and Hoffman. The three marines stayed there for several minutes, studying the landscape below. There were no animals prowling the forests, no signs of even a single human. Fields that had once been meticulously plowed were now overgrown. Fruit lay rotting on the vine or stalk. Strands of withered grain waved back and forth like wisps of graying hair on an old man's head.

Fitz couldn't help but wonder if the weapon they carried was already too late.

"Listen up, everyone: I just got a message from Command," Davis said. "They said the juveniles may have a delivery system for their venom. The science team thinks the little bastards can *shoot* the stuff."

Garcia raised his shotgun. "Great—so if we do get close enough to kill one of 'em, we have to worry about that shit?"

"That's right," Davis replied. "We have no reason to believe there will be any juveniles in the target area, but if we do encounter them, use your M4s. Our new rounds are armor penetrating and should bring them down, but remember you have a limited supply."

"Got it, LT," Murphy said. The others all nodded, but Fitz simply stared ahead. He didn't have a shotgun anyway. He carried an M4 and his staple MK11. Shotguns were for hunting deer, not Variants.

The pilots changed course, directing the bird toward a wall of mountains lining the horizon. Jagged peaks covered in snow reached toward crimson-stained clouds that bulged across the sky like smoke from a raging fire. The stunning sunset signaled the beginning of the end. Somewhere out there, the other strike teams were preparing to land and enter the Earthfall facility.

They were almost there. In minutes, Fitz would be running on his new blades.

"All right, people. Final gear checks. Make sure you're frosty as fuck when we get out there," Davis said.

The lieutenant seemed different than the officer he'd observed on the *GW*. He found her demeanor oddly charming. She was respectful, intelligent, and supportive in front of her superiors. In the field, she was fearless and inspiring. And she clearly cared about her soldiers.

Fitz reached down to check the belts securing his new blades. They fit surprisingly well. He tightened the right strap and smiled at Davis. She winked back.

The troop hold came alive with the routine sounds of pre-combat checks. Magazines were slotted into weapons, bootlaces were pulled tight, and every piece of gear was checked, double-checked, and checked a final time. Fitz tightened Apollo's saddlebag and kissed him on the tuft of brown hair cresting his head.

Rico watched from a few feet away. She winked at Fitz, plucked out her gum and stuck it on the side of her helmet. Then she sat back and closed her eyes. Hoffman, Murphy, and Garcia continued going over their gear while Fitz turned to look at the landscape below.

The shadows of the choppers raced over open fields split by crystal-clear streams. Pine trees reached up at the birds, pointed tips swaying in the wind. A flash of motion commanded Fitz's attention to the edge of a forest. Blurs of white fur darted through the canopy of green.

Fitz hadn't seen a live animal for weeks. Recon reports indicated the Variants had killed almost everything outside the cities. Livestock that had survived the first few weeks of the outbreak were later slaughtered when their owners transformed into monsters.

"You see those?" Fitz asked. He angled the barrel of his MK11 toward the forest. "Whatever those things are, they must have been able to fight off the Variants."

"Could be deer," Davis said.

"Deer aren't white," Rico said.

Fitz moved to the door and zoomed in with his rifle. By the time he had centered the scope on the trees, the beasts had vanished.

"What the hell were those things?" Garcia asked.

Before anyone could reply, a transmission hissed in Fitz's earpiece. "Spartan One, this is Wolverine One. We've landed at..."

Fitz held the scope against his eye. Another creature darted in front of the cross hairs and vanished into the underbrush.

"Wolverine One, Spartan One, come again? Didn't catch your last. Over."

There was a surge of white noise. "Spartan One, Wolverine One. We're approaching the facility. What's your ETA?"

Davis pulled her hand away from her earpiece and moved to the cockpit. "How far out are we?"

"Thirty minutes," one of the pilots replied.

Davis relayed the info to the other three strike teams.

The bird jerked as the pilots twisted to the right. The shadows of the other Black Hawks and the Chinook rolled over the forest floor, darkening Fitz's view. He was lowering his rifle when he saw another streak of motion to the east. This time he had enough time to center the muzzle on the movement.

Apollo nudged up next to Fitz's left blade and barked at a pack of four wolves racing over the forest floor. The majestic creatures took Fitz's breath away. He'd never even seen a wolf before in the wild, and seeing them now defied everything he thought he knew.

Life was still out there.

"Holy shit, you see those?" Rico said. She wedged into the open doorway and pointed. Fitz followed her finger to the thickest pine trees in the north. She wasn't pointing to the wolves. She was looking at something a quarter mile ahead of them. The branches of the trees swayed back and forth as something big moved through the green canopy.

Wolverine One came back online as Fitz zoomed in for a better look. "Spartan One, we're preparing to enter the facility and going dark. See you soon. Over."

"Copy that. Good luck, Wolverine One. If you find any Variants, save a few for us. Over and out," Davis said. She scanned her marines individually. "All right, Spartans. Lock and load. When we hit the ground, I'll take point. Fitz, I want you and Apollo right behind me. Put that MK11 to good use. Rico, you're with us. Garcia, you take Murphy and Hoffman."

Fitz nodded, but he was still searching the trees for whatever prey the wolves were chasing. The muscular back of a Variant suddenly darted in front of his cross hairs.

"Holy shit," he muttered, nearly dropping his rifle.

"Forget the wolves," Davis said, glaring at him. "This isn't a fucking safari."

Sweat cascaded down Fitz's forehead. "LT," he said. "You better—"

Davis cut him off. "When we land, our priority is to help secure the facility. The other teams will guard our batch of Kryptonite."

"LT," Fitz repeated. He had centered his rifle back on the beast.

"What?" Davis said, frustration in her voice.

Fitz pointed, and every marine in the troop hold slowly worked their way to the door to stare. The wolves had closed the distance on the Variant by half now. Apollo watched attentively, his tongue hanging from his mouth.

"Just when I thought I've seen it all," Garcia said. He flipped his guard up to cover his face. The other marines followed suit, and one by one the Spartans secured their armor. Fitz reached down and patted Apollo on the head.

"On second thought, Fitz, let's see what you're made of," Davis said. "Take that monster down."

"With pleasure, LT," Fitz said. He chambered a round and drew in a breath as he zoomed in.

*Steady, Fitz. Steady.*

A flash of ropy muscle blurred in front of his cross hairs. The Variant leaped from branch to branch, trying to escape, but it was running out of room. The forest stopped at the rocky base of a mountain.

"Don't got all day, Fitz. We're almost there," Garcia said.

Fitz exhaled and took in a slow breath. The Variant leaped to another tree and climbed to the very top. It perched there like a bird, tilting its head at the chopper as if it had never seen one.

Crack!

An empty brass casing shot out of his MK11 a millisecond after the Variant's ripe face vanished in a spray of bone and blood. The body slumped over the side of the tree and skidded down the bark, crashing to the dirt below.

"Attaboy!" Garcia shouted.

"Holy fuck." Rico laughed.

The wolves tore into the corpse as the chopper flew overhead.

Fitz lowered his smoking rifle and held back his own grin. For once, he was heading into a mission without feeling like the underdog.

Kate had to wait over an hour to see President Ringgold. She had already met with several high-level officers to discuss her recent findings, but she wanted to talk to the president face-to-face.

The small room in the CIC where she paced back and forth was a mess. The bulkheads were covered in satellite imagery of cities and green night-vision images of Variant lairs. Several maps lay draped in a jumble over a single metal table. Red spots that could have been bloodstains marked the paper.

*How much longer are they going to make me wait?*

The slow burn of solitude ate away at Kate. It opened the door for every negative thought to come rushing back through.

She wasn't going to let that happen.

The trick was keeping her mind off the nightmares, and the images on the walls provided the perfect distraction. As the wall clock ticked, she studied the pictures and maps. There was an entire wall dedicated to different types of Variants: those with camel humps, others covered in fur, some with gills, and, of course, the Alphas. The Bone Collector was there, and so was the White King, but there were others she had never seen.

Kate stopped to examine a thin beast with green skin. Bulging yellow eyes stared back at the camera that had taken the photo. Jointed limbs with triangular forearms were held down by chains. The creature looked remarkably similar to a praying mantis.

According to the accompanying notes, this Alpha hailed from northern Japan. The beast had killed hundreds of Japanese soldiers before finally being captured. Instead of killing the monster, they had tortured him and sliced him into pieces.

The subsequent pictures were of that autopsy. Kate felt no empathy for the Alpha but was startled by the brutality of the Japanese soldiers. The war had reached the point of being one of attrition. She reminded herself that these men weren't the only ones who had tortured Variants. Dr. Yokoyama and his staff had done the exact same thing to Lieutenant Brett. And with the discovery of collaborators around the world, it was hard to keep faith in her species. The one thing she could count on was that there would always be men like Beckham, Horn, and Fitz, as well as women like President Ringgold and Lieutenant Davis, to fight those who would see the world destroyed.

Truthfully, nothing really shocked Kate anymore, but

the juveniles' venom came close. A message had already been transmitted to the strike teams on their way to Colorado, but Kate needed to explain in more detail how this would affect the final stage of Operation Extinction. If the offspring could fire venom that ate through CBRN suits, then flak jackets and helmets weren't going to do much for soldiers in the field.

"I hope this is very important, Doctor Lovato," said a female voice.

Kate expected to see Ringgold, but instead found Lieutenant Colonel Kramer in the entrance to the conference room, a laptop held against her hip. Several other officers followed her inside.

"Where's President Ringgold?" Kate asked.

"She's on her way. We've had pressing matters to deal with."

Kate stepped away from the maps as Kramer took a seat at the table. The woman opened her laptop, the glow illuminating her sharp eyes. She said nothing further to Kate, seeming to forget she was even there. Two soldiers, dressed in black and carrying shotguns, waited just outside the hatch. Kate wasn't sure why Kramer felt the need to march around the *GW* with her own personal armed guards, but it made her uneasy.

A few minutes later, Ringgold and Johnson entered the room. They both offered a smile as they sat, but Kate saw the worry in their features.

"Good evening, Doctor. My apologies for keeping you waiting," Ringgold said. "I'm told you have more information about the venom. Johnson and I got wind of it a few hours ago."

"More bad news, I'm afraid," Kate replied. "We've discovered the offspring may have a delivery system. What we first thought was a self-destruct system is potentially another weapon."

"Christ. What can't these things do?" Kramer asked.

Johnson laced his fingers together and placed his hands on the table. Knitting his brows together, he asked, "Are you absolutely sure?"

"Ninety-nine percent, sir."

Johnson shook his head. "So what does this mean, exactly?"

"It means that whatever you're planning for the final stage of Operation Extinction needs to account for more adaptations like this. We haven't even scratched the surface of what these things are capable of. Lucy was more than just an armored monster. She was able to show emotion and manipulate her captors. Remember when we said the Variants are the perfect killing machines? Well, think of the juveniles as a step above that."

"Another reason to nuke the bastards," Kramer muttered.

Johnson glared at her, but didn't reply. He focused on Kate. "So you're saying they could continue to change?"

"Absolutely. I would put money on it."

"We've already relayed this information to our strike teams and told them to be on the lookout if they encounter juveniles," Kramer said. "So I'm assuming there is something else you want to discuss, since we're all here."

Kate nodded. "There is."

"We're all ears," Ringgold said. She rested her arm in its sling on the edge of the table.

"We found a weakness—something that could work in our favor during the final stage of Operation Extinction."

That got everyone's attention. Several officers repositioned their chairs so they could get a better look at Kate. Kramer folded her arms across her chest and twisted her lips to the side skeptically.

"The juveniles are *extremely* sensitive to radiation. By

*sensitive*, I mean exposure that wouldn't affect a human would kill them. One hundred rads, for example, would not produce any symptoms in a human besides some blood changes. Up that to two hundred over a short period of time, and the human body could suffer from acute radiation syndrome. Anything above two hundred is where we would start to have serious illness."

Kramer scooted closer to the table and stiffened her back, more attentive now. "How many rads do we need to kill a juvenile?"

"Only one hundred. Maybe even less," Kate replied.

Johnson unlaced his fingers and looked at a bald general at the end of the table. "General Kohl, what about that program a few years back? Radiation weaponry, right?"

Kohl stroked his mustache. "Yes, sir, but it wasn't fully funded. Congress got wind of it and decided to shut it down. Some spineless senator from Montana said it was no different than biological or chemical weapons. Hell, what was his name?"

"Senator Bradley," Kramer recalled. "He argued that it broke the Geneva conventions."

"Great," Johnson said. "What else do we have to work with?"

Kate looked at Kramer, expecting the woman to mention their nuclear arsenal, but she said nothing.

"I'll look into it," Kohl said.

"Very good," Johnson replied. "Is there anything else, Doctor?"

Kate shook her head.

"Keep up the good work," Ringgold said.

Kate remained seated as the room emptied. She stared at the map on the table in front of her and traced her finger over the smooth surface. The boot of Italy was marked with red. Rome, Venice, Florence, Naples—they were all covered with the bloody ink that webbed out to surrounding cities.

Her parents had taken her to Naples when she was a child. She would never forget that vacation, or the look on her dad's face when she pulled a chemistry book out of her bag on the beach.

*You're going to make a good scientist someday, Katherine,* he had said.

How she longed to hear his deep voice again. He was the only man on Earth who always referred to her by her birth name.

"Doctor," said a voice from the door.

Kate had been so focused on the map that she hadn't noticed Ringgold had stayed behind after the meeting.

"Mind if I join you?"

"Please." Kate stood and gestured toward the chair next to hers. The president made her way across the room in what felt like slow motion. Maybe it was the lighting, or perhaps Ringgold's injury, but the president looked ten years older.

She sat next to Kate and cradled her sling with her good hand.

"I need to know something, Kate, and I want your honest opinion. Don't sugarcoat your response. Okay?"

Kate felt her insides tighten. She nodded and held the president's gaze.

"Do you think we can defeat the juveniles with bullets and bombs?"

The question caught Kate off guard. She hesitated, her jaw opening but no words forming. A mental image of a Black Hawk landing in DC and disgorging Team Ghost unnerved her. She could picture the armored offspring surrounding Beckham and his men.

"I said what I thought our men and women need to

hear earlier," Ringgold said. "That's the role of a politician sometimes. In the face of such daunting odds, we must remain strong. We must have hope; otherwise we will fail."

In Kate's imagination, the battle against the offspring raged. Beckham and Horn were back to back, firing their rifles at the advancing beasts.

"I really need your scientific opinion," Ringgold said. "If I'm sending our soldiers to their deaths, then I will reevaluate the final stage of Operation Extinction."

A wall of armored flesh closed in on Beckham and Horn in Kate's mind. Fitz was tossed to the ground, his helmet flying off and tumbling away. He was pulled by his blades into the horde. Beckham and Horn ran after him, their weapons blazing.

"Kate?"

The sound of the president's voice pulled Kate from the awful images.

"I'm sorry, Madam President."

"For what?"

Kate wasn't sure how to reply. She wasn't sure what she was apologizing for—not replying right away, or the fact she didn't think it was possible to defeat the offspring with conventional weapons.

She didn't need to reply. Ringgold leaned away, her features hardening with understanding.

"I was afraid you felt this way," Ringgold said. She bowed her head and pressed her lips together. "If you have any better ideas, Doctor, I'm open to hearing them."

Kate shook her head. "I'd love nothing better than to find a way to save our soldiers from the nightmare that awaits them in the cities. Sending Reed and his men back out there hurts more than you know. But I've done everything I can at this point. There's no scientific answer. We're simply out of time."

# 18

Fitz was still high on adrenaline from his kill shot. He never took pleasure from his job when his targets were other human beings, and even now he wouldn't call what he felt *good*. But it was better than the place he'd been after losing Meg and Riley.

As dusk settled over the Rockies, their jagged white tips swallowed the fiery glow of a radiant sunset on the horizon. The Black Hawk carrying Team Spartan raced toward the receding sunlight. From a distance, the Earthfall facility didn't look like much. Most secret facilities didn't. Some were disguised with other structures built over the top, like The Greenbrier in West Virginia. Others were constructed on remote islands or under deserts. Then there were places like this.

A groove three football fields long had been carved into the western edge of the mountain. Peaks towered thousands of feet above an airfield and a single concrete building. Walls of boulders created a natural barrier on the western and southern edges of the terrain. From above, it looked like a miniature high-altitude airport. Anyone flying over the top probably wouldn't think twice about it.

Fitz sucked in a breath of cold air that burned his

lungs and scanned the area with his MK11 as the pilots circled. Patches of snow dotted the brown landscape. Several spindly trees grew out of the gray rocks. A dozen idle helicopters dotted the airfield.

"Where the hell are the other three teams?" Rico shouted. She plucked the bubblegum off her helmet and jammed it back into her mouth, then turned from the open door and looked toward Davis.

Fitz zoomed in on the choppers. Rico had taken the words from his mouth. There was no sign of the soldiers or pilots from the other strike teams in the dim light of the vanishing sunset.

Davis narrowed her brows and stepped closer to Fitz.

"No one's guarding those Chinooks," she said.

Fitz roved his rifle to one of the massive birds. Sure enough, there wasn't a single sentry on duty. He moved his gun to the cockpit, seeing no movement through the windshield.

"Wolverine One, Lightning One, Saber One, do you copy? Over," Davis said on the open channel.

Static hissed into Fitz's ears.

"Does *anyone* copy out there?"

Rico blew a pink bubble and shook her head. "Must still be inside, LT."

"No," Davis said. "Orders were clear. Wolverine would secure the facility while Lightning and Saber guarded the Kryptonite."

Garcia elbowed Fitz in the arm. "You see any sign of Lighting and Saber?"

Fitz zoomed in on the four-story structure. It was devoid of windows, and the only entrances appeared to be sets of double doors on the south and north sides. Both were sealed shut. No marines were standing guard, nor were there signs of the teams returning for the Kryptonite.

"No sign, Sergeant," Fitz replied.

Garcia shook his head. "I don't like this, LT. I got a bad fucking feeling in my guts."

"How could everyone just disappear in half an hour?" Rico asked. "We didn't even hear anything on the comms."

"I'm not sure, but we're going to find out." Davis turned to the cockpit. "Put us down on the south side of the airfield."

The other Black Hawks and the Chinook from the *GW* convoy rolled to the right. Grass whipped back and forth around the base of a patch of stiltlike pine trees whose branches swayed violently in the gusts. Fitz crouch-walked to the other side of the troop hold as the pilots touched down next to the Chinook.

"Go, go, go!" came shouts from the other birds.

The thrill of pre-combat rushed through Fitz, but he remained in the doorway with Apollo to take in his surroundings.

He drew in another cold breath to test it for the sour scent of the Variants. He sensed nothing but the clean, alpine hint of pine needles. He scoped the terrain a fourth time, scanning for bodies or blood.

*Nothing.*

The marines from the other two Black Hawks and the Chinook piled onto the airfield. Davis started shouting orders the moment her boots hit the ground. "Sergeant Adair and Sergeant Lynch, secure that Chinook. Guard the Kryptonite with your lives."

The two marines waved their men over to the big black bird. Amber from the fleeting sunlight reflected off their black armor as they ran.

"Fitz, you afraid to use those or what?" Davis asked.

Still standing in the open doorway, he followed her gaze toward his blades. That kicked him into gear. He whistled to Apollo and jumped onto the snow with a crunch. The bottom of his blades sank a few inches into the soft powder. The German shepherd joined him on the ground.

Fitz flexed his thighs for a moment before bolting after Davis. She was already running across the airfield toward the other birds. Garcia, Rico, Murphy, and Hoffman fell into line behind them, each shouldering their M4s and sweeping muzzles over the terrain for contacts.

With every step closer, Fitz expected to see a mangled human corpse. But there wasn't a single streak of red, nothing to indicate a battle had occurred. It was as if the other three teams had vanished into thin air.

"Radio discipline from here on out," Davis said.

Fitz quickly caught up with the lieutenant. His nimble new blades were much lighter than his old pair. Even Apollo was having a hard time keeping up.

*I could get used to this,* he thought.

Davis held up a hand as the team approached the idle choppers. She then flashed Fitz an advance signal toward the first of the abandoned Black Hawks. He slung his MK11 over his back and pulled his M4. There was just enough light that he didn't need his night-vision goggles to see the blood dripping from the bottom of the left cockpit door. Slightly ajar, it creaked in the cold wind.

He raised his rifle at the window, his finger hovering over the trigger. The dripping blood pooled on the snow. Apollo let out a low growl, fur trembling. Fitz gestured for the dog to get behind him. Taking his left hand off his M4, he put the butt of his weapon into the crook of his right arm. Slowly, he reached for the door handle.

He swung the door open to an empty cockpit. An upside-down helmet sat on the pilot seat. Chunks of gore streaked down the visor, as if the pilot's skull had detonated inside. He grabbed it and held it up so Davis could see from her location.

She pivoted slightly. It was a subtle movement, but Fitz noticed she was nervous as she flashed an order to Garcia. They moved side by side toward the troop hold with weapons raised.

Fitz placed the helmet back on the seat and took in a breath that held a trace of sour, rotting lemons. Apollo smelled it too. His wet nose was working in overdrive, and his tail dropped between his legs.

That was his tell. The Variants had been here.

So why hadn't the soldiers fought back? There wasn't a single empty shell casing. None of it made any sense.

Fitz, Davis, and Garcia returned to Team Spartan. Rico chewed her gum nervously. "I'm officially creeped the fuck out," she said.

"Me too," Murphy said. "Marines don't just disappear without a fight."

Davis paused to think. She checked the Chinook on the south side of the airfield. Lynch and Adair paced back and forth beside it.

"Let's keep moving. We have a mission to complete," Davis said. "Garcia, you and Murphy take those choppers on the left. Rico, you and Hoffman got the right side. Fitz, on me."

Team Spartan examined the final birds lining the airfield slowly. Fitz and Davis cleared each to the same sight—empty cockpits and troop holds. The closer they got to the building, the more agitated Apollo became. His tail dropped farther between his legs and he bared his teeth.

Davis paused at the next bird and said, "Saber One, this is Spartan One. Does anyone copy? Over."

Fitz opened the door to the cockpit and climbed inside. Besides the wrapper from an energy bar, the seats were clean.

No blood. No bullet casings. No footprints in the snow.

"Yo, LT, you better see this," Garcia said over the comm channel.

Fitz spotted the marine through the windshield. He stood with Murphy outside the open door of a Chinook to the west. Davis waved at Fitz, and he jumped back to the snowy ground.

This time Apollo didn't budge. He stood staring at the rocky barrier to the east. His ears pricked just before Fitz heard the guttural howl. It grew into a booming screech that echoed off the rocky peaks.

The dog growled back, fur trembling. Fitz followed Apollo's gaze across the shadowy rock outcroppings. The reverberating screech was only vaguely reminiscent of a typical Variant—it sounded like a cross between a grizzly bear and an enraged human. Whatever was making the high-pitched howl was a beast Fitz had never seen.

Rico raked her M4 in all directions. "What the hell *is* that?"

"Adair, Lynch, you got eyes?" Davis asked.

"Negative, LT."

The howl ended, and with it went the final rays of sunlight. Darkness consumed the mountain.

"Everyone switch to NVGs," Davis ordered.

Fitz flipped his into position, then took off running after her. This time he had a hard time keeping up. In the green hue of his NVGs, Fitz scrutinized the Chinook. He prepared himself for a grisly discovery, but when he reached the bird, he saw nothing but the empty interior of a troop hold.

"What's the problem? I don't see anything," Rico said.

Davis lowered her rifle and turned to look at the building a few hundred feet away.

"That *is* the problem," Garcia said.

"The other strike teams aren't the only things missing,"

Davis said. She kicked at the snow. "The Kryptonite is missing too."

Beckham couldn't believe his eyes.

A soldier holding an IV pole and covered in bandages was walking toward him down the aisle of injured soldiers in beds. If it weren't for the strands of black hair hanging over the man's slashed face, Beckham wouldn't have known it was Chow.

"What are you doing out of bed, brother?" Beckham asked.

"Making the rounds, boss. Can't sit all day or I'm going to lose my muscles."

There was a reason the other men used to refer to Chow as Bruce Lee. He had the same physique as the late martial-arts legend, and he knew about as many moves.

Beckham shook his head. "You're also going to tear your stitches."

"Nah, I'm good. I told you I'd be on my feet in no time." The sutures that ran from Chow's lip to his right eyebrow tightened every time his jaw moved. Beckham gritted his teeth, feeling his friend's pain. He would have taken it from him if he could.

"I'm hopped up on so many drugs I can hardly even feel my dick," Chow said. "And trust me, I would know it if I did. There are some nurses that are hot as—"

Chow grabbed the IV pole again and stepped to the side at the sound of footfalls. Beckham backed up a step too, making room for a pair of doctors rushing down the narrow aisle. He moved to Chow's side, and together they watched as a soldier on a gurney was wheeled out of the room and into surgery. The hatch sealed shut behind the trio. The metal thud echoed through the enclosed space.

The silence that followed made Beckham want to say something, but instead he found himself praying for the soldier who was going under the knife.

Chow broke the silence with a question Beckham had been dreading.

"Meg's gone?" Chow's voice was serious now; he had hardened back into a Delta Force operator.

"She made it back from New York, but..." Beckham paused, then found Chow's gaze. "She died on the operating table."

"I'm sorry. She was a tough chick." Chow tightened his grip on the IV pole as if it was a weapon. They were silent several more moments before he started pulling it down the aisle. "Come on, I want to check on Tank. He just got out of surgery a few hours ago."

It was almost more stressful waiting around with nothing to do but worry. Fitz and Apollo were in Colorado, and Kate was working in the lab. What the hell was he doing?

Helping the injured was honorable, but he wasn't hurt. He could fight.

He *ached* to fight.

The itch crept up so fast he didn't even recognize it at first. It was a messy, addictive feeling that brought with it a rush of adrenaline.

Heart pounding, Beckham approached Tank's bedside, still fighting the urge to run above decks and board a chopper to join Fitz. But it was too late for that. All he could do right now was prepare for the next battle.

The *final* battle.

"You hear anything 'bout Sarge yet?" asked a deep voice. Tank struggled to sit up in a bed that was way too small for him. He traced a finger around a patch covering his right eye.

"Not yet," Beckham replied. He looked at his wristwatch.

"Should hear something soon. They ought to have arrived at the Earthfall facility by now."

Tank swung his legs over the side of his bed, grumbling. "I should fucking be there. This is bullshit."

"Me too," Chow said.

At first Beckham thought they were joking. But looking at them, he saw they too would hop on a chopper in a second if they could.

"We'll all have our chance again," Beckham said. "Very soon."

"I'm ready," Chow and Tank said at the same time.

There was no time to share a laugh. A voice called Beckham's name. "Boss."

Horn was walking down the aisle, his shoulders sagging. Beckham's heart dropped when he saw a man dressed in blue lab scrubs and an apron covered in blood behind him. Horn stopped and put his left hand on Beckham's shoulder.

"They brought the kid back from Plum Island," he said softly. Horn held out his right hand to reveal a pair of dog tags.

Chow looked at the floor.

"I figured you'd want to see him one last time before the ceremony," Horn said.

Beckham took the tags. The cold metal made his gut sink. He closed his eyes and remembered Riley's blue eyes and contagious smile. For a fleeting moment, Beckham couldn't think of anything other than the collection of dog tags in his quarters. He had a feeling that, before the war was over, he would be adding more.

# 19

Davis wasn't sure what to make of it. There was no sign of Teams Wolverine, Saber, or Lightning. That was more than fifty marines and support staff who had vanished into thin air. The only evidence they had even landed were the birds and a single bloody helmet.

There was something that bothered her even more than the missing army—the sensation of eyes on her back, no matter which way she turned. Every time she checked the steep mountain slope to the northeast, she saw nothing but powder and jagged rocks.

The howl they'd heard earlier hadn't been repeated, but that didn't relieve the slimy feeling of being watched. It was starting to eat at her. The thin air made things worse. She was light-headed and nervous as hell. What if the other teams were already dead? What if she was the only one left who knew how to operate the Earthfall facility?

*Shit just got real. So much for an easy in and out.*

A gust of wind bit into Davis's side. The cold air whistled across her armor and kicked up snow at her feet. The wind was growing stronger. She tensed every time she heard it, the same defensive reaction her body made when she saw a Variant. The sudden hiss of static in her ear made her flinch.

"Spartan One, Command, do you copy? Over."

Davis flipped up her face guard and pushed the mini-mic closer to her lips. The damn armor stifled her voice, and she wanted to be very clear in her reply.

"Roger that, Command, this is Spartan One."

A familiar voice spiked over the channel. It was Captain Humphrey, and he was breaking mission protocol.

"Davis, what is going on there? Wolverine, Saber, and Lightning are dark."

"We're not sure, sir. We lost contact with the strike teams approximately thirty minutes ago, sir."

"What the *hell* happened? We have no video feed, no radio transmissions. They just vanished. Something scrambled the network moments after they landed."

Davis scanned the airfield again. If that were true, why was she able to communicate with Command?

"Sir, we're not sure what happened," Davis said. "Last we heard, Wolverine was preparing to enter the facility, but when we landed, all the strike teams were gone. And so is their Kryptonite."

There was a pause that filled the channel with white noise. It lasted several agonizing seconds as Humphrey no doubt consulted with his team aboard the *GW*. Davis used the stolen moment to scrutinize her own team. It was hard to see their features with their NVGs covering most of their faces, but there were small tells that betrayed their nerves. Murphy and Hoffman both flung repeated glances over their shoulders. Rico blew her bubblegum behind her face guard. Fitz and Garcia were the only frosty ones of the bunch. Both men scanned the terrain with their rifles, breath and hands steady.

Humphrey's voice, proud and stern, fired back over the channel. "Your orders just changed, Lieutenant. Find the other batches of Kryptonite. Secure that facility and launch the weapon."

"Understood, sir." She made her voice as confident as possible, but there was no hiding the hint of fear in it. The proud side of her wanted to leave it at that, but the logical side needed to ask, "What about reinforcements, sir?"

There was another pause over the channel.

"There isn't any backup within a hundred-mile radius. If you fail, we will have to retake the facility, but that will further delay the deployment of Kryptonite." Humphrey said. "We're counting on your team, Lieutenant."

In the past, the words might have made Davis's gut churn.

Not today.

She had promised herself a long time ago that she would not let her husband and nephew die in vain. There were survivors out there like those she had helped save from New York. She hadn't been able to save Blake or Ollie, but she could still save others.

She *had* to.

"Roger that, Captain," Davis said. "You can count on us."

Another voice that Davis didn't immediately recognize filled the net. "Lieutenant, this is President Ringgold."

"Oh, uh, hello, ma'am," she said, taken off guard.

"I'm not going to remind you how important this mission is. Captain Humphrey has already made that quite clear. What I will say is that I have the utmost faith in you. I've been watching you, and what you did in New York took guts. I have faith you will finish the work we started. Good luck, Lieutenant."

"Thank you, Madam President," Davis replied. "We won't let you down."

Each member of Team Spartan nodded at Davis to say they were ready. They had all heard Ringgold's words, and they were all prepared to give their lives to ensure the survival of their species.

"Lynch, Adair, you see anything back there?" Davis asked.

"Nothing, LT. All clear," Adair replied. "We'll keep our Kryptonite safe."

Davis glanced back at the team one more time. "Roger that. Stay sharp. We're heading into the facility. Stand by."

Fitz and Apollo pivoted toward the building with the rest of Team Spartan.

Slinging her M4 across her back, Davis pulled out a map of the facility. This wasn't supposed to be their mission, but all the team leads had been handed blueprints back on the *GW*. She studied it for a moment to double-check she had it memorized.

"Fitz, watch our back. The rest of you, huddle around."

Rico, Murphy, Hoffman, and Garcia crouched next to her.

"All right, listen up. Kryptonite and the other soldiers *have* to be inside the structure. My guess is someone went rogue or there was a collaborator in the group. That's the only theory that makes sense. They took the other marines prisoner, stole the Kryptonite, and went inside."

"I was thinking the same thing," Garcia said. "I bet that pilot got his brains blown out when he tried to take off."

"Apollo senses Variants," Fitz said. "I know it doesn't make sense, but that howl we heard came from a beast, not a collaborator."

Davis paused to look at her team. "Whatever happened, we have to deal with it. This is *our* job now—our mission. Once we enter the building, we proceed into this stairwell. It leads fifteen floors down to an open command center. From there, there are two access doors, here and here," Davis said, pointing. "Those directly connect to the tunnels that launch the Earthfall missiles. Once we secure the building and find the Kryptonite, I'll order Lynch and Adair to bring our supply into the facility."

Garcia stood and looked at the building. "What do we do if the other batches of Kryptonite aren't inside?" Garcia asked.

Davis swept her arm in a wide arc. "Where else could it be? We cleared every chopper. Unless our missing strike teams just walked over the ledge to their deaths, they have to be inside that building."

The whistle of the wind was the only reply.

Davis stood, put her map back into her vest, and unslung her M4. "Let's get it done, marines." It was time to stop talking and lead—no matter what waited inside the Earthfall facility.

As she fell into a steady jog, she tried to picture what things looked like inside. But the longer she ran, the less she could seem to imagine the stairwell and command room. Instead, flashes of the missing strike teams filled her thoughts. She could picture human collaborators marching marines toward a hungry pack of Variants waiting in the basement. In her mind, the beasts were stringing prisoners onto walls and ceilings. Others were torn apart by talons and maws rimmed with needle teeth. If that's what they were heading into...

*I have the utmost faith in you.*

Remembering the president's words, Davis swallowed her fear and waved her team forward. They crossed the final stretch of airfield with Apollo out in front. He sniffed the air all the way to the double doors. Then he bent down and scooped something up into his mouth.

Fitz crouched next to the dog's side and whispered, "Whatcha got, boy?"

Apollo looked up with a thick twig in his mouth. He pulled away when Fitz went to grab it from him.

The wind screamed through the jagged peaks, a deep shrieking sound that made Davis shiver. She looked up at the green hue of the silhouetted mountain. Snow drifted across the rocks and vanished into the sky. To the north-east, an elongated rock formation that reminded her of the vertebrae of some prehistoric monster rose toward the skyline. The entire side of the mountain was covered in similar outcroppings.

*Perfect place for Variants or collaborators to hide.*

At this point, she didn't believe a damn thing Command had said. The recon runs had revealed no sign of Variants, but something was watching her team.

*Just because you can't see it doesn't mean it's not there.*

The words from her days at West Point echoed in her mind. Davis flipped up her night-vision goggles and squinted with naked eyes. The rising moon had penetrated the clouds. Another blast of wind swirled across the serrated rocks. Somewhere out there, something was watching and waiting.

Behind her, the sound of crunching boots broke her concentration.

It was Garcia. He stepped up to her side and followed her gaze to the northeast. "You see something, LT?"

Another blast of wind bit into Davis. The icy gust stung her eyes. She shook her head, flipped her NVGs into position, and motioned for Garcia to move to the double doors.

"Drop it, Apollo," Fitz whispered.

The dog reluctantly spit the stick onto the snow. Fitz held it up and studied it in the moonlight while Davis took up position behind Garcia. She handed him the key card for the building.

"Get ready, Fitz," Davis said.

Rico, Murphy, and Hoffman fell into line behind them. Davis could see and feel their tension. It came in puffs of icy breath that rose from the nostril slits in their armor like cigarette smoke. Hoffman's labored breathing rattled in his chest. He had been holding in a cough since they were in the chopper.

"LT," Fitz said. "Take a look at this." He handed her the branch Apollo had picked up. But in the moonlight she saw it wasn't a stick at all.

It was a talon. The largest she'd ever seen. If it weren't for the scaly exterior, it could have been from a grizzly bear.

She dropped it back into the snow, unwilling to hold on to it any longer. "Changes nothing. We still have a mission."

"Thought Command said there aren't supposed to be any Variants out here. Recon came back with nothing, right?" Garcia said in a deliberately soft voice.

Davis rolled her eyes. "You really still believe that, Sergeant?"

"Then what the fuck are we doing here with just one squad?"

"We're supposed to be more than one squad, remember?" Davis said.

Garcia shrugged, then pressed the key card against a rectangular control panel to the right of the door. The glass surface flared red. He pushed the card against the panel a second time.

Davis stepped forward and reached for the card. "Let me."

Each time she waved the card over the panel, it turned red.

"LT," Fitz said.

She continued a fourth and fifth time, growing more frustrated with each swipe.

"Lieutenant Davis," Fitz said, louder this time.

"What, Fitz?" She turned and followed his finger toward a video camera that was angled down on them.

She didn't see anything unusual about the device—until it twisted in her direction. A red light on it blinked, and the lens zoomed in and out.

"Someone's watching us," Fitz whispered.

The slimy feeling from before paralyzed Davis. She staggered backward and motioned for her team to retreat from the door. They raked their weapons over the terrain, from the helicopters to the mountain towering over them.

The howling wind rose to a high-pitched screech that sounded almost like a Variant. Davis searched the jagged rock formations for movement.

*Nothing*...

A rising panic filled Davis. She was used to fighting the monsters head-on, as she had in New York. Variants didn't stalk their prey; they charged. That was what the beasts did. Especially when they were hungry.

Davis had just raised a hand to signal to her team when a gunshot echoed from the peaks above. The blast echoed, making it impossible to pinpoint.

"Man down!" Garcia shouted.

Murphy slumped to his knees, the gaping hole in the middle of his chest armor gushing blood. He choked and fell forward into the snow.

"Ambush!" Davis shouted. "Fall back!" She considered grabbing Murphy and pulling him to safety, but he was already beyond saving. The sheer amount of blood pooling around his body left no question.

Another gunshot rang out, biting into the concrete beside Davis's head. The shrapnel pinged off her helmet. She dove for the ground as two more shots ricocheted above her.

"Eyes? Does anyone have eyes?" Rico shouted. She ducked just as another shot hit the wall where her head had been a second earlier.

Team Spartan scattered for cover. Hoffman ran for the airfield while Rico, Garcia, Fitz, and Apollo bolted for the western side of the building.

Chatter from M4s broke out from the south; Lynch and Adair were opening fire on targets Davis couldn't see. An M240 joined the fight a moment later.

"Multiple contacts!" Adair reported.

"Form a perimeter around the Kryptonite," Davis replied, in the calmest voice she could manage.

The crack from a high-caliber rifle sounded from the northeast. Davis followed a shot streak away from the bluffs.

"Fitz! Two o'clock!" she shouted.

She took a knee and aimed her M4 at the tower of gray rocks just as Hoffman crashed to the ground ten feet from the nearest Black Hawk. Davis looked over to him, but kept her muzzle on the rocks. The marine squirmed on the ground, pressing a hand over his right thigh.

"Hold on, Hoffman!" Davis yelled. She pressed the scope back to her NVGs and centered her cross hairs on the rocky outcropping. The flash of a muzzle illuminated a face in the shadow of a parka's hood. The sniper fired off another round of shots. Two of them punched into the ground around Davis, kicking up dirt and snow. She scrambled for the cover of the building. Another shot silenced Hoffman's screams.

She pushed herself to her feet, raised her rifle, and squeezed off three shots toward the sniper.

Crack!

The reassuring suppressed crack of Fitz's MK11 echoed off the concrete walls around her, yet the sniper continued firing. *How?* Fitz never missed a shot.

Davis resisted the urge to twist to search for Fitz when the same guttural howl from earlier filled the night. She froze in place to search for the source.

The muzzle flashes continued from the northeast, lighting up rock after rock. The sniper was on the move. Davis squeezed off three of her own shots, two of them punching into the serrated formations.

"Fitz! Where are you?" Davis shouted.

Rico and Garcia were firing now too.

"Head shots!" Garcia shouted.

"Watch out!" Rico yelled back.

The deep growl of a beast Davis couldn't see reverberated off the peaks. She gritted her teeth and zoned out the noise to focus on the sniper. Team Spartan was only going to get one chance at this, and a single mistake would put the future of the human race in jeopardy. That was the type of pressure that could make a man's heart pound.

But Davis wasn't a man. And she was ready to give her life to complete this mission.

Another booming screech filled the night, rising into a furious harmony that hurt Davis's ears. Apollo's barks and a slew of gunfire followed.

*What the hell is making that sound?*

Davis made the mistake of twisting to look. The bullet punched through her armor and cut through flesh with such power it took her breath. She fell to her left knee and aimed her rifle, furious at herself and the bastard killing her team. In her cross hairs, she saw the bearded face of a sniper. He closed his right eye, lining up his next shot, at the same second she fired three of her own.

His muzzle flashed as blood blossomed around the hole in his forehead where one of those three shots hit him. The one round he managed to squeeze off streaked toward her. The millisecond that passed before the shot pinged off the top of her helmet wasn't nearly enough time to move or even blink, but plenty to understand she had almost lost the insides of her skull.

The force of the round knocked her NVGs off and spun her helmet sideways. She crashed to her back still holding her rifle, head pounding, stars dancing before her vision.

But all this meant she was still alive.

The high-pitched howl of the monster snapped her back to reality. Fighting the blinding pain, Davis craned her neck for a view of the battle. A figure draped in shadow towered above Rico.

The creature lumbered into the white light cast by the crescent moon overhead. In the glow stood a naked beast covered in silvery fur. A narrow torso connected to barreled chest muscles covered in black hair.

The Variant tilted a massive head toward Davis, narrowing ycllow, slitted eyes. Rico wasted the opportunity to escape, reaching for her side arm instead.

"Move!" Davis managed to shout.

As Rico raised her M9, the creature slashed at her with claws tipped with the same talons Apollo had discovered. The nails knocked away her gun and sent her skidding into the wall of the building.

Davis blinked, and in the next moment took in the entire landscape. Garcia was lying facedown on the ground a few feet away from Fitz. The marine dragged his new blades as he crawled for his MK11, sticking out of the snow just out of reach.

Flipping to her stomach, Davis raised her M4 and held down the trigger. Two shots punched into the beast's upper chest before her magazine went dry. The monster roared in anger, bulging lips opening to reveal a maw studded with four massive canines. Saliva webbed between the barbed teeth.

Apollo latched onto the Alpha's leg from the side. He kicked the dog away with a quick blow to the ribs.

"No!" Fitz shouted.

The German shepherd landed in the snow close to Garcia, turning tail over snout before jumping back to all fours. Apollo let out a low whine that rose into a growl.

"Over here, you ugly son of a bitch!" Fitz shouted. He unslung his M4 and fired a burst into the creature's bulging arm.

Davis reached for another magazine as the Alpha hunched his back and barreled toward Fitz. She slammed it home the same second he bulldozed into the marine's side.

Fitz was launched three feet into the air. He came crashing back down on his side, letting out an *oof* that Davis could hear over the chatter of gunshots.

Apollo rushed to his aid, standing between man and monster, teeth bared. The Alpha dropped to all fours and moved forward, stopping inches from the dog's face. Opening his mouth, he let out a roar that peppered Apollo's muzzle with saliva. The dog's tail dropped between his legs, but he held his ground, barking furiously.

"Fitz, get down!" Davis shouted.

She waited for a shot, but Fitz was in the way. He struggled to push himself up, then fell back to his stomach. In that moment, she fired off a round that lanced into the beast's thick back. The Alpha rose on two feet and clawed at the wound, yelping in pain.

"Contacts! We got multiple contacts!" Adair shouted over the comms. "Can't hold them back for long!"

Gunfire and the shrieks of Variants rose into a macabre chorus that drowned out the transmission. Davis ignored everything but the Alpha. The monster was on the run now, galloping away toward the western ridgeline. She fired off a dozen more shots, but the beast was fast and using the protection of rocky outcroppings. By the time Davis finished her magazine, he was gone.

"Damn," she muttered, reaching for a fresh mag.

"We have to move, LT!" Garcia shouted. He was back on his feet, but had a hand clamped on his helmet as if he were still dazed.

"What...the fuck...was that thing?" Rico gasped. She pushed herself up and grabbed her rifle.

Davis rushed over to Fitz. He was on his knees, clutching his side with one hand and checking Apollo with his other. Garcia met her there. Together, they helped Fitz to his feet.

The gunfire intensified behind them.

Davis turned to the south, looking past Murphy and Hoffman's corpses to the Chinook holding their batch of Kryptonite. Lynch and Adair were retreating toward their Black Hawks, firing on the move. An M240 blazed from the right shoulder window of the Chinook at shadows flashing across the tarmac. Davis could see the shadows belonged to furry abominations advancing on all fours. There were dozens of them. Maybe more.

"Lynch, Adair, get our Kryptonite out of here!" she ordered. "We'll radio you when we clear the facility."

The marines were two steps ahead of her. The rotors of the Chinook had already fired, making their first pass.

"You're shot," Rico said. She grabbed Davis under an arm. "We have to get out of here."

Davis shook her hand away. "No. We have to find the rest of the Kryptonite."

"LT, if we don't move, there won't be anyone to launch it," Rico protested.

"There's nowhere to go," Garcia replied. He raised his rifle and fired at the mountain slope to the north, where another pack of Variants descended the rocks. "We're being surrounded."

Davis looked back at the double doors leading into the facility. She jerked her chin toward the entrance. It was their only option.

"Inside!" Garcia shouted. He slung his M4 over his back and pulled out his shotgun as the team hurried for the locked doors. He fired from a distance, the blast of bullets peppering the steel. Another shot sent the left door swinging open.

"On me," he called. "All it takes is all you got, marine," were his last words as he burst into the darkness.

Davis steeled herself for what came next. Whatever was inside, she could handle it. She had to handle it. She was in charge now.

Fitz and Apollo followed. Rico helped Davis in next. When they were all inside, they came together in a phalanx, weapons raised and searching the walls and ceiling for contacts.

The cold, dark room stank of rotting lemons and wet fur.

Outside, the Chinook and one of the Black Hawks lifted off the ground. Two packs of Variants gathered underneath, all but one set of claws swiping just out of reach. A single beast grabbed onto the side of the Chinook. It clambered toward the open right shoulder window, where it yanked the marine firing the M240 out and tossed him to the field below.

Davis gritted her teeth as the man was consumed. His screams were audible even over the sound of rotors and the bark of gunfire.

Fitz aimed his rifle at the creature still on the Chinook, but didn't fire. If he missed, he could hit the hydraulics, and Davis wasn't going to risk giving that order no matter how good a shot he was.

"Three o'clock," Rico said. She pointed at an abandoned Black Hawk across the airfield, where two human collaborators wearing parkas watched from a distance.

"Get these doors shut and secure," Davis said.

Fitz kicked a blade at the left door while Garcia worked on the right.

As the pilots pulled away from the mountain, a second marine emerged in the open shoulder window of the Chinook. He fired a handgun at the monster, hitting it in the face. It tumbled away, claws slashing at air as it plummeted thousands of feet.

In the final moments of moonlight, Davis glimpsed the maws of a dozen Variants on the south side of the airfield. Fresh blood dripped from their lips as they fed.

"Hurry!" Rico said. She kicked at the left door with Fitz.

The monsters looked away from the remains of the marine, curious now. In seconds, a dozen Variants had stripped away his armor and flesh, leaving only gristle and bone. Their starving eyes homed in on what was left of Team Spartan. All at once, the pack reared their heads back to unleash a chorus of howls. Then they were moving, long limbs pounding the ground as they advanced toward doors Fitz and Garcia were still trying to close.

Beckham and Horn stood beside Riley's body in silence. Neither of them had said a word since the coroner let them into the morgue. A dozen corpses retrieved from Plum Island were in body bags on gurneys throughout the small room. A bank of LEDs illuminated the shapes of men and women who had lost their lives.

Red, Donna's husband and Bo's father, was somewhere among them. So were the marines who had made a valiant last stand against the Bone Collector. Beckham had said a silent prayer for each of them, and especially for Major Smith. The officer had died alongside his soldiers, fighting off the Variants that had swarmed the island.

Horn broke the silence by clearing his throat. "You ready, boss?"

Beckham unzipped the body bag in front of him. Riley's ruffled blond hair popped out of the opening. Blue irises surrounded by broken blood vessels and covered in a milky film stared up at the ceiling.

Beckham's lips quivered, and he almost dropped to his knees. This wasn't the young man Beckham had known. The spark of mischievous humor was gone.

*I'm so fucking sorry, Kid. I'm so fucking sorry.*

Horn put a hand on Beckham's shoulder. They stood there for a few minutes, as tears cascaded down their bruised, scratched faces. A few minutes turned into fifteen. Then thirty. An hour passed, and though their sobs at last subsided, still they remained, Horn's arm around Beckham and Beckham's right hand on Riley's shoulder.

He couldn't bear to look at the bruises around Riley's neck, or the way his blue eyes were bulging from his face. But somehow, standing there in the kid's presence gave Beckham a small sense of comfort.

They stood there unmoving until the hatch clicked open and a voice called into the room.

"Excuse me—I'm sorry to bother you, Master Sergeant."

Beckham kept his gaze on Riley as he closed the kid's eyes. He didn't want anyone else to see him like this.

"Yeah," Beckham replied.

"President Ringgold and Vice President Johnson have asked to see you and your men in the CIC, ASAP."

The hatch closed, sealing him inside with Horn. For them, as soon as possible would be after a few more minutes with Riley. Horn pulled his hand off Beckham's shoulder and wiped his eyes.

"You were a good man. I'll see you again someday. And I'll beat you in the one-hundred-yard dash again." Horn chuckled.

Beckham bit back his own chuckle. "I love you, Kid, but I know you're in a better place. And you're no longer chasing tail, because you finally met someone who could keep up with you. Meg's a hell of a woman, little bro. You better treat her right."

Horn laughed at that too.

They took another few minutes of silence before Beckham zipped the bag back up and put his hands in his pocket to touch Riley's dog tags. Horn opened the hatch, and they left the room together.

Ten minutes later they were in the CIC. It was bustling with activity. The movement, energy, and adrenaline helped Beckham put things into perspective. There was a war going on outside that would determine the fate of the human race. Fitz, Davis, Garcia, Apollo— they were all fighting to ensure there *was* a future.

"Master Sergeant, where are your men?" said a voice. Captain Humphrey eyed Beckham as he turned.

"We're it," Beckham replied, gesturing toward Horn.

Humphrey hesitated before waving them into a conference room. Vice President Johnson and President Ringgold were at the table with Lieutenant Colonel Kramer and General Kohl.

They all looked up when Beckham and Horn entered the room. Johnson wasted no time.

"The Earthfall facility has been compromised," he said. "Davis and her team are trapped inside. We just lost contact with them."

The news hit Beckham like a brick wall. He could only take so much, and after seeing Riley like that, he couldn't hold back his next words. "I thought that area was clear of Variants. This was supposed to be an easy mission, goddamnit!" Beckham stiffened his spine and clasped his hands behind his back. "Sir."

"The Variants had help," Kramer snapped. "We aren't dealing with mindless monsters, Master Sergeant."

Focusing, Beckham put on his game face and dipped his chin. He knew what was coming. They hadn't called him and Horn here to tell them about their fuck-up. The final two members of Team Ghost had been called here because they were about to be sent into the fray, and that made Beckham even more furious.

"What do you know about radiological dispersal devices?" Johnson asked.

Beckham raised a brow and glanced over at Horn, who shrugged. "Dirty bombs? I know they were one of the biggest threats to our national security before the Variants," Beckham replied. "Team Ghost was trained to deal with an RDD scenario where terrorists smuggled them into the United States."

"Good," Johnson said.

A hundred questions danced around Beckham's head, but behind all of them he couldn't help but think of Fitz, Apollo, Garcia, and Davis. They were in trouble, and he was being questioned about dirty bombs?

"We've come up with a plan to sneak RDDs into the major lairs of the juveniles in our target cities. It won't kill all of the bastards, but it puts fewer troops at risk, and the radiation impact is much smaller than that of a nuclear weapon," Johnson said.

"We want you to lead one of those missions," Ringgold said. "We want you to take back our nation's capital. I don't trust anyone else."

"With all due respect, Madam President, what about Kryptonite? I thought Vice President Johnson just said—"

Kramer cut Beckham off. "It's not a matter of *if* we

deploy Kryptonite, it's just a matter of when. If Davis fails, we'll send someone else. In the meantime, we're moving forward with the final stage of Operation Extinction."

Beckham and Horn exchanged an uneasy glance. He was going back out there, but he wasn't heading to Colorado; he was heading to Washington, DC.

"There's another reason I want you two to lead this mission," Johnson continued. He nodded at Kohl. The general crossed the room to flip off the lights, then pointed a remote at the wall projector. Footage from a strike team's helmet cams flashed over the screen.

"This is a team of Navy SEALs inserted in DC earlier this week. Their mission was to document the Variants that have been breeding in the tunnels under the Capitol Building. We've known they're down there for a while, but no team has returned with footage until now."

The video feed flickered, and a three-man squad crouch-walked through a tunnel. They came to an old blast door pockmarked with rust. A few minutes later, they entered a massive, domed chamber. Orange barrels the size of oil drums were stacked twenty feet high. Boxes and crates marked DRY FOOD filled the room.

"This is one of the shelters designed to house members of Congress during a nuclear attack," Johnson said.

As the camera tilted, Beckham saw a room the length of two football fields, full of food and something else...

At the far end, near a pair of blast doors, was a web of human prisoners that climbed one hundred feet up the east wall. Armored Variants skittered about like bees, plucking off chunks of flesh and returning to an area blocked from view behind the crates.

The SEAL team slowly snuck through the room to flank the monsters. Beckham fidgeted as he watched, knowing the men were likely going to die.

They stopped at the edge of a pile of crates and captured the most terrifying image of the Variants Beckham had ever seen. Beyond the stockpiled provisions was a glistening pool of red water, and hundreds of juvenile Variants were swimming in it. Body parts bobbed up and down in the bloody soup. Countless more of the offspring either rested nearby or chased each other around the open space.

The lens zoomed in on a head floating in the water. Beckham squinted at the screen and the bulging lips on the pale, wet face before it was submerged. He realized then why there weren't any adult Variants in the chamber. The limbs, torsos, and heads drifting in the pool weren't all human; some of them were Variants. The beasts were eating their parents.

"Gentleman, this is the largest lair of juveniles ever documented. And this is where we want you to set off the RDD," Johnson said.

"If the SEALs made it out, so can we, sir," Beckham said confidently.

"They made it out, right?" Horn asked.

Johnson nodded. There was no lie in his gaze. Beckham still couldn't quite believe anyone could make it out of there alive, but if there was a job for Team Ghost, this was it, and he was ready to accept the challenge if it meant helping end the war.

# 20

It felt odd not having someone up against his back who wasn't a Variant Hunter. He was used to having Tank or Steve-o next to him. Unlike marines assigned to larger units, Garcia was used to fighting and working in his small recon group. He prided himself on being able to accomplish missions with only a handful of hardened marines.

But now, standing inside the green-hued passage of the Earthfall facility, he wouldn't have turned down a couple extra men and women.

*Or a couple hundred.*

Hell, Garcia would have been happy just having Tank's three hundred pounds at his back—eye or no eye. Fitz and Davis were warriors, and Rico held her own, but Garcia had trusted his men with his life.

A rumble shook the doors as the first of the Variants slammed into the metal. Whoever had taken control of the facility had clearly thought ahead. Several coils of heavy chains sat just inside the door. The only thing missing was a way to tighten them. The loose chains rattled violently as the beasts pounded the exterior.

Garcia checked them a second time, but he could already see they weren't going to hold.

"Other than me, who's hurt and how bad?" Davis asked.

Garcia examined the team with a quick glance. Fitz had a hand on his vest, but shook his head.

"I'm fine."

"Me too," Rico replied.

"Good to go here," Garcia added. He turned back to Davis. She was hurt the worst. Blood seeped from the armor covering her right thigh. There was enough to make Garcia nervous, but she continued to play it off as just a flesh wound.

*She's still in charge, Jose.*

He looked past Fitz at the hallway behind him. It curved and led to another set of doors about two hundred feet away. The white walls were bare, and there wasn't a single window. The structure was hollow, like an empty grain silo. There were only two options now: Fight the beasts outside or descend into the depths of the facility.

"All right," Davis said in her command voice. "Fitz, you and Apollo take point. Garcia, you got rear guard. Rico, stay close to me." She flashed an advance signal and limped forward.

The chains rattled again, metal clanking on metal.

Garcia centered his shotgun on the door. The collaborators he'd seen outside hadn't fired yet, which told him something—they were going to let the Variants do the dirty work.

Four dents appeared on the inside of the door simultaneously. Garcia roved his muzzle from spot to spot, waiting to blow a gaping hole in one of the beasts.

*Come on, you furry fucks.*

Another thud shook the door. There wasn't much standing between what was left of Team Spartan and a dozen hungry Variants, not to mention whatever firepower the collaborators carried.

He took another step backward as the beasts continued ramming the doors. The left one bent inward. Moonlight streamed through the gap. An arm covered in icy fur shot through, claw swiping at the air.

"Garcia!" Davis yelled.

"I'm on it!" Garcia aimed his shotgun at the arm just as the clawed hand wrapped around the frame and pulled. He squeezed the trigger with pleasure. The blast blew the arm off at the elbow. He fired three more shots at the right door, sending several beasts retreating and screeching in agony.

"Come on, Sarge!" Rico shouted.

The sound of boots pounding the floor echoed through the narrow hallway. Garcia backpedaled as fast as he could while keeping his shotgun trained on the door. His mind was working in overdrive, adrenaline dumping into his system at the thought of the human collaborators. They were clearly still outside, but there had to be some inside too. So where the fuck were they?

"Coming up on the stairwell," Fitz said. "Who's got the key card?"

"Me," Davis said.

Garcia whirled at the same second the double doors to the building flew off their hinges and smashed into the wall across the passage. Three Variants on all fours skidded across the floor, their talons drawing sparks.

Outside the open doorway stood the colossal beast that had just about taken Garcia's head off earlier. He flipped up his NVGs to stare into the moonlit night. Fur matted with sticky blood, the creature ducked into the hallway and rose to a full seven feet, his head narrowly missing the ceiling.

Swollen, veiny lips opened as the beast unleashed a roar and extended a claw directly at Garcia. The beast coughed as it tried to speak.

"Get...them..."

*Holy hell. Not just an Alpha, but one that fucking talks!*

Garcia squeezed off a shotgun blast at the beast, his heart firing like the weapon. The spray took off the monster's right ear and punched into the ceiling. The smaller Variants scattered to the walls.

He pumped the gun, firing it over and over at the monsters. The spray clipped their extremities, slowing their advance, but he was too far away for kill shots.

"Hurry up with that door!" Garcia screamed. He plucked an M84 stun grenade off his vest and wrapped a finger through the pin. There was a precise technique to using the grenades, but with his hand shaking and the beasts closing in, he wasn't sure he could execute it perfectly.

The Alpha staggered down the hallway. Rico and Fitz fired on the creatures clambering over the walls. One of them crashed to the floor, coughing up blood and something that looked like a heart. The massive beast kicked the dying creature out of the way as he advanced. It smashed into the wall next to Garcia, bones breaking.

He waited several seconds to toss the M84, his eyes glued to the Alpha. Rounds lanced down the passage around him. Over the gunfire, there was a click.

"It's locked!" Davis shouted.

"Improvise, LT!" Garcia yelled back.

A shotgun blast tore into metal. Two more sounded in unison.

Pulling the pin, Garcia yelled, "Stun grenade out!" He launched it toward the Alpha. The toss was perfect, hitting the monster square in the eyes, then clanking on the floor.

Garcia rushed after Team Spartan into the stairwell. He counted the seconds in his head as he ran.

*One.*

*Two.*

On the third second, he closed his eyes and bolted through the open door. A bang of 180 decibels sounded as he slammed the hatch shut a second too late. The ear-splitting noise sent him dropping to his knees at the top of the landing. The pressure in his pounding head squeezed his brain, and the hazy shapes of his comrades blurred into apparitions. Their voices echoed up the stairwell.

"Sarge, lock that door!"

Garcia brought a hand to his head and tried to stand but lost his balance. He grabbed a railing and closed his eyes.

*All it takes...*

Rising to his feet, Garcia forced his eyes open and fumbled with the lock mechanism. It had been shot to hell, but a security bar was still on the wall, strapped upright beside the door. He batted at it with a clumsy hand, knocking a retaining pin loose and freeing the bar, but it didn't fall. Garcia staggered as he tried to control his arms and get the bar down. His eyes just wouldn't focus.

"Out of the way!" Rico shouted. She grabbed the bar and slammed it into place across the door just as something collided with the metal, sending Garcia stumbling backward and almost down the stairs.

Rico grabbed his right arm and helped him grip the railing. Using the handrail as a guide, Garcia shambled down the stairs away from the noise, dragging his feet like a drunken frat boy. The shrieks of the beasts in the hallway dwindled.

Step by step, the team descended into the darkness. It was too dark for their NVGs, so the other marines switched on their tactical lights. The beams danced over the concrete walls.

Garcia's head was spinning now. Nausea swirled in his gut. He was going to puke. There was no holding it in.

The vomit came out in a stream just as he stopped to flip up his mouth guard. He coughed, wiped off his mouth, and blinked rapidly. Then he clicked on his own light and shouldered his shotgun.

He was still unbalanced, but at least he was able to see in a straight line now. Rico was several steps ahead of him. She looked back and said, "You good, Sarge?"

Garcia opened his mouth to reply but gagged. He swallowed the bile and mumbled, "Good."

"Ten flights to go!" Fitz shouted somewhere ahead of them.

*I'm not going to make it another two.*

Garcia fought the blinding pain in his head as he looked up at the flights above him. He'd bought them some time. The Variants still hadn't broken down the door.

"Stay sharp!" Davis said when they reached the fifth flight.

Garcia pulled shells from his vest and loaded his shotgun as he moved. Several of them slipped from his grip and dropped to the floor.

*Get it together!*

Pumping the gun, Garcia readied himself. The anticipation ate at him with every step. He was a recon marine; his job was to identify danger before they encountered it. But now he couldn't help but feel as if they were escaping one threat only to be led directly into something even worse.

"Two floors to go!" Fitz shouted.

Garcia loped down the next flight. His beam caught the backs of Team Spartan. They were clustered at the final landing, muzzles angled at an open door. Fitz slowly reached up and shut off his light while Davis balled her hand into a fist.

There was a second of silence that was promptly

shattered by the shrieks of the prowling monsters fifteen floors above. Garcia strained to hear over the noise. There were too many sounds from too many directions, all equally distracting, and his ears were ringing as if someone had fired an M249 next to his head.

He stumbled down the final two stairs and braced himself with a hand on Rico's shoulder.

"I'm okay," he panted.

Davis took a second to examine him, then ordered the rest of Team Spartan to retreat up the stairwell. This time she wanted Garcia on point. She shook her head when he pulled an M84 grenade.

"LT, what about hostiles?" he whispered in protest, still clutching the grenade.

"We can't risk damaging any of the equipment."

Garcia clipped the grenade back on his vest. He had been thinking about enemy combatants inside, not electronics. Personally, he didn't give two shits about the computers, but their mission was to launch Kryptonite. Damaging vital equipment could put that goal at risk.

When he finished loading his shotgun, he bounded around the corner. Hurrying down the stairs, he ran into the room and kept as low as possible. He played his tactical light over the space, sweeping it back and forth as he entered a vaulted chamber the size of a hockey arena. Idle computer stations lined the walls.

He angled his light up fifteen floors at the hollow center of the structure to reveal a domed ceiling. Then he worked his gun back to the far end of the room. A platform rose four feet off the ground. A ramp of three stairs led to the carpeted surface, which was furnished with leather chairs positioned in front of five wall-mounted monitors.

Garcia strode toward the platform, sweeping his gun from left to right. The beam cut through the darkness and spread over the hatches leading to the Earthfall missile launch tunnels. Both doors were slightly ajar.

He couldn't hear much past the ringing in his ears, but there was something oddly familiar-sounding, though too faint to make out. He searched for the source, raking his gun back and forth, finger ready to squeeze the trigger.

"Looks clear," Garcia whispered into his headset. He could hardly hear himself speak, but he could make out the reassuring footfalls of Team Spartan entering the room and shutting the door behind them.

Davis, Rico, Fitz, and Apollo fanned out around him.

"What *is* that?" Rico whispered.

A cold screech replied, like the caw of a dying crow, the echoes fading as they bounced off the fifteen floors of circular walls.

Garcia froze and perked his ears, aching to hear. His guts churned and made a gurgling sound.

He could hear that, damn it.

Beams from Team Spartan's guns flickered across the walls and the platform at the other end of the room. Garcia centered his on the leather chairs with their backs facing him. He approached slowly, heel to toe, heel to toe.

*Deliver me from evil, Lord.*

Garcia held his breath as he approached. To his right, Fitz centered his M4 on the ceiling. Apollo's tail suddenly dropped between his legs. He froze next to his handler, his hackles raised as he focused on the two hatches leading into the missile tunnels.

Cracking his jaw from side to side, Garcia's ears popped. The ringing subsided for a fleeting moment, replaced by the stifled sounds he couldn't make out earlier. They were unmistakable now.

The moaning came from everywhere and nowhere.

All at once, the monitors on the platform flashed.

Garcia's heart flipped at the sight. The creak of a chair made it skip a second time. He almost fired off a blast at the leather chair as it turned.

Team Spartan trained their guns on a figure that rose and slowly pivoted toward them. At first, Garcia thought the six-foot-tall man was a Variant. His face was covered in a thick silver beard, and he pulled a hood back to reveal deep eye sockets with dark irises that made his eyes look like black holes.

"Welcome to Earthfall," he said.

"Hands on your head!" Davis shouted.

The man flashed a crooked grin of stained teeth. He slowly raised his shaking hands, then turned to point at the screen to his right.

Apollo let out a low growl at the doors and cowered behind Fitz.

"It's okay, boy," Fitz whispered.

"Command, Spartan One, we have located—"

The man chuckled in a low tone.

"Shut up!" Davis shouted. She paused, then said, "Command, do you copy?"

Static filled Garcia's earpiece, same as before. There had to be some sort of interference in the facility.

"No one's going to help you," the collaborator said. "Or your friends."

Garcia followed the man's finger to the monitor. Now he knew why the German shepherd was hiding behind his handler. Nothing scared the dog, not even the Alpha Variant still pounding the door fifteen floors above them.

"Drop your weapons or die," the man said dryly.

Garcia stared incredulously, his brain unable to process what his eyes were feeding it. On-screen were images of the long, narrow tunnels that led to launch tubes already preloaded with missiles. Every inch of the passages was covered with the bodies of the missing marines, pilots, and support staff from Teams Lightning, Saber, and Wolverine. Some were plastered to the ceilings and walls. Others were stuck to the floor. Most were already dead, limbs missing and flesh torn away. There was some movement as a few of them twitched and squirmed in their gluey traps. Variants prowled the tunnels. Several were hunched and feeding, while others moved lethargically, their bellies full from the feast. Moans ebbed out into the command room, surrounding Team Spartan with ghostly voices.

"Your radios won't work," the collaborator said. "Nor will your video feeds, and by the time reinforcements arrive, you'll all be dead—unless you listen very carefully."

Garcia was only half paying attention. His eyes flitted from screen to screen and finally to the human scum in front of him.

"I said shut the fuck up!" Davis yelled.

The man reached forward and pecked at the keyboard in front of him. Garcia took a discreet step to the right, catching movement in his peripheral. The Earthfall hatches slowly creaked open and disgorged the shadowy shapes of Variants. Dozens of monsters scrambled into the room on all fours, circling Team Spartan. Despite their full stomachs, they moved with astonishing speed.

Garcia could smell the sour stench radiating off their wet fur. Adrenaline quickened in his veins, and for a fleeting moment, an image of his wife and smiling baby girl flashed in his mind.

He knew he would be joining them soon.

The images vanished as a piercing thud sounded above. The Alpha had finally broken through the door leading to the stairwell. Claws screeched over concrete as the monsters scrambled over the walls.

It wasn't hard to calculate the odds. Even if they could fight off the mob surrounding them, there was no way they could kill those advancing down the stairs. The door to the command room wouldn't hold them long. To make things worse, there was also no telling what the collaborator would do, or what he *could* do. Fighting their way out of this one seemed impossible, and Davis seemed to know it too.

"It's over," the collaborator said in the same heartless voice. "Drop your weapons and I might allow some of you to live. We may have some use for you."

Garcia knew what surrender meant. But he was Force Recon. He'd been in enough dicey situations to know there was little chance of shooting their way out of this one.

Davis followed the beasts with her muzzle as she considered the man's offer.

"LT," Rico whispered.

Garcia knew what his men would do. Tank, Steve-o, Morgan, Thomas, and Daniels would fight to the end in order to launch Kryptonite.

But then, they had already fought to the end.

Everyone but Tank was gone now.

And Garcia wasn't in control.

Davis wasn't either. His heart sank as the lieutenant slowly lowered her weapon toward the ground. Rico did the same thing, but Fitz held steady. Garcia's shotgun shook in his hands. He was simply unable to force himself to surrender to a piece of shit like the man standing on the platform.

"Spartans," Davis said.

The collaborator narrowed his pitch-black eyes on Garcia. The cold stare told Garcia that if anyone was truly going to be spared, it wasn't him.

"I said drop your weapons."

Davis continued lowering her M4 toward the floor. The sour-rot stench of the Variants drifted through the chamber as the beasts closed in. They crawled over every surface, snapping joints filling the room with the awful noise Garcia knew all too well. He tightened his grip on his shotgun defiantly.

Never in his career had he surrendered like this.

"I'm losing my patience," the man said.

"So am I!" Davis yelled back.

Garcia barely had a chance to react to what happened next. In a lightning fast motion, she dropped to her uninjured knee and yelled, "Open fire."

The collaborator's expression tightened with shock. As he raised a hand, Davis blew it off with a shot from her rifle.

Garcia quickly squared his shoulders and fired his shotgun at a thin Variant to his left, sending the beast flying through the air in a cloud of bloody mist. No prayer was going to get Team Spartan out of this one, and he doubted bullets would either.

But what the hell—it was worth a shot.

*There's no scientific answer. We're simply out of time.*

Kate still couldn't stomach her words. There had to be some way to kill the juveniles other than dropping nukes or the insane idea of sneaking dirty bombs into their lairs. The thought of Beckham and Horn going back out there to attempt something so suicidal sent her running back to the lab.

She was going to work until she came up with something. There was no preventing Beckham or his men from being deployed to the cities, but maybe, just maybe, she could help them fight the juveniles when they got there.

"Found something, Kate," Ellis said. He waved her over to his laptop.

They were working inside a small conference room aboard the *GW* now. Empty coffee mugs littered the table. The remaining members of Yokoyama's science team were back on the *Cowpens*. With the development of Kryptonite complete and Johnson hell-bent on using RDDs, there wasn't much for them to do anymore.

But Kate wasn't giving up.

"What is it?" she asked.

Ellis swiveled his chair to face her. "Data on the juveniles. The Brits were able to capture one a few days ago, and apparently so were the French."

"Why weren't we informed?"

"I don't—"

"Because we didn't know either," said an authoritative voice. Captain Humphrey entered the room and shut the hatch. Ellis and Kate both stood to greet him.

"What I'm about to tell you is completely confidential." Humphrey parted his thick hair with his fingers as he walked to the table.

So much had been on Kate's mind the past two days, she hadn't thought much about other countries. She'd forced herself to direct her attention to saving the United States. But her family and friends overseas were always in the back of her thoughts.

"This does not leave this room," Humphrey said. "Understood?"

"Yes, sir," Ellis said. Kate simply nodded.

"The French and British both report their juveniles are fully developed now. They do have a delivery system for their venom. Three French soldiers were killed and a dozen more injured trying to take down just one of the beasts."

Humphrey handed Ellis a USB drive. Ellis inserted it into his laptop and clicked on the only file it held. A room full of injured soldiers flashed onto the screen. The men were covered in bandages, but not from deep gashes. These men were burned—their skin melted away by the venom.

The video feed wobbled before centering on a double amputee lying on a bed in the center of the room. The soldier glanced at the camera with droopy basset-hound brown eyes that took Kate's breath away. His chiseled jaw was covered with a five o'clock shadow. If it weren't for his missing legs, Kate might have confused him for Beckham. The man even had the same full lips.

"My God," she gasped.

"This is the work of the devil," Humphrey said. He pointed at the injured man. "The venom inflicts horrific injuries. This poor bastard reported a juvenile hit him in the legs with the liquid from thirty feet away."

"How did these soldiers not die of the toxins?" Ellis asked.

Humphrey scratched at the stubble on his chin. "French scientists are saying the venom eats away the flesh, but takes longer to spread through the human vascular system. It's the only good news I've heard."

"Interesting," Ellis said. "Kate and I will look into it."

"There's something else, Doctors," Humphrey said. "A few hours ago we received word that the juveniles are starting to move in Europe. They're leaving the lairs for extended periods of time. Our drones are reporting the same activity in DC, Atlanta, LA, and Chicago. That's why I'm here. Vice President Johnson wants your opinion: Why are they moving?"

To Kate, the answer was obvious. "Two reasons," she replied. "Like any child, they'll eventually leave the nest, so to speak. In this case, I believe it's to hunt for resources. The second reason is to explore. They're learning. As the offspring evolve, they'll also grow more intelligent."

"That's what I thought," Humphrey said. "They're starving, just like many of the parents. In some cases the freaks are so hungry they're *eating* their parents. Assuming we get Kryptonite in the air sometime soon, we're going to have to move fast here in the States before they leave the lairs for good."

"Assuming?" Kate asked. Her heart did a jumping jack in her chest.

Humphrey frowned. "I'm afraid the Earthfall facility wasn't abandoned. Lieutenant Davis and her team are trapped inside."

Kate closed her eyes. After a moment of despair, she snapped them back open and said, "Have you sent reinforcements?"

"We're working on it."

It took everything in Kate not to rage at the captain. She had to trust the military, despite everything that had happened before, but it was proving more difficult by the minute—especially with the clock counting down on a final battle that would send Beckham and Horn back into that hell.

"Is there any other reason the juveniles might be starting to move?" Humphrey asked, in an obvious effort to change the subject.

Ellis nodded. "I have a theory."

"Let's hear it."

"As Kate stated, the offspring are continuing to evolve and grow more intelligent. They will start doing things their parents aren't capable of—"

"Like what?" Humphrey interrupted.

There was a moment of silence. Kate wasn't sure if she should answer, but she knew her partner well enough to know he was thinking the same thing she was.

"Everything," Ellis and Kate said simultaneously.

Ellis paused to lock eyes with Humphrey. "It's imperative we kill them before they leave the cities, sir. The juveniles will eventually possess an intelligence that matches or exceeds our own."

# 21

Fitz shot the collaborator in the jaw as he scrambled to reach for the computer keyboard with his remaining hand. Shattering bones made a distinct sound that always made Fitz wince. He could still remember the sound when his legs were blown off on that dirt road back in Iraq.

But this time he didn't wince.

The crack of the man's jaw separating from his face and the blood splattering the computer screen filled Fitz with grim satisfaction. The mess streaked down the surface of the monitor as the man's knees crumbled.

Fitz was firing on the Variants streaming from the tunnel before the collaborator's body hit the ground. He wasn't going to get a second chance.

*Every shot has to count.*

He fired his M4 in three short bursts, sending three Variants crashing into computer equipment on the east wall, gaping holes in their furry flesh. A dozen more emerged, squawking and shrieking in their terrifying language.

"Don't hit the equipment!" Davis yelled. "Rico, on me! Garcia, Fitz, take those to the left!"

Garcia hurried over and stood on the other side of

Apollo. He and Fitz stood back to back, armored shoulders clicking. Fitz had seen the sergeant's gaze earlier—a look that had told Fitz he didn't think they were going to make it out of this one. Fitz wasn't sure himself. The odds were grim, but they had been grim many times before.

Across the chamber, Rico and Davis came together side by side. They turned full circle while firing precise bursts at the beasts charging into the room.

"Watch your zones of fire!" Davis shouted.

Muzzles flashed, spent casings clanked, and dead Variants crashed to the ground. Team Spartan fought with the skill and honor of a squad that had been together for years, not just hours.

*Maybe we do have a chance after all.*

A roar boomed from the stairwell behind Fitz, shaking the thought from his head. The Alpha pounded on the locked door relentlessly. Fitz didn't risk a glance; he continued firing on the beasts that moved with blinding speed in the shadows.

*Steady, Fitz. Steady.*

The chatter of gunfire echoed up the concrete walls and resonated at the top, trapped in the chamber just like them. Apollo snapped at the Variants that dared come close to Fitz's smoking M4.

Flickering light from computer monitors and the fiery glow from muzzles illuminated the beasts as they clambered in every direction. All around Fitz, his fellow marines fired calculated shots.

His next two cracked open the heads of a pair of Variants that broke off from the prowling pack. Their jointed limbs gave out, and both crashed to the floor chin first, sliding to a stop a few feet from Fitz's shiny new blades.

And still more continued to emerge from the tunnels. Fitz watched a monster with a swollen stomach stagger out into the room. It dragged a hairy arm across its bloody beard and focused on its next meal. Fitz fired a three-round burst into its gut, then took a mental inventory of the beasts between his next shots. There were sixteen on the left of the platform.

Boom!

Fourteen, after Garcia's shotgun blast sent two spinning away.

A beast with long limbs leaped to the walls and threw back its head to let out a shriek. Fitz shot it in the spine. The creature dropped to the ground, an incredulous look painted across its features.

"Changing!" Rico shouted. She tossed her shotgun away and reached for her M4.

"I got you," Davis yelled back.

Fitz counted at least a dozen on the right side, but Davis and Rico were holding their own, for now.

The Variants on the left moved in a line that twisted like the tentacle of an octopus, making targets more difficult to find in the weak light. Several made dashes for Garcia.

Fitz killed three before pivoting to fire on a scrawny beast covered in patchy fur. He clipped it in the shoulder, throwing it off balance. In a graceful movement it leaped to the right, then to the left, and finally toward him, claws extended.

An empty magazine clicked back as Fitz squeezed the trigger. He raised the gun's butt to block the beast as a flash of brown fur leaped in front of him. Apollo tackled the creature to the ground, snarling and snapping at the monster's neck.

Garcia laid down covering fire as Fitz reached for his MK11. There was no time to change the magazine in his M4. He hefted the big rifle and centered it on the circling monsters. Fitz thought back to the battle topside. There were only five rounds left in the magazine.

*Make 'em count.*

"Behind me, boy," Fitz said. Apollo backed away from the corpse of the Variant he'd killed as four more broke off from the twisting arm of the main pack. They hunched their backs in preparation to strike.

The world slowed to battle time. Every breath and movement became augmented. Fitz could smell the ripe scent of the Variants, could feel his muscles flexing and the adrenaline pumping through his veins.

He fired without thinking, his mind disconnected from his body. The first shot hit a Variant with a mane of black hair. The round struck it in the neck, arterial blood geysering out. The other three let out high-pitched shrieks that threatened Fitz's concentration. He gritted his teeth, narrowed his eyes, and hit the beast on the far left directly in its open maw. Chunks of what had once been a human brain bloomed behind it.

*Three shots left.*

Garcia took the other two creatures down with a single blast. He yelled above the echoing gunfire, "Climbers!"

The formation of moving creatures had broken in half. Five leaped to the walls, while the other five closed in on Fitz and Garcia. Out of the corner of his eye, Fitz saw that Rico and Davis were losing their fight. A Variant made it through their barrage of gunfire with a chest full of gushing wounds. How it was still breathing was a mystery. It reached out with a brown talon and slashed at Rico's leg. She parried the attack with a kick that allowed the beast to grab her boot.

A minute had passed since Davis fired the first shot, and Fitz could see the tide was quickly turning against them. With not even a second to spare, he did the only thing he could think of.

"Apollo, sic!" Fitz shouted, jerking his chin.

The dog lunged at the Variant that had pulled Rico onto her back.

Fitz concentrated on the encroaching monsters. Garcia cut four of them down, but those on the ceiling were close to flanking their position.

"Behind us!" Fitz shouted.

*Three shots. Three breaths.*

"I got this one," Garcia growled.

Fitz spun with his MK11, holding a breath in his chest and lining up a shot that took off the leg of one of the beasts below the kneecap. The second creature leaped just as Fitz pulled the trigger. The shot slammed into the wall above the monster's skull.

*Shit. Shit. Shit.*

Garcia shot it in the chest midair with three rounds from his M9. Then he killed the legless beast crawling across the ground with its stump gushing blood.

Seeing an opportunity, the pack galloped toward Garcia and Fitz. Fur and flesh blurred as the monsters charged. The three remaining Variants were all covered in abrasions and gashes, their fur torn away. Fitz had seen it before. These beasts were low in the hierarchy. They were starving and more desperate than the others. Their bulging lips smacked. Fitz would never get used to that horrifying sound.

*Make. It. Count.*

The final round left Fitz's MK11 and entered the skull of the lead beast right between its reptilian eyes. The creature on the right spun away in a spray of blood and bone as Garcia emptied his shotgun, but the final monster barreled toward Fitz.

"Watch out!" Garcia yelled.

Fitz didn't have time to reach for his knife or M9. His next action wasn't premeditated. He simply planted his left blade and roundhouse kicked with his all of his strength as the beast took to the air. The spike on his right blade connected with its temple, slicing through flesh and bone like a knife cutting into a steak. He hit it with such force that he lost his footing and went down on his left side, along with the shrieking Variant.

Gunfire rang out all around him as he hit the ground. In the pause between the shots, the pounding on the door to the command center intensified. It reverberated through the chamber in a relentless echo—a reminder of the threat outside.

Fitz pushed himself up and yanked the spike on his blade from the creature's skull. His spur free, he took a knee, grabbed his M9, and fired with one eye closed at the beasts closing in on his friends.

Rico was still on her back; the monster that had her boot was tugging on her leg. Apollo had his mouth clamped onto its neck but was struggling. Behind them, another Variant scurried on all fours. Fitz clipped it in the face with two rounds. Then he pivoted and squeezed off two more shots that killed a creature making a run for Davis.

"Garcia, we need you!" Fitz shouted.

"Reloading," Garcia replied. He was hunched over and jamming shells into his shotgun. His eyes widened at the sound of the cracking metal. The door to the room suddenly flew off the hinges.

Fitz holstered his M9, pulled his M4, and slammed in a fresh magazine. He whirled to the entrance while Davis fired on the final three beasts.

Bodies piled on the floor in front of Rico, blood pooling around them. Apollo reared his head back, ragged flesh hanging from his jaw as he finally ripped his prey's jugular vein free from its neck.

"Our six!" Fitz yelled. He raised his rifle at the Alpha lumbering through the open doorway. He stood on the broken door, eyes roving from side to side. Patches of glistening blood dotted the monster's muscular body.

The pop of gunshots sounded across the chamber as Rico and Davis finished off the remaining beasts flanking them. Fitz and Garcia aimed for the Alpha and opened fire.

The creature jerked back and forth, rounds punching through his flesh and slamming into the stairs beyond. He roared in anger and clambered away, exposing the smaller monsters trapped in the stairwell. Fitz held down the trigger without restraint and slaughtered those that didn't retreat.

Garcia strode toward the Alpha, pumping his shotgun and firing off blasts that ricocheted off the walls and floor. The beast was injured, but he was still fast. Garcia finally clipped him in the right leg.

Fitz checked the stairwell one last time. If there were still human collaborators out there, he didn't see them. By the time he killed the last Variant on the steps, the Alpha had crossed half the room. He was running toward Rico and Davis, maimed but deadly as ever. Standing seven feet tall, with talons the length of a buck knife, the abomination was one of the most formidable Variants Fitz had encountered.

"Reloading again!" Garcia shouted.

Fitz reached for a new magazine too, his eye on Davis and Rico. They were down to their side arms. Both women emptied their weapons into the Alpha, but he wouldn't go down. Apollo bared his teeth, saliva dripping from his bloody maw. The monster stopped to shield his face with his massive arms.

For the second time that evening, Davis did something that shocked Fitz. She limped toward the beast with her left hand pressed against her injured thigh and her right holding her M9.

"LT, watch out!" Fitz yelled. He moved to the right to get a shot, bumping into Garcia.

Davis stopped two feet from the monster's face and shouted, "Hey!"

The Alpha pulled his arms away from its face. When he looked up, she raised her gun and shot him first in the right eye, then the left eye. Both rounds punched through skull and brain.

A gurgling sound rose from the Alpha's throat as he slowly fell backward. He hit the ground with the force of a bag of bricks, dust clouds rising into the air around him. The impact rocked the chamber, echoing over and over.

Davis turned to her team as if nothing had happened. In a commanding voice that made Fitz shiver, she said, "Rico, Garcia, find the other crates of Kryptonite and see if there's anyone else alive. Fitz, you and Apollo follow me. We're going topside to flag down Lynch and Adair."

Surrounded by smoking bodies, Fitz drew in the rank aroma of fired weapons, sour fruit, and scorched flesh. More than anything, he was surprised, once again, that he was breathing at all.

President Ringgold stood in the CIC of the *GW*, cupping her injured arm and staring at the curtain of smoke on the horizon, the only lingering evidence of the tanker that had attempted to ram them before being blown to smithereens. Her mind drifted like a cloud. She would never know who had steered the ship packed full of shipping containers. It was obvious there had been civilians on board—survivors who had managed to evade the infected for weeks. She wanted to imagine they had been bad people. Collaborators, maybe. But what if they had just been people trying to survive?

Blowing them out of the water was another decision

she'd made for the future of mankind, and it wasn't the last time she would be responsible for such a choice.

A raised voice that seemed way too young to Ringgold to be in the CIC called out behind her. A freckle-faced petty officer sitting in front of a cluster of monitors stood and turned to face Captain Humphrey and Vice President Johnson. Ringgold watched the young man's movements in the reflection of the glass. She could just make out the nametag on his uniform, which read NAGLE.

"We have a visual from Spartan Two," Nagle said. "The feed just came back online."

Corporal Anderson stood in front of the radio station a few feet away. "Spartan Two just reported in, sir."

Johnson hurried to the monitors. He finished his cup of coffee as he examined the screens. "Madam President, you might want to see this."

Clutching the bottom of her sling, Ringgold worked her way over between the two stations. Johnson offered a reassuring nod that didn't make her feel much better. Everything was riding on this mission. The tension in the room was palpable. No one was spared, not even Lieutenant Colonel Kramer, who stood at the far end of the room watching like a hawk.

"They're back online?" Johnson asked.

Nagle punched at his keyboard. "Bringing up the feed now, sir. Spartan Three is our Chinook. Spartan Two is our Black Hawk."

Leaning closer, Johnson furrowed his bushy eyebrows at the screens. "Well done, son."

Two of the monitors flashed with green-hued video feeds. Ringgold ignored the digital telemetry at the top and bottom of the screens. She didn't care about the time or how many rounds the two gunships carried. She looked past all of it, focusing on the mountain rising over the cross hairs in the center of the second monitor. An airfield dotted with choppers and a windowless building came into focus.

"Spartan Two, this is Command, do you copy?" Corporal Anderson asked.

A second chopper crossed in front of the feed Ringgold was studying. The Black Hawk raced toward the mountain.

"Roger that, Command, Spartan Two here. Good to hear your voice."

Anderson looked back at Humphrey. The Captain reached for the corporal's headset and slipped it over his head.

"Spartan Two, this is Captain Humphrey of the *GW*. Sitrep. Over."

There was a brief pause, static crackling from the speakers. Spartan Two came back a few moments later.

"Captain, the Earthfall facility is compromised. Repeat. The facility is compromised. We came under heavy fire from human collaborators and dozens of Variants twenty minutes ago, suffering several casualties before Davis ordered us away from the mountain."

"What happened to her?"

"Sir, last we saw her, she was entering the building. But we haven't heard from her for fifteen minutes. Something is interfering with our comms, sir."

"No sign of contacts," Nagle whispered. He pointed at the infrared feed to the right. Ringgold followed his finger to an airfield littered with the corpses of dead Variants and several marines.

"How many hostiles are still in the vicinity?" Humphrey asked.

"We cleared the area of collaborators, sir, but there may still be some Variants lingering," replied Spartan Two.

Humphrey cupped his hand over the mini-mic and turned to Johnson. "What do you think, sir?"

"I think Davis and her team are probably dead, but do

we risk sending in Spartan Two and Three? It could be another trap. We still don't know what we're dealing with."

Humphrey turned to look across the room. "What's the status of the new strike teams?"

"They're in the air, sir," Kramer said. "Just took off from Creech Air Force Base."

Ringgold ignored the conversation and took a step closer to the monitors. A tiny flash of red had emerged from the doors of the building. A second darted out behind the first.

"What's that?" she asked.

Humphrey and Johnson were still busy discussing their next move. Ringgold didn't blame them. With Lieutenant Davis, the first three strike teams, and Kryptonite missing, the future of humanity hung in the balance. What happened next would be one of the most important turning points in the war.

Nagle scooted closer to his monitor and examined the moving red dots. He held up a hand at the same moment Spartan Two came back online.

"Command, we have potential hostiles emerging from the target, permission to engage. Over."

Johnson and Humphrey glanced at the screen, both men squinting.

"Shit," the captain said. "I don't like it."

Johnson gave his next order with a half a nod.

"Prepare to engage," said Humphrey.

"Roger that, sir," Spartan Two replied.

The Black Hawk circled the mountain, then hovered in the Chinook's video feed. Ringgold's eyes flitted to the screen with the Black Hawk's cam. The pilots zoomed in on two figures running across the airfield. Both appeared to be carrying weapons, but Ringgold couldn't see their faces. There was a smaller heat signature now too. Something small and running on all fours.

*A Variant and two collaborators?*

"Spartan Two, Command. Do you have eyes?" Humphrey asked.

"Roger that, sir. Three potential hostiles. Got them in our cross hairs. You give us the order and we'll light 'em up."

Ringgold's heart rate increased, sending a jolt of pain across her injured shoulder and down her arm. There was something odd about the third figure. Something she recognized.

"Unable to identify potential human hostiles," Spartan Two said. "But the third appears to be a Variant."

"Can't risk our choppers if they got weapons," Humphrey said. "Spartan Two, permission to engage."

Ringgold held up a hand when she saw the blades one of the targets was running on. It was Corporal Fitzpatrick, and Apollo was right next to him. The Black Hawk turned toward them as the video feed suddenly shut off.

"Hold your fire!" she shouted, a second too late. By the time Humphrey relayed the message to Spartan Two, the video and the audio were down. Static surged from the speakers. The connection was severed again.

"Kate, there's something you need to see," Ellis said. His features were strained in the glow of his laptop. They were still sitting in the cold conference room aboard the *GW.* The big hand on the clock ticked toward 11:00 p.m.

Kate cupped one hand over her mouth to hold back a yawn as she pushed her chair over to Ellis.

"Check this out," he said, spinning his laptop toward her. "These are French paratroopers tracking juvenile movements in Paris. Last night they parachuted into the city under the cover of darkness, wearing camo that was designed to make them nearly invisible to both the adults and juveniles."

Kate couldn't help raising a skeptical brow.

"Apparently, surviving French scientists have designed a liquid that masks the scent of human flesh. It's been lab-tested with good results, but this is the first field trial," Ellis added.

"That's a brilliant idea. I remember reading that Jews used cocaine during WWII to confuse German dogs searching for them. Why didn't we think of something like this?"

"We were too busy trying to find a weapon to kill them."

"If this works, then perhaps we can come up with something similar for Reed, Horn, and all the other soldiers going back out there."

Ellis shrugged. "Better see if it works then." He typed a few commands and pulled up the video.

On-screen, the team of paratroopers dove out of the back of a plane and vanished into the clouds. The man taking the video cast a sidelong glance that revealed nothing but darkness. Everything was pitch black until they shot through the cloud cover and descended over Paris. Kate could make out the Seine snaking through the city in the moonlight. This was not the Paris she remembered. The Eiffel Tower was nothing but a silhouette, and the city of beautiful cathedrals had crumbled as a result of relentless bombing.

The men landed in the middle of the Parc des Princes soccer stadium. They quickly discarded their chutes and sprinted across the field. The team made its way into the streets undetected. Ten minutes and two blocks later, they stopped to watch a pack of Variants prowling in a courtyard. The beasts didn't seem to notice them and moved on.

Flashing a hand signal, the man with the helmet-mounted camera ordered his team forward. They took up position in the husk of a building destroyed by artillery fire. It provided a clear view of the street below.

"Can you speed this up?" Kate asked.

Ellis pushed another button. They sat and watched for another five minutes. The numbers on the clock at the bottom of the screen ticked away. At six in the morning, the team suddenly moved.

"Slow it down," Kate said.

By the time Ellis had slowed the feed, the squad was back on the street below. He turned up the volume. Boots pounded the ground, and a voice in French blared from the speakers. The soldier's helmet cam bobbed as he ran down a street surrounded by neo-Gothic facades tucked between modern buildings. He was heading toward a blackened church. The purple-and-crimson haze of the morning sun rose above the steeple.

Kate could almost smell the charcoaled buildings, the same acrid scent she'd smelled while a prisoner in New York. Those memories once again threatened to break her down. She willed them away by grabbing her coffee mug and taking a swig of the cold, bitter liquid.

She tensed as a soldier covered from head to toe in camouflage sprinted down the street. He had a machine gun leveled at the church. Two more men passed into view, boots leaving tracks on the ash-covered street.

Another voice speaking French crackled from the speakers. Kate had only taken two years in high school, but she got the gist of it: *Run. They're coming.*

She nearly dropped her coffee mug when she heard the low hissing. After setting it down, she wrapped her arms across her sweatshirt and pulled her knees to her chest.

The soldier on screen heard the hissing too. He spun toward the buildings behind him. Flashes of movement darted across rooftop terraces.

The gut-wrenching feeling of hope being stripped away was not new to Kate, but this time it made her ill. She'd wanted desperately for these men to be invisible, for science to give them—and Beckham—a fighting chance against the monsters.

Once, just once, she wanted to find a way to stay a step ahead of the beasts.

These men were supposed to be the hunters. Between their camouflage and the liquid masking their scent, they should have been invisible.

But they were the ones being hunted.

She should have known all along.

Kate continued holding her breath as the men were surrounded by juveniles on every rooftop. The video feed shook as the soldier ordered his team to open fire. They emptied full magazines, but the bullets ricocheted off the creatures' armored plates.

Shadows closed in around the team.

The offspring moved like apparitions. Blurs swooped in and whisked the soldiers away one at a time. Agonizing screams of men being slaughtered rose across the dead city.

The man with the cam was the last to be taken. He fought valiantly, firing with his pistol in one hand and his machine gun in the other. Both guns were stripped away—and with them his arms, ripped clean from their sockets.

The last thing Kate saw was a pair of slimy mandibles snapping at the man's face. She buried her head in her arms, unable to watch.

"Jesus," Ellis whispered in a flat voice.

They sat in silence for several minutes. Kate slowly pulled her head away from her arms and glanced up at the clock. It was almost eleven now. She was exhausted, and yet with that exhaustion, an idea formed in her head.

# 22

"Friendly! Friendly!" Davis shouted at the top of her lungs.

The helicopter hovering over the airfield answered with a barrage of 7.62-millimeter rounds that punched into the dirt around her. She glimpsed Sergeant Lynch behind the M240 right before she dove for the safety of a boulder. The projectiles from Spartan 2 shook the rock. Pieces broke away and exploded all around her.

She had to find a better place to hide, but with her injured leg, moving wasn't going to be easy. Crouching behind the boulder, she scanned the airfield and focused on a Black Hawk sitting fifteen feet away.

Surely Humphrey wouldn't allow his men to destroy one of those.

*You can do this, Rachel. You have to do this.*

With no time to come up with a plan, Davis did the only think she could think of. She ran at an angle toward the bird. Pain immediately lanced up her right thigh. She changed course to distract Lynch. He redirected his fire with the grace of an experienced gunner. She could almost feel those rounds tearing through her flesh, but she hadn't been hit—yet.

The screaming gun kicked up chunks of earth all

around her, peppering her with snow and grit. She dove for the undercarriage of the bird when she was five feet away, but the rounds kept coming.

A stream of bullets shattered the cockpit windows and tore into the troop hold above her.

*Holy shit!*

Davis squirmed under the bird as it was pummeled with projectiles.

"Friendly!" she shouted again. Her muffled voice sounded as if it was coming from a stranger. She couldn't contain her frustration. Spit flew out of her mouth and coated the inside of her face guard.

How could Lynch be so blind?

The answer was in the sky. The moon had slipped behind the clouds, casting a suffocating black curtain over the mountain. She looked down at her armor. Lynch couldn't see it. All he could see was her heat signature. For all Lynch knew, she was a human collaborator, or a Variant.

Anger swirled with the pain inside Davis. She had managed to fight her way out of Earthfall, only to be fired upon by her own men. And now it was only a matter of time before Lynch pumped her full of 7.62-millimeter rounds.

"Fitz!" she screamed. "Fitz, where are you?"

She could hear Apollo barking, but she hadn't heard anything from Fitz since the rounds started flying. Another salvo zipped across the dirt behind her boots. She pulled herself under the chopper.

"GODDAMNIT! STOP FIRING!" she shouted into her headset.

An explosion rocked the ground. The undercarriage of the bird she hid under rumbled from the impact. She craned her neck and watched as another chopper burst into flames. Lynch had directed his fire at a Black Hawk a hundred feet from hers.

He was destroying a lot of precious government property, but for the moment, she was safe. She crawled to the other side of the chopper and searched for Fitz. Rounds whistled all around her, coming in sporadic bursts. Lynch would open fire, then pause, then continue firing at a target Davis couldn't see.

In the respite, she heard Apollo howling. She turned to look for him but then saw something else that caught her eye. The sight of the black blades made her grin.

Fitz ran like a madman from chopper to chopper. He was yelling, waving, and moving as fast as a Variant on his new legs. But all he seemed to be accomplishing was drawing Lynch's fire.

Davis had to do something.

She winced as she squirmed out from under the chopper; her right thigh was screaming from the pain. Pushing herself to her feet, she scanned the airfield for something to use. There were few options. With the radio still not working, she could risk waving some more, or she could find a way to signal Lynch. Both choices seemed suicidal.

Her eyes flitted to the cockpit of the chopper on her right. Without thinking, she opened the door and jumped inside. Lynch continued to fire at Fitz, rounds clipping the ground around him as he ran in zigzags. He was fast, but it was only a matter of time before one of them hit their mark.

And it would take only one shot.

Davis reached for the controls.

*Shit. I should know how to do this.*

The panel looked way more complicated than she remembered. But once she turned the bird on, all she needed was to find the damn lights.

It took her a full minute to fire up the bird. As the rotors made their first pass, she leaned down and searched for the lights. She found them and flipped them on, but nothing happened. When she glanced up, the Black Hawk was coming in for a second pass. Fitz was on the western edge of the airfield now, Apollo right behind him. They hid behind one of the Chinooks. Lynch held his fire and raked the gun back in Davis's direction.

Her heart flipped as she stared at the red hot muzzle of the smoking gun.

*Come on, Lynch, open your fucking eyes.*

She flipped the lights a second and then a third time. Beams suddenly fired from the aircraft. Now if she could just remember the Morse code she learned years ago.

Spartan 2 banked hard to the left. Lynch roved the big gun in her direction again. His green-lit helmet in the open doorway looked inhuman. It was hard to remember this man was her friend.

She continued flashing the lights while waving with her other hand. The bulky black chopper raced toward her. She closed her eyes at the last second, waiting to be torn apart. Instead of rounds slamming the windshield, a gust of cold wind rushed through the gaping holes and cracks in the glass as Spartan 2 passed overhead. The frigid air took her breath away.

Had Lynch finally spotted her?

Davis wasn't about to take any more chances. She continued flashing the light and followed Spartan 2 as it circled for another pass.

*Friendly. Friendly. Friendly.*

The Black Hawk swooped back in, but this time it pulled away from her position. A fiery flash bloomed from the M240 as Lynch fired again, rounds spitting toward the east. Fitz was on the move with Apollo.

"Come on!" Davis shouted. She continued flipping the beams at Spartan 2. Fitz was running toward her now. Apollo was right by his side, his coat covered in icy, matted blood.

"Please," Davis whispered.

Fitz didn't bother waving. He tucked his helmet down and ran, his blades kicking up a snowy exhaust behind him. He moved like a running back, sliding to the left and then the right.

For a second Davis thought he might actually make it to her. He was passing another abandoned chopper when Lynch finally got lucky.

The stream of 7.62-millimeter rounds tore into the troop hold of the Black Hawk, peppering the metal with melon-sized holes. They punched into the engine and cockpit with fiery impacts. Her eyes widened as Fitz and Apollo vanished in the explosion.

"*No!*" Davis shouted.

She slid down into the pilot's chair, beaten and broken. Lynch continued emptying the M240 until the helicopter finally pulled away. The rotors whipped up the smoke from the raging fire below.

"You stupid son of a bitch, Lynch," Davis hissed. The marine had followed orders blindly, unable to think for himself. But could she really blame him? When so much was at risk, what would she have done in his shoes? Davis bowed her head, her finger still flashing the lights haphazardly. She could bail from the chopper and run, but that would only delay the inevitable. She wasn't going to make it far on her leg.

As the Black Hawk closed in, she remained in her seat, staring defiantly at her comrade. Part of her wanted to close her eyes, but instead she narrowed them at Lynch. The muzzle of the massive gun was pointing right at her.

"Do it," Davis whispered. "Fucking get it over with."

But instead of firing, the pilots descended onto the

airfield. Grit and ice swirled through the broken wind-shield and flew into Davis's armor. She continued flashing the chopper's beams, repeating the same message.

*Friendly, friendly.*

The pilots put the bird down a couple hundred feet away. Davis watched, still waiting for the rounds that would shred her to bits. She cautiously took her hand off the lights and shut the bird off. Then she opened the door of the chopper and jumped into the snow. A swirling cloud of smoke surrounded the chopper like a halo. She shielded her helmet from the gust the rotors were kicking up.

"Davis!" shouted a voice stifled by the whoosh of helicopter blades.

Marines hopped out of the Black Hawk, but this voice was coming from the east. Davis ignored Lynch and his men. They were yelling now too. She heard apologies and some other shit she didn't want to deal with at the moment.

She turned toward the wreckage of the helicopter where she had last seen Fitz. A curtain of smoke drifted across the airfield. Tendrils of orange flickered out of gaping bullet holes in the engine hood, licking the barbecued metal.

"Help!" someone shouted.

Davis limped toward the sound.

The words came again, but this time they were strangled by pain.

A blur of dark fur made Davis stop midstride. She gasped when she saw it was not a Variant but Apollo. The dog was dragging Fitz by his right arm, tugging with all of his might as he pulled his handler from the smoke.

"Lynch! We need help!" Davis shouted. Despite her wounded thigh, she started running again the moment she saw Fitz.

Apollo continued dragging him clear. Fitz coughed as the dog yanked on his arm. He was trying to say something, but Davis couldn't make it out. He'd taken in a lot of smoke.

When Fitz saw Lynch and the other marines, the words became a lot clearer and louder.

"You assholes almost killed my dog!" There was anger in his voice, but not nearly as much as Davis would have expected. The man was a gentleman, even when people were trying to murder him.

Davis grabbed Fitz's other arm and pulled him away from the burning wreckage. As he emerged from the smoke, she saw his smoldering blades. They were toast, burned and mangled.

"Are you hurt?" Davis asked, her eyes flitting to the rest of his body.

Fitz flipped up his face guard, hacking and coughing. He struggled to draw in fresh air as he slowly shook his head. "Just... my... blades."

"Holy shit, LT!" Lynch yelled as he approached. Other marines crowded around. Sergeant Adair was there too, shoulders sagging, clearly embarrassed.

"We thought you were collaborators—" Lynch began to say.

"Save it," Davis interrupted. "All that matters now is deploying the weapon. Take your men and the Kryptonite and get inside the facility ASAP. I'll meet you in there."

Davis dropped to her knees, overwhelmed with emotion. Apollo nudged up beside Fitz, then sat down, still protecting his handler.

"Good boy," Fitz said, reaching up to pet the dog.

"Don't worry," Davis said. She pointed to his blades. "I'll get you another pair."

Fitz grinned. "This is becoming a habit, LT."

She patted him on the shoulder and exhaled. Then she glared at Lynch, who was still hovering over them.

"What the hell are you waiting for, marine? We have a mission to complete!" she shouted.

Garcia repeated the Lord's Prayer for the tenth time. He couldn't save them.

They were all dead.

And he couldn't do a damn thing.

The bodies of the other strike teams were everywhere. On the ceiling, the floor, the walls. Plastered by the same glue that had bound Steve-o to the sewer wall in Atlanta.

Garcia hunched down and put his hands on his head. Closing his eyes, he pressed as hard as he could on his temples. The pain felt good. It made him feel alive.

But what kind of life did he have left?

He wanted to scream, but he forced himself to snap his eyes open and respect those who had made the ultimate sacrifice for their country.

Terrified faces, frozen at the moment they were killed, stared back at him. He clenched his fists and continued slopping through the blood. The Variants hadn't spared a single person. They had killed everyone before the attack on Team Spartan.

That had given Garcia and his friends time to hold back the beasts. It was hard to stomach the loss of so many dead marines, but Garcia would not let them die in vain.

"Rico," he shouted, "is Davis back yet?"

"Not yet."

He turned back to the open doorway. The three missing cases of Kryptonite were stacked neatly outside. They were six feet long and three feet wide, but far heavier than they looked. It had taken Garcia and Rico ten minutes to drag them across the room.

Rico stood guard over the precious treasure trove, her shotgun draped across her chest armor. They had located the cases with ease, all Garcia had had to do was replay the video footage. He'd also discovered exactly what had happened in the twenty minutes before Team Spartan landed.

The collaborators had waited for Team Wolverine to enter the building. It was an impressive and coordinated attack. As soon as the marines were inside the command room, they were ambushed and their comms disabled.

Outside, the other collaborators shot a pilot in the head, then forced everyone else from Saber and Lightning to surrender. According to the video feeds, not a single Variant had been involved in the battle—not even the Alpha. The collaborators had done all of the dirty work. But they had failed to take out Team Spartan. Arriving last had probably saved them; by the time the collaborators saw them approaching the building, it was too late. The bastards never accounted for Fitz's MK11 or Apollo. The collaborators had panicked and unleashed the Variants.

He wanted to spit on the leader's corpse, but after Fitz had shot him in the face, there wasn't much left to spit on.

"Garcia, the LT is back!" Rico said.

Garcia said a final prayer for the fallen men and women. They deserved better than this—they should have graves in Arlington National Cemetery, not in some classified government facility with the rotting corpses of a bunch of goddamn monsters.

But that was the grim reality of the world he lived in now.

Making the sign of the cross over his chest, Garcia returned to the chamber. Armor clanked down the stairwell as Davis led a group of marines into the room.

Lynch, Adair, and three other men carried Plum Island's batch of Kryptonite. The crate contained enough diluted Kryptonite to cover a three-hundred-mile radius.

"We found the other cases, LT," Garcia said, pointing. "What the hell took you guys so long? And where are Fitz and Apollo?"

Davis flipped up her face guard and snorted. "Friendly fucking fire. Fitz is getting patched up as we speak."

Garcia's heart thumped. "Is he okay?"

"He'll be fine," Davis said. "Fortunately."

Lynch looked toward the floor and whispered something Garcia couldn't hear. It wasn't hard to put the puzzle together: The comms were still down, and Lynch had accidentally ordered his men to fire on Davis, Fitz, and Apollo.

Garcia released his anger with a sigh. There was no time for it. They needed to finish what they had started.

"Adair, Lynch, get the Kryptonite loaded into the missiles," Davis ordered. "Garcia, Rico, follow me."

"You got it, LT," Adair said.

The other marines fanned out across the room. They sidestepped the corpses of mangled Variants, leaving bloody tracks as they continued toward the tunnels. Garcia couldn't believe they had fought off so many of the beasts without taking a casualty. Even harder to believe was that friendly fire had nearly made it all a waste.

*The fuck is happening to us?* Garcia thought, watching the guys who'd almost turned Fitz and Apollo into hamburger. They couldn't have known, though. *Could they?*

Lynch and Adair quickly vanished into the dark passages with the others. Garcia considered warning them about what they would see, but he held his tongue. A warning wouldn't make it any better.

Davis stepped over the collaborator's body draped across the platform.

"Sergeant Garcia," she said. "C'mon up here and help me."

He sped his walk to a run and loped up the ramp. Together they dragged the man's body away from the computer monitors. Garcia could no longer hold back the anger he felt and spat on the corpse.

Davis didn't seem to notice. She continued to one of the keyboards and brought up an encryption screen. Then she typed in a series of codes. Data fired onto the monitor, numbers scrolling across. She punched in another command.

Rico leaned close to Garcia. "How many marines we got topside? What if the Variants come back?" She was fiercely chewing her gum, and her questions were starting to annoy Garcia.

"A dozen, and Spartan Two is back in the air," Davis answered. She twisted slightly away from the monitor and flashed a grin toward Rico. "Don't worry, we're good. More reinforcements are on the way."

A symbol of a cloud divided by a lightning burst came online. Below the logo, a motto flashed across the screen: *Earthfall—The future of modified-weather warfare.*

Davis's grin widened. "We're in."

Garcia slung his M4 over his shoulder and stepped closer. Blueprints of the facility emerged on screen. Twenty missiles came online, the one-dimensional shapes blinking red.

"How's it coming in there?" Davis shouted.

"Loading almost complete!" Adair yelled back.

One by one, the missiles flashed blue. Ten minutes later they were all ready to fly.

Davis brought up a second screen and punched in another code. Garcia watched, feeling oddly calm. It was hard to fathom they were about to launch a weapon that would kill all the adult Variants. He'd never thought this day would come. It made all of the losses seem as if they counted for something.

For the first time in as long as he could remember, Garcia felt a smile spreading across his bruised face. He could hardly recall what smiling felt like.

"All right," Davis said. "This should do it." Her finger hovered over the Enter key. Garcia watched it with wide eyes.

She looked at Rico and then to Garcia. "Congratulations, Spartans. We did it."

Davis brought her finger down on the button. A countdown began on the wall-mounted monitors.

*100*

*99*

*98…*

Captain Humphrey narrowed his eyes at Kate when she pitched her idea of equipping every soldier heading into the field with R49 grenades. She'd expected that, but she'd never expected him to agree so quickly to the idea.

"I've heard of military units in Africa using something similar to the R49 with some success," Humphrey had said. "If it works on Variants over there, it ought to work here too."

Now, two hours later, Kate was standing in the CIC feeling as if she'd finally come up with an idea to help Beckham and his men when they returned to the field. The R49 was extremely potent. The gas could put an elephant to sleep in less than a minute.

All she could do now was watch and wait. Another weapon, one she had designed, was about to launch into the sky.

Captain Humphrey's team tracked the twenty missiles

carrying Kryptonite as they traveled over North America. The missiles would fall apart as soon as they reached twenty thousand feet over their target zones. The diluted Kryptonite would then mix with Earthfall, the modified-weather agent designed to cause massive rainfall. Rural and urban areas alike would be painted with Kryptonite as it showered the ground, penetrating the soil and the sewers where many of the monsters dwelled.

She was so focused on the monitors that she almost jumped as a strong hand grabbed hers. She recognized the calluses and turned to face Beckham.

"Fitz and Apollo are okay," Beckham said.

Kate kissed him on the cheek. "Thank God."

"You ready for this?"

"Yes," she answered without hesitation.

Kate massaged his rough hands with her thumb. All around them in the cramped CIC, dozens of men and women waited as Davis and her team completed their mission.

"We have a freaking countdown!" Nagle shouted. The young man stood and flashed a pearly white grin. He was so caught up in the excitement that he had forgotten all about military decorum.

The feed from Spartan 2 was displayed on the largest monitor at the front of the room. Everyone squeezed closer to see. The Black Hawk was hovering on the west side of a mountain. Below was an airfield, where the smoking wreckage of destroyed helicopters dotted the terrain. It looked like a war zone.

"Twenty-nine, twenty-eight, twenty-seven," Nagle counted from his station.

Kate clenched Beckham's hand. The Black Hawk hovered closer as marines exited the building. A dozen soldiers ran through the drifting smoke in the glow of moonlight. In the lead was Lieutenant Davis, and she was limping. It didn't seem to be slowing her down much.

"Nineteen, eighteen, seventeen," Nagle continued.

*I can't believe this is finally happening.*

Kate had thought she would feel something: excitement, guilt, fear. But all she felt was the presence of the man standing by her side. She was content with him in a way she'd never been before. With Beckham's hand on hers, Kate was at peace.

The marines continued across the airfield and loaded into a chopper that quickly peeled away from the ground. Spartan 2 continued to hover.

"Five, four, three, two," Nagle said.

Ringgold turned at the last second and smiled at Kate.

A missile suddenly burst above the rocky terrain. Another followed close behind. In seconds, a dozen were streaking toward heaven. The room burst into applause as the final missile shot out of the launch tubes and took to the sky. They'd done it. Kryptonite was on its way.

# 23

Thirty-six hours had passed since Kryptonite had been deployed. The war had entered its seventh week now. Fitz was back on the *GW*, testing out his new blades on the flight deck as he waited for the briefing.

*Third time's a charm.*

It was midafternoon, and the wind was picking up, but it wasn't anything the aircraft carrier couldn't handle. From bow to stern she was 1,092 feet long, and she weighed just over 104,000 tons, depending on how many sailors were on board. Capacity was a little over six thousand, but that was no longer important since the apocalypse. Fitz wasn't even sure there were half that many people on board now, although he would have never known by looking at the deck. It was alive with activity.

Ordnance men carefully pushed carts of missiles. Aviation-fuel handlers juiced up the ninety fixed-wing aircraft. Flight deck crew dressed in yellow and blue vests worked together to stretch a rope across the deck. Pilots checked and double-checked their birds.

Everyone had a job—everyone had a duty.

Beckham, Horn, Rico, Tank, and Garcia were huddled around a crate next to the control tower. Dozens of marines, Rangers, and even some SEALs were spread out behind them. The teams were all examining maps of the cities they were being deployed to in the final stage of Operation Extinction.

Apollo looked up and wagged his tail as Fitz approached.

"How you feeling, little man?" Tank said.

Fitz raised a brow. "You're the one we should be worried about."

Tank grumbled something that Fitz couldn't understand. Garcia chuckled; he was the only one who could seem to understand Tankspeak.

Beckham gave Fitz and Tank his typical elevator-eyes look of scrutiny, then offered a reassuring nod to both men. "You look sharp, marines."

Fitz shrugged. He didn't feel sharp. The long ride back to the *GW* had given him too much time to think.

"Officer on deck!" shouted a voice.

Davis slammed open the hatch to the control tower and limped toward the gathered soldiers. They all looked up as she approached. She had earned everyone's respect after two successful missions for which she'd put her own life on the line. She was the type of leader Fitz would follow into battle without question, just as he'd followed Beckham. She was also a hell of a lot prettier than Beckham.

"Everyone, listen up!" Davis shouted, with her hands cupped over her mouth.

Pilots rose from their cockpits, and ordnance men stopped pushing their carts. Every man and woman halted their work. The wind whistled over the ocean. It was calming, but not near enough to reduce the tension.

"I have news that I'm honored to be able to share with you," Davis said. "We just got word that the Variants are dropping like flies in every major city across the country. The final stage of Operation Extinction has been given the green light."

Davis's voice rose to a crescendo. "Tonight, God willing, we will finally take back some of our cities from the Variants!"

The response shocked Fitz. Applause, whistling, and shouting erupted over the wind. Even Apollo howled his approval.

Fitz clapped slowly, hesitant to rejoice this early. The adults were dying—great. But what about the offspring? What came next would be the most challenging battle yet. The mission wasn't just to kill them, it was to sneak in with RDDs and destroy them in their lairs before they escaped.

"It's almost over," Horn said. He clapped Fitz on the shoulder, a bit too hard. Fitz planted his right blade to brace himself and shot Horn a glare.

"Sorry, brother. I'm just excited. Seven weeks of this shit! And now it's almost over."

Fitz shook his head and glanced toward Beckham. The master sergeant was the only one not grinning as if he'd won the lottery. Like Fitz, he clapped politely, but there was a thoughtful expression on his rugged face.

"Those deploying, report to your CO for orders," Davis said.

She took a moment to scan the soldiers on the deck before returning inside the ship. Fitz watched the hatch close behind her. The click was barely audible over the men and women still celebrating.

Fitz put his hands in his pockets. "So we're heading to DC?"

"That's right," Beckham said. "I'm lead. I've had you, Garcia, Tank, and Rico assigned to Team Ghost. Our orders are to sneak an RDD into the main lair, here."

Fitz followed Beckham's finger across a map of the National Mall until it came down on the Capitol Building.

"Horn and I were briefed earlier on a major juvenile hotspot under the Capitol where they've taken up residence in an old fallout shelter," Beckham said. "I'm still working on the best insertion point. Recon missions have shown increased activity over the past forty-eight hours. Juveniles are coming out of the nest more frequently. That's why we're parachuting in under the cover of darkness."

"How many hostiles do we expect to face?" Rico asked. She was no longer the chipper marine Fitz had met a day earlier. She chewed furiously on a stick of bubblegum, but there were no bubbles now, or jokes.

Horn crossed his tattooed arms. "There's a shit-ton of juveniles down there."

"How many, exactly?" Rico asked.

"Thousands," Beckham said coldly.

Tank was the first to speak up. "How the hell do—"

"With these," Beckham interrupted. He held up a grenade in one hand and a gas mask in the other. "This is an R49, and it contains the most potent sleep gas the military has in its arsenal. This was Kate's idea, and I trust her with my life."

"She's sure this gas will put the juveniles out?" Garcia asked.

Beckham shook his head. "Not one hundred percent."

"Has it been field-tested?" Rico asked.

"*We're* field-testing it," Beckham replied. He continued talking before anyone else could ask a question. "Everyone's wearing a gas mask. It goes on as soon as we hit the ground."

Rico cracked her gum. Tank rubbed at his eye patch and continued grumbling. The rest of the team was silent.

Beckham continued. "The RDD's blast radius will destroy juveniles within half a square mile, and the radiation will be lethal up to another two square miles."

"That's a lot of DC," Rico said. "A lot of history we're going to be blowing up and poisoning."

"I know," Beckham said, his voice tight and flat. For the first time since Fort Bragg, Fitz couldn't get a read on him.

"Any other questions?" Beckham asked.

"What about Chow?" Horn asked.

Beckham shook his head again. "He's in no shape to fight with us. I'm afraid he has to stay behind."

Fitz couldn't think of anything worse; being left behind would have pushed him over the edge. Riley had hated sitting on the sidelines. Now Chow was being forced to do so.

"Get a few hours of shut-eye, if you can," Beckham said. "We ship out at 2000."

Kate grabbed Beckham the moment they were inside their quarters. Both of them knew these could be the last hours they ever spent together.

Kate stripped out of her pants and pulled Beckham's shirt off. She wasn't going to spend the next few hours crying or moping. She knew exactly how she wanted to spend that time.

"Kate, we don't have to," Beckham began to say.

"Shush," Kate said, her lips inches from his. "I want to."

Beckham might have smiled, but Kate didn't wait to find out. She leaned in and pressed her lips against his. He tossed his shirt to the side and unfastened his belt. They fell into bed with their mouths still locked together.

Kate lost herself in Beckham's strong arms. If this was it, if she was never going to see him again, she wanted to remember their final moments together just like this.

She ran her fingers down his muscular back and pulled him into her. Reaching up, she wrapped her arms around his neck and kissed him. She filled her lungs with the scent of him. Kate loved his musk, loved everything about him. It was biology, pheromones, but it was also what love was to her—loving every part of someone, the good and the bad. She tried to memorize the feeling of his hands on her skin, the map of scars and bruises on his muscular body, the balance of strength and vulnerability that she treasured.

"I love you, Reed," Kate whispered afterward, her head pillowed against his chest.

Beckham brushed her hair from her blue eyes. "I love you too." After a pause, he said, "I'm coming back. I promise. I'm going to see our child born."

Kate fought back the tears. She was not going to lose control now. She had to be strong—not just for herself but also for him. This time he needed her just as much as she needed him. She could feel it in his hammering heart.

Even Delta Force operators felt fear.

"You're damn right," Kate said, sitting up. She put a hand on his naked chest, right over his heart. "I can feel it."

Beckham put his hand over hers. They locked eyes, a fleeting moment that felt as if it lasted forever.

"Nothing's going to stop me from coming back to you, Kate."

The confidence in his eyes made her smile. She scooted back to him and rested her head once more on his chest.

For hours they lay there, talking and kissing. They made love a second time, and when they were finished, Beckham asked, "What should we name our baby?"

She looked over at him, smiling. "I haven't had much of a chance to think about it. Got any ideas?"

He hesitated. "I was thinking if it's a boy, we could name him Javier Riley, in memory of your brother and Riley."

Kate's heart kicked harder. "And if it's a girl?"

"How about Meghan Joyce, after Meg and my mother?"

"Reed," Kate whispered. She kissed him on the forehead and wiped away a tear that she couldn't hold inside. "I think those are fantastic choices."

A rap on the door snapped them both to attention. Her heart rate elevated as she looked at the clock. Their time together was up.

For once, luck was on their side. A storm front had carried Kryptonite like wildfire over the states. Beckham had never considered divine intervention before, but it felt like a miracle. The weapon worked better than even the science team had expected, killing over 99 percent of the adult Variants. Just shy of two days after the weapon's launch, virtually every adult Variant in the lower forty-eight states was dead or dying.

Despite the victory, Beckham couldn't bury his dread. He stood on the flight deck next to some of the toughest sons of bitches left in the world. Horn, Fitz, Garcia, Tank, Rico, Davis, and even Chow had made it topside. Apollo sat at Beckham's boots. All around them, soldiers stood at attention. It was hard to tell who was who under their plates of black armor and helmets topped with night-vision goggles. Webbing packed full of flares and gear crisscrossed every soldier's legs and arms. Pouches stuffed with extra magazines covered their extremities. M67 and R49 grenades hung from vests. These were some of the last soldiers in the world, and they were ready to fight against overwhelming odds to save their country.

Armored plates bulwarked vital parts, but Beckham knew it wasn't enough. If they were compromised, if the gas didn't work, the armor would do nothing to stop the juveniles.

He thought bitterly that all the armor really did was cover the injuries these men and women had sustained. What little skin was exposed didn't tell the full story of what they'd been through. But Beckham knew better than anyone.

He eyed an Army Ranger with lacerations on his wrists. The man next to him had bruises on his face that made Garcia look like a model. There wasn't a soldier out here who didn't have an injury of some sort. Beckham's face had mostly healed from the attack of the Variant that had pummeled him at Fort Bragg, but his body was still recovering from the shrapnel wounds. Horn had a bullet hole in his bicep. Chow was covered in deep gashes. Davis had been shot. Fitz was on his third set of blades. Tank was missing an eye. Garcia had a broken nose, and even Apollo had stitches in his back.

But none of the faces Beckham studied betrayed the physical pain of their injuries. The tears and red eyes were results of a different kind of pain.

Coffins draped with American flags rested on the starboard side of the flight deck. These were the men and women they had lost at Plum Island. With Kryptonite deployed and the final stage of Operation Extinction about to get underway, Command had finally prepared a funeral ceremony.

To the right of the soldiers, a crowd of civilians looked on. Beckham could see Tasha and Jenny with Kate out of the corner of his eye. Bo and Donna were there too, along with hundreds of civilians. Even the former

NYPD officer, Jake, and his son Timothy were in the crowd. Beckham hadn't seen either of them since he'd rescued them from Manhattan during Operation Liberty. Timothy already looked taller.

Beckham swallowed hard as he reached into his vest pocket. The tip of his fingers brushed against the picture of his mom, and then the dog tags of every man he'd lost since Building 8. He held the metal in his palm. The faces of those who had perished seemed to appear before him.

Riley was flashing his shit-eating grin as he kicked Team Ghost's ass on a beach run five years ago. Panda was laughingly berating the kid at a strip club for stealing his stripper. Tenor and Edwards were smoking cigars on a sandy tarmac in Iraq after a successful mission that had killed two major terrorists. Jinx was cracking jokes at Fort Bragg in the mess as Chow threw a slice of turkey at him. Timbo was flexing his guns as Horn rolled up his sleeves and flexed back.

Meg was there with her crutches, hopping after Riley in his wheelchair, the two of them shouting and laughing as they chased each other like kids on a playground. And finally, Beckham saw Lieutenant Colonel Jensen, one of the bravest and most noble leaders he'd ever had the privilege to follow. Jensen had handed him his Colt .45 Peacemaker on the tarmac at Plum Island as he took his last breaths, and Beckham had carried it proudly ever since. They would bury Major Smith, his loyal second in command, right next to Jensen in a few hours. Riley and Meg would be laid to rest there too.

But Beckham wouldn't be there to see it. He would be off doing what he did best.

Fighting.

The kind yet commanding voice of President Jan Ringgold pulled him back to reality. She strolled out onto the deck wearing a black suit, a white shawl over her shoulders. It caught in the wind, flapping behind her and exposing the American flag lapel pin on her collar. Vice President Johnson hurried to catch up with her. When he did, he carefully grabbed her shawl and wrapped it back around her neck.

It was a kind gesture that reminded Beckham he didn't need to be constantly wary of his superiors. Johnson was a good man. Humphrey wasn't all that bad either. The captain stood to the left of Johnson. Davis joined them, standing to Humphrey's left. Side by side, Ringgold and Johnson faced the crowd of civilians and soldiers. They were equals. Beckham respected that egalitarian relationship. It was a good sign for the future of American politics.

"Good evening," Ringgold said in a voice that carried over the wind. "Tonight, we gather for two reasons."

She paused to look at the coffins. "The first is to remember those we have lost. These are just a fraction of the men and women who have given their lives so we could be standing right here, right now. They paved the way for the final stage of Operation Extinction, and their sacrifice will never be forgotten. I ask all those who pray, and even those who don't, to bow your heads and remember every one of these brave souls."

An eerie wind rushed across the deck as Beckham and everyone else lowered their eyes. He saw the same faces as before in his mind, but they were defiant now. They wanted to be avenged.

The image chilled Beckham to the core.

He looked at his boots, then locked eyes with Apollo. The dog could sense his handler's pain. He nudged up against Beckham's right leg.

Vice President Johnson's booming voice reminded everyone of the second reason they'd all gathered.

"This evening, we begin taking back our cities from an enemy that has taken so much from us. Tonight we will fight and bleed, as we have since the day we gained our independence over two centuries ago. With the success of Kryptonite, I believe we have reached a turning point. The fate of America rests in the balance, and in your hands."

Johnson pivoted ever so slightly toward the soldiers with a commanding gaze Beckham had never seen from him. It was the type of look that took years to master— the type of look that reassured young men and women that there was hope, that this wasn't a suicide mission.

This time Beckham had more than just skin in the game. He'd helped plan the other missions with Horn. A lot of lives were on the line, and if their plan failed, that was on them. He also had Kate and their unborn child to think about. Johnson threw up a salute and turned to Ringgold. Her shawl flapped behind her shoulders as she focused with narrowed eyes.

"You are all heroes. Your mission will not be easy, but in the end, you will be victorious. And after we take back our country, I promise you, as your president, I will make it my priority to rebuild our beloved nation."

She lowered her gaze for a moment, as if searching for the right words.

"Three weeks ago, when I was locked away at Raven Rock, I had some thoughts I am very ashamed of," Ringgold continued. "When I learned that the hemorrhage virus was engineered by our own government, I thought maybe we didn't deserve to survive as a species. But the bravery of people like Master Sergeant Reed Beckham, Doctor Kate Lovato, and so many others has reminded me this isn't the case."

Beckham felt goose bumps prickle across his flesh, but not because she'd recognized him. He'd struggled with the same sentiments. The Variants hadn't had a choice when they'd turned into monsters. But men like Colonel Wood, Colonel Gibson, and every other bastard who created them had. He knew not all humans were inherently bad by nature, but this war had made Beckham seriously question whether his species was a virus of its own. Kate had reminded him that the human race was worth protecting. Fitz had also played a major role. The marine embodied the very best of what it meant to be human: He was resilient, kind, loyal, and selfless. The president standing in front of him was another example of why Beckham had never given up fighting for a military that had all but betrayed him and his men. She was the leader they needed in this, the most terrible chapter of their history.

"Tonight, we are given a second chance," she said. "Tonight, we are reminded what it means to be human, and tonight, we will take the first step in building a better America, a better place for future generations."

Beckham nodded. Maybe his child and all the other children would have a better world to grow up in after all. That was worth fighting for—worth dying for.

Ringgold scanned the faces on the deck, stopping on Beckham's. A smile touched the corners of her mouth.

"Good luck, and Godspeed!" she shouted after the brief pause.

There was no applause as Beckham led his men to the choppers. As he passed the row of coffins, he opened his hand and examined the dog tags.

"This mission's for all of you," he said under his breath.

"Beckham," said a voice. He halted as Chow limped over to him.

"Wish I was going out there with you, brother."

"Me too. But there will be more cities to clear. When you're better—"

Chow leaned in and gave Beckham a hug. "Save it,

man. Just be safe. Come back in one piece. As soon as I can piss on my own again, I'm gonna be right back out there fighting next to you."

Beckham gave his comrade a half smile. "I'll see you soon, brother."

They parted, and Beckham whistled for Apollo to follow. Most of the soldiers continued past the line of civilians, but Beckham and Horn stopped when they reached Ellis, Kate, and Tasha and Jenny.

Jenny pulled away from Kate and hugged Horn's right leg. Tasha latched onto the other.

"Please don't go," Jenny said.

"You promised you wouldn't go," Tasha whimpered.

Horn patted their backs and looked at Beckham. There wasn't anything that Beckham could say to relieve his pain. He now understood the burden of a father leaving behind a child. He felt the same burn as he looked at Kate, his eyes flitting to her stomach.

"Don't worry, girls, Uncle Reed is going to take good care of me. I'll be back in no time," Horn said, his voice reassuring and calm.

His daughters looked up with glistening eyes. "Promise?" they said at the same time.

"Promise," Horn said. He hunkered down, kissed them both on their foreheads, and then hugged them tight.

"I promise too," Beckham said. He leaned over so he was at eye level with the girls. "I'll take care of your daddy, and your daddy is going to take care of me."

Apollo licked the tears off Tasha's face and then moved on to Jenny. They giggled and stroked his coat.

Fitz smiled at them. "Be good, girls."

Tasha and Jenny smiled shyly, and Kate put her hands on their shoulders.

"I like your robot legs," Tasha said.

Fitz raised his helmet slightly as if he was tipping his hat at the girl. He grinned and hurried to the choppers. Apollo followed him, and Beckham turned back to Kate. Her blue eyes were strong and clear. He knew she was being brave for him, and he loved her even more for it. When they pulled away, he held her gaze and said, "I love you so very much, Kate."

"I love you more."

Beckham smiled. "Impossible."

They hugged one last time, then Beckham backpedaled away, his eyes still on Kate and Horn's girls. Both he and Horn paused to say their final goodbyes. Then they turned and jogged toward the open troop hold of a chopper, just as they had so many times before. There had never been more at risk, but they were still together, and they would be until the end.

# 24

"Team Ghost, this is your pilot speaking. Tonight our beautiful flight crew is serving hand grenades and LAW rockets. Hope y'all like hot sauce."

Fitz laughed and looked toward the cockpit. Tank's cousin Tito Boncs was one of the pilots flying the Osprey. His sarcastic sense of humor helped relieve some of the tension in the troop hold, but he couldn't do anything about the weather. A violent storm hammered the sides of the aircraft.

No one besides Fitz seemed to be paying attention to the storm or Tito's jokes. They were too busy checking and double-checking their chutes.

"I can't believe we're doing this," Tank grumbled. He looked the worst. His dark skin was a shade lighter than usual, and he was wobbling back and forth. "I hate heights. I fucking hate 'em!"

"Don't worry, big guy. You won't see a thing until you're about to splatter on the concrete," Horn joked.

Tank crinkled his massive nostrils. "Not funny, asshole. I only got one eye now, man—not sure if you noticed. It fucks with my depth perception."

"Cut the shit," Beckham said, working his way between the two hulking men. He braced himself as turbulence rocked the Osprey.

"If there was a seat belt sign, it would be flashing," Tito said over the comms. His voice was more serious this time, despite the sarcasm.

After the shaking passed, Beckham said, "I need *both* of you frosty."

"Frosty as fuck, boss," said Horn.

"Well, I'm a goddamn deep freeze," Tank replied. He glared at Horn with his remaining eye and half stood as if he wanted to challenge the other soldier.

Tito's voice came back online. "Sit your ass down, Cuz."

That got Tank's attention. He snorted and went back to fidgeting with his pack.

Beckham drew in a breath. "Listen up, Ghost."

Rico, Garcia, Fitz, and the big lugs stopped their gear checks to listen.

"I'm Ghost One on the comms. Garcia is Two, Horn is Three, Fitz is Four, Rico is Five, and Tank is Six. When we land, we stay in close combat intervals. Fitz has point; Tank, you're on rear guard. Keep low to the ground. You spot anything, you signal it. And keep your distance. The juveniles can shoot their venom up to thirty feet. You are *not* to engage unless it's a last resort. If you see them, we use our R49 grenades first. Complete radio discipline as soon as our boots hit dirt unless you're about to get your arms ripped off. Understood?"

Beckham spoke in a calm yet authoritative voice. It was a tone everyone respected. The members of Team Ghost all dipped their helmets. Apollo even wagged his tail.

"If you get separated below ground, you're to meet at the target," Beckham continued. He pulled his sleeved map and pointed at the location everyone had already memorized. "We'll enter the tunnels through a concealed access point located at the Ulysses S. Grant

Memorial at the east end of the National Mall. Tank and Big Horn are responsible for finding the entrance."

Horn slapped Tank on the shoulder, and Tank nodded back, their macho posturing already forgotten.

Beckham looked toward Horn. "You're responsible for the RDD, code-named Gibson."

Fitz grinned. Naming the bomb that would end this nightmare after the man who started it—hell, maybe Beckham had a sense of humor after all. This time Tank slapped Horn on the shoulder.

"Once we get inside the lair, we plant the bomb, set the timer, and get the hell out of Dodge." Beckham drew in a discreet breath. "Oh, and one last thing: The juveniles are going to be bigger than when you saw them last. Probably a hell of a lot smarter too. So watch your back and watch your buddy's back."

"Great," Garcia muttered. He tapped the side of his M4. Fitz used the stolen moment to scan the firepower in the troop hold. Everyone was equipped with a shotgun as a secondary weapon except for Fitz, who carried his M4 and MK11. Horn and Tank had both selected their usual M249 SAWS. Garcia, Rico, and Beckham carried M4s.

They didn't have mechanized units, rocket launchers, or air support, but they had something even more valuable—trust in the men and women fighting beside them. That was more important than any weapon.

Beckham scanned his team in turn. "Any questions?"

Rico shook her head, then changed her mind. "What happens if we breathe in some of this sleep gas or whatever the hell it is?"

"You hope that someone's there to drag your ass to safety," Beckham replied. "Because you'll be out for hours."

No one said anything for several seconds. Fitz suspected

they were all thinking the same thing he was about the sleep grenades—they were a waste of time.

Tank broke the silence in a shaky voice. "How long till drop?"

Beckham looked at his watch. "Twenty minutes."

"I should have taken a shit when I had the chance," Tank muttered. "Now I think I'm going to puke too."

Horn let out a bellowing laugh. "Better keep your cheeks clenched and your jaw shut on the drop!"

Beckham shook his head, but Fitz saw the ghost of a grin on their leader's face. Fitz let himself chuckle with the rest of them. A bit of humor before the big mission wasn't a bad thing, as long as everyone did their duty when their boots hit solid ground.

After a moment, Beckham grew serious again. "This is a high altitude–low opening drop, and we're doing it at minimum altitude. There's no indication human collaborators have anti-aircraft weapons, but even so, we can't risk being spotted if those assholes are down there. We're jumping at fifteen thousand feet. You've all had the training. You know what to do. I'll take Apollo, and we'll deploy Gibson with an automated chute."

Beckham paused one more time for questions. There weren't any.

"All right, let's get it done, people," he said, clapping his hands together.

"*Oorah*," Tank said.

The troop hold filled with the noises of men and women preparing for the most important mission of their lives. Fitz expected to see urgent movements, but aside from Tank pulling nervously on his pack, everyone else was relaxed.

Weapons and magazines were checked a third time. Armor plates were reclicked into place. Night-vision goggles were tested, and boots were laced and relaced.

Silencers were screwed onto primary weapons with clicks that reverberated throughout the narrow space. The final step was an old Team Ghost ritual—fastening bandannas. Fitz had seen Horn's skull mask before, but he had never seen Beckham wear one. Both men removed their helmets and tied their bandannas around their necks. They pulled the cotton up just below their lips. Then they flicked their mini-mics back into position and slipped their helmets back on.

Fitz didn't mean to stare, but he couldn't look away. From the side, in the dim lighting, all he could see were two matte-black helmets and mirrored visors. Beckham and his second in command looked just like their namesakes.

*Ghosts.*

"Five minutes to drop," Tito said. There was no joking around this time.

Beckham clicked his NVGs back into place and reached into his vest pocket. He strode over to Fitz with something in his hand. Fitz took the crumpled bandanna and opened it to reveal the face of a laughing joker. He looked up, shocked.

"This was—"

"Riley's," Beckham replied. "I thought you might like to wear it."

"I'd be honored to." Fitz tied the bandanna around the back of his neck and pulled it up to his bottom lip, then turned to face the other team members.

Horn dragged his gloved hand over his face, but Fitz saw the glint of tears in the man's eyes. Tank put a hand on Fitz's armored shoulder. "Looks good on ya, little man."

"Two minutes," Tito said.

"Put on your gas masks," Beckham ordered. "And don't forget, you breathe in any R49 and you're toast. So make sure your mask is tight. Check your shit and check your buddy's shit," Beckham said. He bent down to put a mask over Apollo's muzzle. The dog had been trained to use one and didn't resist.

Fitz slid his mask into position and pulled his bandanna up to cover it. He breathed in and picked up a distinct sour smell of sweat. It took his mind a moment to grasp that it was from the bandanna's previous owner. A piece of Riley was going back out there after all.

And so was a piece of Meg.

Glancing down, Fitz admired the hatchet hanging from his belt. He'd sawed the handle down so it would fit over his armor, but that didn't change the fact it had been Meg's. She'd held on to it all the way from New York to the *GW*. When Garcia had given it to him, Fitz had thought he might display it as a memento of her. Then he decided that a better way to honor her memory would be to split some Variant melons with it.

He wasn't much of a religious man, but he did believe the deceased lived on in the hearts and minds of those they left behind. Today, Riley and Meg would join them in battle.

Fitz tightened the bandanna and took a step closer to the back of the troop hold.

"Line up," Beckham ordered. Horn scooped up Apollo and helped Beckham strap the dog to his chest.

Fitz worked his way to the front of the team and grabbed the cable on the starboard side of the aircraft. The rest of Team Ghost fell into line behind him.

"One minute to target," Tito said. "Good luck, Ghost. Love you, Cuz."

"Love you too, Tito," Tank said.

There was no crew chief this time to herd them outside. Beckham gave Fitz a nod. Reaching out, Fitz punched the lift-gate door.

Wind rushed into the troop hold. A pitch-black sky stretched across the horizon like a cape. The rain had stopped, but the swollen clouds blocked out the stars and moon.

"This is it, Ghost. Dive safe and see you on the ground!" Beckham shouted.

"Fifteen seconds," Tito said.

Horn heaved the bag containing Gibson closer to the open door. He pushed it out a moment later. The rest of the team took another step forward and watched the dirty bomb plummet toward a city full of juveniles and dead adult Variants.

Fitz massaged the Delta Force Team Ghost patch he'd fastened onto his right shoulder plate and counted the seconds in his head. He glanced back at Beckham one last time and reached out to stroke Apollo's head. Neither of them had a flicker of fear in their dark eyes.

Oddly, Fitz didn't feel any fear either. In its place was something else—something he didn't recognize at first.

Excitement.

This was it. The end game.

Fitz turned, flipped his NVGs into position, and jumped into the darkness.

"Team Ghost is away," Davis reported.

She shifted in her chair as the live feeds fired onto the operations monitors. Waiting was always the hardest part, but at least she was sitting. If she was standing, she would have likely been pacing back and forth on her injured leg.

All across the country, small strike teams were being deployed. Each one carried an RDD designed to minimize infrastructure damage but produce lethal radiation.

No matter how you pitched it, the dirty bombs were going to blow some gaping holes in cities across America, but it was better than bleeding the streets red with what was left of her soldiers in a battle no one thought they could win. If the operation succeeded, the juveniles would be dealt a severe blow, and then Johnson could deploy troops to kill off the stragglers.

President Ringgold had approved the mission almost immediately upon hearing that pitch, but there was no denying how precarious the situation really was. Command was relying on special operations forces trained to sneak in and out of places without being detected. Team Ghost was one of the best, but Delta operators, SEALs, Green Berets, Rangers, Force Recon, and every other ops group were in short supply. They couldn't afford to fail, because there would be no one left for a second attempt.

"Sitrep?" Johnson asked. He stood behind the command staff next to Ringgold and Humphrey.

"We're all set, sir," Petty Officer Nagle replied. "Everything's looking good. Strike teams are away over Seattle, New York, Los Angeles, San Diego, Portland, Atlanta, and DC. There are still teams en route to Des Moines, St. Louis, Kansas City, Nashville, Denver, Miami, and..." Nagle double-checked his report. "And San Antonio."

"All teams have reported in," Corporal Anderson said from the radio equipment.

"Excellent," Johnson said. He turned to face his team. General Kohl, President Ringgold, and Captain Humphrey all wore the same optimistic look. The vice president shared that look, but his features were more strained. It was small, but Davis picked up on it. She felt the same anxiety. The future of the United States of America rested in the hands of the few. And they were up against overwhelming odds—not to mention a constantly evolving creature that had learned the art of the hunt, something even the American military was still adapting to after hundreds of years of warfare.

A jolt of pain made Davis reach down to touch her thigh. The bullet had only grazed her flesh, but it had cut a deep furrow that had required stitches. Without the injury, she would have been right back out there with Fitz and the others.

She had started to turn away from the monitors when she saw someone was missing from Johnson's staff: Lieutenant Colonel Kramer was absent from the CIC.

*Odd*, Davis thought as she stood and strode over to the portholes on the other side of the radar equipment. She grabbed a pair of binoculars from the ledge and aimed them at the horizon in search of her friends, wishing that she was out there with them.

*Good luck, Ghost.*

A green-tinted city that had been all but destroyed exploded into view as Beckham shot through the clouds. He fell with his arms and legs out. Gravity, as well as Apollo and the rest of the gear strapped to his chest, pulled on the center of his mass. It made maneuvering extremely difficult.

Beckham took a sidelong glance to check on his team. They were all in back-falling positions as he was. Tank was the only one struggling. The massive marine wobbled in the wind.

A web of lightning flashed over the eastern edge of DC. The green glow faded away, and the city once again returned to darkness. Thunder boomed a few seconds later. The storm was moving away from their landing zone. That was good, but the wind showed no sign of letting up.

Beckham fought the force pushing on him and angled his helmet downward. Another network of lighting streaked across the horizon. The brilliant flashes illuminated the ruined metropolis. From above, the nation's capital was scarcely recognizable. Iconic buildings had been reduced to rubble. Green spaces that had once drawn tourists to blooming cherry blossoms were covered in ash, the trees nothing but skeletons. Over two hundred years of the nation's history had almost been destroyed.

The dirty bomb would blow another hole in the historic fabric of DC, but he was confident President Ringgold would come through on her promise.

Humans would rebuild.

In the distance, the Washington Monument rose over the surrounding pools. It was one of the only things still standing, its tip pointing toward the sky Team Ghost was falling from.

The screeching wind was replaced by the distant crack of lightning and rumble of thunder. Beckham's body shook from the sound. Apollo's fur spiked in the wind, but the dog remained calm, hardly even wiggling.

Beckham checked his altimeter.

*Five thousand feet.*

They were already two-thirds of the way through the dive. At terminal velocity, or 120 miles per hour, he was falling 1300 feet every 8 seconds. He had only a few seconds left before he needed to deploy his chute.

Beckham cut through the clouds with a seed of hope forming in him. The seven weeks of hell was almost over. With Ringgold in charge, and men like Horn and Fitz by his side, Beckham allowed the seed to grow. If Ghost and the other teams were successful tonight, America would once again be the great nation it had been since 1776. But first they had to sneak past thousands of juvenile Variants.

The irony wasn't lost on Beckham: The last time an invading force had entered DC was when the British burned the White House to the ground in 1814. Two hundred and one years later, Team Ghost was about to do pretty much the same thing.

The first chute opened below. Gibson floated down to earth, the canopy breaking its descent. Rico pulled her chute a few seconds later. Garcia and Tank went next. The marines fanned out away from one another as they sailed over the Capitol Building toward the National Mall.

Looking up, Beckham saw Fitz and Horn were still in a back-falling position. That was fine. They still had a couple of seconds. He didn't bother signaling or breaking radio discipline. He had his hands full with Apollo anyway.

The wind screamed as Beckham cut through the air. Gusts whistled over his armor. He took in a long breath through his cotton bandanna and watched the city blooming across his field of vision. The dome of the Capitol Building and the long open lawns of the National Mall came into focus. That was their LZ.

"Hold on, boy," Beckham said. The dog had been good on the fall. He had whimpered a few times, but Beckham suspected that was more from the pressure on his injuries than fear.

Apollo was one of a kind.

Beckham reached back and pulled the rip cord of his chute. The straps tightened and yanked on his upper body as the chute fired. He followed his team over the dome of the Capitol, eyeing the gaping holes from large-caliber rounds. As soon as he was over the top, he bent his knees and aimed for a small stretch of green space that had somehow managed to survive the fires.

The single patch of grass was surrounded by death. Variant corpses dotted the landscape in every direction. Humvees, tanks, and other military vehicles of all shapes and sizes clogged the street below. They hadn't surrendered the capitol to the Variants without a fight. There had to be thousands of corpses.

He was glad Kate couldn't see this. The guilt would eat at her. Between her two bioweapons, billions had perished. Monsters or no monsters, it was hard to stomach.

Silent and unseen, they hoped, Team Ghost fell to earth. The comms were silent; Beckham heard nothing but the hiss of the wind and crackle of thunder on the horizon. He looked away from the battlefield and found Fitz and Horn. They glided toward the open space to the east.

Garcia was the first to reach the ground. He bent his knees and performed the two-stage flare. His boots almost caught on the decomposing body of a Variant, but he managed to avoid it and jog out his landing. Beckham couldn't see Rico or Horn, but he kept an eye on Fitz. The marine hit the dirt a few seconds after Garcia. Despite his blades, his landing was surprisingly graceful.

Mimicking Garcia's two-stage flare, Beckham hit the ground with a thud. Apollo and the gear pulled down on his chest, throwing him off balance. A shiver rushed through him as he fought to stay on his feet. He ran it out the best he could, but he finally dropped to his armored kneepads and skidded across the grass with his arms around the German shepherd.

Apollo whined for the first time on the entire drop as the straps tightened around his body.

"Sorry, boy," he whispered.

Beckham pushed himself to his feet and unstrapped

Apollo. All around him, his team cut away their chutes, chambered rounds, and began moving out across the field. Horn had recovered the RDD and was throwing the pack over his shoulders.

A buzzing sound filled the night as Beckham fell into a run. He swept his muzzle across the lawn for contacts, but only saw the twisted corpses of Variants that had puked up their insides. He could smell them through his gas mask, the awful sour scent radiating off their rotting bodies.

The beasts were everywhere, piled on one another. Scars and lacerations covered their diseased flesh. He slowed when he saw a cloud of flies shifting across the mass graveyard. The buzzing was like a lawnmower stuck in the wrong gear. Millions of bloated flies took to the air as Horn and Tank passed. Fitz followed at a crouch-run, with his scope pressed to his eye. He kept his rifle up with one hand and signaled with the other.

*No contacts,* Beckham thought. *Good. That means no venom to worry about. Yet.*

Beckham fired back an advance signal across First Street. Fitz took point and darted over the lawn.

Vehicles completely clogged the road ahead, but it was the quickest way to the tunnels. The Ulysses S. Grant Memorial rose above the other side of First Street. That was their target.

The rest of Ghost continued moving, their footsteps silent and breathing steady. He picked up his pace and hopped over a dead Variant, his boot scraping a taloned hand that reached toward the sky like the branches of a leafless tree. Beckham took a knee a hundred feet from the street and motioned for Fitz, Apollo, and Horn to clear the vehicles. Rico, Tank, and Garcia huddled next to Beckham.

They watched in silence, weapons roving over the terrain

as Fitz worked his way to the first cars with Horn. Apollo trotted alongside, his tail up. The small squad moved quickly, Fitz checking the interiors while Horn checked the undercarriages. They gave the all clear a few minutes later.

Beckham moved into the road cautiously, scrutinizing the statue of Ulysses S. Grant on the other side. There was a statue of four horses pulling a wagon to one side and steps leading to a pool full of murky water.

A slight breeze rippled its surface.

Beyond, the National Mall stretched as far as he could see. His eyes roved back and forth as he took in the sight. Lightning flashed across the skyline. The green electric explosion lit up the city like a bomb.

Beckham focused on the Grant statue. It was surrounded by four lions, and there was a fifth on the steps leading to the pool of water. Another ripple broke across the surface.

In his mind's eye, Beckham reconstructed the picture he'd studied of the memorial. The horses and wagon solidified in his memory. So did the Grant statue and the four lions.

But he couldn't remember the fifth lion.

Team Ghost continued across the street, weapons shouldered. Raising his hand, he attempted to signal Fitz, but Apollo did it for him with a low growl. His tail dropped between his legs.

In the wake of the thunder, clicking armor sounded as the fifth statue slowly rose onto two feet and twisted in Beckham's direction.

The juvenile stood a full six and a half feet tall. Covered in plates of armor, it was thicker, and wider, than Big Horn. The monstrosity blinked almond eyes the size of pomegranates at the team, then cracked its head from side to side. Its plates of thick armor continued clanking as it stretched its muscles and opened its bulging mouth.

A pointed tongue shot out at Beckham, curled, then vanished back in its mouth.

Every member of Team Ghost froze and stared at the massive beast—everyone except for Fitz. He raised his suppressed MK11 and shot it in the face. The creature's tree-trunk arms flew up as it tumbled backward and skidded down the steps all the way to the pool of water.

Beckham wasted no time giving the advance signal. The team continued to the monument and set up a perimeter as Horn and Tank searched for the entry into the tunnels.

He didn't need to tell the men they didn't have much time.

Beckham angled his M4 toward the rippling pool where the dead juvenile was lying next to the carmine water.

As soon as Beckham looked past the beast, his heart flipped. The ripples weren't from the impact of the monster's body. Curved skulls slowly rose from the other end of the pool, steam rising off the heads. More juveniles emerged, dripping wet.

"Everyone back," Beckham said, breaking radio discipline. He plucked an R49 grenade off his vest, but hesitated. The gas wouldn't deploy if he threw it in the pool. And Ghost was just within striking distance of their venom.

He pivoted away and pointed at the monument. "Get behind the statue."

Rico, Garcia, and Fitz took refuge on the other side. Tank and Horn were already prying up a stone slab covering the hidden entrance to the tunnels on the street side of the monument. Together, they hefted the three-foot square and slid it across the ground.

No one said a word as the juveniles charged through the water on two feet, even as the hissing shrieks of the evolved monsters sounded all at once. Weapons were raised and readied, but everyone remained calm. Team Ghost was prepared for this. They had expected it. Everyone knew exactly what to do.

A whistling rose over the discord. Something hit the statue on top of the monument. Beckham looked up to see venom eating away at the top of Grant's face.

*Hurry, Big Horn!*

Tank pulled open a metal door and waved the others inside. Rico, Fitz, and Garcia darted over to the entrance. Garcia was the first inside. He reached up for the bomb. Horn grabbed it and handed it down. Rico and Fitz went next, boots clanking on a skeletal ladder that hadn't been used in decades.

Apollo nearly jumped into Beckham's arms when he reached down for the dog. He tightened his grip and leaned down to climb into the opening just as another stream of venom splattered the stone next to Tank. The massive marine let out a screech and stumbled away from the safety of the monument.

Horn grabbed at his arm, but it was too late. Three different shots of the corrosive liquid slammed into Tank's armor, hitting him in the chest, face, and right thigh. He let out an agonizing cry and crumbled to his knees, armor crackling as the venom ate right through the plates.

Beckham watched in horror as Tank grabbed at his smoldering chest. He plucked an object from a pouch and reached for it with his other hand as a second round of venom plastered his body. The scream that came from Tank's mouth sounded inhuman, like that of a desperate, dying animal. His left hand melted and fell away. That was when Beckham saw the M67 grenade still clutched in his right fist.

Horn fired on the advancing beasts that Beckham

could no longer see from his position. Tank pushed his face guard up and met Beckham's gaze as he plucked the pin away with his teeth. They shared a moment of understanding, and despite the overwhelming pain from the venom, Tank somehow managed to speak.

"Tell Tito…" Tank's voice trailed off, but Beckham understood. He nodded and yelled for Horn to get inside. Horn fired off another few bursts and hesitated, looking at Tank.

"Get out of here, you big, stupid shit," Tank growled.

Horn wasn't moving. He reached out as if he wanted to haul Tank to his feet, but the big marine slumped to his left as his guts spilled from his stomach.

Garcia was shouting from below. "What's happening? Where the fuck is Tank?"

The situation was crumbling, and Beckham couldn't do a damn thing to stop it. He felt someone tap his leg, but he didn't move. His eyes were locked on Tank. The marine was somehow still alive, even though his flesh was melting.

Horn fired off a final shot, then climbed into the passage with Beckham. Both men watched as a third salvo of venom peppered Tank. The marine finally fell. Smoke rose off his smoldering armor, and the primed grenade rolled away from his body.

Horn slammed the hatch shut and twisted the wheel to seal them in as Garcia continued shouting over the comm. A massive detonation rocked the monument above with a rumble that shook the entire passage. The explosion from the M67 drowned out Garcia's frantic voice.

Beckham and Horn fell from the ladder's rungs, crashing into one another at the bottom. Someone grabbed Beckham under the arms and hoisted him to his feet. It was Garcia, and his eyes were wide and wet.

As the ringing passed and the last dying groans of the juveniles above faded into the night, Team Ghost looked into the dark tunnels. Beckham offered his silent condolences to Garcia with a pat on the shoulder. The sergeant trembled with anger, but it wasn't directed at anyone. There was no time to mourn Tank, and both of them knew that.

Rico and Fitz stood ahead in the tunnel, awaiting Beckham's order. He flashed an advance signal and they hurried into the darkness. Horn heaved the pack with Gibson over his shoulders and followed the marines, but Garcia hesitated.

Beckham patted Garcia on the shoulder a second time. It took a third to get the sergeant to move.

"Should have been me," Garcia whispered, turning and locking eyes with Beckham. "Why the fuck is it always someone else?"

Beckham shook his head, although he understood exactly what Garcia meant. Both of them had lost almost every man in their squad since the beginning of the war. As leaders, they felt responsible for those deaths. Beckham would lay down his life to protect Team Ghost, and he knew Garcia felt the same way about the Variant Hunters. But there was nothing they could do to change the past.

Right now, they had bigger problems than their grief and guilt over losing Tank. The blast from his grenade had saved Ghost from the pack of monsters, but it had also told every other beast in the city exactly where they were.

# 25

Ringgold's heart ached. She'd watched Corporal "Tank" Talon fall on the live feed, cut down before he'd even made it below ground. She wasn't used to the horrors of war. Years ago, when she had first stepped into the world of politics, she'd found a way to shut off her emotions in order to do battle with her political opponents over important issues. But real war was much different than war over laws and taxes. She couldn't unsee what she had just witnessed.

Watching Tank die had taken away her breath. Now she was holding it as strike teams all over the country entered underground bunkers, tunnels, sewers—wherever the monsters dwelled. The adults were dead, but the offspring were larger and more dangerous than ever before. These brave men and women were likely heading to their deaths—and she had sent them there.

Ringgold paced back and forth as she waited for the feed from Team Ghost to come back online. As soon as they'd entered the tunnels, the transmission had cut out. Nagle said the bunkers were probably blocking the signals.

Across the room, Lieutenant Davis searched the ocean with a pair of binoculars. Rain cascaded down the glass, but she continued raking them back and forth.

"Keeping busy?" Ringgold asked as she strolled over.

Davis lowered the binoculars. "Trying to, Madam President."

"It's the wait that kills us, isn't it? I can still remember those walls closing in around me at Raven Rock. Every day I was trapped there, I thought it would be my last. At times I *wanted* it to be my last, but then Beckham showed up. If anyone can survive out there, it's him and his men."

"He's a fine soldier. I have the utmost confidence…" Davis's voice trailed off.

"Are you all right, Lieutenant?"

In the reflection of the glass, Ringgold saw what Davis must have noticed a moment earlier. Figures were rushing into the room, and they appeared to be armed. Davis reached for her side arm just as a deafening blast rang out.

Ringgold didn't have time to turn before Davis tackled her to the ground. They landed in a heap. Pain streaked across the president's collarbone. The gunshot rang off the metal walls like a church bell, lingering in her ears.

From the floor, Ringgold watched men in black armor rush into the CIC. Their leader held a smoking shotgun. The marine who had been standing guard at the entryway was sprawled on his back, a gaping hole blown in his chest.

"Nobody move!" someone shouted.

Johnson and Humphrey were hunched next to Nagle's monitors. Several officers reached for weapons but were quickly disarmed. Two more marines rushed into the room, weapons raised. Neither of them got off a shot before they were blown away. Blood splattered the bulkheads.

Davis hovered over Ringgold. "Shit, shit, shit," she kept repeating.

Despite the pain of her injured arm, a dozen questions swam in Ringgold's mind. As soon as she saw Lieutenant Colonel Kramer stride into the room, it all made sense.

"No one else has to die," Kramer said.

"What the *hell* is this?" Johnson yelled, getting to his feet. Humphrey stood too, his hands raised in the air. A soldier silenced Johnson by roving a shotgun in his direction.

"Madam President," Davis whispered. "When I tell you to move, you move, but stay low. I'm getting you out of here."

Ringgold couldn't believe the response she whispered back. "Okay."

Corporal Anderson crawled across the ground after a pistol, moaning and muttering, "You bastards."

Kramer looked at one of her men and nodded. The soldier, faceless behind the black helmet, walked over and aimed a pistol at Anderson's head.

"No!" Davis yelled at the same moment as the gunshot. Ringgold flinched as the bullet punched through the birthmark above Anderson's right eyebrow. His head bounced off the ground and a geyser of blood hit the overhead.

Kramer and her troops turned toward the radio station Ringgold and Davis were hiding behind.

"Don't," Ringgold insisted when she saw Davis raising her handgun.

"Be quiet and stay here, Madam President," Davis whispered. "I'm going to get help."

Before Ringgold could reply, Davis jumped to her feet and ran for the other side of the room like a track-and-field star. She fired off three shots as she ran, aiming for Kramer but taking out one of her men instead.

Gunfire lanced into a wall of equipment and shattered portholes behind Davis. She ducked behind a station, popped off two random shots for covering fire, then bolted through the open door that led to the passage outside the CIC.

Ringgold swallowed her thumping heart.

"After her!" Kramer shouted. "Don't let her escape."

Two of her men took off after Davis.

"Why, Kramer? Why the hell would you do this?" Johnson said, his voice low. There was sadness there that took Ringgold by surprise.

Kramer grabbed a shotgun from the soldier closest to her, pumped it, and aimed it at Johnson's chest.

"I've been monitoring the strike teams over the comm channels. They. Are. Failing. So now I'm taking control of this mission." She paused and searched the room. "Where's President Ringgold?"

Johnson did not so much as glance in her direction, and she knew he wouldn't give her up. Ringgold worried it was going to get him killed. She pushed herself to her feet—partly out of defiance and partly because she wanted to look the mutinous bitch in the eye.

"Ah, there you are," Kramer said. She walked over calmly—so calmly it made Ringgold furious. As soon as Kramer was two feet away, Ringgold cocked her good hand and smacked the lieutenant colonel across her jaw.

"How *dare you*!" Ringgold shouted.

The echo of the slap reverberated through the room like the shotgun blasts. Kramer reared back and regarded Ringgold with a pair of wide eyes. She wiped away blood from her lip with the back of her hand. For a moment Ringgold thought she was going to shoot her, but instead, Kramer simply tossed the shotgun back to the man she had gotten it from, straightened her collar, and narrowed her cold eyes.

"Madam President, I'm going to need the launch codes."

Ringgold narrowed her eyes right back at Kramer. "What codes?"

"The codes to our nuclear arsenal, Madam President. I'm not just taking control of this vessel. I'm doing what you and Johnson lack the courage to do: I'm ending this war."

Garcia didn't bother saying any prayers. None of them were ever answered. He was the last Variant Hunter alive. His family, his friends, and every man he had fought with were gone.

He was the last man standing. Why? Why had he survived when better men had fallen?

*Don't do that. You don't get to do that. You keep fighting, Marine. All it takes...*

Fitz stopped at the intersection ahead. He balled his hand into a fist and signaled for everyone to get down. Garcia took a knee and waited.

He was furious—at himself, at the men who created the hemorrhage virus, at God. But the anger wasn't doing him any good.

*You stupid son of a bitch. God is still on your side.*

A distant shriek reverberated through the tunnels. Garcia was only half listening. Every death had tested his faith, and now he was close to the edge of losing it in this dark tomb.

*Lord, I have been your servant for so long. Now I have one final request: Please let us complete this mission. I won't beg, Lord, but I am on my knees. I am yours, Lord. Do what you want with me, but let me finish this.*

As the words went through his mind, he felt his doubt and anger trying to resurface, but saying the prayer also filled Garcia with relief. He had been wrong to doubt his savior. God was always listening, even if Garcia couldn't hear a response.

A hand patted his knee. His eyes flitted to Rico. She flipped up her face guard and gave him a kind and reassuring smile that reminded Garcia of his wife. In his mind, he was suddenly no longer in the cold, damp tunnels beneath the Capitol. He was back on his ranch in North Carolina, watching a brilliant sunset. The fiery glow lowered over their acre of apple trees, the light slowly receding like the surf returning to sea. Ashley was sitting on the porch swing, rocking their daughter, Leslie, to sleep. Garcia stood with his palms on the railing that overlooked the lush hills in the distance. But he wasn't admiring the beauty of the trees or the sunset—he was mesmerized by the tiny life in front of him.

"Jose, she's beautiful," Ashley said with a wide smile. She rocked Leslie back and forth across her chest.

*My beautiful girls.*

"Garcia," someone whispered.

A tap on his armored shoulder pulled him back to the underground tomb. The North Carolina sunset from his memory was replaced by a chain of light bulbs hanging from the ceiling, only half of which were still glowing. He felt cheated. He wanted to lose himself in those sweet memories for just a moment longer.

Closing his eyes, Garcia pictured his men and his family one last time, then tucked the memories safely away. He was a marine, and he had a job to complete—with or without God's help.

Beckham was looking down at him and pointing to the next bend. Fitz hugged the wall as he approached the corner with his rifle shouldered.

Horn, Rico, and Garcia took up position on the opposite wall of the passage, and Beckham gestured for Apollo to follow him toward Fitz.

They paused to listen to a distant humming that sounded like a generator. Now Garcia knew what was keeping the lights on. Bunkers were designed to function for years after a catastrophic event. It had only been seven weeks since the hemorrhage virus emerged from Building 8, so the systems were still operational in places like this.

Horn heaved Gibson higher onto his shoulders and tightened the straps as they waited.

Garcia was sweating his balls off under his armor. After seeing what had happened to Tank, the plates seemed pointless. The venom was more potent than sulfuric acid, and he doubted that anything less than inch-thick steel would stop it.

A distant thud broke Garcia's concentration. It echoed for several seconds before fading away. He trained his eyes on shadows darting back and forth. The tunnel seemed to go on forever, like an open portal with no end. Had the juveniles entered through the same secret passage at the Grant memorial?

Garcia scoped the tunnel behind him, but there was no sign of movement—no armored bodies clambering across the ceiling or pointed tongues firing off venom, only the dark, damp walls of a place built to protect humans from radioactive fallout. He turned back to Team Ghost. They waited several more minutes before continuing.

Rico was the first to move. She inched closer to the corner ahead. Garcia put his hand on her shoulder and walked with her. Fitz and Beckham were doing the same thing across the corridor. When they got to the corner, Beckham knelt and lifted Apollo's gas mask. The dog sniffed at the air. He trotted forward a few steps, sniffed again, and then wagged his tail.

The coast was clear.

Beckham lowered the mask back over Apollo's face and looked at Fitz. They paused to listen again, but there was nothing besides the distant hum of the generator.

Fitz pointed to his eyes, then to the left. Garcia nodded and repeated the gesture, pointing to the right. Fitz nodded back and moved out.

Garcia stepped in front of Rico and pushed the butt of his M4 into his shoulder, where the gun felt at home. He crouched down and then moved into the tunnel. A quick sweep revealed that Apollo's nose still worked: The passage was empty.

"Clear," he heard Fitz whisper.

Fitz continued down the left corridor with Apollo by his side. Everyone else filed behind them. Horn walked backward with his M249 raised to cover their rear.

In his mind's eye, Garcia brought up the map he'd memorized. They were approximately a quarter mile from the entrance to the underground bunker. At this rate it would only be a few more minutes before they reached the blast doors. There they would have the opportunity to deal a severe blow to an enemy that had taken everything from him. The thought filled him with adrenaline that quickened in his veins with every step.

The next several minutes became a blur. Garcia's arms and legs moved without thought, and he aimed his rifle out of habit.

All around him, Team Ghost moved with that same precision. They hugged the sides of the passage as they worked their way beneath a city that had been the symbol of liberty for the free world. God willing, DC would once again be that beacon.

Garcia tightened his grip on his M4.

*Heel to toe.*

*Deep breath.*

*Exhale.*

*Check your line of fire.*

*What the fuck is that?*

*Just a shadow. Calm down, Jose.*

*Steady breath.*

*Keep moving.*

In his peripheral, Apollo trotted along, his tail still up. Fitz followed a few feet behind. Even in the enclosed space, the marine opted for his MK11. Garcia was really starting to trust that gun and the man carrying it. He was a hell of a shot.

Fitz suddenly halted, and Garcia realized the clicking sound he'd thought was from Fitz's blades was something else. A raucous noise came without warning. It sounded like a landslide, as if jagged boulders were crashing down the side of a mountain.

Garcia pushed the scope to his naked eye. The end of the passage darkened as the long, thick shapes of juveniles filled the tunnel. Their joints snapped beneath their plates of heavy armor.

The tightness of Garcia's muscles wasn't from fear, as he would have expected. It was from excitement. He was so primed for action that his trigger finger quivered.

Rico, on the other hand, caved to her fear. She fumbled for an R49 grenade but dropped it on the ground. She bent down to scoop it up, cursing as she accidentally kicked it away.

"Apollo, back," Beckham ordered. "Fitz, Garcia, suppressing fire." He plucked an R49 off his vest, pulled the pin, and chucked it toward the beasts. They were two hundred feet away, maybe closer, and closing in fast. In the glow of the lights, Garcia counted a total of five: two on the ceiling, one on the right wall, and two more on the floor.

Fitz quickly reduced the number to four with one round. His first shot sent the leader crashing into a wall.

It stood, clutching a gaping hole in its chest armor where one of the 7.62-millimeter rounds had penetrated. The abomination slumped to the ground, shock painted across its inhuman face.

Taking a knee, Garcia opened up with his M4. The rounds lanced into the skull of a juvenile racing across the ceiling. He got lucky when one of those shots found the soft flesh of an eye socket. He could almost hear the wet thunk of the bullet entering the creature's yellow iris.

The creature dropped and landed on its belly with such force that its armor sent up a cloud of dust from the concrete floor. Angry shrieks followed. The juveniles increased their pace. Dozens of talons slashed the walls, drawing sparks and creating a high-pitched whine that threw off Garcia's aim.

His next shots chipped away the floor as the enraged monsters leaped over their fallen siblings and jumped to the ceiling. They were moving into striking distance, and yet the R49 grenade still sat idly on the floor.

"Fuck, it's a dud!" Beckham shouted. He reached for another, but Fitz had already launched one into the air.

Garcia pulled his spent magazine.

The beasts on the ceiling knocked the chain of lights loose. The cord snaked to the right, then dropped to the floor. Shadows filled the tunnel as bulbs smashed beneath the feet of a juvenile that had dropped back to the ground. Their armored bodies became distorted in the dim lighting.

Garcia slammed a fresh magazine into his M4 and fired a burst into the leader. It leaped to the side, avoiding the rounds. Snarling, Garcia gripped his rifle tighter and fired again. This time his aim was true, blowing off the plating covering the beast's back.

*That's for Steve-o.*

The next burst hit the monster in the gut.

*That's for Tank!*

In the brief pauses between bursts, he thought of his men. Muzzle flashes lit up the tunnel, but in the strobing light, the three creatures continued to charge, relentless, rounds cracking armor and tearing through flesh.

Fitz's grenade rolled to a stop about twenty feet in front of the juveniles. That put Ghost in striking distance.

Gas hissed out of the grenade.

All at once, the clank of the juveniles' armor stopped.

The cloud of white drifted across the floor and rose to the ceiling, forming a solid wall that Garcia couldn't see through. He held his fire and waited for a target, but the juveniles had stopped on the other side, hissing as if taunting Team Ghost.

*Come on, you bastards. I got something for you.*

Beckham raised a hand and ordered the team to retreat.

Garcia almost asked where they were retreating to, but he kept his mouth shut and his muzzle trained on the cloud of gas. A massive body that could have only been Horn filled his peripheral on the left.

Garcia was glad to have the big man next to him, but he wasn't Tank, and Beckham wasn't Steve-o. He had to accept they were gone now. Team Ghost were his new brothers and sisters.

With deliberate care, the team slowly backed away, making sure each footstep was as silent as possible. Garcia wasn't sure it mattered. The freaks could probably hear the sweat cascading down his forehead.

They were almost out of striking distance when he heard the telltale whistle of the launching venom.

A flash of liquid streaked through the air and whizzed past Garcia's helmet. He ducked down and fired into the mist. Retreat wasn't an option. They had to kill the beasts here.

The rattle of suppressed gunfire sounded all around him. Team Ghost unloaded magazines into the cloud as the juveniles fired back.

Rico let out a shriek and dropped to her knees. Garcia hesitated, watching from the corner of his eye. She pawed at her chest plates. He pushed his scope back to his eye. There wasn't anything he could do to help her right now.

He searched the cloud for a target.

*Come on, show yourselves, you bastards.*

One of the grotesque creatures surfaced for a moment, and Garcia blew its lips off. The creature let out a roar, and so did Horn. Garcia heard shuffling behind him, and kneepads scraping across the floor.

Whistling venom and gunfire filled the passage. The sounds hit his ears like stones, but Garcia stayed on one knee, praying as he fired.

*Please, Lord, I'm yours and always will be. Please don't take more of my friends before we complete this mission.*

Slowly, the gunfire silenced around him. Garcia ached to turn and see who had been hit, but he kept firing. The cloud of gas lifted, dissipating into the air. He finished off his magazine, pulled it, and jammed in a fresh one. Then he was firing again. The ringing in his ears made it impossible to hear much of anything besides the faint, muffled screams of injured soldiers.

By the time he finished it off, every other gun was silent. He blinked rapidly and rose to his feet, his muzzle still on the unmoving armored corpses of the three juveniles sprawled across the ground. He backed up, afraid to look behind him. An awful feeling gripped him. Was he truly the last human standing?

*Keep moving. There will be more contacts. There are always more.*

Popping his ears, Garcia tried to hear past the ringing in them. There were stifled voices, and then someone shouting at him. He caught Fitz's Southern drawl and Horn's deep voice.

When Garcia was certain the juveniles were dead, he turned to face his team. Horn was crouching over the bag containing the dirty bomb. Beckham and Fitz were bending down next to Rico. Her chest plate hissed on the ground next to her. Apollo sat behind them.

Garcia drew in a deep breath.

"I said hold your fucking fire, Garcia," Beckham snapped. He looked up from Rico and caught Garcia's gaze.

"Sorry. I couldn't hear shit," Garcia replied. He changed his magazine and glanced back at the juveniles. Blood had pooled around their bodies. The remaining lights flickered down the hall, creating more shadows that made Garcia's heart kick. "We need to move, ASAP."

"I know," Beckham said. "Can you walk, Rico?"

"I think so. None of that shit got on me, right?" She tilted her visor to scan her body.

Fitz patted her on the shoulder. "If it did, you wouldn't be talking."

"That shit may not have gotten on her, but it did get on Gibson," Horn said with a snort.

Every helmet turned in his direction.

The bag was smoking next to Horn. He pulled out the dirty bomb and placed it on the ground, but the metal case was smoldering on top.

"Looks as if we have a major problem." Horn flipped his face guard up and shook his head as he glared at

Beckham. "The timer is fucking toast, boss. Someone's going to have to stay behind and set it off manually."

Davis ran from the CIC at a breakneck pace. Her leg screamed with every stride, but the pain was a small sacrifice. She'd already lost the two soldiers from Kramer's detail who had been trailing her.

At the next bulkhead she slipped into an empty security station. She carefully shut the hatch behind her and turned to the video monitors.

*Holy shit. I can't believe this is happening.*

She pulled her hair back into a ponytail and wrapped it tight.

*Believe it, Rachel. And do something to fucking stop it. You can't lose control of your ship.*

Reaching out, she clicked on the monitors. Davis already knew that Kramer had the most loyal soldiers under her umbrella out of any high-ranking officer left on the *GW*, but seeing them taking over the ship was unreal.

Squads of soldiers in black armor patrolled nearly every deck. They herded marines away with hands bound. Davis's gaze flitted from screen to screen, pausing on the mess hall. Two marines were facedown on the ground, their backs peppered with blooming bullet wounds.

"No." Davis said, tears welling in her eyes.

The sight of dead marines made her heart hurt. She had to do something. But what could she do against Kramer's loyal army?

There had never been so much at risk. Davis knew exactly what Kramer was after, and if she got those codes, she would rain down nuclear fire on the United States, destroying everything they were fighting for.

Davis checked the monitors for an escape route. She noted the empty passages, then ran back into the corridor. As she ran, questions swirled in her mind. How could Kramer be so fucking blind? Did she really think she was going to save them with the nukes? Then again, Colonel Gibson, Colonel Wood, and General Kennor had shared the same grand delusions of saving the world. Gibson had aimed to create a supersoldier to keep American soldiers off foreign battlefields. Kennor had fought the only way he'd ever known—with bombs and boots instead of science. And Wood? He'd just been fucking insane.

She took a right at the next bulkhead, lost in her thoughts but focused on her mental map of the ship. All men and women were created equal in Davis's book, but some chose a path that made them less human. She would be damned if she let anything happen to the people who were really trying to save the human race. She was going to save President Ringgold and Vice President Johnson, even if she died in the attempt.

"You two clear that passage," someone said up ahead.

A dozen pairs of boots pounded the deck as soldiers searched the ship for her. Davis ducked through an open hatch and hid behind a bunk in an empty cabin. She slowly pulled the magazine from her M9 to check the rounds. Only five, plus one in the chamber.

It wasn't much against well-trained men in armor with shotguns and M4s.

The sound of stomping boots faded away from her position, but the coast wasn't clear yet. A voice echoed down the passage. "This shit is cray, man. Is Kramer really going to launch those missiles?"

"She ain't playin', Rice," said a second, softer voice. "But maybe it's the only way."

"I don't like it. There have to be survivors out there, right?"

The rap of footfalls resumed, heading in her direction. Davis slowly slid the magazine back into her gun and raised it toward the hatch leading into the cabin. The idea of killing another human unnerved her. Killing Variants was easy, but humans were a precious commodity, and these men were just following orders because they were too frightened to do anything else.

*Maybe they'll pass me by.*

*Please pass me by.*

The man with a kind voice spoke again. "Rice, you take the cabins to the left, I'll get the right."

"You got it, Mark."

Davis tensed.

A shadow moved down the corridor outside the open hatch. She crouched down behind the bunk, her right thigh burning as if someone was driving a knife into it.

*Don't come in here, please.*

She could hear the two soldiers clearing the rooms. Hatches opened and clicked shut. Bunks slid across the deck, the metal scraping as the soldiers searched.

Davis made a decision: She holstered her weapon as Mark's shadow stopped outside her door. Shooting him wasn't going to do anything but reveal her location.

A man no older than twenty stepped into the glow of the light inside the cabin. Mark wasn't wearing the same type of helmet Kramer's guards had worn in the CIC. Seeing his youthful brown eyes made what Davis had to do even more difficult. They widened as she bolted around the side of the bed. In three swift motions, she slapped his M4 aside, grabbed his right arm, and wrapped her left arm around his neck. He let out a whimper as she dragged him into the cabin with her.

She had him in a chokehold, but his neck was so thick she could hardly get her arm around it. He kicked and squirmed in her grip as she pushed with her other hand on a pressure point at the back of his neck.

*Go to sleep, dammit.*

Mark let out a whimper but simply would not give up. He elbowed, kicked, and squirmed in her grip. They collapsed to the floor, Davis on her back, the man's weight crushing her body. She wrapped her legs around his and tightened her arm around his neck. He brought his helmet back on her head, smashing her in the nose. Pain flared up her nasal passages.

The young man twisted his right hand free of her grip and reached for his pistol. By the time her vision cleared, he had unholstered the weapon. Wheezing for air, he struggled to point the gun at her head.

She wasn't afraid to die, but if he killed her, there would be no one left to save the ship and stop Kramer from turning the major cities of the United States into so many radioactive craters.

Her training took over, and her body reacted on instinct to the threat. She reached down and grabbed the knife from his belt, unsheathed it, and jammed it into the soft flesh below his Adam's apple.

There was a gurgling sound as he tried to scream.

Even as the blade pierced his skin, Davis wished she could take it back. His eyes turned desperate and pleading, and she almost pulled the knife out to put pressure on the wound and try to stop the bleeding. But it was already too late. A quick death was the only mercy she could show him now. She swiftly traced the knife across his throat, severing his jugular vein. He bled out in seconds, and she held him as the life flooded out of his body.

Davis knew that if she lived through the day, this moment would haunt her. For now, she sealed it away in the vault where she stored the rest of her most painful memories.

She loosened her grip around his neck with her left arm, but left the blade inside. Then she slid out from under him, grabbed his M4, and raised it at the hatch. The second soldier, the man she'd heard referred to as Rice, strode up right into her line of fire.

His eyes flitted to Davis's gun, then to Mark's motionless body.

"Don't," Davis whispered.

Rice lowered his carbine.

Davis pushed herself up with the gun still on him, then herded him into the cabin. He bent down to help his friend, but they both knew there wasn't anything that could be done. Rice looked up, his eyes pleading for mercy.

Davis wondered if he'd shown any of the dead marines on board the same courtesy. Killing Mark had been necessary, but she couldn't kill Rice in cold blood.

She extended mercy to the man with a butt of her rifle to his face. Rice fell to his back, unconscious. She reached down, grabbed his extra magazines and radio, then proceeded back into the passage.

Her heart pumped adrenaline through her like a river fueled by a broken dam. She had lost a part of herself in that cabin that she would never get back, but she'd done what had to be done.

Now she needed to find help.

But where?

*Think, Rachel, think.*

She shouldered her M4 and continued down the next passage at a crouch. She could try to make it to the flight deck to free some marines, but she would have to get past a dozen or more of Kramer's men. Those were impossible odds. Going deeper into the ship would take her to an infirmary full of civilians and injured soldiers.

Injured—but still soldiers.

There were men and women in there who could fight.

Davis slowed to a halt outside the next ladder. She slung the M4 across her back, grabbed the handle with one hand, and raised her M9 with the other. Pulling the hatch open, she slipped inside with her gun raised. She swept the weapon over an empty ladder. Gritting her teeth, she loped down the ladder and paused at the open hatch.

When she peeked outside, she saw only one of Kramer's guards. One she could deal with. Leaving the infirmary guarded by a single sentry would be the move that took Kramer down.

"Rice and Mark were wounded," Davis called out. "I need assistance back here." Then she ducked back inside the ladder. With her back to the bulkhead, she waited.

Kramer's soldier strode inside with his gun lowered. Pistol-whipping him in the face was the easiest thing Davis had done all evening. The man slumped to the floor, and she relieved him of his M4 and M9.

Davis hurried into the passage outside the infirmary. She slung the second carbine over her back as she prepared to enter the room. Coughing and a few hushed voices could be heard on the other side of the open hatch.

"You can do this, Rachel," she whispered. Raising both M9s, she entered the room and swept the pistols from side to side, prepared to shoot any of Kramer's men if necessary. But there were no men in black armor inside, only the frightened faces of injured soldiers, civilians, and medical staff staring back at her.

"What's going on?" someone asked.

"We heard gunfire," said another.

Davis holstered one of her M9s and crossed the room. "Who can fight?"

Several raised voices replied.

"Fight what?" a man yelled.

A nurse gasped. "What's happening? Are there Variants on board?"

Davis ignored them and continued through the room at a clip. She stopped at the foot of Staff Sergeant Jay Chow's bed. He swung his bandaged legs over the side and stepped onto the cold floor, his eyes locking with hers. She handed him her extra M9, then turned to face the rest of the room.

In her most commanding voice, Davis said, "There has been a mutiny. The *GW* has been taken over by Lieutenant Colonel Marsha Kramer, and I need your help to take it back."

# 26

Beckham unfastened the clasps on his chest plate and handed the piece to Rico. "Don't protest, just take it. We don't have much time."

"Thank you," Rico said. Her eyes were still wide from the shock of being hit, but Beckham could see she was going to be fine. She positioned the plate over the front of her fatigues and clasped the ends. It looked a bit loose on her, but it would have to do.

Team Ghost was moving two minutes after the final juvenile corpse hit the ground. This time Beckham took point. They were lucky to have lost only Tank so far, but *luck* was a relative term in the apocalypse.

The automatic timer on the dirty bomb was destroyed. Someone was going to have to stay behind to set it off.

Beckham tried not to think about that. Their mission hadn't changed, and they were almost to the blast doors. A thousand more juveniles were prowling the miles of tunnels that stretched beneath the Capitol complex.

The closer he got, the more the slow burn ate him. Sweat bled down his forehead as he considered their options. If no one volunteered to stay behind, they would have to draw straws. Either way, Horn was definitely out. Beckham wouldn't let him stay behind no matter how hard he pushed back. Not a chance. Apollo was trained to follow more than a hundred commands, but none of those included setting off an RDD. Not that Beckham would let the dog do it anyway. That left Beckham, Garcia, Rico, and Fitz.

Everyone was likely thinking the same thing as they jogged down the final tunnel and eyed the double set of rusted blast doors. Their mission was almost complete, but one way or another, they wouldn't all be going home. They'd known that when they signed on, and each of them had their own reasons being there. Horn wanted a better world for his daughters, Beckham wanted to give Kate and their unborn child a chance at life, Fitz wanted to make up for what he considered his sins, Garcia wanted revenge, and Rico? Beckham wasn't exactly sure what drove her. She seemed a bit crazy, if he was honest. It was endearing, but he still wasn't going to ask her to volunteer to kill herself.

The ten-foot-high doors loomed above Team Ghost—a gateway that led to a fortress of monsters. Beckham balled his hand into a fist, stopping just outside. Everyone huddled around him like a football team about to discuss a play. He flipped up his face guard and looked at his friends in turn. "Someone is going to have to stay behind to manually detonate Gibson."

Anxious eyes stared back at him. No one immediately volunteered, but no one resisted either. Sweat dripped off foreheads; Beckham could hear the plops. He could hear everything: his thumping heart, the team's stifled breathing, and the snap of joints from juveniles on the other side of the doors.

"I'll do it."

Beckham hardly recognized the voice at first.

It was his.

Before Building 8, he'd never lost a man. Now he

had a vest pocket full of dog tags. He was going to be damned if he let anyone else do this.

"No," Garcia said. "I'll do it."

Helmets roved in the marine's direction, but he kept his gaze on Beckham.

"You can still have what I lost, brother. You and that doctor, you got a future together. I'm ready to be with my family again. I've done some bad shit in my day, but I have faith. I'll be seeing them again soon."

Beckham narrowed his eyes. Garcia was a deeply religious man, and Beckham respected that. But just because he believed in an afterlife didn't mean the burden was his to carry alone.

"It's okay," Garcia reassured everyone. "I want to do this. For my men, my family, and my country." Horn exchanged a glance with Beckham, but the big man's face was unreadable.

The screech of talons skittering across the floor drew everyone's attention. Fitz jerked his MK11 toward the door to stand guard, but didn't say a word. This decision was on Beckham.

He reluctantly nodded at Horn to give Garcia the bomb. He couldn't deny the relief he felt, but there was a deep shame that went along with it. Letting Garcia do this was one of the most difficult decisions of his life. It all went down in a matter of seconds, but it felt like an eternity. Horn handed Garcia the bag and patted him on the helmet as he heaved it onto his shoulders.

"You're sure?" Beckham asked.

Garcia replied by making the sign of the cross over his chest.

"Okay, Ghost. Stay low, and keep on me," Beckham whispered. "We guard Garcia while he plants the bomb. Then we deploy our R49 grenades and seal the chamber behind us."

No other orders were needed. Every member of the team knew exactly what needed to be done. One by one, they followed Beckham through the gap in the blast doors.

The wide gashes in the metal and the click-clack of joints didn't deter him. After he ensured the entry was clear, he entered the chamber on the west side and bolted for the cover of a forklift.

The room was larger than it had appeared in the video, but everything was right where it was supposed to be. Blocks of hundreds of orange barrels rose toward the ceiling. Crates full of food and medical supplies were stacked beyond those, and row after row of shelves lined the center of the room. He couldn't see the pool of filthy water or the decomposing bodies, but he could see the wall where the juveniles kept their human food. The top was a lumpy spider web. Arms and legs protruded from the white goo.

Beckham was glad he had a gas mask.

*It's almost over, Reed. This nightmare is almost over.*

He continued at a crouch, keeping as low and close to the barrels as he could. When he reached the edge, he stopped and peered around the corner. The coast was clear. He was running for the next set of barrels when the concrete began to rumble under Beckham's boots. He ducked behind a forklift, holding the air in his chest as a group of juveniles walked on all fours across the floor in front of the machine.

They tilted their heads every few feet, stopping to listen with pointy ears. The largest beast was the size of a rhino. It sniffed at the air with a nose encased in armor. Beckham pulled back to hide behind the forklift, slowly letting out his breath.

*Mom, I sure hope you're watching over me right now.*

He rubbed the outside of his vest pocket containing

her picture as he waited. The thud of clawed hands and feet grew fainter. The monsters were moving on.

Beckham checked with a quick glance. The curved back of the final beast vanished around a corner. When they were gone, he darted toward a mountain of boxes. Apollo, Fitz, Rico, Garcia, and Horn followed him.

They remained there for several seconds.

Command had made it very clear: deploy the R49 grenades near the wall of human prisoners and plant the bomb there. Beckham was going to make sure he followed those orders. He pointed to the next crate of boxes, gazed around the corner, then took off running.

Team Ghost continued moving across the room with a precision that reminded Beckham of the old days, when his only job was to sneak in and out of places. But those memories seemed so long ago. Most of those recon missions were against untrained enemies with obsolete weapons—not Variants and juveniles that had evolved into the perfect predators.

Beckham bolted toward a row of crates he remembered from the video. They were the same boxes the Navy SEALs had hidden behind when they documented the lair. Those men had made it out of here, and Beckham was starting to think Ghost might too.

Once he was at the crates, he would be able to see the entire north end of the room, including the wall of human prisoners and the pool of crimson water. The grotesque image from the video footage entered his mind the same moment a shadow crossed his path.

There wasn't enough time to take cover. He glanced to the left at nothing but rows of shelves. It took him two full strides to pass through the length of the shadow. That was when he realized it was coming from above him.

Beckham didn't have a chance to react as a juvenile

dropped from the ceiling and landed on Rico. A guttural crack sounded, and she let out a strangled howl.

The chatter of suppressed gunfire sounded as Beckham whirled with his M4. Fitz and Horn were already firing on the massive juvenile. Rico's right leg was twisted underneath her like a pretzel. Saliva cascaded from the beast's open mouth, leaving a slimy trail on Rico's body.

Beckham snapped into operator mode in a single heartbeat, instinct taking over.

"Horn, Fitz, take it out and get Rico the hell out of here," he shouted. "Garcia, on me!"

The creature clamped down on Rico's chest plate with bulging lips. If it weren't for the armor Beckham had given her, it would have ripped her heart out. Instead, it just pulled the plate off as if it was a Band-Aid. A 7.62-millimeter round shattered the top of the juvenile's skull as it tossed the armor away.

The creature reared back and released a roar. Fitz used the stolen moment to jam his muzzle in its open mouth and fire off a shot that blew a hole through the opposite side.

Garcia turned and ran toward Beckham. Together, they bolted for the final row of crates. Beckham could hear the monsters on the other side. He pulled the pin from an R49 and let it sail long before he saw them. Garcia launched one into the air a moment later, then raised his rifle.

The sight of the monsters around the corner hit him with the weight of a bullet against his flak jacket, bringing him to a skidding halt.

"Holy shit!" Beckham cried.

"My God in heaven," Garcia added.

The leaders of Team Ghost and the Variant Hunters slid to a stop two hundred feet from the greatest number of juveniles either of them had ever seen. The entire north corridor was crawling with the abominations. Some appeared to be waking from a deep slumber. Others were prowling, heads tilting from side to side curiously.

The only thing separating the beasts from Beckham and Garcia was the pool of crimson water. Body parts floated in the filth like buoys in a hellish sea. To the east, the hands of the hundreds of human prisoners attached to a wall seemed to reach down. Their moans merged into an eerie wail that made Beckham shudder.

Beckham wanted to throw up. Instead, he pulled another R49 grenade and tossed it at the army of monsters across the water. He lobbed another toward the wall of prisoners, a merciful act that would put them to sleep long before Garcia set off the bomb. He grabbed a third grenade and was preparing to throw it when something hit him, first in the right wrist and then in the left leg.

Garcia was shouting, but Beckham wasn't able to register the words. He couldn't seem to focus on anything besides the most severe burning he'd ever felt in his life. His body was on fire, as if the marrow of his bones was melting from the inside. In Delta Force training, he'd read that was what being hit by lighting felt like. But this was much, much worse.

Beckham watched the third R49 grenade spin across the floor, stopping hundreds of feet from the pool. The first two grenades were already hissing gas. Tendrils of smoke twisted like miniature tornadoes in the meat of the juveniles' nest and near the wall of prisoners. Some of the monsters dropped where they stood, but others leaped into the water.

Garcia was screaming and firing his M4. Beckham could see the muzzle flash, but he couldn't hear the words. He looked over at the marine. They were no longer at eye level.

Looking down, Beckham saw why.

He had dropped to his right knee. At first he couldn't understand what he was seeing. His left leg looked like a limp snake, and his boot was turned at an impossible angle. Then he understood. His leg hung useless because the venom was dissolving both armor and flesh.

A powerful stench found its way into his mask. He knew the smell of burning flesh, and it wasn't coming from the outside. It was coming from his own body.

*Shit. God. No.*

Rounds zipped past his helmet. It took every ounce of concentration to move his head to follow them. His pounding heart seemed to burst when he saw the giant juvenile charging at him from the west. Three others were right behind it. They crashed into shelves, knocking them over and spilling the contents across the floor.

*You can survive this. You just need to remove your armor and grab your rifle.*

Despite the pain, Beckham knew how delusional the thought sounded. The venom was already burning through his flesh. He would have to cut off his entire leg to stop the toxins from reaching his heart.

His M4 lay several feet in front of him, just out of reach. He had to get to it—if he was going to die, he was at least going to take some of the monsters with him. But his arms and legs wouldn't respond. He could only feel panic as it rolled over him in numbing waves that seemed to be coming in slow motion.

That was how he knew he was dying. He had known right away the wound was bad, but now he knew there was no coming back from it. There was nothing anyone could do for him now.

And yet he still fought. He fought for himself, for his family, and for his brothers and sisters. He reached down with his left hand to remove the armor on his leg, but he couldn't feel his limbs anymore. They wouldn't respond.

Beckham slumped face first to the ground, falling on his side, his eyes locked on the beast that galloped toward him. He convulsed, helplessly, unable to control the tremors as the toxins ate away his flesh and poisoned his ruined body.

The lead juvenile pounded the concrete from the west with its massive horned paws. Beckham was going to die, but he would not give up until his final breath. He tried to reach for his rifle again, managing to move his left arm a little before his muscles contracted, then locked up. The resulting seizure was agonizing. He could feel every muscle fiber trying to extend.

A flash of brown-and-black fur suddenly bolted in front of him as the monsters galloped closer.

"Apollo," Beckham groaned. "Get out of here, boy..."

The dog stood his ground, tail raised, teeth bared, back ridged as he faced an enemy twenty times his size.

*No. Get out of the way, boy.*

Beckham squirmed, unable to speak. His broken body partially responded. He moved like a worm, wiggling closer to Apollo. He could see the Delta Force Team Ghost patch on the dog's collar now.

Apollo howled at the armored skulls barreling toward him. Horned feet and hands stampeded over the concrete, leaving a trail of cracks. They had already closed the gap in a matter of seconds, and Beckham couldn't even fire a shot.

*Big Horn, Fitz, where are you guys?*

To the north, in front of the pool, Beckham's last R49 grenade released its load of sleeping gas. What had seemed like a horrible toss had ended up providing a barrier that protected Garcia and Beckham from the army that had made it into the pool. The creatures jumped out of the bloody water right into the cloud of gray mist. As soon as they breathed it in, they crashed to the floor and skidded over the concrete.

Shades of red encroached on the sides of Beckham's eyes. His entire body was shutting down, but his mind was still aware of what was happening to him.

He sucked in a gasp of air, his heart working in overdrive. Each breath was harder than the last. The fight flooded out of him with each gasp.

"Apollo, please. *Please* run. Run!"

The four beasts closed in. Perhaps six seconds had passed, maybe more, maybe less. He couldn't focus his thoughts. He could barely see or breathe.

Beckham blinked away the red, and as his vision cleared momentarily, he saw the monster rushing toward him suddenly take a round in the side of its head. Chips of armor flew into the air, but the creature ignored the first shot. A second slammed into its spine, drawing an angry roar. The creature craned its neck to look at Fitz as the marine ran out from the safety of the orange barrels. It launched a salvo of venom at Fitz, then continued toward Beckham.

Fitz dropped to the ground and fired from a prone position. Beckham lost sight of him as the invading red flashed across his vision.

Beyond the crimson blur, Beckham watched the juvenile approach. Apollo continued to stand between him and the beast. He couldn't watch his dog ripped apart right in front of him. He refused to let that be the last image he ever saw.

*Get up, Reed. You have to get up!*

The creature couldn't have been more than five feet away when a wall of black armor crashed into the monster's right side. Horn tackled it to the ground, rolling with it over and over until he came up on top. He wrapped his hands around the beast's neck, trying to find a grip. It clawed him in the side of the head, denting his helmet and jerking him to the left, but Horn stood right back up.

"Big Horn, catch!" Fitz shouted. He tossed Meg's hatchet through the air.

Horn caught it with his left hand and brought it down on the monster's face. He pulled it loose, and then brought it down again and again until there was no face left at all. Leaving the hatchet in the skull, he grabbed at the beast's snapping mandibles.

Beckham hardly heard the shrieks of the dying monster, but he watched in awe as Horn ripped all four mandibles from its face as if they were crab legs. The beast twitched under him a few more times before finally going limp.

"Damn right, motherfucker!" Horn shouted. He ripped the hatchet from the dead juvenile's face and rose to his feet, caked in blood and gore.

Beckham felt something then. Not pain. Not fear.

Pride.

He couldn't believe Horn had killed one of those things with his bare fucking hands. He'd saved Beckham— and now Beckham would save everyone else. He would set off the bomb. He would stay behind to ensure that Kate and his child had a world to grow up in.

Clouds of gray filled his field of vision, but it wasn't because he was losing consciousness. The R49 gas swirled throughout the chamber. Thuds echoed as monsters crashed to the ground all around him.

Horn came back into view, Rico slumped over his back. Fitz was right behind them. He'd stopped to toss an R49 grenade at the other three beasts that had been charging at Beckham. They were all squirming on the ground, blood gushing from holes in their plated armor.

"Brother!" Horn yelled. He set Meg's hatchet down on the ground and crouched at Beckham's side.

"Help me get this shit off him!" Fitz shouted.

"I've already got his leg armor off," someone yelled back. It was Garcia, but Beckham hadn't seen or felt him removing the armor.

Apollo whined and licked Beckham's face. The dog couldn't do anything to save him, not this time, but he was there to comfort his handler in Beckham's last moments.

"It's already eaten his leg!" Horn yelled. There was a panicked note in his shaky voice that Beckham understood. Horn knew Beckham wasn't coming home with him this time.

Horn grabbed Meg's hatchet and bent down to hover in front of Beckham's helmet. "This is going to hurt, boss."

Beckham couldn't even open his mouth to protest. His body had been numb until Horn brought the hatchet down on his leg. He screeched in a voice he didn't want to be his own.

Another blade cut at his arm.

"Garcia, take my R49s!" Fitz shouted. "Launch every single one we got."

Pain tore through Beckham's body. His heart thumped so hard he thought it was going to explode.

*Kate, baby, I'm so sorry I broke my promise.*

He shifted in and out of the nightmare as he fought to remain conscious. But he was tired. He couldn't keep his eyes open. His eyelids were weights, and the red wouldn't go away.

"Beckham!" someone shouted.

Garcia's bruised face was looking down at him. The sleeping gas swirled around Team Ghost, a barrier to protect them from the monsters. Horn was putting a tourniquet around bloodied flesh connecting to a riven stump.

Beckham almost choked when he saw that the stump

was his left leg. He twisted in horror to see Fitz doing the same thing to his arm.

"It's okay," Garcia said. "Hang in there, brother!"

Beckham couldn't form words. He slipped out of consciousness and into the most vivid memory from his childhood, the moment that had set him on the course to becoming a Delta Force operator. He had been ten years old, standing with his mom on the summit of a trail overlooking Rocky Mountain National Park. He hadn't known it then, but she had already been sick. In another six months, she would barely be able to walk, let alone hike, but that day she had taken him to their favorite place in the world to watch the sun set over the peaks. As the setting sun painted the heavens rose and gold, she said something that would stick with him forever:

*Reed, someday people will depend on you, and I know that you will grow up to be a brave and loyal man. Will you promise me that you will always do the right thing, no matter how hard it is?*

Beckham hadn't understood then, but he did now. He'd done everything he could to keep his promise to her, but now his body was failing, just as hers had done so many years ago.

"Get him out of here!" Garcia shouted.

The ground seemed to fall away as Beckham opened his eyes. Horn was scooping him up carefully, but quickly. Fitz was working on picking Rico up a few feet away.

"Good luck, Garcia!" Fitz shouted.

"I got you, boss!" Horn yelled as he draped Beckham over his back. "You're a good man, Garcia. Give 'em hell!"

Beckham tried to speak, but his lips felt disconnected from his body. He'd lost a lot of blood. He watched helplessly as Garcia lugged the dirty bomb toward the wall of human prisoners.

Horn was running now, Beckham bobbing up and down on his shoulders. He squinted and watched as Garcia knelt to set up the device. When he was finished, he turned and locked eyes with Beckham.

In a final moment of clarity, Beckham and Garcia shared an understanding. Garcia was doing what Beckham's mom had spoken of to him on that mountainside—something that Beckham had done so many times before, but that he couldn't do this time. The last Variant Hunter threw up a salute, and Beckham slowly raised his left arm to return the gesture.

# 27

Kate and Ellis were pushed forward with gun muzzles pointed at their spines.

"Hurry up, Doc," said a guard in black body armor.

Ellis kept his hands in the air but turned slightly toward the two soldiers. Kate resisted the urge to do the same thing. If Beckham were here, he would have snapped their damn necks.

But he wasn't here.

He was out there, fighting, while these cowards herded her and Ellis toward the bridge like sheep. Her stomach churned with disgust and anger.

The squealing of wheels sounded in the next passage as a second pair of guards rolled a gurney around the corner. She clenched her firsts when she saw the bloody sheet draped over the body.

*How can this be happening?*

The guards escorting Kate and Ellis motioned them to get out of the way. Kate stepped back to watch as the soldiers whisked away a fresh corpse. Blood dripped off a limp arm hanging over the side of the gurney.

"Keep moving," the guard with the gun on Kate said.

She pushed on, drawing in a breath that smelled like

gunpowder. As soon as they approached the CIC, she saw why.

A battle had been fought here.

Empty bullet casings and pools of blood littered the floor. It was quiet inside the room, aside from the beep of computers and monitoring equipment. Lieutenant Colonel Kramer had her arms folded across her chest as she stood in the center of the space. She was surrounded by an entourage of soldiers decked out all in black. President Ringgold, Vice President Johnson, and Captain Humphrey were on their knees a few feet away.

"Ah, Doctor Lovato and Doctor Ellis," Kramer said calmly as she pointed a pistol at Kate's head.

"Don't you dare," Ringgold hissed. She rose to her feet, but one of the guards pushed down by her shoulders. Ringgold winced and favored her good arm as she went back down on her knees.

"President Ringgold apparently needs some motivation to hand over the launch codes," Kramer said.

Kate's eyes flitted from Ringgold to Kramer. "What launch codes?"

"Don't play games. You know better than anyone that the strike teams out there aren't going to complete their missions. The monsters *you* created are killing them." Kramer pointed to a cluster of monitors.

Kramer jerked the gun at the screens. "Go ahead; take a look for yourself."

Kate unclenched her firsts and slowly walked over to the monitors. The gun pointed at her back wasn't the only thing making her heart kick. She had to force herself to look at the images. She squinted as she got closer, as if she was about to watch a scary scene in a horror movie.

"As you can see, all but one of our teams has gone dark," Kramer said.

Kate forced herself to look. The lieutenant colonel was right: All but one monitor was off-line. A single green-hued feed from Los Angeles rolled across the screen on the far left. A soldier wearing a helmet-mounted camera was scaling a ladder in some sort of tunnel.

"They could still be alive," Nagle said. The young petty officer was tied up with a dozen other staff from Humphrey's crew. A guard with a machine gun angled his weapon at Nagle.

A few feet away from the prisoners, the floor was covered in blood. Corporal Anderson's station sat empty. The tears streaking down Nagle's face made sense then. With his hands bound, they rolled freely down his face to the deck.

Kramer regarded the man, shaking her head. "I highly doubt that. There are thousands of juveniles out there, and a few canisters of sleeping gas aren't going to hold them back while our teams plant the RDDs."

"That's bullshit, Kramer, and you know it. Our men and women are trained for missions just like this," Johnson shot back. He fought his restraints, looking up with furious eyes.

"They're already dead. God, Johnson, you're just like the others—weak. Colonel Wood was the only man who could have won this war," Kramer said. She shook her head again and directed her gaze at Kate. "You people simply don't understand."

"Colonel Wood was a goddamn madman. Now I see he wasn't the only one," Johnson said. He bowed his head, and when he looked up the anger was gone. He no longer had the hardened look of a general. His worried eyes reminded Kate of her own father.

"Please, Kramer, just give our boys a chance," Johnson pleaded. "How can you nuke the cities while they're still out there?"

As Kate looked around the room, she saw the same bewildered expression on Johnson's staff. They were all shocked—and that was exactly why Kramer's plan had worked so flawlessly. She'd waited until the strike group wasn't guarded and surprised her superiors.

Kramer stopped shaking her head to stare coldly at the vice president. "Maybe you didn't see the same intel reports I did. Once the juveniles leave those nests, we won't be able to stop them. They'll move out of the cities. Nowhere will be spared. This is our last chance to destroy them before that happens. We *must* launch our nuclear arsenal while your strike teams are keeping them busy below ground."

"You crazy bitch." Kate hissed. Hearing Beckham was being used as bait was the last straw. "You can't do this!"

Kramer ignored Kate. She turned and pointed the gun toward Ringgold.

"Now, Madam President, I need those launch codes, or things are going to get a lot worse. I really don't want to hurt Doctor Lovato, but I'll do what it takes to ensure the Variant threat is defeated once and for all."

Kate knew what was coming, but she was more concerned with Beckham's fate than her own. She searched the monitors a second time and stopped on the digital text that read, *Team Ghost/Washington, DC*.

Seeing the blank screen was too much. She dropped her hand to her stomach, cupping the body of the child who she feared she would have to raise on her own. Overcome with dread and anger, she couldn't stop the wave of light-headedness that overwhelmed her.

"Kate," Ellis said. He rushed over to her side as she fell to her knees, but Kramer beat him there.

She grabbed Kate roughly and hauled her upright. Pulling back the slide on her gun, Kramer pointed it at Kate's temple. Kate spat in Kramer's face without thinking.

Kramer used the back of her hand to wipe the spit off. "That wasn't very smart."

"If you hurt her, you'll never get the codes," Ringgold said defiantly.

"Okay," Kramer said. She pushed the barrel at Kate's temple.

Kate locked eyes with the president, a woman she considered a friend. There was strength in Ringgold's gaze, but Kate knew it wasn't enough. Ringgold wouldn't let her die.

"I'll give you the codes if you give the strike teams another hour to complete their mission," Ringgold said.

"Half an hour," Kramer said. "And that's me being generous." She looked toward her guards. "Get Doctor Lovato up and—"

"Ma'am." A male officer with a sharp widow's peak cut Kramer off. We have movement on Feeds Two and Three."

Kate followed the man's finger to the screens monitoring Operation Extinction. It was directed at Atlanta and Des Moines.

"What you got, Nelson?" Kramer asked.

"Looks like juveniles, ma'am."

The feed for Des Moines had come back online. A camera bobbed up and down as the soldier wearing it ran for his life. He looked over his shoulder to reveal three beasts trailing him. He emerged from a sewer opening and pulled himself onto a street.

"Shit, those things are everywhere," Nelson said.

Kramer holstered her gun and folded her arms across her chest. "Just as I said: It was suicide from the beginning."

"No, no...*No!*" shrieked a voice from the speakers.

Nelson went to reach for the audio control, but Kramer stopped him.

"Let them hear every word."

Hesitating, Nelson withdrew his hand.

There was no trace of emotion on Kramer's face as the man on-screen was ripped limb from limb. She didn't care about the soldier dying on the screen in front of her. She just wanted to nuke the monsters—to obliterate the enemy, no matter what it cost.

The feed from Atlanta went dark again a few minutes later.

"Are you starting to understand, Madam President?" Kramer asked. She looked down and tapped her watch. "Looks as if Des Moines and Atlanta will be our first targets. The rest of the teams have approximately fifteen minutes to complete their mission."

Kate looked at the clock and then stared at the feed from DC.

*Come on, Reed. I know you can do this.*

Davis had had no idea what she was getting herself into when she asked a room full of injured soldiers to fight. A dozen men had immediately volunteered. But there were two major problems.

They only had four guns.

And the clock was ticking.

Davis was running out of time to stop Kramer from launching nukes from the USS *Florida*. She scrutinized the soldiers in front of her. They were all in pretty bad shape: A few could stand without assistance, but most needed crutches. One man who looked as if he was in his fifties had rolled up in a wheelchair.

Davis couldn't hold back a smile. The courage of

wounded vets always amazed and inspired her. She needed that reassurance now more than ever. More blood was about to be spilled on the *GW*.

It was an odd feeling, knowing that she could have only a few minutes to live, but Davis was about to spend them with some of the world's finest men in uniform.

She picked out two marine PFCs she remembered from Operation Liberty. Both were young, no older than twenty-five. Lee Bryant had thin blond hair that he wore high and tight. Pete Kehoe didn't have any hair at all. He had a cast on his left arm, and a long scar divided his face. It ran from his hairline down his nose, all the way to his chin. Bryant didn't look much better. His chest was wrapped to protect broken ribs, and his legs were bandaged from ankle to crotch. Variants had carved them up pretty good in Nashville during Operation Liberty. They had later been assigned to the *GW* and had volunteered for a mission in Miami, where they were injured a second time.

Now they were volunteering again.

Davis jerked her chin at the two marines. "Kramer and her men have taken over the *GW* strike group. I need your help taking back the CIC."

Bryant arched a brow. "The lieutenant colonel? How the hell—"

"No time for questions," Davis said. "And she's just Kramer as far as I'm concerned. She lost her rank when she killed your brothers who didn't want to join her gang." She handed an M9 his way. "You in?"

He took a second to think, then accepted the weapon.

"How about you, Kehoe?" Davis asked.

Kehoe extended his hand. "Hell yeah, I'm with you, LT."

"You're *sure* you can fight?" Davis asked. She didn't mean to come across as condescending, but both men shot her a glare.

"What about us?" the man in the wheelchair said.

Davis paused to think. "I don't have any more weapons, but I could use your help with something else."

The man's brown eyes lit up. He was eager for a fight.

"We need a distraction," Davis said. "Ten minutes after we leave, you guys make as much racket down here as possible. That should attract some of Kramer's goons."

"You got it, ma'am," the man in the chair replied. He wheeled away, already ordering the other patients to get ready to make some noise.

Davis had a feeling they were going to be doing more than making some ruckus. She hated leaving them behind, but she simply couldn't risk bringing them along without weapons. It would be suicide.

"Follow me," Davis said to her new team. She led them down the aisles of the infirmary. Chow stood as straight as he could, holding the M9 she'd given him earlier. He pulled the magazine to check the rounds while Davis went over the plan with Kehoe and Bryant.

Ten minutes after entering the infirmary, she left, with a Delta Force operator who looked like a mummy and two marines with multiple broken bones. But hell, she wasn't in the best shape either. She had been slashed, shot, and nearly blown to pieces in Colorado.

They hustled out of the room with every eye following them. Davis caught the gaze of a young boy wrapped up in his mother's arms on her way out. She recognized him as one of the Plum Island survivors, but couldn't remember his name. The child raised a hand and waved. She halted in the doorway and waved back.

More determined than ever, Davis hurried into the passage with her new team. Chow was the first inside the ladder. He directed his M4 at the guard Davis had knocked out earlier. The man was groaning on the floor. She smacked him with her M4 a second time.

"Stay down, asshole," Davis said.

Chow continued up the ladder and halted at the top. Once Davis had ascended, she pulled her radio and turned the knob to listen to chatter. A few seconds later, a voice crackled over the channel.

"Fox Four, this is Lynx One. We're making a pass of Quadrant Three. Still no sign of Lieutenant Davis—please advise. Over."

"Copy that, Lynx One. Proceed to Quadrant Four. We have squads sweeping One and Two. Better check the infirmary too. Oscar Two missed their last radio check."

Davis pulled back the slide on her M4 to chamber a round. "Shit. That's three patrols, and we're about to have company. We need to move fast."

"We should split up," Chow said.

Kehoe and Bryant exchanged a meaningful look.

"Agreed," Davis replied. "Kehoe, you and Bryant take the starboard passage. Chow and I'll take the port side. We'll meet at the CIC."

She raised her hand as they turned to leave. "Wait—take this." She handed Kehoe her M4 and took his M9. "You'll need the extra firepower."

Kehoe nodded. "Thanks, LT."

"Good luck," Davis replied.

The two marines went down the passage, slow and careful, nursing their injuries but looking strong and determined just the same. Chow limped after Davis, the same determination showing in his stride and stance. Still, she turned every few minutes to make sure he was okay. His jet-black hair hung over his bandaged face. He brushed it away so she could see his eyes. Chow winked, a reassuring gesture that told her to focus on the path ahead.

Davis moved quickly. She stopped at every corner

to listen for Kramer's men. The soldiers were far from being special-ops soldiers, and they acted like it. Most were administrative staff who didn't know how to fight. Since there wasn't much need for their skills in the new world, Kramer had given them guns.

But in close corridors, the untrained cowards only needed to get lucky once. Davis tightened her grip on her M9. She wasn't going to give them the opportunity.

She increased her pace toward the next four-way intersection, where she heard distant voices coming from another passage—three of them. She slowed, pointed to the corner, then held up three fingers and signaled the direction the voices were approaching from.

Chow slipped into a cabin across from Davis. She darted after him just as a trio of soldiers came striding around the corner. Chow crouched down and angled his M4 toward the hatch. Davis took up position with her back to the bulkhead.

She swallowed hard as the soldiers approached. A firefight here would bring every one of Kramer's men down on them. There would be no way they could battle their way to the CIC if they were pinned down this far away.

"Got reports of a couple marines who are still causing trouble on the *Cowpens*," someone said. "The other ships are all secure except for this one. Most of 'em hardly even put up a fight."

A second voice, muffled by a mask, growled back, "Lieutenant Colonel Kramer wants Lieutenant Davis found."

"Copy that, sir," said a third.

The rap of boots passed the cabin and continued down the passage, but Davis couldn't relax. Kramer had taken over all the other ships? *How the hell?*

It was partly Davis's fault. She had signed off on the

major deployment that sent most of the *GW*'s soldiers to the Marine Corps Recruit Depot at Parris Island. It was one of the last military strongholds left and a staging ground for the final phase of Operation Extinction. Davis cursed her luck. She should have known better. She should have seen this coming.

"LT," Chow whispered.

Davis glanced over.

"You got a plan when we get to the CIC?"

"Yeah. Don't shoot anyone important."

Chow cracked a pained grin. "How many hostiles?"

"At least six."

His grin vanished, but he nodded. "I can handle that."

"Figured as much. Let's keep moving."

"Hold on," Chow whispered. "Any word on Team Ghost?"

Davis hesitated. She could see the pain in Chow's eyes. He was desperate for news about his brothers.

"We'll find out as soon as we get to the CIC."

Chow scratched at one of his facial bandages and wiped the blood on his shirt. He wasn't good at hiding his anxiety, but he was damn good at disguising his physical pain.

As soon as the footfalls of Kramer's men faded away, Davis crouch-walked back into the passage. She kept low, her M9 raised close to her right eye as she swept for contacts.

Chow moved on her left side with his M4 shouldered. Several of the bandages on his legs were weeping blood. He caught her looking at the wounds, but offered no wink of reassurance this time. Adjusting his grip on his rifle, he exhaled a short breath and pushed on.

They worked forward, watching the passages through their gun sights, boots scarcely making a sound. The security cabin came into view around the next corner. She pointed at the hatch that was now sealed. Chow moved across the corridor and took up position to the right of the hatch while Davis tried the handle.

It was unlocked.

Chow took a step backward with his rifle. Beads of sweat crawled down his bandaged face. He blinked them away, then pressed his scope back to his right eye.

Davis twisted the handle and pushed the hatch open, expecting to hear gunfire as Chow rushed inside, but he cleared the cabin with a quick sweep. She motioned for him to hold security. Then she moved to check the monitors again. Kramer's men really were amateurs: If Davis were taking over a ship, she'd have this room on lockdown. But she wasn't about to complain.

Her eyes flitted from screen to screen. As she suspected, there were six soldiers in the CIC, but they were spread out, and one had a shotgun angled at Dr. Lovato's head.

"Shit," Davis said. "They have more hostages."

She turned up the audio and leaned closer to the monitor.

"You can't give her the codes!" Kate shouted.

Ringgold bowed her head toward the ground and then glanced up. "I'm sorry, Kate, but I have no choice."

"You said there's always a choice," Kate fired back. "That there's always hope."

"Not this time." Ringgold accepted a pad of paper and a pen from one of Kramer's men.

Davis couldn't believe her eyes. This was not the president she had come to know. Ringgold suddenly shot a discreet look at the video camera, then looked back at Kramer. "You don't have to do this. There's still time to change your mind. To do what's right," she said.

"This is the only way," Kramer said. "In the end, you will see that."

Ringgold pushed the pen to the paper but hesitated. "You're wrong. You're wrong about all of this."

"Come on," Chow whispered.

Davis nodded. The president, she saw now, wasn't weak at all; she was stalling to give Davis and whoever else was out there a chance. She must have known Kramer's men hadn't captured everyone yet.

*I'll be damned. You're one hell of a lady*, Davis thought with a smile. She quickly checked the other monitors. Kehoe and Bryant were sneaking down the passage that led to the CIC. They stopped at the next four-way intersection and waited. Twenty feet away, around the next bulkhead, two of Kramer's men guarded the hatch to the bridge. There were two patrols working down other corridors, and they were both closing in on Davis's position.

"Let's move," she said.

Chow stepped into the hallway and waved her forward. She limped after him, gun sight pressed to her eye as she kept close to the bulkhead. The burn of anxiety rushed through her. They had been lucky so far to have avoided most of Kramer's troops, but the men holding down the fort in the CIC would likely be the best. Davis's small team was injured, outgunned, and facing a hostage situation.

Chow and Davis rounded the next corridor from the south. Kehoe and Bryant came into focus at the north end. The west passage led to the CIC. One of Kramer's teams would be working its way down the east passage.

Shit was about to go down. They couldn't avoid a showdown with Kramer's men any longer.

Davis's muscles tightened in anticipation, as if she was preparing to be punched. She took a knee halfway down the corridor next to Chow. Kehoe raised his left arm to wave when he saw them coming. He stood and took a step toward the corner.

Davis gestured to the marines, telling the story with her fingers.

*Six hostiles in the CIC. Two more patrols on the way.*

Kehoe took another small step in her direction that exposed part of his body to the firing lines from the west and east. The small movement cost him his face. It disintegrated in an explosion of bone and blood before Davis could react. Rounds punched into the bulkhead. His chest and torso jerked from the impacts.

"No!" Bryant yelled.

He grabbed Kehoe's wrist and pulled him around the corner as another salvo of rounds slammed into the overhead.

Davis stared, unbelieving, at Kehoe's convulsing, faceless body. It took her a moment to comprehend the fact that such a small mistake had cost him his life. The shock of watching him die vanished as anger took control. Chow was back on his feet and working toward the four-way intersection at a cautious pace.

The two soldiers who had been guarding the entrance to the CIC rushed into Chow's line of fire—a fatal mistake of their own. Without hesitation, the Delta Force operator fired two quick bursts into their backs as they directed their weapons toward Bryant.

Chow was running again before Kramer's men hit the ground. "Bryant, on me!"

The marine scrambled away from Kehoe's broken body and rushed into the intersection. He immediately dropped to his stomach and fired from a prone position at a target around the corner from Davis.

She whirled with her M9 raised at the corridor behind her to check their six. Confirming it was clear, she continued to Chow. He had his back against the left-side bulkhead.

Rounds lanced into the deck around the corner, but

Chow kept back. He waited a beat, then turned and fired off a burst. Davis took up position next to him and tapped him on the shoulder.

"Changing," Chow said. She traded places with him and twisted to the side just as a round bit into the metal next to her face. A crack echoed in her ear, but adrenaline pushed her forward.

She fired off several shots at the two men outside of the CIC, hitting one in the leg. He crashed to the floor while his partner fired on Bryant's position.

The marine fired back, hitting the second guard between the eyes with a three round burst that blew off the top of his head and helmet.

Davis patted Chow on the shoulder again, motioning for him to move. They hurried into the intersection side by side.

The crack of gunfire echoed through the passages, and a round whizzed past Davis's face as all hell broke loose. She ducked down to avoid the bullets that punched into the overhead.

Raised voices followed the gunshots, and her heart rose in her throat.

*Shit. We're being flanked.*

The guard who Davis had shot in the leg managed to push himself up in front of the CIC. Bryant took him down with a shot to the throat. The man crumpled in the open hatch, blocking it from being shut.

Now was their chance.

"Inside!" Davis shouted.

Bryant had just jumped to his knees to make a run for the hatch when three rounds hit him in the torso. He crashed into the bulkhead, blood gushing from his wounds as he slumped to the floor.

Chow turned to fire on the patrol flanking them. "Go, Davis! I'm right behind you!"

She was already running. Bending down, she grabbed an M4 lying on the deck. It felt heavy, but she didn't have time to check the magazine. She only had seconds to think as she bolted for the CIC.

Training, habit, and a dash of insanity drove her next actions. She grabbed the armored body of the dead guard blocking the entry under his armpits and hoisted him to his feet.

The chatter of gunfire amplified behind her. More voices called out.

"Stop them! Stop them *now*!"

She positioned the dead soldier against the bulkhead and held him there while Chow, lying on his belly, fired at targets in the south passage. He used the two dead guards as cover, but it wasn't enough. Blood blossomed across his left shoulder from a bullet wound.

Flashes from two muzzles came from the north firing lane, and a second round hit Chow in the back of his right leg. He fired off a burst toward the flanking soldiers and yelled, "Make it count, Davis!"

She nodded grimly. The Delta operator was making a heroic last stand to give her a chance at this. She had seconds to make a move. She pushed the dead guard through the open hatch.

Rounds immediately peppered his armor.

Everything that happened next seemed to move in slow motion. Davis bolted into the room with her gun shouldered. She drew in a breath, slid on her knees, and made a mental inventory of the space. Two of the remaining four guards were still firing on the poor bastard Davis had pushed into the room. She killed them both with two short bursts.

Davis shot a third guard in the face as he trained his weapon on her. There was a muzzle flash from his gun, but he missed. Sliding to a stop on her knees, Davis pivoted her gun to the fourth guard, hiding behind a radar station. He squeezed off a burst before she could.

She felt the hot rounds before she heard them. They bit into her left shoulder, stinging as if the biggest bug on earth had sunk a needle into her flesh. The impact threw off her aim, allowing the soldier to fire again. She rolled to the right to avoid the spray, landing on her stomach and pushing the gun's sight to her eye. She fired a shot that hit the guard just above his heart. He crashed into a monitor, the screen cracking from the impact.

Another round tore into her side as she pushed herself up. It hit her with such force she was slammed into the bottom of a station. The air exploded from her lungs, and she collapsed to the deck, her vision blurring with shades of red.

*Get up, Rachel. You aren't finished.*

Davis palmed at the ground, pushing herself to her feet to the sight of a woman staring down at her. At first, she thought it was President Ringgold, but her vision cleared to Kramer's stern face.

The lieutenant colonel aimed a pistol down at her head.

"A brave attempt," Kramer said. "But you're too late."

Davis eyed her M4, a few feet away. It was so close, but she knew the moment she reached for it she would have a bullet in her skull.

There was screaming and gunshots in the passage outside the CIC. Davis strained to hear Chow's voice but couldn't make it out over the ringing in her ears.

He was a Delta operator, but she knew the chances of him holding back two squads was unlikely, especially since he was already injured.

No, Davis was on her own now.

Alone, cornered, and bleeding from multiple gunshots.

She fought the rising panic, knowing that if she gave

in she was dead. But what could she do? Her body was already numb, and she could feel the blood pumping out of her. Her arms wobbled as she struggled to stay on her knees. She strained to look past the barrel angled down at her, searching the room frantically for President Ringgold.

Instead, she looked through the portholes and saw a cloud of exhaust ripping across the sky. Davis couldn't see the USS *Florida*, but she heard each of the missiles launching.

*One.*

*Two.*

*Three.*

There were a total of ten, peeling off in different directions to destroy the cities Davis had tried so desperately to save. Her failure hurt worse than the gunshots. She battled her heavy eyelids, trying to keep them open, but no matter how hard she tried, she couldn't hold back the darkness. It washed over her.

No.

No—she would *not* let the bitch win.

Davis snapped her eyes open. She pushed at the deck with a groan. Blood soaked her uniform, pooling on the ground, but it didn't matter. There were raised voices all around her, but she was focused only on Kramer.

"We're finally taking our country back," Kramer said as she turned to watch the missiles.

A second voice said, "Not like this, we're not."

Kramer's eyes suddenly widened.

Davis saw Ringgold come from the side with a revolver. She pulled the hammer back with her thumb, pointed it at Kramer's head, and pulled the trigger without hesitation. Kramer blinked right before the bullet entered her left temple, realizing just a millisecond before her life ended that she'd failed.

Time ground to a halt in the CIC, as if Davis was watching everything happen from inside a fishbowl. A hot, sticky spray of blood hit her in the face. She blinked it away as Kramer's body thudded onto the deck in front of her. A team of marines rushed into the room, weapons raking over the space.

"Hostiles down!" one of the men shouted.

Time snapped back into motion as Ringgold dropped the pistol and crouched down in front of Davis. The president wiped blood gently from Davis's face.

"We have to stop the missiles!" someone shouted.

"I'm on it," called another voice.

"There isn't enough time," said a third.

"Make time!" yelled Captain Humphrey.

The voices blended together as Davis struggled to stay conscious. But there was one voice that was louder than the others. She couldn't see Ringgold's face, but she could feel the president's breath against her as the woman took off her jacket and pressed it against the wound in her side.

"Hold on," President Ringgold said. "Hold on."

# 28

The rap of footsteps filled the tunnel as Fitz and Horn carried Rico and Beckham away from the chamber of sleeping monsters. Apollo trotted ahead, looking behind him every few feet to make sure his handlers were still there.

Fitz was struggling to carry Rico, but Horn was moving at a fast clip. His best friend was unconscious and limp across his back. It was a sight that made Fitz's heart ache.

Beckham's right hand had been severed at the wrist, and he'd lost his left leg just below the knee. Between the blood loss and the toxins, he was in bad shape. Fitz remembered what it had been like to lose his legs in Iraq, the terrible pain and horror he'd felt, but the medevac had been only fifteen minutes away then. Help was over an hour away for Beckham—and that was if Ghost even made it out of the tunnels.

The pain of seeing a brother injured was always worse than his own pain. Part of that pain was knowing what Beckham would have to deal with if he did survive. His trigger finger and knife hand were gone. He would have to learn how to shoot all over again with his left. He'd have to adjust to walking with a prosthetic too. Nothing about it would be easy.

Fitz knew he was getting way ahead of himself. They weren't even close to being out of the blast zone, and he wasn't sure how long Garcia could last before setting off the bomb. If the monsters woke up—

"Hurry the fuck up!" Horn shouted.

Fitz pushed Rico's body higher up on his shoulders. She screeched in pain.

"Raven One, this is Ghost Three, do you copy?" Horn said into the comms.

It was the first time anyone from Team Ghost had attempted a transmission since they'd jumped from the Osprey. White noise hissed back. They were still too far underground.

Fitz ran as fast as his blades would carry him. He didn't know how long the R49 gas would keep the monsters down, but he guessed it wasn't long. Garcia wouldn't be able to hold them back more than a few moments when they did wake. Ghost had to be well out of the blast zone before that happened.

"You see anything back there?" Horn shouted.

Fitz could hardly twist his head, but he checked the shadowed passages with a quick glance.

"Looks clear!"

"Almost to the ladder," Horn said, his voice tight with the strain of carrying Beckham.

For a fleeting moment, Fitz thought he saw Beckham look up, but it was just his helmet bouncing on Horn's back. He had no way of knowing if Beckham was even still alive. Judging by his gray skin and bleeding stumps, he was slipping away from this world fast—if he hadn't already.

"Beckham!" Fitz shouted without thinking. "Stay with us, goddamnit!"

Thighs burning, chest heaving, and heart aching, Fitz pushed on. Garcia's voice popped into his head: *All it takes is all you got, Marine.*

Beckham had a lot—much more than most men. *More than me.*

The skeletal ladder came into focus at the end of the tunnel. Fitz ran harder, his blades creaking with each step. They were halfway to the ladder when the bark of a shotgun echoed from the chamber they'd left behind.

The sound spurred Fitz. They were running out of time.

"Hurry, Fitz!" Horn yelled. "Garcia's got company."

Apollo circled at the bottom of the ladder; whining and growling at the noise. Horn slowed as he approached. When he was under the bottom rung, he stopped and repositioned Beckham on his back.

"Hang on, boss! We're getting you out of here," Horn said. He turned to look over his shoulder. "Boss, can you hear me?"

Fitz glimpsed the cavernous wrinkles on Horn's forehead and the sweat bleeding out of them. Horn continued to shout his friend's name, but the only response came in the hiss of static over the comms.

"Fitz…Horn…multiple contacts. Can't hold…hur—" Garcia's voice cut off.

Another shotgun blast echoed down the hall from the chamber. Fitz turned to scan the shadows. When he turned back to the ladder, Horn was already climbing.

"I'll be right back for you," Fitz said, looking down at Apollo. The dog's tail made a single pass, and he sat on his haunches.

Garcia fired off three more shots. "Hurry!" he said over the channel, clearer this time. "I can't hold them back for long."

The boom from a hand grenade shook dust from the ceiling. Fitz grabbed the bottom rung and started climbing with Rico hanging over his back. Moonlight steamed into the tunnel as Horn pushed the hatch open above.

He slid Beckham's body onto the concrete and pulled himself up, vanishing into the night.

"Almost there, Rico," he whispered. His arms were shaking, his thighs were on fire, and he struggled to breathe. He focused on the sliver of moon peeking out from behind the clouds, blinking away the sweat dripping into his eyes.

*Almost there. Three more rungs. Just three…*

A face emerged over the open hatch. Horn reached inside. "Give her to me!"

Fitz locked the spikes tipping his blades onto the rungs and used the power of his thighs and back to push her limp body up toward Horn.

"I'm going back for Apollo," Fitz said.

He unlocked his blades and slid down the skeletal ladder to the bottom, sparks streaking down the metal as another explosion rocked the chamber. Four shotgun blasts followed. Garcia was putting up one hell of a fight, but he couldn't hold on forever.

Apollo jumped into Fitz's arms. He wrapped his left arm around the dog and grabbed the ladder with his right. The German shepherd was much lighter than Rico, but Fitz's muscles had already been pushed to their limits. Every fiber seemed to stretch as he climbed.

Halfway up, he froze at the rattle of suppressed gunfire.

Apollo let out a low whine, looking up with Fitz at rounds spitting across the sky. This gunfire wasn't coming from the chamber or the comms. Horn was firing on a target.

*Shit, Shit. Shit. Keep moving!*

Fitz pushed Apollo out of the tunnel and onto the concrete. The dog hurried over to Beckham, stopping to nudge the unconscious soldier with the muzzle of his gas mask.

Climbing out of the hole, Fitz clambered across the ground toward Beckham, Rico, and Apollo. His hands and blades slid through the gory remains of juveniles. Fitz wanted to close his eyes, especially when he saw the remains of what had once been his friend Tank.

There was no time for emotions right now. The world was crashing down around Fitz, and if he didn't get out of here now, he wouldn't be getting out at all.

Rico reached up as Fitz approached. Her lips were as blue as the highlights in her hair. "Hang in there, kiddo," Fitz said. He moved over to Beckham and put a finger on his neck to check for a pulse. For several seconds Fitz couldn't feel anything. It was only the slight movement of his chest moving up and down that told him Beckham was still alive.

"Fitz, get your ass over here!" Horn shouted. He was unloading his M249 on targets across First Street. In between bursts he yelled, "Raven One, Ghost Three. We're outside the Grant Memorial. We got two injured and have *multiple* contacts closing in. Need extraction, ASAP."

Fitz almost choked on adrenaline when he saw the lawn around the Capitol. It was full of monsters. Hundreds of dark, jagged shapes rushed across the charcoaled grass. The light of the moon illuminated the rugged armor of the beasts darting toward them. Shadows Fitz knew to be more of the juveniles came loping down the Capitol steps.

In a few seconds, the Capitol Building and the monsters would disappear in a fiery explosion—but Fitz and his friends were still in the blast zone.

Tito's familiar voice flared over the open channel. "Copy that, Ghost Three. Raven One. Where the fuck you been? We got a major problem!" There was a pause, and Fitz looked toward the sky to search for the Osprey. Had he seen his cousin fall?

The next transmission nearly stopped Fitz's thumping heart.

"There's a nuclear-tipped ballistic missile on its way to DC," Tito said. "We got maybe five minutes to get the hell out of here!"

Horn glanced back at Fitz. They exchanged a horrified, confused look.

Fitz pushed himself to his feet and unslung his MK11. Tito had to be wrong. There was no way the military would nuke this city, unless...

"They fucking used us as bait, Big Horn!" Fitz shouted. He knew it was paranoid, but shit, nothing else made sense. They'd sent the strike teams into the cities to keep the juveniles occupied while they prepped the nukes.

"What the fuck!" Horn growled. He fired off another burst that peppered the side of a Humvee, shattering windows and deflating the front tire as a juvenile loped by. Cursing, he squeezed off another shot that finally hit the beast in the spine. It crashed to the ground, flopping and shrieking.

"Get your ass down here!" Horn yelled, stopping to scan the sky for the Osprey.

Another voice surged over the channel. "Fitz, Horn, are you out of the blast—" There was gunfire, and then, "I can't hold—"

"A few more minutes, Sarge," Horn said. "Hang in there, brother!"

White noise filled the comms between the gunshots. Fitz strained to hear Garcia's response.

"Can't...No more...*Hurry!*"

The words made Fitz's heart fire like Horn's SAW. He pushed the scope of his MK11 to his eye, squared his shoulders, tightened his grip on the stock, and lined up the cross hairs on a juvenile that had reached the street that separated Ghost from the Capitol lawn. The creature mounted a vehicle and tilted its curved skull. Fitz shot it in the mouth as it opened its mandibles and let out a howl. It slid down the windshield, leaving a trail of blood.

The shadows of more abominations stretched across the lawn as more of the beasts raced toward the street. There were dozens of them. Fitz fired shot after shot, but the rounds only slowed them down. Nailing head shots was nearly impossible when they were moving so fast, especially at this range.

Fitz counted the seconds, panic growing inside him like a tumor. Thirty seconds had passed since Tito's last transmission, but there was no sign of the Osprey. If the chopper didn't get there soon, they'd be caught in the blast of the dirty bomb.

Or, apparently, a goddamn nuclear explosion.

*Hold on, Garcia. Just hold on, brother.*

"Where the hell is Tito?" Horn shouted.

Another salvo of gunshots popped behind Fitz. Rico had her back against the south side of the Grant Memorial. She wielded dual M9s from a sitting position at the juveniles flanking them across the pool.

"Behind us, Big Horn!" Fitz shouted.

Three more of the beasts had reached First Street. They clambered over vehicles, setting off car alarms. The shrieking sirens nearly put Fitz back on his ass in shock until he realized what they were.

Horn fired without restraint, rounds shattering windshields and punching through metal. The muzzle flashes from his M249 cast a glow over his armor. He'd removed his face guard and torn away his gas mask, leaving just his skull bandanna. Each muzzle flash lit up his crazed features, as if he were the Angel of Death himself.

Fitz blinked the sweat from his bulging eyes.

A brass casing ejected from his gun in slow motion. He heard it clank off the monument behind him. Two more steps backward and his blades nudged a body that had to be Beckham. After chambering another round, he grabbed Beckham by his left wrist and dragged him to the base of the monument. Apollo darted after them.

"Big Horn, over here!" Fitz shouted.

"Raven One, where the fuck are you?" Horn yelled into his mini-mic.

Team Ghost came together on the south side of the Grant Memorial as they waited for a miracle. Fitz, Horn, Rico, and Apollo formed a perimeter around Beckham's limp body. Gunshots lanced out in every direction as the juveniles closed in.

Fitz imagined it looked a lot like the Battle of Thermopylae. But unlike the three hundred Spartan warriors protecting King Leonidas, not all of Team Ghost was here to protect Master Sergeant Beckham. A half mile away, in the nightmarish chamber below, Sergeant Garcia must have been fighting valiantly. Fitz could only imagine the fear the marine felt as he too was surrounded.

Or maybe he didn't feel any at all. The sergeant had developed a death wish. Everyone had seen it. And Fitz didn't blame him. He'd lost everyone he cared about: his family, his team, maybe even part of his soul.

All at once, a mechanical noise roared over the National Mall. An Osprey flew over Capitol Hill, its dual rotors making a mechanical thundering that masked the high-pitched screeches of the monsters. The creatures paused to look up, heads tilting and almond-shaped eyes following the aircraft.

"Let's move!" Horn shouted.

Fitz flung his rifle over his back and bent down for Rico. She reached up and grabbed him around the neck. Horn already had Beckham over his shoulders.

A scream that sounded like a freight train's whistle commanded Fitz's attention to the east. At first he thought that Garcia had detonated the dirty bomb.

Then he recognized the source of the noise. It was about to make a much bigger explosion than their RDD.

Thousands of times more powerful.

In the sky to the north, a streak of red split through the drifting storm clouds. The ballistic missile heading for DC was reentering the atmosphere. Pieces of the rocket tumbled away as the heat vehicle carrying the nuclear warhead raced across the skyline.

"Move your ass, marine!" Horn shouted.

A cold spray of water snapped Fitz back to reality, and he forced himself to look away from the missile. Tito and his copilot slowly lowered the Osprey over the pool, churning the water into mist. Juveniles charged from all directions, racing across First Street, barreling across the dead grass of the National Mall and leaping into the pool.

Fitz tightened his grip on Rico's legs and bolted for the steps at the bottom of the memorial. The whine of a mini-gun sounded over the discord of the hissing monsters. Fire flashed from the remote-controlled gun attached to the underbelly of the Osprey. Firing three thousand rounds per minute, the weapon tore the beasts to shreds. The sight filled Fitz with hope, but even if Ghost could make it into the troop hold in time to escape the dirty bomb, there was no way they could make it out of the city before the nuke leveled it.

And yet Fitz continued running, knowing each second could be his last. He was fueled by a single objective: to save his friends. Every breath came out in a labored puff and his blades creaked, straining under Rico's weight.

Apollo ran ahead, his tail up now, oblivious to the nuclear holocaust barreling down on them. Fitz closed his eyes in prayer, running blindly through the water.

His eyes snapped open as the Osprey's lift gate hit the pool. The splash soaked Fitz as he waded into the water. Horn powered his way to the troop hold, set Beckham softly on the floor, then climbed inside. Apollo hopped in after him with an impressive leap. Horn scrambled back to the edge of the gate and reached for Rico. As soon as she was inside, he reached for Fitz and shouted for Tito to take off.

Fitz jumped and grabbed Horn's hand as the craft lifted into the air. Both men scooted away from the open door and watched the National Mall filling with monsters. Hundreds of the beasts came streaming out of the surrounding buildings.

Had Garcia failed?

Fitz hadn't heard a word or gunshot from the marine for over a minute. Reaching up, he pulled away his gas mask and repositioned his headset.

"Garcia, do you copy?"

Static burped over the channel.

Several seconds of silence passed. Fitz moved closer to Rico. She was gripping her injured leg and staring out the open door.

"Tito, get us the hell out of here!" Horn yelled.

The Osprey rolled to the right, passing over waves of frantic monsters. They clawed at the sky, hate-filled eyes following the bird as it pulled away.

"My God," Rico breathed. Her eyes fixated on the skyline, where the nuke cut through the storm clouds like a bullet in slow motion.

"Hurry, Tito!" Fitz yelled. As he crawled over to Beckham, everything seemed to slow down, and the absurdity of what they'd been through hit him in his gut. He had seen a lot in the past seven weeks, but this was too much. A nuclear explosion was the last way he'd imagined things would end.

"Garcia…" Fitz repeated.

Fitz finally realized that it didn't matter if Garcia was successful or not. In a few minutes, DC would be a smoldering crater, with or without the dirty bomb.

"Boss," Horn said. He removed Beckham's helmet and carefully pulled it away from his friend's matted hair. With deliberate care, Horn maneuvered Beckham's head into his lap.

"It's okay, Reed, we're going home," Horn said.

Beckham's eyelids fluttered for a moment, then slowly opened. Grimacing, he strained to look up at Horn's face.

"Why you crying, Big Horn?" Beckham whispered.

Fitz put a hand on Beckham's left shoulder, trying not to look at the bandages covering his stumps.

"I'm not," Horn said. He wiped a tear away from his freckled face.

"You're almost as bad a liar as Chow," Beckham said, coughing.

Horn chuckled and sniffled at the same time. "Just hang in there, brother. Don't try and talk. Kate's waiting for you. So are my girls."

Beckham's gaze flitted to Fitz.

"Did we complete the mission?"

Fitz rubbed the plate of armor covering Beckham's left shoulder. He couldn't disrespect Beckham by lying. Before he could reply with the truth, the Capitol Building vanished in a massive explosion that filled the dark sky with fire. Fitz shielded his face from the heat of the blast. It rushed outward, incinerating every monster on the grounds within seconds.

"Hold on!" Tito shouted. The Osprey jerked to the left, then pulled up.

"He did it," Fitz whispered. "Garcia fucking did it."

Flames licked at the sky as Raven 1 rushed away from the National Mall. When the light from the explosion faded, the nuke once again came into focus. It sailed across the skyline at a ninety-degree angle. From a distance, the Washington Monument looked like the point of impact.

Fitz squeezed Beckham's shoulder and reached for Rico with his other hand. Horn kept a hand on Beckham's head as it rested on his chest. Apollo curled up among the survivors of Team Ghost. Together, they watched the rocket scream toward the nation's capital.

The Osprey carried them away at max speed, but to Fitz, it felt as if they were crawling through the clouds. In a few seconds, everything they'd just fought and bled for would vanish in a nuclear fire.

It wasn't fair. They'd come all this way, completed their mission— only to be killed by their own damn military. Considering the origin of the war, the irony no longer surprised Fitz, but he did wonder who had given the order this time, and why. He guessed it didn't matter any longer.

Fitz gripped his friends tighter, taking comfort in their presence during the final moments of his life. Rico plucked up the wad of chewed gum stuck on her helmet and jammed it into her mouth. Beckham struggled to sit up, asking again if Ghost had completed their mission. Horn whispered prayers to see his girls again. Fitz felt the urge to pray too, but something held him back. Did he deserve to make it, after everything he'd done and everyone he'd lost? All those lives he couldn't save . . . maybe it was time to finally pay the price for his failures.

*Don't let it win, Fitz. You're a good man. The* best, *just like Riley. You didn't fail us. You saved us with your friendship and kindness.*

Meg's final words brought him back from the edge of despair, and, looking around, he saw he hadn't failed after all. Fitz had helped save Beckham and Rico, and Apollo too. And they'd saved him. That was the way things were with family. Feeling a sense of peace that had eluded him ever since Iraq, he bowed his head, held his brothers and sister close, and prayed.

# Epilogue

Two weeks later

A brilliant sunrise crested the North Atlantic. The rays sparkled over the water and banished the darkness. As the crimson sun slowly climbed higher into the sky, the light carpeted a lone island. Waves slapped against the shore. On a hill overlooking the surf were the graves of men and women who had lost their lives defending their country during the war against the Variants. The sun continued to rise, the light illuminating fresh dirt and dozens of new white crosses.

Tears fell from Master Sergeant Reed Beckham's eyes. He tried wiping them away but had to switch hands in the middle of the motion. His new right hand hung heavy by his hip, feeling unnatural and awkward. He knew he'd get used to it someday, but he didn't know when.

Beckham dried his tears, pushed away his own discomfort, and put his thoughts back where they belonged. Plum Island was a beautiful yet poignant sight—one that he'd never thought he would see again.

He could see for miles from the top of the command center of the *GW*. Cool spring air rustled his uniform as he stood there, looking out over the waves. Seven other vessels trailed the flagship of the strike group as the aircraft carrier split the water.

Drawing in a breath, Beckham took a cautious step with the blade on his left leg. Metal clanked on metal as he carefully made his way down the ladder leading to the flight deck. Every step was tedious and painful. He was learning to walk again with the prosthetic. It was an extremely slow and nerve-racking process, but he wasn't alone.

A hand touched his back, remaining there for just a second. Kate had given Beckham the support he'd needed over the past two weeks, but she never made him feel helpless.

"Do you know what you're going to say?" Kate asked.

Beckham grabbed the railing with his left hand and turned to face her. Her blue eyes searched his as they stood in the breeze, her hair blowing in a halo behind her head. Without Kate, he would never have made it home after Horn, Fitz, Rico, and Garcia had brought him out of that hellhole in DC, but she had given him something worth living for when his body was shutting down from the venom and blood loss. He only vaguely remembered the last moments inside the chamber, but one image was seared in his memory: the look on Garcia's face when Ghost left him there to detonate the bomb.

*I hope he found his peace.*

Kate massaged Beckham's left hand with her thumb. "Reed?"

"Sorry," he replied, turning back to the view of the flight deck. "Yes, I know what I'm going to say. It's funny though: I've fought against the Taliban with nothing but a bayonet and I've killed Variants with my bare hands, but public speaking scares the hell out of me."

Kate smiled and stood on her tiptoes to reach his lips. "You'll do just fine."

A raucous mechanical noise suddenly sounded from the western sky. Beckham and Kate turned to watch a squadron of F-16s explode from the clouds. The jets screamed over the strike group, leaving a white streak of exhaust as they raced away.

Beckham's mind slipped again, returning to that night in DC.

*"Hurry, Tito!" Fitz screamed.*

*Beckham struggled to focus on the nuke whizzing through the clouds. It was moving at an astounding speed, and in a few seconds it would level the city. Their nation's capital would disappear in a massive mushroom cloud.*

*The pain from his injuries was overwhelming, but he was aware of what he was witnessing, even though it was difficult to understand.*

*"Hold on, everyone!" Tito ordered.*

*Rattling, the Osprey jerked, rolled, and pulled higher into the sky.*

*Tito was still trying to save them, but Beckham knew they weren't far enough away. In a few moments, the nuclear explosion would engulf the helicopter.*

*Beckham blinked, and in that fraction of a second, the nuke shot through the final clouds that lay between it and the city. Two more heartbeats passed before it plowed into the lawn next to the Washington Monument. Even from a distance, Beckham could see the plume of black dirt that was hurled into the sky by the impact. The warhead skipped once, sailed into the air, and came crashing back to the ground, where it dug a shallow grave and came at last to rest.*

The ocean breeze and Kate's soft touch brought him back to the *GW*. He used his left hand to brush the hair from his forehead, his mind still partially focused on the memory.

It wasn't a miracle that had caused the nuke not to

detonate—it was a few brave soldiers in the CIC who had fought to retake the *GW* and disarm the weapon and others like it. Soldiers he was here to honor.

"Let's go," Beckham said to Kate. He clutched her hand and they walked side by side down the ladder. He stumbled slightly when he saw the crowd gathered at the far starboard side of the flight deck. They were just silhouettes, faces hidden by the shadows cast by the line of Super Hornets, Ospreys, and Black Hawks.

"Slower, Reed. This isn't a race," Kate said soothingly.

Nodding, Beckham paused to catch his breath. Walking down the ladder felt like going on a ten-mile run. His body still hadn't healed from the toxins, but he was getting better every day.

Two weeks from now, he would be running with Fitz. The wounded warrior had already put together a training schedule for them, eager to help Beckham adjust to his prosthetic leg.

Beckham put his left arm around Kate when they reached the bottom of the ladder and pulled her close as they crossed the deck. To the east, a Black Hawk pulled away from the USS *Chancellorsville*. He eyed the troop hold, which was filled with civilians. The aircraft was ferrying the survivors to their new home at Plum Island.

In the past two weeks, they'd found several more groups of holdouts living in New York high rises; the same had been true in other cities around the country. There had been more survivors than anyone had dared hope.

By the time Beckham and Kate reached the crowd gathered on the flight deck of the *GW*, the sun had fully enveloped the ship. Apollo came running toward them, his tail whipping back and forth.

Beckham grimaced as he took a knee. The German shepherd licked his face joyfully, unburdened by the weight of the terrible memories that would never fully fade for his human friends. Beckham would be living with those nightmares—but at least he was alive.

A youthful voice snapped him from his trance.

"Uncle Reed!"

The vision in his right eye was permanently damaged from the toxins that had destroyed the nerves, but Beckham didn't have to see to know the small shapes running away from the crowd were Tasha and Jenny. Their freckled faces beamed up at him as they threw their arms around him.

Behind them stood Horn, his tattooed arms folded across his chest. He looked out of place in a T-shirt that read, JUST ANOTHER DAY IN PARADISE. Rico and Fitzpatrick were in neatly pressed uniforms, and Ellis wore a button-down shirt and slacks. President Ringgold and Vice President Johnson stood with an entourage of marines to the right.

There were dozens of civilians too. Donna held Bo in her arms, and Jake stood holding Timothy's hand. The boy wasn't much younger than Beckham had been when he'd lost his mother to cancer.

Several wounded warriors in wheelchairs and leaning on crutches were mixed throughout the crowd. Lieutenant Davis, uniform full of shiny new medals, sat in one of the wheelchairs, scowling and fidgeting with the wheels as if she wanted to leap to her feet. But that was it. The group was much smaller than the one that had gathered before the mission to DC.

So many faces were missing.

Beckham reached into his pocket and pulled out the picture of his mom and the handful of dog tags he'd collected. He needed their strength to get through what came next.

A gust of wind suddenly plucked the picture of his

mom from his fingers. It sailed away, whirling and flapping over the deck. Beckham tried to lope after it, but with the sudden movement, he lost his balance and crashed to the deck. The dog tags spilled across the ground. The sight made him cry out. They were all he had left of his men, and the picture all he had left of his mom, besides memories.

Beckham reached for the picture, but his hand came up empty, his depth perception off due to his damaged vision. He scrambled after it, moving into a large shadow. Horn crouched down in front of him, holding the picture out in his huge hand.

"Here you go, boss."

"Thanks," Beckham said, exhaling. He kissed the picture, then carefully tucked it back in his pocket.

Fitz was scooping up the dog tags a few feet away. After he collected them, he walked over to Beckham's left side. Horn moved to his right. The two men reached down and grabbed Beckham under his armpits without a word. Apollo wagged his tail as they hoisted their leader to his feet.

Ringgold and Johnson were standing next to Kate. They didn't ask if he was okay, or stare at him as if he was disabled. Their gazes were empathetic, not pitying, and full of respect. Everyone knew what he had been through and the sacrifices he'd made.

Beckham brushed off his uniform and took the dog tags back from Fitz. The cold metal went back into his pocket.

*These are the last dog tags I'll ever have to collect*, he realized.

Ringgold and Beckham exchanged a glance. He saw her brush the American flag lapel on her collar with a finger as she walked back to the crowd. It was the slightest of gestures, one that the average onlooker wouldn't have noticed. Despite Beckham's limited vision, he homed right in on it. The president was the first politician he'd ever truly trusted, and once again she was about to prove why. She raised a hand to shield her face from the radiant sunlight and smiled at the crowd.

In a commanding but kind voice, Ringgold said, "Several weeks ago, I made two promises to you. The first was to take back our country. The battle for America isn't over, and the fight for Europe, South America, and Asia is just beginning, but we have already cleared many of our cities. The surviving juveniles are on the run, and it's just a matter of time before we defeat them once and for all."

Horn was the first to clap. The smack of his paws heralded a roar of applause. Bo pulled away from Donna's neck and clapped with his tiny hands. Timothy hugged his father, grinning. Rico hollered like a madwoman, and next to her Fitz clapped with tears in his eyes.

Ringgold's smile widened. She waited a few moments before continuing.

"The second promise was to rebuild. The island you see in front of you is one of many outposts where survivors can live safely as our cities are reconstructed. These outposts will support a local economy and will be protected by well-trained military forces."

Beckham turned with the rest of the crowd for a better look at Plum Island. There were already dozens of civilian and naval vessels docked in the new harbor. Construction equipment growled to life on the shoreline as crews prepared for work. Row after row of makeshift shelters had been constructed. Plots of land had been cleared to make way for community gardens. The island had already transformed from the grim Medical Corps lab facility and military outpost Beckham remembered. To the east, the white-domed Medical Corps buildings had been torn down, replaced by the skeletal wood frames of new structures that would serve as governmental buildings.

But evidence of the nightmares that had occurred on the island was far from erased. Electric fences and guard towers had also been rebuilt. It was a poignant reminder that, despite the overwhelming victories across the country, there were still juveniles out there. The threat wasn't over.

"As you can see, there's a lot to celebrate," Ringgold said. "But today we also mourn those who can't be here with us."

The crowd's mood turned solemn. No one had escaped the war without loss. Beckham's heart broke for the kids who'd had to grow up too fast, like Bo, Timothy, Tasha, and Jenny. Other children had lost their entire families. Beckham closed his eyes, wishing that he had been able to save just one more.

"Today, I'm making a third promise to you. While our grief will never truly go away, I promise you will have the community and support to help you heal. Together we *will* make it through this." Ringgold gestured at Beckham and Kate. "I'm already surrounded by new friends and people I now consider family. We've gathered here to honor the men and women who made this all possible through their sacrifice. But first, I've been told Master Sergeant Reed Beckham would like to say a few words."

Clearing his throat, Beckham grabbed Kate's hand and walked in front of the small crowd. Apollo trotted over and sat beside them.

Beckham took a moment to review his speech for the third time that morning. He'd never been big on words. His actions had always spoken louder. But his fighting days were over now; words were all he had left.

"Nine weeks ago, Staff Sergeant Parker Horn and I led Delta Force Team Ghost into the depths of Building Eight. It was there the military secretly authorized and designed a bioweapon that has since decimated the human race. Since then, we've lost almost everything: our friends, our families, and, at times, our hope. That we stand here today is a testament to human resilience, but it's also a testament to love. The love of a father for his daughters." Beckham regarded Horn with a nod. Then he looked at Kate. "The love between a man and a woman." Finally, he looked at Ringgold. "And the love of a leader for her country."

A smile touched the president's lips.

"Our standing here today is also a testament to the brave men and women who made victory in America possible. Staff Sergeant Jay Chow, Corporal Bruce Anderson, PFC Lee Bryant, PFC Pete Kehoe, and a handful of other men and women gave their lives to take back the *George Washington*. Without their sacrifice, the missiles Kramer fired would have made their targets. It was their valiant efforts that allowed Vice President Johnson's staff to disarm the nukes at the last moment."

Beckham took a moment to give the crowd time to remember the fallen. He gazed at the hundreds of white crosses protruding from the dirt of Plum Island and remembered every face buried there, including the one that wasn't marked with a cross. Jinx and his best friend Chow were both gone. Beckham hadn't seen Chow in his final moments, but he could imagine how Chow had died.

The same way he'd lived: furiously.

Flashbacks to every battle of the past two months rose in Beckham's memory. Chow and Jinx's Delta Force Team Titanium had been wiped out, and so had the Variant Hunters. He had seen Jensen gunned down on the tarmac of Plum Island. He pictured Meg dying on the operating table. He watched half of Team Ghost slaughtered in Building 8, and he imagined Riley being strangled by the Bone Collector on Plum Island. There was a memory of Timbo transforming into a Variant before Jensen took him out. And then there was Garcia, surrounded by monsters, his finger on the button of the RDD.

Beckham blinked the thoughts away. His eyes flitted to Jensen's Colt .45, which he still carried on his hip. He could no longer fire it with his right hand, but he would learn to use his left.

He felt fingers lace through his own. Kate was looking at him with her brilliant, kind blue eyes. He hadn't realized that a long moment of silence had passed.

Beckham squeezed her hand and looked back at the crowd. "It will never be easy to understand, but it's important to remember that members of our military and government betrayed us by creating VX-99 and the hemorrhage virus. They betrayed us further with Operation Liberty, and then again during Operation Extinction. We must remember so we never make the same mistakes again. For many of us, Plum Island will be our new home. It's a reminder of everything we've lost, but it's also a beacon of hope. Kate and I will raise our child there, and hopefully, so will many other families."

Beckham paused again. He felt as if he should say a prayer, but he'd never been good at that sort of thing. Out of respect for Garcia, he decided to give it a shot.

"I ask you all to join me in prayer for our lost brothers and sisters and for the new world we're creating together, here on Plum Island and at other outposts across the country."

Another moment of silence passed as the crowd bowed their heads. Beckham thought he might just get used to the quiet. It was a nice change of pace from shrieking monsters and gunfire.

"Thank you, Master Sergeant," Ringgold said. "Thank you for everything you've done for us. Now it's our turn to show you how much your country appreciates your service."

Beckham saw that she was holding a pale blue ribbon with a star and wreath hanging from it. Without a second thought, Beckham stood at attention.

"Master Sergeant Reed Beckham," Vice President Johnson began, "it is our privilege, as a nation, to have men such as yourself defending us."

Ringgold took over, lifting the medal to slip it over his head, but in that instant Beckham took a step back, his heart thumping.

He stood there for a moment in shock. Somehow, he hadn't realized that the Medal of Honor was meant for him.

"I know it's a surprise, Master Sergeant, but you deserve this."

Beckham could feel Kate's hand tighten around his. Had she known?

"Thank you, Madam President," he said at last. He closed his eyes as he felt the ribbon settle around his neck.

"President Ringgold?" he said after the applause died down.

"Yes, Master Sergeant?"

"I—I'd respectfully request that the medal be awarded to Marine Sergeant Jose Garcia instead. His actions during his final moments exemplify the personal sacrifice and valor the medal was created to honor."

Ringgold smiled. "How did I know you were going to say that?"

Johnson gave a serious nod. "We've thought of that, already, Master Sergeant. Sergeant Jose Garcia will receive the medal posthumously."

"Thank you, sir," Beckham said, still shaken, but comforted knowing that the people around him remembered those who had fallen.

Ringgold put a hand on Beckham's shoulder. "You're a good man," she said. Her eyes flitted to Kate. "I don't suppose you're going to accept the Medal of Valor for citizens who go above and beyond in the face of danger, are you?"

It was Beckham's turn to give Kate a knowing look. Even though she shook her head at first, he knew she understood the burden of honor as well as he did. "Absolutely, not," Kate started to say. Then, clearly holding her emotions in, she continued. "I mean, yes, Madam President. And thank you."

"You two were meant for one another." Ringgold chuckled. She lifted the second medal from Johnson's hand and draped the ribbon over Kate's head. The assembled crowd applauded, and Beckham felt a surge of warmth as the woman by his side stood with quiet dignity. If there was one good thing to come out of this nightmare, it was that he'd met Dr. Kate Lovato.

Beckham leaned in to kiss Kate as the crowd cheered. He savored the moment, goose bumps prickling across his skin. When Kate took his left hand in hers and placed it over her stomach, he almost broke down in tears.

Ringgold smiled and clapped him on the shoulder. "Hope, my friends. Courage and hope," she said, just loud enough for them both to hear.

Beckham turned to gaze at the island where they would make a home for their little family. Knowing they had a safe place for their child to grow up made all of the pain more bearable. Nothing could take away the loss, but Ringgold was right. Hope would keep them all alive.

"Vice President Johnson!" The raised voice came from the ladder at the top of the command center. It carried over the wind, and the applause abruptly cut off as everyone turned to look at Captain Humphrey.

"We just got a transmission from England, sir!" he shouted.

Johnson nodded curtly. "Meet me on the deck."

The crowd continued to celebrate their heroes and honor their fallen, but Ringgold and Johnson hurried away, recalled to their duty. Kate and Beckham followed, and in a few moments Davis, Fitz, Horn, and Rico caught up with them.

Humphrey met them at the bottom of the ladder. The marines and members of Team Ghost remained at a distance, but Beckham and Kate came up next to Johnson and Ringgold. Davis wheeled over at the same hurried pace that she walked. She nearly fell out of her chair when she stopped and stiffened her back at attention.

"Madam President, Mister Vice President," Humphrey panted, winded from his quick descent to the deck. "We just got word that England, France, Italy, and a dozen other countries are putting together a coalition called the European Unified Forces. They're preparing to take back their cities from the juveniles."

"About time," said Davis. Then she seemed to remember that she was in the presence of her superiors and added, "That's the news we've been waiting for, sir."

Beckham looked at Kate. There was a flicker of hope in her blue eyes—hope that her parents were still out there.

"They're asking for our help," Humphrey said. "Ships, aircraft, and troops."

Ringgold didn't take a single moment to think.

"And the United States of America will answer their call. Start the preparations."

Beckham turned to look at Fitz. He'd hoped the marine would help him with rehab, but he could see Fitz was itching to get back out there. Some men didn't know what to do with their lives in times of peace. Hell, Beckham wasn't sure he'd be able to adapt either. But unlike Fitz, Beckham had to accept he was no longer the man he'd been. The toxins had ruined his body, and his war was over.

"Fitz," Beckham whispered.

Fitz continued to cavesdrop on the discussion among Ringgold, Johnson, Humphrey, and Davis.

"Fitzpatrick," Beckham said, louder this time.

The marine caught his gaze, his eyebrows raised.

"There's something I need to ask you, brother."

The two injured warriors took a step closer to one another, blades creaking. Beckham glanced back at Kate. She was focused on the leaders' conversation, her features pinched, desperate for news. Her hand slowly massaged her belly through her shirt.

Seeing her standing there made up his mind that he was doing the right thing. His family was his first priority now.

"Fitz. I've got a lot of respect for you, and I can't thank you enough for everything you've done since I met you at Bragg."

Cheeks flaring red, Fitz looked down at the deck. "Just doing my duty."

"More than your duty, Fitz. You've gone above and beyond on every single mission. That's why I'd like you to take over for me."

Fitz glanced up sharply. "What do you mean?"

"How would you feel about being the new lead for Team Ghost?"

A grin slowly stretched across Fitz's face. "You serious?"

Horn clapped Fitz on the back, and Rico reached up to give him a high five. Davis beamed at Fitz in a way that told Beckham there was something beyond friendship there.

Beckham smiled at that and reached out to shake Fitz's hand. "Absolutely. It sounds as if Team Ghost is needed in Europe."

Kate, Ringgold, Johnson, Humphrey, and Davis were the ones eavesdropping now. They all watched, smiles on their faces.

Beckham shook Fitz's hand with his left, trying to make his grip as tight as possible. Fitz squeezed back, then leaned in to hug Beckham.

When they pulled apart, Beckham said, "You can pick your own team, but Big Horn and I are going to take a vacation for a while. We'll be here when you need us."

Fitz nodded, tears glinting in his eyes.

"I'm with you, Fitz," Rico said. "If you want me." She smiled broadly, but stopped when she saw Davis glaring at her. "If that's okay with you, LT."

Beckham chuckled, even though the movement hurt. Davis was marking her territory after all. The lieutenant gripped the handles on her wheelchair and said, "When I get out of this damn thing, I'll be right there with you two."

Beckham didn't doubt that. Davis was a lot like Fitz: Nothing kept her down for long.

"Oh, one more thing," Beckham said. He reached down to pet Apollo's head. "You aren't taking my dog this time."

There were several laughs, and more than a few sniffles. Beckham finished petting Apollo and grabbed Kate's hand. He whistled at the dog to follow, dipped his chin respectfully at Ringgold, then kissed Kate on the cheek.

"Ready, my love?" he whispered into her ear. "Let's go home."

*If you want to hear more about Nicholas Sansbury Smith's upcoming books, join his newsletter or follow him on social media. He just might keep you from the brink of extinction!*

**Newsletter:** www.eepurl.com/bggNg9

**Twitter:** www.twitter.com/greatwaveink

**Facebook:** www.facebook.com/Nicholas -Sansbury-Smith-124009881117534

**Website:** www.nicholassansbury.com

For those who'd like to personally contact Nicholas, he would love to hear from you.

**Greatwaveink@gmail.com**

# Acknowledgments

It's always hard for me to write this section for fear of leaving someone out. So many people had a hand in the creation of the Extinction Cycle and I know these stories would not be worth reading if I didn't have the overwhelming support of family, friends, and readers.

Before I thank those people, I wanted to give a bit of background on how the Extinction Cycle was conceived and the journey it has been on since I started writing. The story began more than five years ago, when I was still working as a planner for the state of Iowa and also during my time as a project officer for Iowa Homeland Security and Emergency Management. I had several duties throughout my tenure with the state, but my primary focus was protecting infrastructure and working on the state hazard mitigation plan. After several years of working in the disaster mitigation field, I learned of countless threats: from natural disasters to manmade weapons, and one of the most horrifying threats of all—a lab-created biological weapon.

Fast-forward to 2014, when my writing career started to take off. I was working on the Orbs series and brainstorming my next science fiction adventure. Back then, the genre was saturated with zombie books. I wanted to write something unique and different, a story that explained, scientifically, how a virus could turn men into monsters. During this time, the Ebola virus was raging through western Africa and several cases showed up in the continental United States for the first time.

After talking with my biomedical-engineer friend, Tony Melchiorri, an idea formed for a book that played on the risk the Ebola virus posed. That idea blossomed after I started researching chemical and biological weapons, many of which dated back to the Cold War. In March of 2014, I sat down to pen the first pages of *Extinction Horizon*, the first book in what would become the Extinction Cycle. Using real science and the terrifying premise of a government-made bioweapon, I set out to tell my story.

The Extinction Cycle quickly found an audience. The first three novels came out in rapid succession and seemed to spark life back into the zombie craze. The audiobook, narrated by the award-winning Bronson Pinchot climbed the charts, hitting the top spot on Audible. As I released books four and five, more readers discovered the Extinction Cycle—more than three hundred thousand to date. The German translation was released in November 2016 and Amazon's Kindle Worlds has opened the Extinction universe to other authors.

Even more exciting, two years after I published *Extinction Horizon*, Orbit decided to purchase and rerelease the series. The copy you are reading is the newly edited and polished version. I hope you've enjoyed it. I want to thank everyone who helped me create the Extinction Cycle.

I couldn't have done it without the help of a small army of editors, beta readers, and the support of my family and friends. I also owe a great deal of gratitude to my initial editors, Aaron Sikes and Erin Elizabeth Long, as well as my good author-friend Tony Melchiorri. The trio spent countless hours on the Extinction Cycle books. Without them these stories would not be what they are.

Erin also helped edit *Orbs* and *Hell Divers*. She's been with me pretty much since day one, and I appreciate her more than she knows. So, thanks Erin, Tony, and Aaron.

A special thanks goes to David Fugate, my agent, who provided valuable feedback on the early version of *Extinction Horizon* and the entire Extinction Cycle series. I'm grateful for his support and guidance.

Another special thanks goes to Blackstone Audio for their support of the audio version. Narrator Bronson Pinchot also played, and continues to play, a vital role in bringing the story to life.

I'm also extremely honored for the support I have received from the military community over the course of the series. I've heard from countless veterans, many of them wounded warriors who grew to love Corporal Joe Fitzpatrick and Team Ghost. I even heard from a few Delta Force operators. Many of these readers went on to serve as beta readers, and I'm forever grateful for their support and feedback.

They say a person is only as good as those that they surround themselves with. I've been fortunate to surround myself with talented people much smarter than myself. I've also had the support from excellent publishers like Blackstone and Orbit.

I would be remiss if I didn't also thank the people for whom I write: the readers. I've been blessed to have my work read in countries around the world by wonderful people. If you are reading this, know that I truly appreciate you for trying my stories.

To my family, friends, and everyone else who has supported me on this journey, I thank you.

# extras

# meet the author

NICHOLAS SANSBURY SMITH is the *USA Today* bestselling author of *Hell Divers*, the Orbs trilogy, and the Extinction Cycle. He worked for Iowa Homeland Security and Emergency Management in disaster mitigation before switching careers to focus on his one true passion: writing. When he isn't writing or daydreaming about the apocalypse, he enjoys running, biking, spending time with his family, and traveling the world. He is an Ironman triathlete and lives in Iowa with his fiancée, their dogs, and a houseful of books.

if you enjoyed

**EXTINCTION END**

look out for

# EXTINCTION AFTERMATH

**The Extinction Cycle**

by

**Nicholas Sansbury Smith**

*A new monster emerges.*

*The newly christened leader of Delta Force Team Ghost, Master Sergeant Joe Fitzpatrick, arrives in Normandy over seventy years after Allied forces joined the fight against the Nazis. The war to free survivors and eradicate pockets of adult Variants and their offspring is under way, led by the European Unified Forces. But as the troops push east, rumors of a new type of monster spread through the ranks. Fitz and his new team quickly realize that the fight for Europe might be harder than anyone ever imagined.*

*Back in the States, Captain Reed Beckham and Dr. Kate
Lovato are settling into a new life on Plum Island.
Across the United States, the adult Variants have all been
wiped out, and the juveniles are on the run.
But the survivors soon realize there are other monsters
at home, and they may be human.*

The boat jolted again as the bottom scraped over a rock.

Fitz cupped his hand over the radio to hear an incoming transmission over the distant explosions and the exhaust from the turbo fans at the rear of the LCAC.

"Command, this is Fox One. We've reached the shore. No sign of contacts. Preparing to disembark. Over."

"Copy that, Fox One. You have a green light to proceed. Stay frosty."

Fitz patted Rico's shoulder and took his rifle back. He walked to the metal landing ramp at the right side of the craft. A middle-aged marine with his arm in a sling stood at the gate, his helmet and flak jacket soaked with salt water from the spray. Through the mist, Fitz could see the first wave of boats running ashore. The ramps opened, and Humvees shot out onto the beach. The tankers followed in the M1A1s, plowing over the sand.

"Master Sergeant, you're supposed to stay in your vehicle until we beach," the marine said. "Please get back to—"

A thud rocked the side of the landing craft, cutting the man off midsentence. He glanced over his shoulder, then back at Fitz. "You hear that?"

"Just a wave," Fitz said. He looked past the sentry, focusing on the ocean. It was difficult to see in the darkness, and he could spot only the outlines of the other

LCACs to the east. Rico joined him at the ramp and grabbed the railing.

"Please return to your vehicle," said the marine guard. "We're going to be on the beach in a couple minutes."

"We're going. Just give me a second," Fitz replied. He scoped the shoreline again and zoomed in on the tanks. They were crawling across the beach toward a dirt ramp that curved up and over the cliffs.

Fitz was roving his rifle back and forth when he saw a sudden flash of motion at the top of one of those cliffs. He jerked the gun back to a figure skittering up a jagged summit like a spider. The monster crested the peak and perched.

"Command, this is Fox One. Beach is clear of contacts. Repeat—"

Another jolt hit the side of the LCAC.

"What the hell are we hitting?" Rico asked. "It's not supposed to be shallow out here."

Fitz didn't reply. Instead, he zoomed in on the biggest juvenile Variant he had ever seen. The beast, covered from head to feet in plates of armor, was crouched like a gargoyle on the rocks over the beach.

Fitz had just pushed his mini-mic into position to report the contact when another transmission came over the net.

"Command, this is Fox One. Our tracks are stuck in something."

"Come again, Fox One?"

Fitz centered his gun on the Abrams tanks. Several of them were stopped about halfway up the beach, not far from the natural sandy incline leading out. Steam from the engines rose around them as if they were steaks cooking in a skillet.

White noise crackled from his headset, the spotty transmissions breaking up.

"Tracks...stuck in some sort of oil..." the tank commander replied over the comms. "Something's burning."

Fitz aimed back at the Variant. It was gone now. A pair of Black Hawks swooped over the spot where it had been and headed back to sea.

"This is all wrong," Fitz whispered. He lowered his rifle and opened the channel to Command. "This is Ghost One, reporting hostiles on the cliffs. Over."

"Copy that, Ghost One. How many did you see?"

"One," Fitz replied, realizing how silly it sounded.

The reply was briefly delayed. "Ghost One, Command. Advise if you spot anything else. Over."

Fitz's cheeks burned with embarrassment. He turned to move back to his vehicle, but then he saw something that made him stop. The whitecaps near the LCAC looked strange. He elbowed the marine out of the way, squinting for a better look at what could have been fins in the water.

Flares suddenly shot into the sky in all directions from the second wave of the marine expeditionary unit. Their red light illuminated the water and the beach.

*Boom, boom, boom.*

The sound of more flares rang above, and in their wake came a sight that seized the breath from Fitz's lungs. Those weren't waves at all—they were the turtle-like shells of juveniles swimming just beneath the water. Hundreds of them.

All at once they seemed to jump from the water, claws extended and puckered mouths smacking. The beasts leaped onto the sides of the LCACs and clung like barnacles.

"*Contacts!*" Fitz screamed. He swung his MK11 up just as one of the creatures grabbed the marine guard by the back of the neck. The monster plucked his head off with the ease of a man popping the tail off a shrimp. The sound of the man's skull disconnecting from his spine made Fitz's stomach roll. He angled his MK11 upward, chambered a round, and shot the monster in the right eye, blowing out the back of its head over the water.

Rico grabbed Fitz and pulled him away from the ramp as two more of the beasts emerged, their claws gripping the top gate of the landing craft. Their talons shrieked over the metal as they pulled themselves up.

"Move!" Rico screamed. "Get back to the M-ATV!"

Fitz fired off two more rounds as soon as a pair of bulbous eyes emerged over the side of the ramp. One of the creatures opened its mouth and sucked down a round that exited through the armor lining its neck. The second juvenile jerked to the left an instant too late, and Fitz shot it in the skull. Chunks of armor and flesh peppered his helmet.

"On the 240s!" he yelled, waving to the other vehicles. He pushed his mini-mic to his lips and opened the channel to Team Ghost. "Dohi, get on the big gun!"

Marines emerged from their M-ATVs and climbed into the turrets, swerving the automatic weapons into position. Within seconds the whine of 7.62-millimeter rounds sounded, echoing in the enclosed space. They streaked in all directions, smashing through armored plates and sending juveniles spinning down to watery graves.

"Don't hit the sides of the ship!" Fitz yelled. But it wasn't just the rounds he was worried about cutting through the delicate landing craft—there was also the talons of the juveniles to consider. He ran back to his M-ATV and opened the passenger's-side door.

Stevenson beat on the wheel. "Close the door!"

Apollo was barking at the approaching monsters, saliva dripping from his maw. Fitz turned where he stood and fired. Two more of the juveniles vanished over the high walls of the LCAC. He chambered another round and was moving into the vehicle when an explosion on the beach commanded his attention. The Abrams tanks had opened fire. Fitz zoomed in with his rifle on dozens of creatures mounting the bluffs. Several of the beasts jumped into the air as the shells punched into the cliffs, blowing pieces of rock sky high.

Another explosion flashed in his peripheral. He pulled his scope away to see the beach ignite in a massive blue fireball. The heat was fast and intense, and he could feel it on his face even a quarter mile from shore.

He shielded his eyes, squinting through a fort of fingers.

Fitz jumped into the M-ATV and slammed the door as the explosion died down, revealing the tanks, Humvees, and other vehicles caught in an inferno. A tank commander opened the hatch of his Abrams, his skin melting off like candle wax as Fitz watched helplessly through his scope. The man fell limply over the side of his tank, and Fitz lowered his rifle in horror.

"Jesus, this isn't happening!" Rico said.

Tanaka leaned forward. "It was a trap all along. That's juvenile toxin on the beach, isn't it? They knew we were coming."

Fitz couldn't wrap his mind around the facts. More of the juveniles were climbing the side of the landing craft. They were almost inside.

*Lead, Fitz. You have to lead.*

Black Hawks and Vipers returned to the fight. They flew over the smoldering wrecks of the first wave of the MEU, door gunners firing—but they were aiming into the sky. So what the hell were they shooting at?

Fitz pushed his scope to his eye and leaned back so he had room to move his rifle in the front seat. Something flapped across his cross hairs toward the Black Hawks, but it was too fast to capture.

One of the juveniles made it over the ramp and landed in front of their bumper. It let out a screech that opened a trio of armored slits on both sides of its neck. Fitz knew then how the monsters had avoided detection in the water: They had gills.

Dohi centered his gun on it and fired rounds that lanced into the creature's chest plate, punching through vital organs.

Fitz exhaled and raised his MK11. The Black Hawks were circling now, and their gunners were still firing into the sky. He zoomed in on the door gunner of the closest helicopter just as a batlike creature twice the size of a man yanked the marine out of the chopper. It flapped away, holding the man in its talons.

*Not bats. Juveniles. They can fly!*

More of the beasts launched from the cliffs and took to the sky, plucking out door gunners and tossing them aside like rag dolls. The Vipers gave chase, guns blazing and missiles streaking away. The winged Variants were massive, but they were no match for a missile. Several of the creatures windmilled to the ground, frayed wings smoking as they plummeted.

A flurry of transmissions from Command overwhelmed Fitz's earpiece.

"What the hell is happening out there?"

# if you enjoyed
# EXTINCTION END
## look out for

# THE LAZARUS WAR: ARTEFACT

### by

# Jamie Sawyer

*Mankind has spread to the stars, only to become locked in warfare with an insidious alien race. All that stands against the alien menace are the soldiers of the Simulant Operation Programme, an elite military team remotely operating avatars in the most dangerous theatres of war.*

*Captain Conrad Harris has died hundreds of times—running suicide missions in simulant bodies. Known as Lazarus, he is a man addicted to death. So when a secret research station deep in alien territory suddenly goes dark, there is no other man who could possibly lead a rescue mission.*

*But Harris hasn't been trained for what he's about to find. And this time, he may not be coming back...*

# CHAPTER ONE

## *NEW HAVEN*

Radio chatter filled my ears. Different voices, speaking over one another.

*Is this it?* I asked myself. *Will I find her?*

"*That's a confirm on the identification: AFS* New Haven. *She went dark three years ago.*"

"*Null-shields are blown. You have a clean approach.*"

It was a friendly, at least. Nationality: Arab Free-worlds. But it wasn't her. A spike of disappointment ran through me. *What did I expect?* She was gone.

"*Arab Freeworlds Starship* New Haven, *this is Alliance FOB* Liberty Point: *do you copy? Repeat, this is FOB* Liberty Point: *do you copy?*"

"*Bird's not squawking.*"

"*That's a negative on the hail. No response to automated or manual contact.*"

I patched into the external cameras to get a better view of the target. She was a big starship, a thousand metres long. NEW HAVEN had been stencilled on the hull, but the white lettering was chipped and worn. Underneath the name was a numerical ID tag and a bar-code with a corporate sponsor logo – an advert for some long-forgotten mining corporation. As an afterthought something in Arabic had been scrawled beside the logo.

*New Haven* was a civilian-class colony vessel; one of the mass-produced models commonly seen throughout the border systems, capable of long-range quantum-space jumps but with precious little defensive capability. Probably older than me, retrofitted by a dozen governments and corporations before she became known by her current name. The ship looked painfully vulnerable, to my military eye: with a huge globe-like bridge and command module at the nose, a slender midsection and an ugly drive propulsion unit at the aft.

She wouldn't be any good in a fight, that was for sure.

*"Reading remote sensors now. I can't get a clean internal analysis from the bio-scanner."*

On closer inspection, there was evidence to explain the lifeless state of the ship. Puckered rips in the hull-plating suggested that she had been fired upon by a spaceborne weapon. Nothing catastrophic, but enough to disable the main drive: as though whoever, or whatever, had attacked the ship had been toying with her. Like the hunter that only cripples its prey, but chooses not to deliver the killing blow.

*"AFS* New Haven, *this is* Liberty Point. *You are about to be boarded in accordance with military code alpha-zeroniner. You have trespassed into the Krell Quarantine Zone. Under military law in force in this sector we have authority to board your craft, in order to ensure your safety."*

The ship had probably been drifting aimlessly for months, maybe even years. There was surely nothing alive within that blasted metal shell.

*"That's a continued no response to the hail. Authorising weapons-free for away team. Proceed with mission as briefed."*

"This is Captain Harris," I said. "Reading you loud and clear. That's an affirmative on approach."

*"Copy that. Mission is good to go, good to go. Over to you, Captain. Wireless silence from here on in."*

Then the communication-link was severed and there was a moment of silence. *Liberty Point*, and all of the protections that the station brought with it, suddenly felt a very long way away.

Our Wildcat armoured personnel shuttle rapidly advanced on the *New Haven*. The APS was an ugly, functional vessel – made to ferry us from the base of operations to the insertion point, and nothing more. It was heavily armoured but completely unarmed; the hope was that, under enemy fire, the triple-reinforced armour would prevent a hull breach before we reached the objective. Compared to the goliath civilian vessel, it was an insignificant dot.

I sat upright in the troop compartment, strapped into a safety harness. On the approach to the target, the Wildcat APS gravity drive cancelled completely: everything not strapped down drifted in free fall. There were no windows or view-screens, and so I relied on the external camera-feeds to track our progress. This was proper cattle-class, even in deep-space.

I wore a tactical combat helmet, for more than just protection. Various technical data was being relayed to the heads-up display – projected directly onto the interior of the face-plate. Swarms of glowing icons, warnings and data-reads scrolled overhead. For a rookie, the flow of information would've been overwhelming but to me this was second nature. Jacked directly into my combat-armour, with a thought I cancelled some data-streams, examined others.

Satisfied with what I saw, I yelled into the communicator: "Squad, sound off."

Five members of the unit called out in turn, their respective life-signs appearing on my HUD.

"Jenkins." The only woman on the team; small, fast and sparky. Jenkins was a gun nut, and when it came to military operations obsessive-compulsive was an understatement. She served as the corporal of the squad and I wouldn't have had it any other way.

"Blake." Youngest member of the team, barely out of basic training when he was inducted. Fresh-faced and always eager. His defining characteristics were extraordinary skill with a sniper rifle, and an incredible talent with the opposite sex.

"Martinez." He had a background in the Alliance Marine Corps. With his dark eyes and darker fuzz of hair, he was Venusian American stock. He promised that he had Hispanic blood, but I doubted that the last few generations of Martinez's family had even set foot on Earth.

"Kaminski." Quick-witted; a fast technician as well as a good shot. Kaminski had been with me from the start. Like me, he had been Alliance Special Forces. He and Jenkins rubbed each other up the wrong way, like brother and sister. Expertly printed above the face-shield of his helmet were the words BORN TO KILL.

Then, finally: "Science Officer Olsen, ah, alive."

Our guest for this mission sat to my left – the science officer attached to my squad. He shook uncontrollably, alternating between breathing hard and retching hard. Olsen's communicator was tuned to an open channel, and none of us were spared his pain. I remotely monitored his vital signs on my suit display – he was in a bad way. I was going to have to keep him close during the op.

"First contact for you, Mr Olsen?" Blake asked over the general squad comms channel.

Olsen gave an exaggerated nod.

"Yes, but I've conducted extensive laboratory studies of the enemy." He paused to retch some more, then blurted: "And I've read many mission debriefs on the subject."

"That counts for nothing out here, my friend," said Jenkins. "You need to face off against the enemy. Go toe to toe, in our space."

"That's the problem, Jenkins," Blake said. "This isn't our space, according to the Treaty."

"You mean the Treaty that was signed off before you were born, Kid?" Kaminski added, with a dry snigger. "We have company this mission – it's a special occasion. How about you tell us how old you are?"

As squad leader, I knew Blake's age but the others didn't. The mystery had become a source of amusement to the rest of the unit. I could've given Kaminski the answer easily enough, but that would have spoiled the entertainment. This was a topic to which he returned every time we were operational.

"Isn't this getting old?" said Blake.

"No, it isn't – just like you, Kid."

Blake gave him the finger – his hands chunky and oversized inside heavily armoured gauntlets.

"Cut that shit out," I growled over the communicator. "I need you all frosty and on point. I don't want things turning nasty out there. We get aboard the *Haven*, download the route data, then bail out."

I'd already briefed the team back at the *Liberty Point*, but no operation was routine where the Krell were concerned. Just the possibility of an encounter changed the game. I scanned the interior of the darkened shuttle, taking in the faces of each of my team. As I did so, my suit streamed combat statistics on each of them – enough for me to know that they were on edge, that they were ready for this.

"If we stay together and stay cool, then no one needs to get hurt," I said. "That includes you, Olsen."

The science officer gave another nod. His biorhythms were most worrying but there was nothing I could do about that. His inclusion on the team hadn't been my choice, after all.

"You heard the man," Jenkins echoed. "Meaning no fuck-ups."

Couldn't have put it better myself. If I bought it on the op, Jenkins would be responsible for getting the rest of the squad home.

The Wildcat shuttle selected an appropriate docking portal on the *New Haven*. Data imported from the APS automated pilot told me that trajectory and approach vector were good. We would board the ship from the main corridor. According to our intelligence, based on schematics of similar starships, this corridor formed the spine of the ship. It would give access to all major tactical objectives – the bridge, the drive chamber, and the hypersleep suite.

A chime sounded in my helmet and the APS updated me on our progress – T-MINUS TEN SECONDS UNTIL IMPACT.

"Here we go!" I declared.

The Wildcat APS retro-thrusters kicked in, and suddenly we were decelerating rapidly. My head thumped against the padded neck-rest and my body juddered. Despite the reduced-gravity of the cabin, the sensation was gut wrenching. My heart hammered in my chest, even though I had done this hundreds of times before. My helmet informed me that a fresh batch of synthetic combat-drug – a cocktail of endorphins and adrenaline, carefully mixed to keep me at optimum combat performance – was being injected into my system to compensate. The armour carried a full medical suite, patched directly into my body, and automatically provided assistance when necessary. Distance to target rapidly decreased.

"Brace for impact."

Through the APS-mounted cameras, I saw the rough-and-ready docking procedure. The APS literally bumped against the outer hull, and unceremoniously lined up our airlock with the *Haven*'s. With an explosive roar and a wave of kinetic force, the shuttle connected with the hull. The Wildcat airlock cycled open.

We moved like a well-oiled mechanism, a well-used machine. Except for Olsen, we'd all done this before. Martinez was first up, out of his safety harness. He took up point. Jenkins and Blake were next; they would provide covering fire if we met resistance. Then Kaminski, escorting Olsen. I was always last out of the cabin.

"Boarding successful," I said. "We're on the *Haven*."

That was just a formality for my combat-suit recorder.

As I moved out into the corridor, my weapon auto-linked with my HUD and displayed targeting data. We were armed with Westington-Haslake M95 plasma battle-rifles – the favoured long-arm for hostile starship engagements. It was a large and weighty weapon, and fired phased plasma pulses, fuelled by an onboard power cell. Range was limited but it had an incredible rate of fire and the sheer stopping power of an energy weapon of this magnitude was worth the compromise. We carried other weapons as well, according to preference – Jenkins favoured an Armant-pattern incinerator unit as her primary weapon, and we all wore plasma pistol sidearms.

"Take up covering positions – overlap arcs of fire," I whispered, into the communicator. The squad obeyed. "Wide dispersal, and get me some proper light."

Bobbing shoulder-lamps illuminated, flashing over the battered interior of the starship. The suits were equipped with infrared, night-vision, and electro-magnetic sighting, but the Krell didn't emit much body heat and nothing beat good old-fashioned eyesight.

Without being ordered, Kaminski moved up on one of the wall-mounted control panels. He accessed the ship's mainframe with a portable PDU from his kit.

"Let there be light," Martinez whispered, in heavily accented Standard.

Strip lights popped on overhead, flashing in sequence, dowsing the corridor in ugly electric illumination. Some flickered erratically, other didn't light at all. Something began humming in the belly of the ship: maybe dormant life-support systems. A sinister calmness permeated the main corridor. It was utterly utilitarian, with bare metal-plated walls and floors. My suit reported that the temperature was uncomfortably low, but within acceptable tolerances.

"Gravity drive is operational," Kaminski said. "They've left the atmospherics untouched. We'll be okay here for a few hours."

"I don't plan on staying that long," Jenkins said.

Simultaneously, we all broke the seals on our helmets. The atmosphere carried twin but contradictory scents: the stink of burning plastic and fetid water. *The ship has been on fire, and a recycling tank has blown somewhere nearby.* Liquid *plink-plink-plinked* softly in the distance.

"I'll stay sealed, if you don't mind," Olsen clumsily added. "The subjects have been known to harbour cross-species contaminants."

"Christo, this guy is unbelievable," Kaminski said, shaking his head.

"Hey, watch your tongue, *mano*," Martinez said to Kaminski. He motioned to a crude white cross, painted onto the chest-plate of his combat-suit. "Don't use His name in vain."

None of us really knew what religion Martinez followed,

but he did it with admirable vigour. It seemed to permit gambling, women and drinking, whereas blaspheming on a mission was always unacceptable.

"Not this shit again," Kaminski said. "It's all I ever hear from you. We get back to the *Point* without you, I'll comm God personally. You Venusians are all the same."

"I'm an American," Martinez started. Venusians were very conscious of their roots; this was an argument I'd arbitrated far too many times between the two soldiers.

"Shut the fuck up," Jenkins said. "He wants to believe, leave him to it." The others respected her word almost as much as mine, and immediately fell silent. "It's nice to have faith in something. Orders, Cap?"

"Fireteam Alpha – Jenkins, Martinez – get down to the hypersleep chamber and report on the status of these colonists. Fireteam Bravo, form up on me."

Nods of approval from the squad. This was standard operating procedure: get onboard the target ship, hit the key locations and get back out as soon as possible.

"And the quantum-drive?" Jenkins asked. She had powered up her flamethrower, and the glow from the pilot-light danced over her face. Her expression looked positively malicious.

"We'll converge on the location in fifteen minutes. Let's get some recon on the place before we check out."

"Solid copy, Captain."

The troopers began a steady jog into the gloomy aft of the starship, their heavy armour and weapons clanking noisily as they went.

It wasn't fear that I felt in my gut. Not trepidation, either; this was something worse. It was excitement – polluting my thought process, strong enough that it was almost intoxicating. This was what I was made for. I steadied my pulse and concentrated on the mission at hand.

*Something* stirred in the ship – I felt it.